# THE LOST WAR

## The Eidyn Saga: Book One

# JUSTIN LEE ANDERSON

orbitbooks.net

Copyright © 2019 by King Lot Publishing Ltd.
Excerpt from *The Bitter Crown* copyright © 2023 by King Lot Publishing Ltd.
Excerpt from *The Sword Defiant* copyright © 2023 by Gareth Ryder-Hanrahan

Cover design by Lauren Panepinto
Cover illustration by Jeremy Wilson
Cover copyright © 2022 by Hachette Book Group, Inc
Map by Tim Paul
Author photograph by Melody Joy Co.

Orbit
Hachette Book Group
1290 Avenue of the Americas
New York, NY 10104
orbitbooks.net

First Orbit Paperback Edition: May 2023
First Orbit Ebook Edition: December 2022
Originally published in Great Britain by King Lot Publishing in August 2019

Orbit is an imprint of Hachette Book Group.
The Orbit name and logo are trademarks of Little, Brown Book Group Limited.

The publisher is not responsible for websites (or their content) that are not owned by the publisher.

The Hachette Speakers Bureau provides a wide range of authors for speaking events. To find out more, go to hachettespeakersbureau.com or email HachetteSpeakers@hbgusa.com.

Orbit books may be purchased in bulk for business, educational, or promotional use. For information, please contact your local bookseller or the Hachette Book Group Special Markets Department at special.markets@hbgusa.com.

Library of Congress Cataloging-in-Publication Data
Names: Anderson, Justin Lee, author.
Title: The lost war / Justin Lee Anderson.
Description: First edition. | New York : Orbit, 2023. | Series: The Eidyn Saga |
   "Originally published in Great Britain by King Lot Publishing in August 2019."
Identifiers: LCCN 2022037814 | ISBN 9780316454070 (trade paperback) |
   ISBN 9780316454179 (ebook)
Subjects: LCGFT: Fantasy fiction. | Novels.
Classification: LCC PR6101.A53 L67 2023 | DDC 823/.92—dc23/eng/20220816
LC record available at https://lccn.loc.gov/2022037814

ISBN: 9780316454070 (trade paperback), 9780316454179 (ebook)

Printed in the United States of America

LSC-C

Printing 1, 2023

**Cargill fired into life, brandishing his sword high.**

"I'll cut your fucking head off right now if you don't walk away!" His bravado was fragile, though. He didn't know what Aranok could do—what his *draoidh* skill was. Aranok enjoyed the thought that, if he did, he'd only be more scared.

"Allandria!" he called over his shoulder.

"Aranok?"

"This gentleman says he's going to cut my head off."

"Already?" She laughed. "We just got here."

All eyes were on them now. The tavern was silent, the crowd an audience. People were flooding out into the square, drinks still in hand. Others stood in shop doors, careful not to stray too far from safety. Windows filled with shadows.

Cargill's bravado disappeared in the half-light. "You...you're... we're on the same side!"

"Can't say I'm on the side of stealing from orphans." Aranok stared hard into his eyes. Fear had taken the man.

"We've got a warrant." Cargill pulled a crumpled mess from his belt and waved it like a flag of surrender. Now he was keen to do the paperwork.

**By Justin Lee Anderson**

THE EIDYN SAGA

*The Lost War*
*The Bitter Crown*

*For Sean, Kirsten, Juliet, Craig, Neith, and Jan*

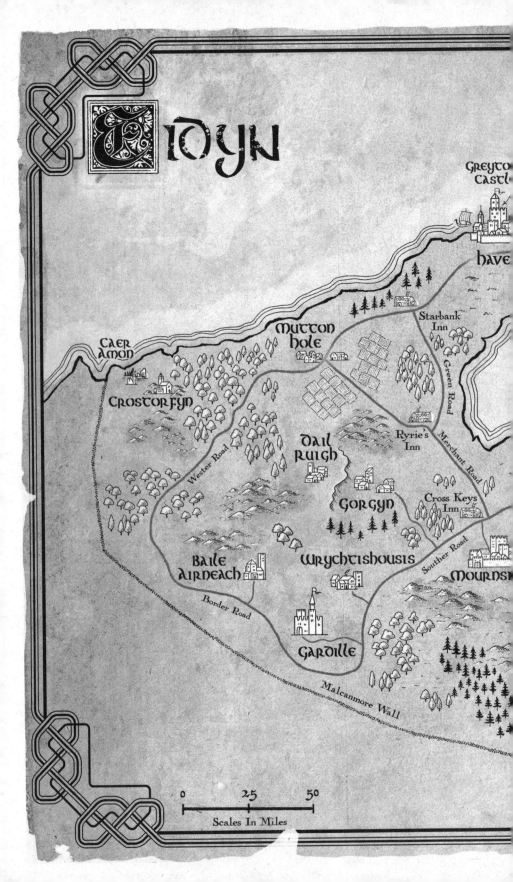

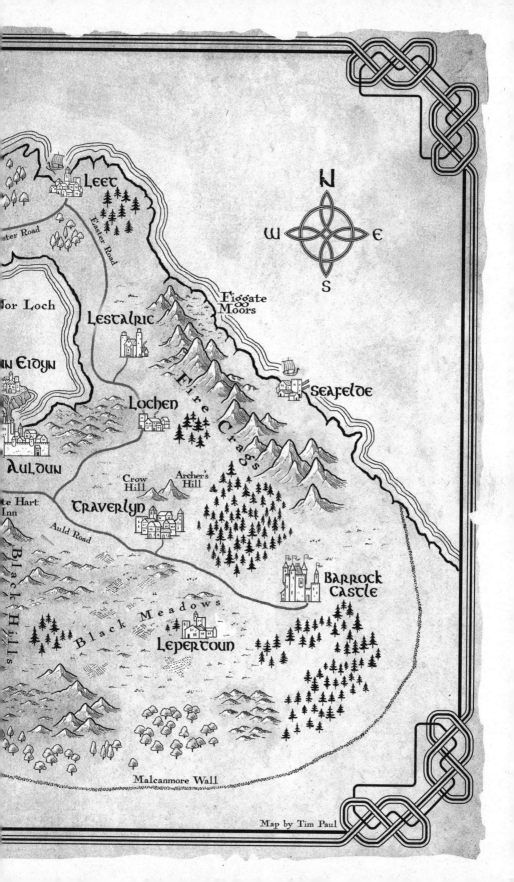

# CHAPTER 1

*F*uck.

The boy was going to get himself killed.

"Back off!"

Aranok put down his drink, leaned back and rubbed his dusty, mottled brown hands across his face and behind his neck. He was tired and sore. He wanted to sit here with Allandria, drink beer, take a hot bath, collapse into a soft, clean bed and feel her skin against his. The last thing he wanted was a fight. Not here.

They'd made it back to Haven. This was their territory, the new capital of Eidyn, the safest place in the kingdom—for what that was worth. He'd done enough fighting, enough killing. His shoulders ached and his back was stiff. He looked up at the darkening sky, spectacularly lit with pinks and oranges.

The wooden balcony of the Chain Pier Tavern jutted out over the main door along the front length of the building. Aranok had thought it an optimistic idea by the landlord, considering Eidyn's usual weather, but there were about thirty patrons overlooking the main square with their beers, wines and whiskies.

Allandria looked at him from across the table, chin resting on her hand. He met her deep brown eyes, pleading with her to give him another option. She looked down at the boy arguing with the two thugs in front of the blacksmith's forge, then back at him. She shrugged, resigned, and tied back her hair.

*Bollocks.*

Aranok knocked back the last of his beer and clunked the empty tankard back on the table. As Allandria reached for her bow, he signalled to the serving girl.

"Two more." He gestured to their drinks. "I'll be back in a minute."

The girl furrowed her brow, confused.

He stood abruptly to overcome the stiffness of his muscles. The chair clattered against the wooden deck, drawing some attention. Aranok was used to being eyed with suspicion, but it still rankled. If they knew what they owed him—owed both of them…

He leaned on the rail, feeling the splintered, weather-beaten wood under his palms; breathing in the smoky, sweaty smell of the bar. Funny how welcome those odours were; he'd been away for so long. With a sigh, Aranok twisted and turned his hands, making the necessary gestures, vaulted over the banister and said, "*Gaoth.*" Air burst from his palms, kicking up a cloud of dirt and cushioning his landing. Drinkers who had spilled out the front of the inn coughed, spluttered and raised hands in defence. A chorus of gasps and grumbles, but nobody dared complain. Instead, they watched.

Anticipating.

Fearing.

Aranok breathed deeply, stretching his arms, steeling himself as he passed the newly constructed stone well—one of many, he assumed, since the population had probably doubled recently. A lot of eyes were on him now. Maybe that was a good thing. Maybe they needed to see this.

As he approached the forge, Aranok sized up his task. One of the men was big, carrying a large, well-used sword. A club hung from his belt, but he looked slow and cumbersome, more a butcher than a soldier. The other was sleek, though—wiry. There was something ratlike about him. He stood well-balanced on the balls of his feet, dagger twitching eagerly. A thief most likely. Released from prison and pressed into the king's service? Surely not. Hells. Were they really this short of men? Was this what they'd bought with their blood?

"You've got the count of three to drop your weapons and move," the fat one wheezed. "King's orders."

"Go to Hell!" The boy's voice cracked. He backed a few steps toward the door. He couldn't be more than fifteen, defending his father's business with a pair of swords he'd probably made himself. His stance was clumsy, but he knew how to hold them. He'd had some training, if not any actual experience. Enough to make him think he could fight, not enough to win.

The rat rocked on his feet, the fingertips of his right hand frantically rubbing together. Any town guard could resolve this without blood. If it was just the fat one, he might manage it. But this man was dangerous.

Now or never.

"Can I help?" Aranok asked loudly enough for the whole square to hear.

All three swung to look at him. The thief's eyes ran him up and down. Aranok watched him instinctively look for pockets, coin purses, weapons—assess how quickly Aranok would move. He trusted the rat would underestimate him.

"Back away, *draoidh*!" snarled the butcher. The runes inscribed in Aranok's leather armour made it clear to anyone with even a passing awareness of magic what he was. *Draoidh* was generally spat as an insult, rarely welcoming. He understood the fear. People weren't comfortable with someone who could do things they couldn't. He only wore the armour when he knew it might be necessary. He couldn't remember the last day he'd gone without it.

"This is king's business. We've got a warrant," grunted the big man.

"May I see it?" Aranok asked calmly.

"I said piss off." He was getting tetchy now. Aranok began to wonder if he might have made things worse. It wouldn't be the first time.

He took a gentle step toward the man, palms open in a gesture of peace.

The rat smiled a confident grin, showing him the curved blade as if it were a jewel for sale. Aranok smiled pleasantly back at him and gestured to the balcony. The thief's face confirmed he was looking at the point of Allandria's arrow.

"Shit," the rat hissed. "Cargill. Cargill!"

"What?" Cargill barked grumpily back at him. The thief mimicked Aranok's gesture and the fat man also looked up. He spun around to face Aranok, raising his sword—half in threat, half in defence. Nobody likes an arrow trained on them. The boy took another step back—probably unsure who was on his side, if anyone.

"You'll swing for this," Cargill growled. "We've got orders from the king. Confiscate the stock of any business that can't pay taxes. The boy owes!"

"Surely his father owes?" Aranok asked.

"No, sir," the boy said quietly. "Father's dead. The war."

Aranok felt the words in his chest. "Your mother?"

The boy shook his head. His lips trembled until he pressed them together. *Damn it.*

Aranok had seen a lot of death. He'd held friends as they bled out, watching their eyes turn dark; he'd stumbled over their mangled bodies, fighting for his life. Sometimes they cried out, or whimpered as he passed—clinging desperately to the notion they could still see tomorrow.

Bile rose in his gullet. He turned back to Cargill. Now it was a fight.

"If you close his business, how do you propose he pays his taxes?" Aranok struggled to maintain an even tone.

"I don't know," the thug answered. "Ask the king."

Aranok looked up the rocky crag toward Greytoun Castle. Rising out of the middle of Haven, it cast a shadow over half the town. "I will."

There was a hiss of air and a thud to Aranok's right. He turned to see an arrow embedded in the ground at the thief's feet. He must have crept a little closer than Allandria liked. The rat was lucky she'd given him a warning shot. Many didn't know she was there until they were dead. Eyes wide, he sidled back under the small canopy at the front of the forge.

Cargill fired into life, brandishing his sword high. "I'll cut your fucking head off right now if you don't walk away!" His bravado was fragile, though. He didn't know what Aranok could do—what his *draoidh* skill was. Aranok enjoyed the thought that, if he did, he'd only be more scared.

"Allandria!" he called over his shoulder.

"Aranok?"

"This gentleman says he's going to cut my head off."

"Already?" She laughed. "We just got here."

All eyes were on them now. The tavern was silent, the crowd an audience. People were flooding out into the square, drinks still in hand.

Others stood in shop doors, careful not to stray too far from safety. Windows filled with shadows.

Cargill's bravado disappeared in the half-light. "You...you're... we're on the same side!"

"Can't say I'm on the side of stealing from orphans." Aranok stared hard into his eyes. Fear had taken the man.

"We've got a warrant." Cargill pulled a crumpled mess from his belt and waved it like a flag of surrender. Now he was keen to do the paperwork.

Perhaps they'd get out of this without a fight after all. Unusually, he was grateful for the embellishments of legend. He'd once heard a story about himself, in a Leet tavern, in which he killed three demons on his own. The downside was that every braggart and mercenary in the kingdom fancied a shot at him, which was why he tended to travel quietly—and anonymously. But now and again...

"How much does he owe?" Aranok asked.

"Eight crowns." Cargill proffered the warrant in evidence. Aranok took it, glancing up to see where the rat had got to. He was too near the wall for Aranok's liking. The boy was vulnerable.

"Out here," Aranok ordered. "Now."

"With that crazy bitch shooting at me?" he whined.

"Thül!" Cargill snapped.

Thül slunk back out into the open, watching the balcony. Sensible boy. Though if this went on much longer, Allandria might struggle to see clearly across the square. He needed to wrap it up.

The warrant was clear. The business owed eight crowns in unpaid taxes and was to be closed unless payment was made in full. Eight bloody crowns. Hardly a king's ransom—except it was.

Aranok looked up at the boy. "What can you pay?"

"I've got three..." he answered.

"You've got three or you can pay three?"

"I've got three, sir."

"And food?"

The boy shrugged.

"A bit."

"Why do you care?" Thül sneered. "Is he yours?"

Aranok closed the ground between them in two steps, grabbed the thief by the throat and squeezed—enough to hurt, not enough to suffocate him. He pulled the angular, dirty face toward his own. Rank breath escaping yellow teeth made Aranok recoil momentarily.

"Why do I care?" he growled.

The thief trembled. He'd definitely underestimated Aranok's speed.

"I care because I've spent a year fighting to protect him. I care because I've watched others die to protect him." He stabbed a finger toward the young blacksmith. "And his parents died protecting you, you piece of shit!"

There were smatterings of applause from somewhere. He released the rat, who dropped to his knees, dramatically gasping for air. Digging some coins out of his purse, Aranok turned to the boy.

"Here. Ten crowns as a deposit against future work for me. Deal?"

The boy looked at the gold coins, up at Aranok's face and back down again. "Really?"

"You any good?"

"Yes, sir." The boy nodded. "Did a lot of Father's work. Ran the business since he went away."

"How is business?"

"Slow," the boy answered quietly.

Aranok nodded. "So do we have a deal?" He thrust his hand toward the blacksmith again.

Nervously, the boy put down one sword and took the coins from Aranok's hand, tentatively, as though they might burn. He put the other sword down to take two coins from the pile in his left hand, looking to Aranok for reassurance. He clearly didn't like being defenceless. Aranok nodded. The boy turned to Cargill and slowly offered the hand with the bulk of the coins. Pleasingly, the thug looked to Aranok for approval. He nodded permission gravely. Cargill took the coins and gestured to Thül. They walked quickly back toward the castle, the thief looking up at Allandria as they passed underneath. She smiled and waved him off like an old friend.

Aranok clapped the boy on the shoulder and walked back toward the tavern, now very aware of being watched. It had cost him ten crowns to avoid a fight... and probably a lecture from the king. It was worth it. He really was tired. The crowd returned to life—most likely chattering in hushed tones about what they'd just seen. One man even offered a hand to shake as Aranok walked past; quite a gesture—to a *draoidh*. Aranok smiled and nodded politely but didn't take the hand. He shouldn't have to perform a grand, charitable act before people engaged with him.

The man looked surprised, smiled nervously and ran his hand through his hair, as if that had always been his intention.

Aranok felt a hand on his elbow. He turned to find the boy looking up at him, eyes glistening. "Thank you," he said. "I...thank you."

"What's your name?" Aranok asked. He tried to look comforting, but he could feel the heavy dark bags under his eyes.

"Vastin," the boy answered.

Aranok shook his hand.

"Congratulations, Vastin. You're the official blacksmith to the king's envoy."

———

Aranok righted his chair and dramatically slumped down opposite Allandria. The idiot was playing up the grumpy misanthrope because every eye on the top floor was watching him. He looked uncomfortable. Secretly, she was certain he enjoyed it.

Allandria raised an eyebrow. "Was that our drinking money, by any chance?"

"Some of it..." he answered, more wearily than necessary.

Despite his reluctance, Allandria knew part of him had enjoyed the confrontation—especially since it had ended bloodless. The man loved a good argument, if not a good fight—particularly one where he outsmarted his opponent. Not that she'd had any desire to kill the two thugs, but she would have, to save the boy. It was better that Aranok had been able to talk them down and pay them off.

"You could have brought my arrow back," she teased.

He looked down to where the arrow still stood, proudly embedded in the dirt. It was a powerful little memento of what had happened. Interesting that the boy had left it there too...maybe to remind people he had a new patron.

"Sorry." He smiled. "Forgot."

She returned the smile. "No, you didn't."

"You missed, by the way."

Allandria stuck out her tongue. "I couldn't decide who I wanted to shoot more, the greasy little one or the big head in the fancy armour." The infuriating bugger had an answer to everything. But for all his arrogance, she loved him. He'd looked better, certainly. The war had been kind to no one. His unkempt brown hair was flecked with grey now—even more so the straggly beard he'd grown in the wild. Leathery skin hid under a layer of road dust; green eyes were hooded and dark. But they still glinted with devilment when the two sparred.

"Excuse me..." The serving girl arrived with their drinks. She was a slight, blonde thing, hardly in her teens if Allandria guessed right. Were there any adults left? Aranok reached for his coin purse.

"No, sir." The girl stopped him, nervously putting the drinks on the table. "Pa says your money's no good here."

Aranok looked up at Allandria, incredulous. When they'd come in, he wasn't even certain they'd be served. *Draoidhs* sometimes weren't. Innkeepers worried they would put off other customers. She'd seen it more than once.

Aranok tossed down two coppers on the table. "Thank you, but tell your pa he'll get no special treatment from the king on my say-so, or anyone else's."

It was harsh to assume they were trying to curry favour with the king now they knew who he was. Allandria hoped that wasn't it. She still had faith in people, in human kindness. She'd seen enough of it in the last year. Still, she understood his bitterness.

"No, sir," the girl said. "Vastin's my friend. His folks were good people. We need more people like you. Pa says so."

"Doesn't seem many places want people like me..."

"Hey..." Allandria frowned at him. He was punishing the girl for other people's sins now. He looked back at her, his eyes tired, resentful. But he knew he was wrong.

"Way I see it"—the girl shifted from foot to foot, holding one elbow protectively in her other hand—"you've no need of a blacksmith. A fletcher, maybe"—she glanced at Allandria—"but not a blacksmith. So I want more people like you."

*Good for you, girl.*

Allandria smiled at her. Aranok finally succumbed too.

"Thank you." He picked up the coins and held them out to her. "What's your name?"

"Amollari," she said quietly.

"Take them for yourself, Amollari, if not for your pa. Take them as an apology from a grumpy old man."

*Grumpy* was fair; *old* was harsh. He was barely forty—two years younger than Allandria.

Amollari lowered her head. "Pa'll be angry."

"I won't tell him if you don't," said Aranok.

Tentatively, the girl took the coins, slipping them into an apron pocket. She gave a rough little curtsy with a low "thank you" and turned to clear the empty mugs from a table back inside the tavern.

The girl was right. Aranok carried no weapons and his armour was well beyond the abilities of any common blacksmith to replicate or repair. He probably had no idea what he'd use the boy for.

Allandria raised the mug to her lips and felt beer wash over her tongue. It tasted of home and comfort, of warm fires and restful sleep. It really was good to be here.

"Balls." A crack resonated from Aranok's neck as he tilted his head first one way, then the other.

"What?" Allandria leaned back in her chair.

"I really wanted a night off."

"Isn't that what we're having?" She brandished her drink as evidence. "With our free beer?" She hoped the smile would cheer him. He was being pointlessly miserable.

Aranok rubbed his neck. "We have to see the king. He's being an arsehole."

A few ears pricked up at the nearest tables, but he hadn't said it loudly.

"It can't wait until tomorrow?" Allandria might have phrased it as a question, but she knew he'd be up all night thinking about it if they waited. "Of course it can't," she answered when he didn't. "Shall we go, then?"

"Let's finish these first," Aranok said, lifting his own mug.

"Well, rude not to, really."

Her warm bed seemed a lot further away than it had a few minutes ago.

# CHAPTER 2

"Demon's balls, woman, how are you still standing?" Glorbad's orotund belly laugh echoed off the damp stone walls of the Anchor Inn.

Nirea slammed the glass back down on the bar, shook off the burning in her throat and stared triumphantly at the old soldier. He had the gut of a man used to drinking beer. He might be able to drink more than her tonight, but her leaner body would burn it off quicker and leave her feeling fine in the morning. She doubted he'd be able to say the same.

"Live at sea, drink rum," she slurred. The floor lurched unpleasantly toward her. She leaned heavily on the dark wooden bar until the room went back to its natural shape.

"Whoa, there, Captain!" Glorbad was playing to the crowd. "Don't spew on my new boots!"

He waggled his battered old leather footwear around for the others to see. They were filthy. There might even have been blood on them, but Nirea's balance wouldn't tolerate bending over for a better look. She was in no fit state for... anything. Getting this drunk hadn't been the plan, but the soldier had a way of making you forget yourself—and a lot of the evening. They should have eaten.

"Shite," she said, a little louder than she'd intended. "What if we're summoned tonight? I can't see the king in this state."

"It's past sunset," the soldier answered. "All the king will want tonight is a bottle of wine and a good seeing to—and I'm not giving him either!"

Glorbad roared again and a number of others joined him.

"Seriously, though…" Nirea tried again. "We're liaisons to the court now. Should we be more…sober?"

Glorbad put his drink on the bar and drew himself up to his full height. It wasn't quite Nirea's, but she was taller than average, and his bulk was mostly horizontal—the stocky chest and rounded belly making him look like a barrel in uniform.

"A year of war is over. The people we've lost…I'd rather drink to their memories than lament their deaths."

A wave of ice swept through Nirea. They'd lost so many. The mood in the bar quickly turned sombre, until Glorbad smiled that infectious, disarming grin again, raising his cup in salute before draining the contents. But when he caught her eyes, the facade wavered, and she saw the same pain, the same horrors buried in shallow graves.

Glorbad waved his cup at the innkeeper and plonked it on the bar for a refill. "Mind that horde of Dead south of Leet?" His voice quiet now. This was not for the crowd.

"Aye." Of course she remembered. She remembered everything. Every misshapen demon, every shambling corpse. "The bloody stench."

Glorbad wrinkled his nose. "Fuck, don't. I'll lose my lunch." The stink was the thing people didn't expect. They'd recount the horror of a man with his guts dangling round his knees or a woman with her ribs split open like some gaping, demonic mouth, but they rarely talked about the absolute reek of decay that crept like fog with the Dead. Half a dozen soldiers emptied their guts before the fight began.

Their ranks seemed endless. Dragged from graves, some fresh from other battles—their own dead sent to wear them down. And how many soldiers survived the battle only to die of infection from filthy, rusted weapons, rotting flesh, or the thick black syrup of Dead blood?

And then they came back.

Another day; another field; another fight. The ones they lost, raised to come against them.

The fresh dead were the greatest danger. They moved faster, fought harder. The armour that failed them in life made them lethal in death. It had taken months to realise what needed done. Well, months to accept it.

Decapitating their own dead. Hacking their bodies beyond use. Preventing their fallen from being used against them. Burning them, when they had time. When it was safe. Whole fields aflame in the dying light, before demons came with the dark.

"Gershin was a good man." Glorbad's voice was morose now.

"Aye. Deserved better." Her second had taken an axe in the neck at Leet. A good man. A good friend. She'd watched the life drain from him and then, screaming, crying, wailing, she'd finished the axe's work. Watched the blood mat his thick grey beard.

She remembered too much. So she drank rum. "Fuck. We're getting miserable again. Let's not get miserable again."

Glorbad supped from his newly filled cup and found a twinkle of a smile. "Aye. Fucking cheer up, ye miserable bitch."

Nirea carved a smile on her face and slapped the old goat's shoulder. "Barkeep! Barkeep! Food, for fuck's sake. This idiot is trying to kill me!"

The noise of the huge oak doors swinging open echoed around the chamber. Aranok strode in as if he were the king. Allandria followed a few steps behind, nodding apologetically to the two kingsguards he'd completely ignored. She'd never been in Greytoun before. Having lived in Dun Eidyn for so long, she'd come to think of it as home, though her real home was on the other side of the country.

The throne room was longer than Dun Eidyn's, with pillars stretching along both sides like a guard of honour. Ironic, since the real guards who would have populated the throne room in the kingdom's traditional seat of power were absent. Only two stood either side of the throne at the far end of the room, silhouetted against the huge fireplace, which burned with the familiar smell of peat.

Eidyn's colours hung above the hearth. This was the capital—for now.

King Janaeus looked up from the map on the table in front of him as Aranok approached. The soldier next to him swung round, hand on the

pommel of his sword. Allandria didn't recognise him. She hadn't recognised anyone since they entered the castle, which made her wonder
what had happened to all the kingsguards she knew. Janaeus placed a
calming hand on the soldier's arm and nodded. The man stepped back.

Aranok strode forward. "How are they supposed to pay taxes if you
shut them all down?"

The king cocked a disapproving eyebrow. "Aranok. Welcome back. I
see you've been to the tavern."

"I have," he answered. "Pleased to see it's still open."

Allandria winced. He was pushing his luck—but he had a lot of it
here. Still, there were ears that ought not to hear their king addressed
this way. Janaeus's look changed from indulgence to irritation. He
turned to the soldier.

"Give us the chamber."

"Sire." The man rolled up the map and backed out of the room, the
pair of kingsguards following. One glowered at Aranok as he did—the
*draoidh* didn't notice.

As soon as the doors were shut, Janaeus sat on his throne. "What are
you doing?"

"What are you doing?" Aranok barked in return. "Destroying the
kingdom yourself now we've saved it?"

He was irritated, tired and a little drunk. Whatever safeguards he
usually had in place to remind him to speak to the king like a monarch
and not as his closest friend were apparently not working.

"What are you talking about?" Janaeus looked genuinely confused.

"I just paid eight crowns in taxes for a fifteen-year-old blacksmith
whose parents died in your war, to keep your men from stealing his
stock and shutting him down," Aranok answered. "On top of that, I
reckon at least one of the men came from our dungeons. Is that who
we are now? We send criminals to steal from honest merchants? You
should melt down that fucking crown and call yourself Robber Baron
Janaeus!"

The king leaned back in his chair, gesturing to the pair to take two
seats alongside the long table. Allandria happily took the invitation
to get off her feet. Aranok paused, probably considering whether to
remain standing just for the sake of defiance, but finally sat.

Janaeus looked unsure of himself—almost nervous, which was out of character for the man she knew. The lines on the king's face had deepened substantially since she last saw him, and his hair had whitened. He looked thinner than she remembered. Smaller. His rich blue cloak seemed too big for him, the crown loose on his brow. His thin blonde beard framed gaunt cheeks. It had been a hard year for everyone.

"First of all, keep your voice down." Janaeus nodded at the chamber doors—and the guards on the other side of them. "You've missed a lot." The king fixed his envoy with a hard stare. "There's a great deal you don't understand."

"Clearly," Aranok said with equal gravity. "Come on, then…?"

Allandria sat quietly. She knew when not to get involved between these two. She'd been privy to a lot of conversations most bodyguards would not have heard. But it had been a long time since she was just the envoy's bodyguard.

Janaeus scratched at the table absentmindedly. "The kingdom is a god-awful mess, Aranok. It took everything we had to repel Mynygogg—and more. We've only been able to contain him in Dun Eidyn. The evil bastard's not going anywhere, but we're not getting to him either, with Auldun overrun by Dead. But that's good. It's a victory. For now. We have time to lick our wounds. To figure out what we do next. But we've had to abandon Auldun and squeeze the residents of our two largest towns into one."

Only half the population of Auldun, though. Mynygogg had laid siege to the city with demons, then raised the dead to murder the living. Husbands killing wives, mothers killing children. Mynygogg was the first *draoidh* known to have more than one skill. That they were the two worst—demon summoning and necromancy—was why it had cost them half a kingdom to defeat him. The *draoidh* had come from nowhere, the reasons for his hatred a mystery. At first, they'd assumed him a conqueror. But all he appeared to want was razing the country to ash and mud.

"The soldiers we have left are starved of supplies and Gardille needs to be almost completely rebuilt," Janaeus continued. "The Malcanmore Wall is breached in God knows how many places, so the Wilds are teeming with Reivers. The White Thorns are helping, but we are indebted to their faith for their assistance. We can't pay them. Their own home, Baile Airneach, is under repair by the monks. In the meantime, the demons the Thorns are trained to fight are running free outside the city walls. Right now, what Eidyn needs is soldiers—bodies—not blacksmiths who can't pay taxes."

Janaeus breathed out heavily. Aranok stared back across the table. It was as bad as—and worse than—they'd feared. Bloody Reivers. Scavengers from the south who'd been raiding Eidyn for generations. The history books said Auld King Malcanmore had built a wall along the southern border in an attempt to keep them out. What they didn't say was that *draoidhs* like Aranok probably did the bulk of the work. Something of that size could never have been built by hand alone—not even allowing for the slave labour that was common back then.

Allandria's parents had been nomads. They'd passed through the Reiver Lands on their way to settle in Eidyn while she was too young to remember. They had little good to speak about Reivers. A council of chieftains was as close as they had to organised rule. Instead of siding with their fellow humans when Mynygogg's demons were laying waste to the country, the bastards had plundered what was left while Eidyn was crippled. Parasites.

Aranok sighed before finally speaking again. "And when we run out of weapons to fight with? When our soldiers have no swords and shields—no armour—what then?"

"Aranok, we lost too many people," the king replied quietly. "I wish we had a soldier for every sword in the kingdom..."

He didn't need to finish the sentence. The population of Eidyn had been near a million a year ago, at its height. Now it might be half that. The army had taken the brunt of the losses. The strongest, the bravest.

"All right, but come on, Jan. Taxing businesses to death? Mercenary thugs acting as guards? This is the shit we rebelled against Hofnag for! The new Eidyn was supposed to be for the people, wasn't it?"

Janaeus sighed heavily and spoke slowly. "Yes, Aranok. But as we both know, it's a lot easier to fire arrows from the dark than to stand in the light and run a country. Sometimes you have to commit a small evil for a great good."

"Where's the good here? He's a teenage orphan whose parents died protecting your throne. He's been raised forging weapons and armour. What's he supposed to do?"

The king put a hand across his mouth and looked hard at his friend, as though considering not so much what the blacksmith should do, as what he should do with his envoy. "We need stonemasons. It's not so different from smithing."

"So we give up?" Aranok asked. "If all the merchants fail, the people will starve. They are Eidyn. Without them, what are we protecting? Land? Dirt?"

"And if the soldiers desert because they have no food? And the people are slaughtered by Reivers? If Mynygogg escapes Dun Eidyn and rallies his demons? Do we take comfort that the people will die fat?" Janaeus countered.

Aranok shook his head. "This isn't right. Those people didn't die so their son could live in poverty—or slavery."

Janaeus looked to the ceiling. "Slavery," he said incredulously. "It's hardly slavery."

"What would you call being pressed into work against your will?"

Janaeus reached up and adjusted his crown. "You've always been my better angel, Aranok. But there are practical considerations."

The two stared at each other intensely. Allandria's breathing was suddenly too loud. She picked up an apple from the table, nervously turning it over in her hands. Finally, something changed in the king's face.

"All right, I'll give new orders. Businesses failing to pay taxes are not to be closed, but they must surrender stock equivalent to twice the value of their dues."

"Twice?" the *draoidh* demanded. "Why twice?"

"If they can't sell them at market value, what makes you think I can?" It was the first time the king had raised his voice. Aranok had pushed it as far as he should dare. Allandria hoped he saw that.

"Fine. I'm buying the boy's business. You can take his taxes out of my wage."

He didn't see it.

Janaeus frowned. "I don't pay you a 'wage.' You take what you need."

"I need a blacksmith." Aranok said it as if it were the simplest thing in the world.

Janaeus sighed again. "Aranok, you're lucky to come from a wealthy family. You supported a boy today and maybe he'll benefit from that. But the truth is, we need his hands more than his weapons."

The *draoidh*'s face changed at the mention of his home. He hadn't spoken of his family in some time, but she knew he worried. His parents were old, especially his father. Even their wealth and the walls around Mournside might not have shielded them from the war.

"Have we heard from them?"

Janaeus visibly wilted. "Reports say the town walls are breached."

"No...Reivers? Demons?" Aranok's voice cracked. Allandria instinctively put her hand on his. There were no kingsguards to see it, and their relationship was no secret from Janaeus.

The king noticed, and the first hint of a smile played at his mouth. "Worse. Blackened."

Aranok sucked in a hard breath.

"What?" Allandria's stomach churned. "How?"

The Meadows had once been a vibrant farming community. Sometime before the war, a vicious plague had broken out, a plague that maddened its victims, leaving them with no thought other than to spread the plague. New victims' skin blackened immediately under their touch, as if burned, and they too were driven to spread it. They did not eat; they did not sleep; they did not rest. Their bodies withered and died, though the plague somehow kept them alive longer than natural. Untended and abandoned, the Meadows became a wasteland, rechristened the Black Meadows.

The Blackened had made the Black Meadows impassable, but the wasting nature of the disease seemed to prevent its victims from travelling far. They'd never crossed the Black Hills, as they would have to, to reach Mournside.

"Maybe the plague has mutated," the king answered. "Maybe it has slowed, allowing the carriers to travel farther. Hells, maybe Mynygogg has something to do with it. I honestly don't know."

"Lepertoun?" Aranok had found his voice.

The town at the centre of the original outbreak had become an improvised hospice, attracting many of the kingdom's medics, attempting to find a cure. Allandria hadn't heard of any contact with them since the war began.

"Nothing," said Janaeus. "We have to assume they're dead."

"All of them? Is nowhere safe outside of Haven? What about Leet?" asked Aranok.

"The port is under siege from pirates. For now, they're on their own. We can barely protect ourselves. The farmlands at Mutton Hole are plagued by a demon. Crops burned, animals slaughtered. We're getting sporadic deliveries, but nothing like we need."

"What are we doing about it?" Aranok's frustration was visibly growing with each new problem. Allandria squeezed his thigh, hoping to calm him. She was trying to dam a river with a twig.

"Aranok, we're critically shorthanded. We retreated here. We have to regroup, to rebuild. We need houses—two and three families are sharing one roof. After that, we'll address one thing at a time."

Aranok's fingers drummed on the table. "Let us go, then."

Janaeus's eyes widened as he sat up. "Go where?"

"I don't know! To the farms! We'll do what we can, then see if we can reach Mournside."

Allandria didn't like that. It sounded like a very good way to get killed.

The king waved one hand dismissively. "No. I need you here."

"I'm useless here. People are dying out there!" Aranok jolted to his feet and pointed out the window, his cheeks flushed red.

The two stared at each other again. The king finally broke the silence.

"Let me think about it. Give me some time." Janaeus gestured up and down at his friend. "Take a bath. Shave. Rest."

Aranok nodded—the fire burned out, for now. A bath sounded fabulous to Allandria. She was sure she probably stank to Heaven, but surrounded by others who all smelled as bad, it had been hard to tell.

"Tomorrow," said Aranok.

Janaeus rolled his eyes. "One night?"

Aranok's voice dropped low. "My family's probably dead if the Blackened are in Mournside. I'm not going to get much rest."

Janaeus looked hard at Aranok, as if contemplating some greater issue than letting his envoy leave the castle. He had more to consider than his friend's safety. Finally, he nodded silently. Aranok turned and started back toward the doors.

"Your Majesty?" Allandria's mouth was horribly dry. She swallowed, wondering whether she'd even be able to get the question out, but the subject hadn't come up naturally. "Lochen?"

Janaeus smiled. It was the first time she'd seen anything like genuine pleasure in his light blue eyes since they arrived. "As far as I know, Lochen stands."

Allandria breathed again. The tightness in her chest relaxed. Her home was safe—as safe as anywhere in Eidyn. She crossed her hands on her chest and gave a slight bow. "Thank you."

Aranok had stopped at the door, waiting for her to join him. As she moved to catch up, Janaeus called to him. "Aranok."

"What?"

"You're not going to Mournside. It's too dangerous. I'll think about the rest."

Aranok cocked his head in a noncommittal way.

Janaeus softened. "It really is good to see you again." There was an odd sadness in his eyes, Allandria thought. A bittersweet look, as if he were seeing a childhood toy.

"You too." Aranok's answer lacked the same warmth.

<hr />

Samily listened to the crackle of the fire. She breathed in the thick, earthy smell of the burning peat and felt the warmth tingling across her skin, raising the hair on her arms. It was good to be warm. It was good to sit on a rug. She breathed deeply, slowly, expanding her belly with each breath as she'd been taught. Light and shadow danced together across her eyelids. She relaxed every muscle, let every aching joint rest. She was liquid, melting ice. Free and floating.

Gentle footsteps behind her. She breathed deeply one last time and opened her eyes.

"Good evening, Brother. How may I serve you?"

"Hello, Samily. How are you?" Brother Meristan's deep, soothing voice.

She uncrossed her legs and stood, turning to face him in one movement. "I am well, thank God." In outside society, it was impolite not to ask after the health of someone who had done so for you, but the Order of the White Thorns was not the rest of the world. For a knight to ask any question of their masters, they had to have an extremely good reason. Otherwise, they answered what they were asked.

"Good, good. I have whisky. May I offer you a glass?" He raised the bottle, amber liquid sparkling in the firelight.

"Thank you, Brother, but not tonight." She was tired, and sitting up drinking whisky with Meristan never ended early.

The monk poured himself a measure and swilled it around the glass. He ran his hand over his bald head, considering some imponderable mystery in the drink. Meristan was a huge man, strongly built, with a thick beard that, combined with his lack of hair, had made the young Samily think God had put his face on upside down. She'd sometimes stood on her head, just to see how he looked. Meristan had pretended not to notice her giggles, but she was sure he'd known. He was a perceptive man.

Samily's feet began to throb again, being forced to stand still so soon after getting off them. But it was not for her to move the conversation forward. Meristan would address her, or he would leave, and she would stand there until he did one or the other.

"Sit, Samily, please."

He indicated a chair next to the fire. She took it and he slowly sank into the one opposite. His large frame made it look tiny compared with her identical one. The chamber was simple, but warm and comfortable. Normally, knights were not permitted in a brother's rooms, but so much of Baile Airneach was damaged that rooms with intact roofs were somewhat rare—hence why he'd invited her here when she'd arrived that evening, wet, dirty and exhausted.

"May I ask you a question, Samily?"

She had never been asked permission by a monk of the Order to do anything.

"Of course, Brother."

"What do you think of me?"

"I'm sorry?" Samily asked, confused.

"It's all right, I give you permission to speak honestly. Please. I want to know."

Meristan sipped at his drink and looked across at her with something unfamiliar in his eyes. Had she to guess, she'd have called it loss.

"You are an excellent master, Brother Meristan. I could ask for no better." Of course, he was so much more than that. He'd found her. Raised her. Made her who she was.

Meristan shook his head.

"No...no, that's not what I mean." He sighed. "I'm asking the wrong person."

Meristan stood and crossed to the door. "I'm sorry. Go back to your meditation."

"Brother?" Samily didn't understand what was happening. What did he want her to say?

Meristan turned back to her. "You've given me the only answer you can, Samily. I understand. It just isn't what I need."

Meristan opened the door and stepped out.

"You're wise!" Samily shouted after him, before she even realised she intended to speak. Instinctively, she clapped a hand across her mouth, looking at the back of his head for some trace of reaction.

He turned back into the room. "Go on."

She slowly moved the hand from her mouth. "And kind. Caring... caring too."

Without a word, he returned to his chair and gazed at the fire. Samily sat on the edge of her seat, wondering whether she should speak again but terrified of saying the wrong thing.

"I have been summoned by the king, Samily," he said, not looking up. "He is forming some sort of council and has asked me to represent the Order. I don't know why. I'm no warrior, no politician."

Despite his size and strength, Meristan had always been a man of peace. Samily couldn't remember seeing him raise even his voice in anger, never mind a weapon.

"There is so much to do here. I'm more use with stone and mortar— not sitting in a castle pushing pieces around a map."

"The king is also wise, Brother. If he sees a need for your counsel, perhaps you have more to offer than you imagine. There are others here who can do your work. I will stay, if you like."

"Actually, I was hoping you wouldn't."

That wasn't the reaction she'd expected. "Brother?"

"I should have left already, Samily, but...I didn't. I was waiting for something, I suppose. And here you are. I'd like you to come with me, if you will."

"Of course. The Wilds are treacherous. You should have an escort."

Meristan smiled. "Thank you, Samily. I hoped you would agree."

He had no need to hope. No knight of the White Thorns would refuse a brother of the Order. They spoke with the voice of God. To say no would be heresy.

"Of course." She bowed her head.

"We'll leave in the morning. I'm sorry you won't get more rest. I hope the clean clothes and polished armour will help to make up for it."

The fresh garments did feel good, and she looked forward to seeing her pure white armour shine in the sun tomorrow, once the apprentices had finished with it. The armour of the White Thorns was legendary and as much a part of their weaponry as their blades, their skill and their faith. Many enemies had surrendered or run upon seeing the White. Even demons had learned to be wary of them, as much as their largely mindless nature allowed. But the Reivers she'd been clearing from the Wilds on the way home—they knew better. They attacked in numbers. Even then, sometimes they ran.

"Brother? Perhaps you should wear armour for the journey? It could help us to pass unmolested."

Meristan smiled at her—again with that odd look in his eyes.

Sadness? What was it?

"Thank you, child. As much as it would be an honour, none but an ordained knight can wear the armour of the White Thorns. It would be an insult to the memory of those who died wearing it if anyone could pick it up and pretend to be their equal."

"But you are not any man! You are the leader of the Holy Council. The head of the Order."

"Only because I survived, Samily. Only because I did not die protecting our country, when better people did."

"You guided our forces. Without you, more would have been lost!"

Meristan looked again into the fire. "I'm not sure. It doesn't feel vital."

He stood, waving Samily back to her seat when she instinctively moved as well. He looked down at her for a moment, then reached out to caress her cheek, as he'd often done when she was little. It was familiar and comforting. He gave her a watery smile, crossed the room and exited silently.

What in Heaven's name was wrong? She'd never seen him so small, so beaten. His body had survived, but his spirit? There was one thing she could do for him. She returned to her meditation and prayed—prayed that the greatest man she'd ever known would remember who he was.

---

"Something's wrong."

Aranok sat up. It was good to feel a soft bed beneath him. But odd. It had been a long time. The clean sheets were a pleasure. The warm bath had scrubbed the dirt from him and revealed a few injuries he hadn't been aware of. At least one, a gash on his ankle, probably should have been sewn at the time. Hardly worth worrying about now. It wasn't infected and would heal.

"What do you mean?" Allandria too was now clean. As she slipped out of her robe by the fire, Aranok found himself watching her intently. It had been so long since they were together like this. It was almost as if he were seeing her for the first time; he couldn't remember the last. His eyes traced the crisscrossing scars on her back and shoulders; on her arms; across her breast. The biggest one, the jagged tear on her stomach, which had a match on her lower back—the time she'd taken an arrow meant for him. He'd pressed a torn scrap of cloth against it, screaming for a medic, begging her not to go.

There was nobody he trusted more. In the firelight the scars were not so vivid. If he squinted, he imagined he could see her body the way it once was: smooth, undamaged, innocent. He felt an adolescent rush of anticipation as she walked toward him.

"With Janaeus," he finally replied. "He's keeping something from me."

Allandria lifted the blanket and slipped in beside him, putting her head on his chest. Where her olive skin came against his, he felt a spark, raising the hairs on his neck. She was warm, safe, exciting. Her leg moved across his and he felt a tingling in response to the smoothness of her inner thigh. Tilting his head, he breathed in the lavender smell of her.

"You're thinking too much," she said. "You haven't seen him in an age and he's just finished waging a war. With all he's got to consider, is it any wonder he's on edge?"

She didn't sound sure. She sounded like she wanted that to be true. Truth was, so did he. But it wasn't.

"It's not that. I'm worried it's…" He couldn't finish the sentence. Speaking his fear out loud would make it real.

"Mournside?"

He nodded, clenching and unclenching his fist.

"You think he knows more about your family?"

"I can't think of anything else he'd be afraid to tell me. You saw how much he doesn't want me to go."

Allandria propped her forearm across his chest and looked directly into his eyes. "I understand you're worried. But please don't look for more reasons to fret. Take your friend at his word. Let's try to relax. We have this beautiful room."

It was a lovely room. The wooden four-poster bed sat against one wall, draped with deep red curtains. There was a large, ornate wardrobe opposite, a dressing table with a mirror by the window, and a chest of drawers beyond that. In the corner were wooden doors opening onto a balcony that looked out to sea. Only Janaeus's room was likely grander than this. He'd forgotten, over the past year, what it was like to have the practical comforts of his position. He'd been used to sleeping in an inn if he was lucky, and on the ground more often than not.

"There's plenty of time for worrying tomorrow." She stroked the back of her hand across his cheek. "And you're all smooth."

"Aye." He smiled. "The beard had to go."

"Were we calling that a beard?" Allandria frowned in mock curiosity.

"Ouch." She giggled. Her laugh was contagious and there was little more he wanted in the world right now than to listen to it. She smiled up at him, and he traced the line of her elegant cheekbone with the back of his finger. "I love you."

"Quite right." She leaned up and kissed him. Lightning spread across his lips.

They spent the next hours lost in each other, forgetting everything else. The war, Mournside, the Blackened, all of it was gone as her love soothed him. It was exhilarating, wonderful and completely right.

Then they slept like the dead.

# CHAPTER 3

T he sickly sweet air of alcohol and sweat turned Aranok's stomach. Across the table sat what he assumed was the primary source: a fat, bearded man with a ripe nose. The woman next to him wasn't quite as grey, though the bloodshot eyes that matched her shock of red hair betrayed she should still be asleep.

The main door of the small, round chamber opened and a kingsguard rigidly stepped in. The man and woman stood immediately; Allandria followed them a moment later. Aranok reluctantly got to his feet too. For appearances. The guard stepped back and held the door for the king, then closed it behind him. Janaeus gave Aranok a slightly perturbed look, not marked enough that anyone but he—and maybe Allandria—would notice. All four remained standing until the king sat and gestured for them to do the same. "Ladies, gentlemen."

"Your Majesty," the others replied.

Janaeus turned to him. "Aranok, in your absence, I began forming a new advisory council. This is Glorbad, representing the army, and Nirea, for the navy. I've also sent for a representative from the White Thorns."

Allandria's raised eyebrows suggested she was as surprised as Aranok. They didn't seem like leaders. It didn't matter much anyway—he was leaving today, and Janaeus could spend his time with whatever drunkards he liked.

"Aranok," the king continued, "is my envoy. This is his personal bodyguard, Allandria."

Nirea stood and offered her hand across the table. "Heard of you, of course. Good to meet you."

Aranok accepted the handshake. "And you."

She repeated the gesture with Allandria. Glorbad did not rise, only nodding at Aranok.

"Bodyguard…" he said ambiguously.

Aranok smiled and cocked his head. He wasn't sure what to make of the soldier. Was he mocking him, or was it just the usual army bravado? Was he an arsehole or just a soldier?

"Have we met?"

"I doubt it, son. I'd remember meeting somebody as famous as you."

*Arsehole.*

Aranok said nothing for long enough that the silence became awkward.

"You're doing well if you can remember where you live." Nirea slapped his arm playfully.

The king reclaimed control of the conversation. "Aranok, you asked for permission to do something."

"I did." Aranok turned to him, unsure of where this was going. Did Janaeus expect him to convince this "council" before he left? That wasn't going to happen. He was going either way—it would just be easier when he came back if Janaeus gave permission now.

"There is a way you could help the kingdom," Janaeus continued, "but it's dangerous. I won't order you to go."

"Everything is dangerous at the moment," said Aranok.

The king nodded gravely and tapped a finger on the table.

"All right then. Taneitheia, the deposed queen of Gaulle, is in hiding at Barrock Castle with a small retinue. I allowed it to be thought she was gone, for her own safety, but she remains there under guard."

"She does?" Nirea was clearly surprised.

Glorbad stifled a burp. "What use is a deposed queen?"

Janaeus ignored the interruption. "I understand that there is an uprising amongst her people. They want her back. Her son has not been a popular monarch. If you can get her safely home to her country…"

Aranok looked at him questioningly. How was this helpful?

"We need allies." The king answered his unspoken question.

"You want us to take her to Gaulle?" Aranok asked.

"I've been considering it for a while. If we put her back on the throne of Gaulle, she'd be even more indebted to us. We'd have a powerful ally against the Reivers. And Mynygogg, should it come to that."

*When it comes to that.*

"Aye, makes sense." Glorbad pursed his mouth thoughtfully.

"No," Aranok replied flatly. "We'll be days sailing to Gaulle. Putting her back on the throne could take months. Years. You said yourself the farmlands are urgent."

Janaeus regarded him curiously. Nirea's face drained of what little colour it had, just as Glorbad's somehow got redder. Allandria had heard the two speak frankly before. To the others, this probably seemed treasonous. But Aranok wasn't going to be battered into a bad plan for fear of embarrassing his king.

"All right, go to the farms first. Do what you can about the demon. Then go to Barrock."

Aranok took a long, deep breath, never taking his eyes off his old friend.

"What about Mournside?"

Jan swiped the air with his hand as if to cut off some phantom's head. "Absolutely not. If the Blackened are in there…Get Taneitheia from Barrock. Do not go to Mournside."

Aranok looked across at the other two. How far could he push Janaeus without undermining his friend's authority? Well, it was permission to leave. Aranok nodded silently, making sure to seem a little put out at the rebuttal.

The king smiled. "Excellent. You should go tonight. There's a new moon. You have the best chance of getting out of the walls undetected in the dark."

Aranok turned to Allandria. She shrugged and nodded.

"We'll be ready," he said.

"Thank you." Janaeus sat looking at Aranok thoughtfully, as if considering whether to say something else. Aranok stayed quiet—if this was a contest, he had no intention of losing.

"Are we adjourned, Your Majesty?" Glorbad shifted uncomfortably in his seat.

Janaeus's gaze lingered on Aranok a moment longer before he turned to the soldier. "We are. You should prepare."

"Prepare?" The soldier paused as he stood.

"We're going with them," Nirea answered. "Why else would we be here?"

"You are," the king confirmed. "We can't spare any soldiers, Aranok, but a small band can travel more quickly and quietly anyway. These two will provide you with all you should need to survive, whatever you face."

Aranok looked at his new companions. They would make it more complicated. Disobeying orders wasn't an issue for him, and he could easily make a troop of grunts do what he said—but these two?

"They're under my command?" He was asking the king, but he looked directly into Glorbad's eyes as he spoke.

"Yes," Janaeus answered. Glorbad bristled, the corner of his mouth curling.

"Fine." Aranok held the soldier's gaze a moment before turning to the women. "We leave at nightfall. Meet at the West Gate. Pack light." He turned back to the soldier. "Come sober."

Aranok made to leave, but the king's voice stopped him. "Aranok. Please stay a moment. The rest of you are dismissed."

So he wanted to talk to him in private after all. Aranok stood with his arms crossed as the other three passed out of the room. Allandria closed the door behind them. He waited a moment for them to move away from the door. "What?"

Janaeus still looked tired, haunted. "I'm sorry. About Mournside. I really am. I hoped things would be better. But what I've...what we've built here, what we've accomplished, it's vulnerable. It's fragile. One crack could bring it all down. I wanted things to go differently; I hoped there was a way to make it work, but..." He looked to the ceiling.

"But what?" Aranok asked, sitting again. "Tell me."

"Aranok, I've had to make decisions. Choices I didn't want to make. The world is complex. There are no simple answers. I know you think I'm wrong—I've made mistakes. And you're right. I have. But here we are. We have to work with what we have. I'm trying to make a better world. For *draoidhs*. For all of us."

"I know." Aranok softened. "The better Eidyn."

"Yes." The king lit up enthusiastically. "Yes. The better Eidyn. You understand."

Of course he understood. They'd talked for years about how they wanted to improve the country. It was why they'd risen up against Hofnag, deposed the old bastard and taken the throne for Janaeus. To make a country where people earned enough to live, could be educated and healthy. Where taxes were affordable. Where landed lairds couldn't extract punitive rents and live fat off their tenants' labour. Where *draoidhs* were protected from ignorance and poison. Where the law was decent and just, not a weapon for the crown to subjugate dissent.

The better Eidyn.

People had died for that vision. Had the end been worth the price?

Maybe it was just too early to say. Or too late for regrets.

---

Allandria followed the other two down the corridor. They were conspicuously quiet—obviously waiting for her to be out of earshot before they discussed what had happened. It was an awkward situation, and it was only going to get worse. Maybe she could salve a few wounds now, before they festered. "Listen, don't take it personally. He doesn't trust new people."

Glorbad turned back to her. "That's fine. I don't trust him either."

"What the fuck is wrong with you?" Nirea slapped the soldier's arm.

"What?" Glorbad snapped back. "I don't."

"He's the envoy and he's just been put in charge of us. You're supposed to be a soldier. Show some respect."

"I'll maybe show some deference when he gives the king due respect. And if you don't think I'm behaving like a soldier, captain, you don't know enough soldiers." Glorbad puffed out his chest like a rooster.

Aranok had a bad habit of leaving arguments in his wake. The inevitable outcome of being pissed off by someone you couldn't tell to go to Hell was that you'd do exactly that to the next person who gave you a reason—even if they didn't.

Allandria put out her hands, gesturing for calm. "Just give him time, please. He can be difficult but he's"—*extremely irritating?*—"sort of brilliant, in his own way. You have to get to know him."

Nirea nodded quietly.

"You know what? I don't." The soldier turned and bustled away. Allandria could almost hear his teeth grinding. She looked at Nirea and sighed.

"He can be a prick, but he's all right really," the sailor said.

"I know the type."

This was definitely going to get worse.

---

Darginn Argyll's knees creaked worse than the wooden steps. Too many damned stairs in this building. When the king's messengers had to evacuate Auldun, they'd taken on the old customs building in Havenport. He'd have been grateful if Madu had chosen an office on the ground floor. Instead, his summons from the head messenger dragged him up three flights to take orders.

The real shite of it was, coming back down would be worse. Made his knees burn like they'd been stabbed with a hot poker. He could've done with more rest before being sent back out.

During the war, a messenger's job had been vital. Rather than delivering news to the country, he'd been delivering orders to troops. Damn sight more dangerous than messengering was meant to be.

His main worry was normally bandits. Though most knew the penalty for interfering with a king's messenger was execution, the Reivers had no care for Eidyn's laws. They raided for whatever they wanted—and sometimes knowing the news of the land was useful.

Darginn might not be a fighter, but he was wily—and that had served him well when negotiating Dead and demons as well as Reivers.

Staying off main roads—listening, watching, always alert. Always quiet. That was how he stayed alive.

Plenty of his fellows hadn't. Sent out with orders that never arrived—what was left of them likely joining Mynygogg's putrid army. A chill crept up Darginn's skull at the thought of the *draoidh*. How he could do what he'd done—slaughter innocent folk, women and children turned to shambling corpses. What sort of a man could do that?

Darginn was a man of peace. Damn sight easier than war. Live free and tread lightly. A lot of people didn't like *draoidhs*. Some thought they were "ungodly." Some called them inhuman. Some were just scared. Maybe all of them were, he reckoned. Seemed like most things people hated were just what scared them. Darginn reckoned maybe those who screamed about what a *draoidh* might do were just telling what they might do themselves, granted the power.

But Hells if Mynygogg hadn't proved them right. Damn shame too.

Mynygogg had never asked for aught. Never negotiated. Never demanded. Just killed.

The *draoidh* must once have been a man, but there couldn't be much man left to commit such evil. No man's soul could withstand that weight. Maybe the magic took him. Demonology *and* necromancy? Maybe his mind was broken. Maybe he was born bad.

Whatever he'd been, he was a monster now.

Darginn rapped lightly on the office door.

"Come." Madu's voice was flat, efficient. She'd been the calm at the centre of the war. Always in control, never flustered. The woman had iron nerves.

The chamber was an odd hybrid of office and living quarters. The main area was a cluttered mess of clothes and furniture. Ornate sofa. Silk scarves. But a regal old desk surveyed the room from a raised bit of floor to Darginn's right, where Madu studied some curiosity. Younger than him, but not much, the head messenger wore a cream dress with navy trim, her greying hair up in something between a braid and a bun.

"Darginn. Good. This is for you." She folded the paper she'd been reading, stamped it with the royal seal and proffered it. "Take it directly to Lestalric, for the baroness only. Leave immediately."

"Immediately? I'd hoped…" He'd hardly been home five minutes. Barely seen his family. He'd hoped to spend more time with them. Eat Isadona's sausage casserole. See Liana while she was still young enough to laugh at her grandad's silly faces. But mostly, aye mostly, to rest. Darginn's bones ached with the memories of war.

"Immediately, I'm afraid. King's orders." Madu's eyes seemed to soften, just a touch. Just for a moment. Her life had been chaos as much as his—the mess of her chambers was testament to that. She was usually one for impeccable standards, her office a beacon of order. "All right. Go home. Say goodbye to your family. But be on the Nor Loch ferry tonight. Without fail."

It was better than nothing. He'd hoped whatever was needed from him would keep a few days. But Lestalric wasn't too bad. Deliver the message, stay a night—he'd be back within the week.

He could do that.

Darginn stuffed the missive in his vest and nodded graciously. "Thank you, messenger."

"Thank you, Darginn. The king appreciates your service."

Darginn turned and braced his old knees for the stairs.

---

Vastin carefully put his face over the bubbling pot and felt the warm steam flow over his face. His stomach grumbled as the weak aroma of chicken and vegetables reached his nostrils. The broth was a few days old, so he was careful to boil it long enough. He drew back, stirring it gently—the way his mother had taught him, to keep any meat left in it from sticking to the bottom.

It had been a quiet day. He'd seen little benefit in trade from his new benefactor. Just a woman looking for a knife sharpened. Should he bother to open the forge tomorrow? Maybe he'd spend the day hunting instead. It was supposed to be safer inside the city walls, but safety was little use to him if he starved to death. He sat back and looked around the small stone room. The firelight made it look warm—almost inviting—but in every stone, every piece of furniture, he saw his parents. Childhood memories he would never make again. As he grew older, they would only become more distant. He'd think about them less. Staying here was difficult, but it kept his memories crisp. The pain made them sharp.

He cocked his head. Footsteps approaching the door. He'd closed up at sunset. There was no reason for anyone to be coming here now. They stopped, as far as he could tell, right outside. Then nothing. Vastin sat perfectly still, listening.

Who comes to a door and doesn't knock? Nobody with good intentions.

Quietly, the boy put his spoon back in the pot and lifted the large silver axe from near the fire. It could be the men from yesterday, or thieves taking advantage of him being alone, knowing he had come into some coin. He crept to the side of the door as silently as possible and lifted the weapon over his shoulder. He might not have much, but damned if he was going to let anyone take it. Not while there was breath in his body.

Finally, a gentle knocking.

"Vastin?"

The voice was familiar, friendly, but he couldn't place it.

"Vastin. Are you there?"

That was enough. Vastin felt a wave of relief. He sighed, lowered the axe and warmly opened the door. It was a voice he would not forget as long as he lived.

"Sire! Please, come in."

---

Aranok smiled as he entered the blacksmith's home. It was basic and efficient: bed in the corner with a cloth sheet hung as a makeshift curtain. The workshop took up most of the space, along with the stock Vastin couldn't sell to buy the food that should have been over the fire. There was a weak smell of something, though.

The boy put down an impressive axe and closed the door behind him. He obviously wasn't expecting visitors. Not friendly ones anyway. Understandable.

"Don't call me sire, please."

"All right," Vastin agreed, slightly timidly. "What may I call you?"

"My friends just use my name."

Vastin smiled broadly. Aranok had debated with himself for most of the day whether this was a good idea, and changed his mind several times. The boy was young and deserved to get older. But Janaeus, he hated to concede, had a point. If nobody was buying weapons and armour, how could a blacksmith make a living? Pots and door hinges might just keep him alive—but they clearly weren't where the boy's talents lay. There was a good chance he'd end up press-ganged into the army one way or another. At best, that might be a few years off.

Was it a good idea?

"I have a proposition for you." Aranok idly stroked the edge of the fireplace.

"Yes, sire…" Vastin paused, realising his error. "I mean…what may I do for you, Laird Aranok? Do you need repairs?"

"No." Aranok winced at *laird*. It was strictly accurate, but he had never been comfortable with it. His father was the laird.

The boy looked up at him patiently. Aranok watched the fire dance around the old black pot for a moment, then turned to the rack of weapons. Better he learn how to fight now, while Aranok could at least keep an eye on him.

"Did your father teach you how to use these?"

"He did," the boy answered. "Knowing how to use a weapon gives a better understanding of how to make it—you get the balance."

"Your father was a wise man." Aranok smiled at him uncomfortably. He'd never been good with grief, his own or anyone else's. "Which are you most competent with?"

"I'm good with a short sword, but I prefer the axe." He nodded at the weapon he'd just put down.

"And armour? Do you have armour?"

"Yes, sir. My father adjusted his old set for me before he left."

"Excellent. Come on." Aranok set off back to the door.

"Where are we going?" the boy asked, confused. "What should I bring?"

"You hungry?"

"I have some chicken broth." Vastin nodded to the thin concoction bubbling in the pot.

Aranok looked at it with a mixture of disdain and self-consciousness. He didn't want to insult the boy, but it was a pitiful excuse for a meal. "Douse the fire. We're going to the tavern for roast lamb."

"I can't afford lamb," Vastin protested quietly.

"I know," said Aranok. "But I can't have my new personal blacksmith travelling on an empty stomach."

# CHAPTER 4

Vastin's stomach threatened to crawl growling up his gullet as the sweet smell of roast lamb and rosemary breathed into him. For a moment, he all but forgot he was sitting across from one of the most powerful people in Eidyn. But if he wasn't, he'd not have been anywhere near the steaming plate that had appeared in front of him.

"Thank you, Amollari." Laird Aranok winked and pushed his cupped hand across the table. Amollari's eyes widened and she glanced over her shoulder before quickly picking up whatever he'd been covering and slipping it into her apron. A tip, likely. He'd heard the wealthy did that sometimes—gave extra money for good service. Vastin had never had that kind of coin. But if he had, Amollari would have earned it. She was always smiling and somehow smelled of heather and sunshine despite her work. And she was kind. Always kind. More than once in the last months she'd slipped Vastin some offcut meat or a chunk of pie. Days he'd really needed it. It had often been her packages that kept his stew more than broth, that kept his stomach from cramping.

Vastin didn't know if her da knew what she was doing, and he was afraid to ask in case...in case he broke it, somehow. In case he made it awkward for her—for both of them. So he just thanked her and took what she was able to give him with good grace.

The way his mother would have.

Amollari smiled and curtseyed to Laird Aranok, gave Vastin a quick glance—did her smile widen a little?—and disappeared back through the crowd.

People had been watching them since they arrived. A pair of old women at the bar had abruptly stopped twittering and spoken to each other in hushed tones behind hands when they'd ordered food. A man with a thin beard and weathered cheeks had almost choked on his ale when they sat down. And even now, Vastin felt eyes on the back of his head. But it didn't matter.

In front of him was the finest meal he'd seen in an age, and he was all but drooling over it.

But was it rude to eat before his host? He was sure that was something he'd been told, once. He didn't know how lairds and ladies dined, and he'd no desire to embarrass himself in the Chain Pier of all places. So he sat with his head slightly bowed, looking for a sign from the king's envoy that he should eat.

"Hells, don't wait for an invitation, tuck in!" Laird Aranok waved a hand at the plate.

The first mouthful fell apart between his teeth and he felt the heat of it slide down into his stomach. It grumbled in appreciation and desire.

God it was good.

There was little conversation then, as he wolfed down the plate. A slight bout of nausea nearly stopped him at one point, but a timely burp disguised as a cough had him quickly settled.

Laird Aranok still had half a plate left when Vastin finished, leaving him sitting in awkward silence, watching his benefactor eat and wondering why he was there. The silence quickly became painful.

"Laird...may I ask you a question?" Why had he said that? What in Hells was he going to ask?

The envoy nodded. Now what? What conversation could he start that would interest a man like him? He should ask about him. Something he'd enjoy talking about. The war...? No, Vastin didn't want to hear about that. Not yet. The rebellion. He could ask about the rebellion.

"You helped Janaeus take the throne? From Hofnag?"

Laird Aranok's eyebrows rose and he paused chewing a moment to smile gently. "I did."

"Why'd everyone hate him? I mean, I hear talk—people say he was a right…um, bastard. But, I mean, how…?"

"How was he a bastard?"

"Aye."

The envoy swallowed, took a deep breath and sat back. "How old are you? Fifteen?" Vastin nodded. "So you'd have been, what, ten, eleven during the rebellion?" Another nod. He remembered it, but it had felt distanced from his life. Vastin's parents had stayed home and the fighting never really reached Haven. Mostly, he remembered business was good. The king was all but ordering weaponry by weight.

*Oh.*

That meant his father had made the weapons used against King Janaeus and Laird Aranok. He'd probably not mention that.

Aranok leaned forward, beckoning Vastin to do the same. "There were a lot of reasons," he said quietly. "He was bigoted against *draoidhs*, for a start. When he inherited the throne from his mother, he could have repealed a lot of the old laws about performing magic, but he didn't. If anything, he enforced them harder. And at the same time, there wasn't much protection for us either." A waver in the envoy's eyes suggested something difficult, and Vastin regretted asking the question. This wasn't where he'd thought it would lead. "If a *draoidh* was attacked—even killed—there wasn't much effort made to find the criminal. It was a bad time to be *draoidh*."

Vastin hadn't known that. He hadn't really known a *draoidh* before—that he was aware of. All he'd heard about Hofnag were complaints about taxes—and his own experience didn't suggest Janaeus was any better about that. There must have been more, though, he thought. But this line of conversation had already gotten a bit uncomfortable. Maybe he could change the course a bit.

"How does magic work? Like, how do you make stuff just"—Vastin waved a hand—"happen?"

Aranok laughed warmly. That was good. "What do you want to know?"

Vastin shrugged. He hadn't really thought any further than that.

When he said nothing, the envoy spoke anyway. "Well, we don't know everything. There are masters at the university dedicated to expanding our knowledge of magic—where it comes from, why it works, why only some people can access it. What we know is that there are different skills. I'm an earth *draoidh*, which gives me power over the elements: earth, air, fire, water, light and gravity—the force that pulls us to earth. But there are others—physic, energy, illusion, nature, metamorph—those are the most common. And there are the darker skills, necromancy and demonology. Rarer."

"Mynygogg has both?"

"Mmm. Unique, as far as we know. No *draoidh* has ever had more than one skill."

He didn't want to talk about Mynygogg. Not yet. Laird Aranok picked at the remnants of his dinner. But he hadn't really answered Vastin's question. At least, not in the way he now realised he meant.

"But, how do you...? Is it like speaking? Or breathing? Can you just do it?"

The envoy nodded and swallowed his mouthful. "I see what you're asking. Sort of, yes. In that, at first, you can just do it. One day, as a child, you do something—a reflex, an instinct. Then you know. But you can't control it. When you're young, it just...happens, sporadically. Dangerously. So we learn to control it. With gestures and incantations—words used to focus the magic."

"Oh." That was pretty interesting, actually. He hadn't seen the envoy do magic, but he wanted to. Part of him wished the big bastard who'd tried to rob him hadn't backed down. It would have been interesting to see what Laird Aranok could have done. If he was honest, though, at the time, he'd probably been too scared to appreciate it.

"Does that answer your question?" The envoy picked up his knife and stabbed the final stray piece of lamb.

"I think so." He had more questions now. Like how did they know what gestures and words to use, and who first made them and why did they work? But he didn't want to be the annoying schoolchild, so he stowed them for another time.

Aranok wiped an edge of gravy off the little blade and set it beside his plate.

"Good. Because I have a question for you."

The moon rose, a light sliver over the dark trees. Nirea watched through the slit in the West Gate. It was eerily beautiful. The night air smelled of grass and mud over the nearby torches. She stood near enough one to feel its heat.

There should have been several large, experienced guards here, but the solitary soul on duty was barely a man. Thin and hawkish, he hardly looked capable of lifting his sword over his head, never mind fighting anything that breached the gate. Thankfully, the massive, dark oak barrier was engraved with runes that made it near impossible to break through. Nirea traced one with her finger, black where the hot blade had scorched the wood. Had Aranok himself dug these intricate patterns?

Nirea hadn't known many *draoidhs*, but those she'd met had been decent folk. She'd had a girl on one of her boats for a while, Mirala. She was handy with water and wind, useful talents at sea. But her romantic vision of life on the wave hadn't braced her for the crude reality. The sea made you hard, and hard men were cruel. Mirala had barely lasted one season. Last Nirea heard she'd gone back to the university in Traverlyn.

Damned shame. She was a hell of an asset in battle.

"Bloody magic."

Nirea turned to see her drinking companion had joined her. He cut a more impressive figure in his armour. He also looked as if, like her, he'd spent much of the day sleeping. Still a grumpy sod, though. "It's bloody magic that's keeping us safe."

Glorbad shook his head. "We put too much faith in that stuff. We're lazy, off guard. Who knows when something like that"—he stabbed a finger at the gate—"might fail and leave us with just this to protect us?"

The guard looked down from the wall to see Glorbad's accusatory hand waving in his direction. He stood up straight and threw back his shoulders but still looked like a wee boy in his daddy's armour.

Nirea put an arm around Glorbad's shoulders, turned him away and whispered, "Can we try not to offend *everyone*? I'd like to be welcome when we get back. He's on our side, remember?"

"If that's the best we've got," Glorbad mock-whispered back at her, "then our side is in deep shit."

"Were you of the idea that we weren't in deep shit?" She smiled.

The old goat snorted in reply. "Fair."

"The shit is not as deep as it was." A woman's voice.

Nirea turned toward it, instinctively putting her hand on her sword hilt. Glorbad and the guard had done the same. They'd thought themselves alone. Allandria stepped from a dark corner with a crooked smile. When he saw who it was, the guard replaced the sword he'd half drawn from its sheath.

"Where the fuck did you come from?" Glorbad asked.

"Just there." Allandria jerked her thumb at the shadows. Nirea made a note to be careful what she said in future unless they were definitely alone. She didn't like being spied on.

"Come on." Allandria gestured to them. "We're meeting Aranok in town."

"I thought we were leaving from here?" Nirea asked, confused.

"We're not." The archer carried on walking.

"Then why the Hell tell us to meet here?" Glorbad demanded, his cheeks turning a florid shade of rouge.

"So I knew where to find you," she answered.

Nirea looked at him and rolled her eyes. They might as well just follow her.

"He better have a good explanation," Glorbad grumbled.

"I guess we'll see." Nirea was beginning to wonder what she'd got herself into. Why was the king's envoy playing games with them?

"Bloody *draoidhs*," the soldier mumbled.

"Hey," said Nirea. "Enough of that." They didn't need the soldier's careless prejudice. There were plenty of people who disliked *draoidhs* just for what they were. If the envoy pegged Glorbad for a bigot, any chance of this group coming together would be ended.

"Keep up!" Allandria called cheerily from the junction where she'd stopped to wait.

Glorbad growled. "I hate this assignment."

———◆———

"What are you playing at?" the fat soldier demanded. "Why tell us to meet you at the West Gate, then bring us to a blacksmith's in the dark?"

Vastin looked nervously to the envoy. He'd told him to put on his armour but hadn't explained why. Was he expecting a fight? Laird Aranok calmly leaned forward in his chair.

"I met you this morning. I have no idea whether I can trust you. I don't like people knowing where I'm going to be. And while you're with me, I know you can't be telling anyone else."

That wasn't reassuring.

"What about her?" The soldier pointed accusatorily at the archer. Vastin recognised her from the previous day. Even if he hadn't, most people knew that where the envoy went, Allandria's bow followed. The bodyguard leaned casually against the cool forge.

"*Her,*" the envoy answered, "I have known for a long time. If *her* wanted to betray me, I'd already be dead. Her name is Allandria. I expect you to show her the same respect you show me. I expect you to show her more."

Allandria's eyes lit up with mirth. She didn't seem to be as worried that this was going to turn into a fight. In fact, she seemed completely at home. The other woman—a sailor, by the look of her red leathers—said nothing. Her lips were tight as her eyes darted back and forth between the men.

"How are we supposed to work together if you don't trust us?" the soldier continued. "We're the king's council!"

Vastin suddenly felt his legs become unsteady. The king's council? What Laird Aranok had told him over dinner was a lot. Now it seemed he had some of the most important people in Eidyn in his home. And the envoy had only just met them? What had he got himself into?

"Janaeus makes his judgements," Aranok replied. "We don't always agree."

"Your king's word is not good enough?" the soldier asked.

"The only person whose word I take for anything is standing behind you," the envoy answered, "and I doubt you've done yourself any favours there."

The soldier briefly turned to look at Allandria but said nothing. She smiled a little once he looked away. The archer was attractive for an older woman. About his mum's age, he reckoned. The age she would be.

"So why are we here?" The sailor's voice was commanding, as if she was used to being listened to. Made sense if she was on the council that she must have been a captain or something.

The envoy stood and extended a hand toward him. "This is Vastin, one of the best blacksmiths in Eidyn. Vastin, this is Allandria, Nirea and Glorbad."

Vastin felt his cheeks flush at the compliment. He was good, but not exceptional. His father had been better. He bowed sheepishly. "Good evening, sire, m'ladies."

"Hello," said Nirea politely. The others nodded in acknowledgement.

"As you can see," Aranok continued, "he has a stock of excellent, unused weaponry here. Take your pick."

"Seriously?" Nirea asked. "Who's paying?"

"I am," said Aranok. "I've enlisted Vastin as my personal smith for the foreseeable future. He'll also be travelling with us to effect repairs as we need them." Hearing him say it out loud again made Vastin shiver. He'd agreed, because how could he not? The man to whom he probably owed his life had said it was a good idea. That he needed him. Now he could see some part of why. Glorbad and Nirea at least had need of a blacksmith.

"Oh, will he?" Glorbad asked. "Look at him! He'll be eaten by the first dog we come across!"

Vastin felt his face flush again, but Aranok just smiled. "He can look after himself. Can't you?"

Vastin steeled himself and stood up to his full height. "Aye."

Glorbad laughed. Faster than Vastin could have imagined, the soldier stepped forward and swung his blade. Vastin instinctively fell to one knee and raised his arm in defence, but the blow never landed. Instead, it glanced off the arm the envoy had thrust in front of him.

"What the Hells!?" Vastin reached for a weapon of his own. His hand landed on a broadsword—not ideal for fighting at close quarters like this. But it would do.

He looked up to see Allandria had drawn her bow and stepped toward the soldier. Aranok stayed her with a raised hand. She no longer looked relaxed.

"Magic armour," the soldier grumbled. "Going to spend every battle standing next to him, are you? He'd be dead if I'd been trying to hit him."

"You'd be dead if you'd been trying to hit him," said Aranok.

Glorbad turned to see the arrow.

Allandria shot Nirea a dark look, and the sailor nodded warily. She put a hand on Glorbad's arm, and he shrank back from the envoy. Vastin kept hold of the sword. He didn't fancy being caught unawares like that again. If the old bastard had another go at him, he'd be ready.

"Very good," Glorbad said, taking a seat. "But you know what I mean. You just trying to get him killed, or all of us?"

Nirea slapped him across the back of the head. He looked round in surprise and she glowered darkly at him. But he didn't complain.

"Well, you're going to take this as an opportunity to further his training, Glorbad," said Aranok. "Give him the benefit of your many years' experience."

Vastin looked to the envoy. He wanted this arse to train him?

"Are you calling me old?" Glorbad narrowed his eyes. The tense silence only broke when the soldier burst with laughter. Nirea joined in tentatively. Allandria replaced her arrow in its quiver, shaking her head at Aranok.

"Fine." Glorbad nodded thoughtfully. "We'll see what we can make of the boy. What's your favourite weapon, wee man?"

*Wee man.*

The soldier stood no more than an inch or two taller than Vastin. Warily, he put down the sword and reached across the bench for his axe. "This." He held the weapon out for inspection.

Glorbad weighed it up loosely in his hands. "Interesting. Nice weight. Good balance. Fine edge. Make it yourself?"

"No. It was my father's." His father had been better with a sword, which was the only reason he'd left the axe behind.

"Well, if you've your father's skill, boy, maybe you won't be dead weight after all."

Vastin's stomach lurched. He wasn't his father, not as a smith or as a fighter. The envoy might have said nice things about him, but he'd never seen him in a fight. Except for when they met—and that barely counted. The only person Vastin had ever really sparred with was his father.

A clatter of metal made Vastin look up. Nirea was examining a pair of scimitars. "I'll have these, if you don't mind?"

"Of course." He looked to Aranok for confirmation.

Glorbad lifted a large shield from behind a stack. "This is far too light. Is it just for decoration?"

Vastin smiled. These were his speciality. Now he was in his element.

"That's one of our best shields. Made using a special folding technique. There are multiple layers of thin metal in there. It's light, but hard as any traditional shield. Father learned the technique in the east."

"Did he now?" Glorbad knocked suspiciously on the front of the shield, which clanged satisfyingly in return. "You're trying to get me killed too, aren't you?"

"No, sir," Vastin answered seriously. "I wouldn't do that."

Glorbad looked at him curiously. "All right, I'll take this—as long as you take one the same."

Vastin lifted his own shield and threw it to Glorbad, who dropped the other with a jolt. Its sharp edge marked the wooden floor. Glorbad tested the weight of the shield he'd been thrown, nodding.

"That's mine," Vastin said proudly. The front bore two crossed hammers, the crest he and his father had chosen.

Glorbad looked down appreciatively at the scar in the floor. "Aye, all right."

Laird Aranok had remained silent during the discussions. "No sword?" he asked, after a moment's quiet.

Glorbad put his hand on the hilt of his sword. "Me and this beast have been through a lot together. She'll see me right."

"Fine," said Aranok. "Gather your things and let's go. Leave anything here that you don't need—we'll come back for it."

"Where are we going?" Nirea leaned her old swords against the rack.

"South Gate," said Aranok.

"Our horses are at the West Gate," Glorbad protested.

"No, they're not." The *draoidh* walked out the door. Vastin picked up his keys and followed, pausing to wait for the others.

Glorbad turned to Nirea. "Bloody *draoidhs*."

She hit him. Vastin smiled.

Darginn stepped cautiously onto the ferry. The old wooden boards groaned as his balance adjusted to the bobbing of the Nor Loch. The light of the boatman's torch flickered on the lapping waves.

"Late crossing the night," the old man said.

"Aye," Darginn replied flatly, making it clear he wasn't going to expand on the subject.

"Won't be long," said the boatman, releasing the ropes that anchored the ferry to the western shore. Darginn watched as his gnarled hands fumbled with the ropes, resisting an urge to push him out of the way and do the job himself. It would have been a damn sight quicker. But he wasn't in all that much of a hurry to get going, truth be told.

"Do we still pass close to Dun Eidyn?" Darginn looked ahead into the darkness. Somewhere out there, the castle's imperious towers loomed over the loch, dominating the night sky. Was there a flicker of light?

"Aye, sir. The chains are anchored against Castle Rock." A definite note of discomfort in the boatman's voice. "He can't get out, though, right?"

"No," Darginn answered, fingering the parchment in his pocket. "The castle is off-limits, but not the loch. It's perfectly safe." He hoped he sounded more convinced than he was. He'd never seen Myny-gogg personally, but he knew what he could do—had done. Conjuring demons, raising the dead, turning men into monsters—even at Darginn's age, with a grandchild, he'd lost a lot of sleep during the war. He'd largely avoided battle, but the one fight he happened upon… God, he'd never forget it.

That boy.

Eyes torn from their sockets, jaw hanging limp and half the back of his head missing. Poor bastard couldn't even have known his own name—just reaching out on instinct—a baby searching for his mother's tit. He'd never forget that face, or the slavering, horned thing that mauled it. That was as close to actual fighting as he'd come, and he'd pissed himself the moment that beast looked straight at him. Even now, his heart faltered and his chest tightened.

Thank God for the White Thorns.

With a jerk, the ferry began to move as the boatman pulled the chains and dragged the ferry across the quiet water. Darginn exhaled mist with each breath.

The message he carried to Baroness de Lestalric must be extremely urgent. He'd ridden hard all day to reach the ferry. Sleeping on the crossing had occurred to him, but the rocking of the boat and the dragging of the chains would likely keep him awake.

Even if they didn't, he intended to be alert when they passed Dun Eidyn.

# CHAPTER 5

The fire crackled into life. Samily sat back, relieved it had finally taken. The wood was still damp from the rain a few days before. She'd been at it a while and her hands ached from the effort.

"Well done, child." Meristan was setting up the spit to cook the rabbit she'd caught earlier.

Samily smiled her appreciation, rubbing her palms with her fingers.

The day's travel had been simple and quiet. They'd cut straight through the Wilds, trusting that Reivers would know well enough to keep their distance. So far, they had. It had been nice just to spend time travelling with her master—almost as if the last year had not happened.

They sat in silence for some time, watching the rabbit's flesh brown.

"Samily?" Meristan asked. "What are your memories of the war?"

*Where to begin?*

"Fighting, mostly, I suppose. And walking. A lot of walking. And cold. And wet. We killed a pair of snake demons in Glabertoun. They were quick."

Meristan nodded thoughtfully. "Do you know, I remember very little. It's like a blur. I remember meetings, discussions, some travelling. But I've lost so much. And I have dreams."

The monk looked up at the night sky.

"Dreams of things that never happened, of demons clawing at my legs. I don't sleep well."

Samily stared awkwardly back at him. She should say something, something to make it better. What would make it better?

"God watches over you. Always."

Meristan looked back at her sadly. "Of course." He stood, brushing down his robes. "Excuse me, Samily. Nature requires."

Samily nodded gently and watched him disappear into the thicket of trees.

"Turn the rabbit!" he called from the darkness.

If she'd had doubts before, she was sure now. Something was very wrong. Memory loss and nightmares? He had always been so strong—the rock the Order leaned on. What had reduced him to this?

She leaned forward and carefully turned the spit. Juices dripped into the fire, spitting and hissing in protest. It was already nearing black on the underside—it would not be long before they could share it. Good thing too—she was hungry, and it smelled good.

"Samily!" The shriek was panicked and urgent.

Heaven, no! A Reiver party waiting in the trees? Worse, a demon?

Samily sprang to her feet and lifted her sword, rushing to the space Meristan had left through. She could hear him crashing toward her. He wasn't far. Best she stepped back and allowed him into the clearing—she'd be able to see what she was fighting.

The monk stumbled into the firelight. She glanced at him to assess if he'd been wounded, but he fell with a thud at the other side of the fire.

Had he already taken a mortal blow? What was coming?

She focused on the enemy, as she'd been taught. Her breathing slowed.

*Clear your mind, trust in God and stand your ground.*

She heard a low growling from the darkness and stepped back a few paces, giving herself room to swing. She could hear Meristan moving, scrambling behind her. He was still alive.

Eyes in the dark, reflecting the firelight. Low to the ground—a bear? Or a wolf? She stared back at it, daring it to move. Hoping it might decide to hunt elsewhere tonight.

With a low growl, it leapt. She stepped across its trajectory, drawing her blade with her, and turned. She felt the tug of flesh against the

edge, the crunch of bone as the blade sliced through the beast. She
heard its awful whimper and the wet crunch as it landed on the dirt.
Her blade ran with blood. She turned to see their attacker.

A dog.

A wild, starved dog, split from mouth to lungs. It was skin and
bone—probably hadn't eaten in days, attracted by the smell of their
rabbit.

Involuntarily, she laughed—more with relief than amusement.
She turned to Meristan, smiling, but her face fell when she saw him.
He sat backed up against a tree, one hand over his mouth. His eyes
streamed with tears and he shook with terror, staring at the mangled
carcass.

"It's only a dog," she said quietly. "It's…all right."

Meristan put his face in his hands and sobbed.

—————◦—————

Nirea couldn't even see the bugs she was swatting at, but she could
hear them, and they made her scalp itch. Crouched in the undergrowth
was the worst place to be. The ground was soft and damp, making it
hard even to lift her boots, and squatting was only digging them in
deeper.

"Why in Hell did we leave out the South Gate if we were just going
to skirt the city walls and practically pass the West Gate anyway?"
Glorbad bristled.

Dragging his horse off the roadway in the dark had not improved his
mood. In some ways, she liked him better drunk. He complained less.
But he had a point. The envoy wasn't making this easy.

"I don't know, but stop aggravating him."

"He's aggravating me," the soldier replied.

Nirea sighed. "If I was to guess, I'd say he's testing if he can trust us."

"How?"

"He sent the archer ahead to scout the road and he's separated himself with the boy on the other side. If she comes back and tells him
there was an ambush waiting for us on the road out of the West Gate,
he's going to wonder if we had anything to do with it."

"Hell's arse!" Glorbad grumbled. "I could be three beers down by now!" He looked up to the sky, hidden by the canopy of trees. "What did I do to deserve this?"

———

Allandria crept quietly back through the trees. She was at home outside the city walls. Learning to survive in the Wilds was natural to all children of Lochen, along with archery. The bow had long been the town's traditional weapon and the nearby Archer's Hill, the ancient volcano, was named for it. She'd been given her first bow at the age of seven. At twenty-two, she'd handcrafted her own, as was tradition. Twenty years later, it served her as well as the first day. It was like an extension of her arm now. She didn't think about using it, simply focused on where she needed to put an arrow. She'd made it well. Hours spent rubbing oil into the wood kept it supple.

Tonight, it had taken two more Reiver lives. Aranok would not be pleased, except insofar as it justified his irritatingly cautious approach to everything. She'd long since stopped trying to argue. He'd been right too often.

"Aranok," she whispered, as loud as she dared. "Aranok...?"

"Yes?"

Damn the irritating Hell out of him, he was behind her. She sighed and turned.

"Well?" the *draoidh* asked quietly.

"Two Reivers. In the trees, two miles from the gate."

"Damn it," said Aranok.

"What does that mean?" asked Vastin, who had stayed dutifully quiet until now.

"It might mean nothing," said the *draoidh*. "It might mean the kingdom is so crawling with bandits that we're going to encounter them everywhere. Or it might mean one of them"—he nodded across the road—"is not to be trusted."

Vastin's eyes widened. "You think...?"

"Don't worry," Allandria reassured him, "he assumes everyone is an enemy until proven otherwise."

"Oh," Vastin said uncomfortably. "Including me?"

"Vastin, I'll owe you a small fortune between the weapons and what I'm paying you for this trip. You'd be an idiot to want me dead," said Aranok.

"Oh, yeah." The boy smiled, presumably considering the small fortune, and what he'd spend it on. Maybe a drink with the young barmaid from the Chain Pier.

"So do we join the others and tell them we're onto them?" Allandria asked sarcastically.

"No." Aranok frowned. "It's enough that we know. Watch your backs, both of you—and don't be alone with either of them. Especially the sailor."

"Why the sailor?" asked Vastin. "She seems nice."

"It's always the nice ones," he said, pulling his horse back toward the road.

---

"What is the value of a man, Samily?"

The knight opened her eyes. She'd only been in a light meditation, but it still took her a moment to process what had been said. "Brother?"

The monk stared vacantly at the flames. "If a man does good all his life, does it matter what he thinks? Do his feelings, his desires, condemn him regardless, do you think?"

Samily shifted awkwardly. Her back was stiff. "Brother, I do not think I understand the question."

Meristan looked up at her, his eyes pale.

"I am afraid, Samily. I am afraid that I am a coward. I have trained children to fight the battles I am too scared to fight myself. And I am afraid of what that makes me."

Samily breathed deeply, uncrossed her legs and rose. She moved next to her master and gently took his hand. Under any other circumstances, this would have been an unforgivable breach of her station.

"Brother, if not for you, I would have remained an orphan. Penniless, begging for food—likely dead. You took me in. You raised me and made me strong. Without you, I am nothing. God protects us, as we protect God's children. You act to win all the battles, not just one. There is no more noble cause."

For the first time since she had returned, Meristan smiled.

"You are extremely kind, child. Someone raised you well."

Samily's head snapped round to stare into the trees. They'd both heard it. Something was moving. She was on her feet and wearing her helm in seconds.

"Show yourself!" she bellowed into the dark. They were in a vulnerable position if they were surrounded. She could only hope her bravado and the armour might make them think twice. Meristan stood with his staff raised, backed against her.

"I am with you, girl." His voice cracked only slightly. "Whatever comes."

"Help." The weak voice was barely audible. He staggered toward them, head lolling like a tavern drunk.

"What is it?" Meristan asked. "Surely the Blackened have not come this far west?"

It was no plague carrier. As the Reiver staggered into the light, it became obvious why he moved as he did—his right arm had been torn from the socket and his entire side was a sticky mess of blood.

"Help," he gasped again.

Samily moved instinctively to catch him as he stumbled toward her. Before she could ask what to do, Meristan was ripping cloth from his robe. "Lie him down there, against the tree. We need to pack that wound."

Samily did as she was told. The monk frantically pressed the material against what was left of the Reiver's shoulder.

"Brother, I can…"

"No," he cut her off. "Whatever did this to him could be near. If you're weakened, none of us will survive. God delivered him to us. God will decide what happens to him."

Blood seeped through the cloth. It wasn't going to be enough.

"Damn it!" Meristan reached out a hand. "Quick, bring me wood from the fire."

Samily carefully grabbed the end of a charred piece of wood and drew it from the flames. It still burned gently at the end. Meristan took the soaked cloths from the wound and wrapped them round his hand to grab the makeshift torch. He closed his eyes, seemingly uttering a silent prayer. Placing his right hand over the Reiver's eyes, he pressed the smouldering wood against the wound.

The screaming didn't last long.

Meristan looked back at her, his eyes wide and his face slick with sweat.

"Now what?" Samily asked.

"Now we wait. And watch."

———✧———

The campfire burned low by the time the man woke. Meristan snored loudly.

"Help," he murmured again, trying to sit up. But he had no strength. Samily moved quickly to cradle his head and protect him from injuring himself further.

"Shh," she said. "It's all right. You're safe. Sleep." It broke her heart to see a man so injured, so much in pain. She wanted more than anything, in that moment, to make it better.

"Wha's...happ'ning?" His glazed eyes searched for something familiar. "Don't understand...wha's happ'ning?" He could barely take in enough breath to make the words audible.

"You're wounded," Samily answered gently. "Don't try to move. Just sleep. I will protect you."

Sweat glistened on his pale face. He might have a fever. That was a bad sign.

The man reached for Samily's face with his remaining hand, his eyes still fighting to focus. "Are you...my enemy?"

"It doesn't matter." She placed his hand back on his chest. "Just sleep."

He gazed down at the space where his arm should have been. Samily had never seen someone look so confused, so lost—as if he'd dreamt himself a fish and woke to find a man. Finally, his eyes rolled back and closed again. Samily put his head down carefully and moved back to her seat by the fire. Dawn wasn't far. She should wake Meristan and get some sleep herself.

The Reiver shifted one more time, as though his body was determined to survive, to stay here, in this moment, to fight some unseen battle. He mumbled something Samily could not hear.

She hoped it wasn't important. She prayed it wasn't his last.

# CHAPTER 6

The Starbank Inn had once been a bustling hive of travellers. It sat about a day's ride from Haven, at the crossroads of the Wester Road and the Green Road. The inn's high-quality food and ale were legend throughout the kingdom, as were its hospitality and entertainment. Nowhere else paid musicians so well as the Starbank, meaning nowhere else attracted such wonderful music. Aranok had enjoyed many memorable nights there—and some he could barely remember at all. This morning, with the sun rising over the remnants of its roof, it looked a sad, burnt-out ruin, long abandoned to decay.

He'd known well the family that ran the inn. Craddock was a good man. Treated people right, regardless of their station. Even offered cheap food at the end of the night for those who couldn't afford the full price. His daughters, Esra and Sarro, were kind, intelligent girls who'd helped him run the inn after their mother died. That was before Aranok knew them, but they all spoke of her generosity. Aranok suspected it might have been her idea to offer the cheap meals, and that Craddock honoured her by keeping up the practice.

What was her name? Shalla? Saya? Something like that. He regretted never having met her.

"There's not much left of the top floor." Allandria stifled a yawn. They were all tired.

Aranok dismounted and approached slowly. A body lay to the side of the door. It had been there some time.

"Is that a person?" Vastin asked.

"I knew the owner." Aranok crouched next to the body. It was charred black, but there was enough left for Aranok to see it had been a large man, stockily built. Like Craddock.

"What happened here?" the boy asked.

Nobody answered. But Aranok suspected they were all thinking the same thing: demon. The scorch marks on the ground, the haphazard nature of the fire damage—it all pointed to something breathing flames.

The other, more worrying possibility was a *draoidh*. An earth *draoidh*, like Aranok, could throw fire in a way that would leave these marks. He hoped not. He didn't need another rogue *draoidh* to deal with. A quick glance at Glorbad made him wonder what the soldier was thinking. Allandria had said the man was complaining about magic. He half expected to see Glorbad glowering back at him, but his face was as sombre as the rest.

"I had good times here," he said wistfully. "Good people..."

"The stables are around back," Aranok said to Nirea.

She nodded, dismounted and gestured to Glorbad to join her.

"Why me?" he grumbled.

Nirea cocked her head and he followed her with the horses. Maybe the old goat could be civilised after all. It would certainly be helpful.

"What do you think?" Allandria asked.

Aranok ran his hand over one of the shutters. "This has been repaired. Quickly. Poorly."

"You think somebody could be inside?" Vastin asked.

Aranok nodded. "Maybe."

Or something.

"How do you want to go in?" Allandria asked.

"Vastin, you're out here. Watch our backs." The boy needed to be as far from a fight as possible, at least until he'd had half a chance to learn something from the soldier. He lifted his shield in assent and took a step back to draw the axe from its place on his back. He almost looked like he'd be able to use it.

Aranok moved to a position about ten yards from the door, in a direct line of sight. "Door's not locked. I'll open it; be ready for anything that comes out." Allandria stood behind him, arrow nocked. He crouched in the dirt, made the gestures and spoke the word *gluais*, then thrust his hand at the door. It groaned open, half hanging from the upper hinge.

"Wow," the boy whispered. It was better than the reactions Aranok was used to.

They stood on guard, waiting for whatever came at them.

Nothing.

"Right," Allandria finally said. "I suppose we're going in, then."

The two of them crept warily to the door. It creaked in protest and dug into the dirt as Aranok tried to pull it open farther. The smell was bad. Something acrid. Something rotten.

He put a shoulder against the edge of the door and pushed. It creaked but didn't move.

"I don't like this," Allandria whispered.

Aranok grunted in agreement. She swapped her bow for the sword she used only when necessary. She was good with it, a match for most soldiers, but her archery skills usually made it unnecessary—no enemy lived to get close to her.

"*Solas.*" Aranok quickly conjured a small, glowing orb and cast it into the room. Benches were overturned. Tables held remnants of meals, covered in mould, crawling with life. That explained the smell. Well, some of it. The fire must have stayed mostly upstairs, because a lot of the floor was undamaged. The beams in the ceiling were buckled and blackened in places, but mostly intact. It was unlikely that it could have been so contained upstairs, and Aranok wondered whether a *draoidh* had something to do with extinguishing it—which made him wonder, again, about who had started it.

"Stay here," he said quietly to Vastin. "Wait for the others."

He and Allandria crept into the dank space. Aranok coughed as dust hit the back of his throat. He pulled his scarf up over his mouth.

"Where are the bodies?" Allandria asked.

It was a good question. People had died here. The dark-stained wood was testament to it. Why was there just the body outside?

The *draoidh* gestured at the orb and it split in two—one gravitated to his bodyguard.

"Kitchen," he said. The orb followed as Allandria moved behind the bar and disappeared through the archway.

The room looked largely intact. Apart from one corner where the ceiling bowed heavily and appeared to have something wet growing on it, it seemed sturdy enough to get them through the day.

They needed shelter during daylight. The journey through the night had been slow but quiet, as Aranok had hoped. They were more likely to be targeted by Reivers during the day, so they might as well sleep through the sunlit hours.

"Nobody in there." Allandria came back into the room. "Just some rotten food. Looks like somebody tried to eat it anyway—and regretted it." She screwed up her face in disgust.

That explained the other smell—rotten food and stale vomit. It was an effort not to gag.

"Recently?"

She shook her head. "Days."

"Well, let's make ourselves at home, then."

---

Samily woke to birdsong, the smell of morning dew and woodsmoke. She lay with her eyes closed, drinking in the forest atmosphere. The birds punctuated a constant buzz of insect life. There was a river somewhere near.

Meristan's breathing came into focus. It sounded laboured, tired. Opening her eyes, she sat up to find him leaning over the Reiver.

"How is he, Brother?"

Meristan turned and looked at her sadly. He shook his head. It was a punch to the gut.

"He was lucky to make it as far as he did with his injury," the monk said.

Samily nodded. She would not cry.

"At least we made him comfortable," he added.

"I could have saved him," she said quietly, then gasped, quickly realising her mistake. In her grief, she'd questioned her master's decision. "I'm sorry, Brother. I spoke out of turn."

"It's all right, child," he said. "Please, you have my permission to speak freely at all times on this journey. I want your counsel. I need it."

Samily blinked, trying to understand. She had been taught to respect the brothers as she respected God. To follow orders and speak when spoken to. There were times, like the frenzy of battle, when rules were flexible. But to be granted this freedom was almost unheard of.

"I...thank you, Brother," she said, careful not to repeat her mistake. Then, after a moment's pause: "I think I could have saved him."

"You don't know that," said Meristan, "and if you'd tried, it could have killed all three of us."

"Yes, Brother," she said flatly.

After a largely wordless breakfast, they buried the dead man. Meristan spoke of God's grace and love. It was as good an end as any Reiver was likely to find in Eidyn.

If only they would stop their raids. So much needless death.

When they were packed up and ready to move again, Meristan produced something from a pocket. "Samily, you remember your heraldry studies?"

"Yes, Brother."

"What does it mean when two different crests appear together?"

"The combination of two countries' crests can be formed in a number of ways. If they are at war, they're shown adjacent and reversed, away from each other. If one has conquered the other, the conqueror's crest is placed above the other, usually masking the top of the conquered crest."

"Indeed," answered Meristan. "So what does this mean?"

Meristan handed her a scrap of cloth. The edges were roughly cut, ripped, but she could easily make out the crest. The Reiver symbol of a gauntlet holding a sword was transposed over the top of the crest of Eidyn: a maiden and a doe flanking an image of Dun Eidyn.

"I know what it should mean," said the knight. "Where did you find this?"

"It was on the man's clothing, under his leathers," said Meristan. "I was looking for other injuries, and I found this."

Samily shook her head, trying to clear her eyes, to force this symbol to make sense. The Reivers had been at war with Eidyn for a generation. Their culture recognised no central ruler, rather numerous clans who raided their neighbours instead of building and farming for themselves. They were the reason the Malcanmore Wall had been built—to protect Eidyn's borders.

Meristan nodded at her, silently imploring her to share her thoughts. It would take time to undo her training and learn to speak openly.

"It would mean the Reivers were in alliance with Eidyn."

Meristan fixed her with a hard stare, as if waiting for her to grasp something she could not see.

"It's a trick, obviously," the monk finally spoke. "But by whom—and why? Who benefits from anyone believing the Reivers are allied with Eidyn?"

"Perhaps the Reivers have other enemies who they would prefer to believe they are in league with Eidyn? Or they hope their enemies might attack Eidyn instead?" Neither seemed especially likely.

"Maybe," Meristan answered. "But it's a lot of trouble to go to. These joined crests are a display of alliance, of joined power. The only people who will see them are those who get up close to Reiver soldiers— mostly the ones who defeat them. What's the point?"

"I don't know, Brother."

Meristan slipped the crest back into his pocket. "For now, we keep this to ourselves. Perhaps King Janaeus will be able to explain it."

———

Aranok breathed in deeply. The mixture of wild mint, rosemary and basil tingled like ice water, startling his senses and clearing his head. His mother had taught him about herbology and oils, and he always carried a small vial of this mix to keep him alert on watch. It also helped to cover the rank air. Even after they'd cleaned up the source, the smell of vomit lingered. Aranok wondered if it was just one of those pungent smells that had got into his head, which he would imagine himself noticing for days.

Nirea looked at him curiously in the half-light. He smiled and handed her the vial, gesturing for her to inhale it. She did and recoiled, wide-eyed.

"Wow," she whispered, handing it back to him. "Thanks." The sailor shook her head and returned to whittling at a piece of wood with a small, curved knife. Aranok couldn't tell whether she was making something or if the act itself was her way of staying awake.

He had volunteered to take the first shift with the sailor. He always slept opposite Allandria when a watch was required. She, Vastin and

Glorbad had all fallen asleep quickly, the dark inside the inn mimicking night. They'd agreed torches were only likely to attract attention—and it wasn't especially cold.

Aranok settled into a comfortable position and leaned back against the wall. But something niggled at him. In the silence, behind the sound of Vastin's gentle snoring, something was dripping.

In the corner. They'd stayed away from the damaged roof at that end of the building. If it caved in suddenly, they didn't want to be underneath it. Aranok peered into the dark, trying to see what was leaking and where it was landing. It sounded odd, viscous. Mostly, it sounded like it was getting worse.

He got up, indicating to Nirea that he could hear something. If water had pooled upstairs and was seeping through the ceiling, there was a decent chance the roof would cave in sooner rather than later. The inn was an odd shape, with a number of small nooks tucked away off the main body of the bar. It allowed people who wanted a quieter drink, or a more intimate meal, to get away from the noisy heart of the festivities. Where the main room held about two dozen or so large tables with benches, the nooks each had a few round tables, with four seats each. There was even a separate room, accessible beside the stage, where those with the coin could choose complete privacy.

The noise seemed to be coming from the farthest nook, in the back left corner. At least if the roof did cave in there they could use a table to barricade it against the elements. As Aranok approached the opening, he noticed an odd smell: pungent old meat and stale sweat. How had he not noticed it before? Even over the other stench, this should have been discernible.

He stepped through the doorway into pitch-black. The shutters over the only window were still intact. This was one of the smaller, more intimate nooks, as he remembered it, so there wasn't much to explore. The ceiling was obviously hanging very low, though, and the dripping was definitely getting worse. But it wasn't the rhythmic *tup tup tup* that made his breath catch in his throat; it was the distinct sound of something wet, something alive, moving in the dark.

Suddenly extremely aware of how vulnerable he was, how unprepared he was for a fight, Aranok stepped carefully backwards out into the main room, never taking his eyes off the arch in the dingy light.

"Nirea," he whispered urgently, stepping back toward the slightly brighter section of the main bar. "Nirea!"

A sickly, wet splat, like a pig's organs spilling onto a butcher's floor, got her attention. She stalked quickly toward him, meeting him just in front of the stage.

"What the fuck was that?" she whispered as the sound came again. It was followed by something quiet—chittering, like insects. It didn't sound like anything Aranok had heard before, but there was one obvious and—in these close quarters—terrifying probability.

*Demons.*

They needed light; there was no point now in hoping they could have the element of surprise—they had to know what they were facing.

"*Solas,*" he said quietly. An orb of light appeared before them.

Aranok's eyes barely focused in time to see it coming—a dark mass of limbs barrelling toward him from the corner, screeching like metal dragged on stone. He raised his arms as it hammered into him, knocking him onto his back.

"Arms! Arms!" Nirea bellowed.

With Aranok's concentration broken, the light blinked out. The thing clawed and battered at his armour.

"*Gluais,*" he said, thrusting his arms upwards. His hand brushed against it as it was thrown back. It was slick, cold and hard, like wet stone.

The sound of metal on metal. Nirea must have attacked. She would need help. He touched a flagstone. "*Luisnich.*" The stone glowed, lighting the room again. It would stay lit without his focus. Now he could see.

Nirea was backed against the wall, scimitars repelling attacks from the armoured grey thing. Its slatted skin glistened like metal as its four arms swung for her. It wasn't the biggest danger, though—the one crawling across the ceiling above her was. She had moments before it was in reach of her head.

"*Gluais.*" He pulled it from the ceiling. It landed with a thud, shrieking with rage. It rolled to its feet and Aranok finally got a good look at it. It was about the size of a human, but completely hairless. Its grey skin was indeed slatted like armour and covered with a layer of transparent ooze. Two extra limbs jutted from its abdomen. But the face: hooded red eyes and a wide mouth full of daggers.

It was a nightmare. And it was angry.

He'd planned to avoid invoking *teine* in here—too much wood—but fear drove him to his strongest weapon. Fire flowed from his hands, buffeting the thing. It stepped back, raising all four arms defensively. When Aranok stopped, it stood unbent, unburned.

The hard skin glowed like a sword in a forge. Metallic eyelids clicked open to reveal smoking eyes.

He'd only made it angrier.

An arrow thunked off its temple. Allandria was up. The creature shook its head and returned its attention to him. Aranok braced himself as a hulk of metal battered into it shield first. Vastin.

The boy rolled away from the creature, which used its extra limbs to quickly right itself. Aranok glanced up. Nirea vaulted over a table as Glorbad slashed at the other thing's back.

"What are they?" screamed the boy, crouching behind his shield.

"Don't know!" Aranok answered. "Hard!"

"No shit!" Glorbad bellowed, bringing his sword round again.

The creature lunged toward Vastin. Aranok instinctively stepped forward, raising an arm. It was a mistake.

The thing pushed off its back foot and leapt at Aranok instead. It was on him before he had time to think. He raised his arms to protect his face, but its lower arms hammered into his chest. Off-balance, he fell backwards, landing hard. The stone floor punched the air from his lungs.

He opened his mouth to cast *gluais*. Nothing.

He couldn't breathe.

Panicking, he thrashed against the thing, desperate to get back to his feet, to reach some air. His chest tightened. He would lose consciousness in a moment and then he'd be dead. His legs kicked of their own accord as his whole body spasmed in a desperate search for air.

*Breathe.*

*Breathe!*

Something hammered against the monster, distracting it. It was enough. Aranok pushed hard with his right leg and rolled to his left, throwing the creature off. The jolt was enough to open his chest. His body trembled as he gulped in precious air.

It was only a moment's reprieve. The beast was on him again, claws searching for his face. His armour was all that was keeping him alive. Another arrow bounced off the thing's head, then another. The monster turned its head and screeched at the archer.

It stopped with a wet thunk as an arrow slammed into its open mouth. The thing clawed desperately, gurgling, drowning in its own blood. A second arrow hammered into its eye and it slumped.

Aranok pushed the corpse off. He dragged himself up on a table, lungs heaving. Vastin stood over the dead thing, eyes wide, axe raised.

Nirea and Glorbad were still battering the other, but every blow bounced off. Allandria scrambled over a table, searching for a better angle.

If he used *gluais* to hold it, she'd have a better chance of hitting a vulnerable spot.

Nirea's scimitar bounced off the thing's shoulder and lodged in a shutter. She pulled it free, bringing a chunk of the wood with it.

The creature screamed. Pushing Glorbad away and leaping to the ceiling, it scrambled away.

What the Hell happened?

Nirea realised first.

"The shutters!" she cried, tearing at the rest of the wood.

Sunlight.

It feared the sunlight.

Aranok used *gluais* to tear open the shutter behind him. Glorbad and Vastin took another two. Allandria kept her bow on the thing frantically crawling around the ceiling, chattering urgently. Shutter after shutter came off and the room was bathed in light. Smoke rose from its sleek skin. The dead one smouldered and ignited.

Aranok grabbed the live one with *gluais* and pulled with everything he had left. Surprised, the creature lost its grip and slammed to the floor, bathed in light. Vastin moved to hit it, but Allandria's raised hand stopped him.

The beast wriggled and burst violently into green flames, screeching like the gates of Hell. It took all of Aranok's concentration to hold it, but it was over in a moment. The flames burned bright, dimmed and died.

The charred thing on the floor convulsed, smoking, and was still.

# CHAPTER 7

Aranok's legs trembled as he slumped onto a seat. He'd used a lot of energy and taken a beating in the process. Tenderly, he prodded the ribs on his left. Probably not broken, but he'd have some nasty bruising.

"What . . . what were those?" Vastin stared wide-eyed at the smoking corpse before him.

"Bastard demons," said Glorbad. "Nasty ones."

"I don't think so," Aranok disagreed.

Nirea poked at one with a scimitar. Her lip curled as it crumbled under her touch. "Why not?"

Because Aranok had worked out what was in the nook. "Look in the corner, where they came from. Carefully!"

Nirea was closest. She opened the shutters in the little corner and Aranok heard her intake of breath from across the room. "Are these what they look like?"

"Fuck me," said Glorbad. "They're huge!"

"What is it?" Allandria asked.

"Cocoons," said Aranok.

"Cocoons?" Vastin asked. "Like butterflies?"

Aranok nodded. "I think so."

Glorbad came back into the room. "I've never seen a demon come out of a cocoon!"

"No," said Aranok. That wasn't how demonology worked. They were summoned, not grown.

Allandria was crouched over a body. She held her fist against her mouth as though contemplating some curiosity. Aranok forced himself to his feet and walked to her. "You recognise something?"

"Maybe. There's something familiar about them."

Vastin had gone to the corner for a look. "If they're cocoons, what went in them?"

That was the question Aranok had been trying not to ask himself. Because now that he was closer, he could see that this one, like the other, was female. And that fit just a bit too well with what he already half suspected. "He had two daughters."

"Who?" asked Nirea.

"Craddock. The owner. He had two daughters."

Nirea groaned and put her hands on her head.

"Bloody Hell," said Glorbad.

"Thank God we ran into them now." Nirea changed the subject.

"Why?" asked Vastin.

Nirea raised an eyebrow. "If it had been at night…"

"We might be dead," said Aranok. "And we have no way of knowing how many more of them there are. Especially if they can make more…" His stomach dropped as a sickening thought occurred to him. "The horses!"

Nirea was already ahead of him and out the door. The others followed.

As they approached the stable, Aranok could already tell it was too quiet. There was only half a roof left. To keep the horses out of sight, they'd stabled them as far back under it as they could—out of the sunlight.

"Stay in the light!" he called. Nirea halted suddenly, nearly toppling over with momentum as she stopped right on the edge of the shade. She turned, hand over her mouth. Her eyes told them.

They'd have to walk from here.

"Bloody, bloody Hell," Glorbad grumbled.

They stood for a moment in silence. There was a scuttling noise from the back, in the dark.

"What do we do?" asked Nirea.

Aranok turned and walked back toward the inn.

"Burn it."

---

"Thakhati." The word scratched at Allandria's brain.

"Pardon?" said Aranok.

"Thakhati," she repeated. "I think they're called Thakhati." She had no idea where the name came from, but it was there, along with a weird sense of familiarity with these creatures. Surely she would remember if she'd seen these things before.

"Never heard of them," he said.

"Nor I," said Nirea. "What are they?"

That was the question. "I don't know. I'm not even sure where I know the name from. Maybe from my childhood?" A bedtime story maybe? Where would she have come across such nightmares and yet not be able to remember them clearly?

"Well, that's something." Aranok tapped on the table.

"Is it?" Allandria asked.

"If you've heard of them, they're not new. That means somebody knows what they are. Maybe in Lochen?"

"I suppose." Maybe it was even farther back. Before Lochen. She had very little memory of her first home, but she'd been so young when she left. Could she be remembering something from so long ago?

"Glorbad." Aranok turned to the soldier.

"Aye?"

"You're the tactician. We're exposed here. We've got no horses. Travelling during the day risks Reiver attacks. But at night..." He gestured to one of the corpses.

"Aye. Damned by day or night." Glorbad scratched at his thick beard. "I say better the devils we know than the ones we don't."

"Agreed." Aranok nodded.

"But you two need sleep," the soldier said. "At least a few hours, if we're going to travel this afternoon. The archer and I can keep watch, if that's all right with you."

Allandria knew Aranok would be exhausted after the magic he'd used and being up all night. He didn't even pretend to protest, just quietly nodded.

He handed Allandria his vial of oil, which she took gratefully. It would keep her wits about her.

"What about me?" Vastin asked.

"You might as well sleep too, son," said Glorbad. "Growing boy and all that. Besides, more than two on a watch is bad luck."

"Oh, all right." The boy sounded relieved. He was probably keen to get more sleep. The soldier knew how to manage his men. He'd all but ordered the boy to rest, taking the burden of responsibility off his young shoulders. It was a kindness, and good leadership. Was this a little of what the king saw in him?

As Nirea settled onto the bedroll Allandria had been sleeping on, Aranok knelt and picked up a stone from the floor. He gestured at it and said, "*Sùgh*." Nothing happened. He produced a small metal cage from his belt, into which he put the stone, and hung it from a chain around his neck. She hadn't seen him do that before. What was it?

"Good luck charm?" Allandria smiled.

Aranok looked up at her, more seriously than she felt the question merited.

"I hope so."

She nudged him playfully. "Hey. Saved your life." She said it quietly, so only he could hear.

He smiled. "Congratulations, you did your job."

"Where's my reward?" she asked, eyebrows raised.

He looked around the room, feigning shock. "What? Here?"

"We're amongst friends," she said coyly.

"I don't think we would be for long."

"Nah, it's all right," she said. "I think I'd like a bath first."

"Well, that would certainly be a kindness." He lay back, settled onto the remaining bedroll and closed his eyes, grinning.

—◦—

Allandria gripped her bow, careful to stay out of sight behind the remains of the shutter. A few hours had passed unhindered, but someone had inevitably come to investigate the stable fire. It had mostly burned itself out, but smoke still billowed up like a beacon.

Footsteps padded around the main inn, coming close to the window. As far as she could tell, there were only two of them. Not worth waking anyone up for. She just had to wait until they were in sight. The footsteps approached slowly. They weren't an idiot. Shame.

She waited, holding her breath.

"Now," a voice whispered from inside the room. Stepping out from the wall, bow raised, she found her target and released. Having opened his mouth to call out, the Reiver took the arrow right in the throat.

"Thanks," Allandria whispered.

"Pleasure," the soldier replied. "There's another one, aye?"

Allandria nodded. Glorbad drew his sword and moved toward the door. Allandria looked out the window and gestured for him to go. He opened the door and stepped out, with her covering him from the window. Against the remaining fire, she could make out the shape of the other Reiver. It was a lot of ground to make up, quietly, before he turned. Glorbad backed up and signalled Allandria to come out. Quietly, she joined him and appraised the distance. She should be able to make the shot, but a little closer would be more comfortable—the heat haze was a slight distraction. She moved forward about ten yards, set herself and nocked an arrow. He'd be an easy shot from here.

*Just don't turn around.*

The clanking noise from behind her made her turn—Glorbad was running toward her. The Reiver heard it and turned. He drew his sword and ran at them.

*What the Hell?*

Allandria turned and quickly fired at the Reiver. The arrow hit him in the leg. He stumbled but stayed upright.

"Down!" Glorbad ordered. Allandria ducked as he leapt toward her, grabbed her, and rolled her away. Two arrows clanked off his armour. There was a third! How had they been so quiet?

Allandria regained her balance, Glorbad's shield acting as a blind to protect her.

"The roof," he breathed heavily.

Allandria nodded and he turned the shield. She quickly released two arrows back at the inn. The first was high, but the second hit, knocking the Reiver backwards. The roof creaked in disapproval.

Before Allandria could stand, Glorbad pulled her over and stepped behind her, shield raised against the sword blow from the first Reiver, who had recovered and continued his run. Deflecting the weapon away with his left arm, Glorbad deftly drove his sword into the man's stomach, with more agility than she would have given him.

Allandria stood again, bow raised. Scanning for another. She felt Glorbad's back against her own. They turned slowly, carefully, her eyes flitting to every bush, every possible hide.

Nothing.

When she was satisfied they were alone, she offered the soldier a hand.

"I'm glad you stayed awake." Again, she'd seen some of what made the man a soldier, beyond his boorish behaviour. He had good instincts, and he could fight.

"So am I." He smiled. "Back inside?"

"Better make sure the one on the roof is done."

As it turned out, the arrow, buried deep in her chest, had finished her already.

# CHAPTER 8

Aranok felt his back click as he rolled his shoulders. Walking was exhausting, especially carrying their gear, but at least they were moving. It had been hours since they left the Starbank. Nobody was complaining, but nobody was talking either. Probably best—it reduced their chances of drawing attention.

"Are we going to stop soon?" If anyone was going to tell him they needed a break, it was Allandria.

"You tired?" he asked sarcastically.

"I'm just worried about your old legs. You're not used to carrying… anything."

He smiled. Although she was slightly older, she liked to remind him she was fitter. "If you were as clever as me, you'd have someone to fetch and carry for you too."

"Don't you mean 'as clever as I'?"

"Do I?" he asked, furrowing his brow. "Doesn't sound right."

"Stop," Nirea hissed from behind them. She stepped up to the front pair and pointed ahead. "What's that?"

Ahead, against the trunk of a tree and spilling onto the path, something the size and shape of a body lay completely still.

"Bushes. Now," Aranok ordered.

Everyone moved to the right—the side opposite the body. They huddled together in the shade.

"Stay here, I'm going for a look." Aranok took off his pack.

"Like Hell you are," said Allandria. "Not on your own."

He shrugged. "Fine. Don't get seen."

Allandria's look of absolute disgust was not lost on him. She was at home in the wild, and stealth was something they taught alongside reading in Lochen. Archers learned to hunt early. Of the two of them, he was more likely to be seen than her, and they both knew it.

They slipped quietly up the side of the path, until they drew level with the figure.

"Is that what I think it is?" she asked.

The armour, the sword. Yes. They were looking at a White Thorn. The head lolled at a nauseating angle and the limbs were not right. The knight had been mangled. Aranok was not in a hurry to meet whatever had done this. White Thorns were the greatest warriors in the kingdom, trained from youth to fight demons.

"Cover me." Allandria slipped onto the road before Aranok could protest. She approached with a dagger drawn. Finally, when the knight would likely have felt her breath, she gestured to Aranok to follow.

When he reached her, she wore an incongruous grin. "Good news."

"What?"

Aranok stumbled backwards as Allandria lifted the knight's head clean off and offered it to him.

"It's empty."

———◦———

Samily was glad to get out of the forest. Armour was not well suited to trudging across the soft, damp floor. The road into Gorgyn had been rocky but more stable.

The twin market towns of Gorgyn and Dail Ruigh were separated by a cliff face, with the higher elevation of Dail Ruigh giving the residents a greater sense of self-importance. As the towns had grown, Dail Ruigh had become home to the more upmarket traders in cloth and jewellery, while the messier business of the farmer's market settled down in Gorgyn. Samily did not understand the classification. Food was important; dresses were frippery. She rarely visited Dail Ruigh.

It took about half an hour to reach the market square. Two sides were lined with wooden stands, while the opposite two each housed a series of stone arches, with alcoves where traders could store larger quantities of grain or meat. These were fronted by tables from which they conducted negotiations. In the middle, there was room for three rows of carts, but Samily counted maybe half of what there was space for. The usual stink of faeces, blood, sweat and fish was muted. Before the war, this market had teemed with life. Now only half the stands were manned—and many of them barely stocked. There were no animals to be seen. One cart offered salted fish, one a small selection of bread, and several held a ragtag bunch of vegetables and fruit. The drains designed to carry spilt blood away from the butchers' tables were a dry, dark brown.

There were maybe two dozen other people there. Nothing like the normal, busy hum of a market afternoon.

"Well." Meristan stood in the middle of the square, considering his options. "I fancy some fruit, Samily. What do you think?"

Samily nodded reverently. Meristan crossed to a stall manned by a girl who couldn't have been more than ten.

"Master, mistress." The girl effected a small bow as they approached. It was considered an honour that they had chosen her stall. In truth, Samily thought, Meristan had picked the best-stocked one.

"Hello, child." Her master smiled. "May we take an offering?"

It was tradition that traders offered a reasonable amount of goods to the Order for free, as thanks for their service. The Thorns had strict rules about not abusing this kindness and only ever taking what was needed from those who could afford it.

"Of course, master." But something about the girl's eyes bothered Samily. Her voice had cracked, just the tiniest bit. Something was wrong. She tapped Meristan's arm as he selected a few apples for their sack. He turned, curious, and saw the tears welling in the girl's eyes.

"What's wrong, child?" Meristan gently touched her cheek.

"I'm sorry, Brother, it's just—we don't have much. The demon..."

"What demon?" he asked.

Samily felt the hairs on her neck rise. She scanned the market again, now looking for signs of an attack.

"It burns the crops," the girl said, tears creeping down her cheeks.

Meristan's face turned dark. "Where?"

Her voice trembled. "Mutton Hole."

Meristan considered a moment and carefully put the apples back on the cart.

"Oh, no," the girl protested. "Please, it's our duty..."

"No, child. Your need is greater." He gently wiped the tears from her cheeks, squeezed her shoulder and turned to go.

Samily wondered how many of her family had survived the war. Probably not many if she was the one sent to tend the stall. The journey from home, setting up the cart, sleeping alone in it for several days before heading back. The other market traders would look out for her, Samily hoped, but this was no life for a child. The girl looked up at her, silently questioning why she wasn't following her master. Samily didn't truly know herself, until she spoke.

"What is your name?"

"Mhara." The girl's voice was tiny.

"Mhara, you are stronger than you think," she said, smiling.

The girl's eyes lit up, their green even more vibrant for the tears.

"I was an orphan. Now I am a knight. Stay strong, Mhara. God is always with you."

She leaned forward and kissed the girl on the forehead before following Meristan. She couldn't look back, but she hoped, maybe, she had cast a little light into Mhara's bleak world. She would pray for her.

"Your empathy is a credit to you, Samily," Meristan said without looking round.

"I learned it from you, Brother."

She couldn't be sure, and she dared not look closely, but Samily thought she saw her master smile.

"Samily, how many demons did you kill in the war?"

She did a quick mental count. "Seven, I think, Brother."

"On your own?"

"No, Brother. Not alone."

They walked silently for a time, before Meristan cleared his throat.

"You have always been exceptional, Samily. I have more faith in you than any other. We're going to Mutton Hole."

"Brother?"

"Speak freely, Samily. Remember?"

"What about the king?" They'd been ordered to Haven. Well, he had. Refusing a royal order was a dangerous thing. Meristan stopped and turned to her.

"To whom is your first duty, knight?"

"God." She recited the response automatically.

"And your second?"

"God's children."

Meristan smiled.

"Then the king can wait."

---

"There's no sign of a fight. It's like he just took it off and…left," said Allandria. The size and shape of the armour definitely suggested a man. A large one.

"Never." Glorbad examined the armour. "I've met Thorns—fought with them—and there's cock all chance any one of them willingly abandoned their armour."

"Well, what happened, then? Did he melt?" asked Nirea.

*Eesh.* That was a hideous image.

Allandria looked down into the neck. Nothing to see. She sniffed apprehensively. There was a slight, lingering smell of—she assumed—whoever had been wearing the armour, but nothing putrid, no stench of death. "Nope, nothing in there."

"I don't like it," said Aranok. "What could kill a White Thorn and leave no trace?"

"Those things? Thakhati?" Nirea suggested. The name crept up Allandria's arms like bugs, and she clenched her fists to ward off a shiver. Where did she remember it from?

"What did they do? Eat him very carefully?" Glorbad laughed.

Nirea smacked his arm. "Maybe he went into one of those cocoons."

That was a sobering thought. Allandria scanned the trees. The two they'd fought had been bad enough. A giant White Thorn turned into one of them…?

Aranok weighed up a vambrace. "Can we use any of the armour? It looks lighter than yours, Glorbad. And Vastin's."

The soldier's eyes darkened. "Aye, it is. Stronger too. But only Thorns wear the White."

Aranok cocked his head. "You worried about upsetting 'God'?"

Allandria tutted before she could help herself. He had a horrible habit of provoking people unnecessarily. Especially those who had faith. It was not her favourite thing about him. He'd stopped trying to drag her into theological campfire debates when she'd lost patience with his niggling and barked at him that she'd changed her mind and that he was obviously right about everything. It was the first time she remembered him looking genuinely chastened. And probably when their relationship changed. She spoke more freely after that, and he warmed to it. It was as if an unseen barrier had broken. She'd stopped being just his bodyguard.

"God's long given up on me, son," Glorbad answered. "But I haven't earned the right to wear that armour, and I'm not about to piss on the memory of the man who did."

Aranok stared back at him for a moment, studying him.

"Besides, have you seen the fucking size of it? You'd fit me and the boy in there!" Glorbad slapped Vastin's arm and laughed. The blacksmith joined him. It looked as though they were getting on better, which was good.

"Fair enough," Aranok finally said. "Then we leave it here."

"No. We need to rest," said Nirea. "We're not horses."

"No, we're not." The *draoidh* pointed to the armour. "But if we're in the hunting grounds of whatever did that, or what he became, then we've got more to worry about than sore backs."

Nirea scowled but didn't argue. She was right, they did need to rest, but so was Aranok. This wasn't the place. The sailor hefted her pack onto her shoulders.

Allandria shivered in her bones. First Thakhati and now, maybe, something else?

What the Hell was going on?

"D'you want me to take that for a bit?" Vastin asked. It was nearing dusk and Glorbad was lagging behind. Not really surprising. He was older and heavier than the rest, and he was wearing armour. For all smithing work was hard, it had made Vastin strong enough for a march like this. And he could manage a second pack for a while if it helped the old man. Carrying two might help his balance.

"Fuck off." The soldier grinned, stopping. "You think I can't pull my weight?"

Vastin gestured up the road to the others. He assumed the distance made his meaning clear. Glorbad chortled, but his face was redder than it should be. "Let me tell you something, wee man. When an army marches, do you know the most important thing they have to remember?"

"Where they're going?"

Glorbad snorted. "To pace themselves. You march your army too hard, they arrive exhausted and you've lost before you begin. These three"—he jerked his thumb up the road—"don't know how to pace themselves. It'll be you and me who're ready to fight when those three are panting on their knees."

He lifted his silver flask and took a long glug from it. "And we have to drink. It's not called water of life for nothing!"

For all his grumpiness, he was all right. Now that he wasn't swinging a sword at Vastin, anyway. They started walking again and he matched the soldier's pace, glancing up to see the others were still in sight. Aranok's warning about not being alone with him seemed less important now. Vastin wondered if that was always the way; once you've fought alongside someone, it changes you both.

"You ever fought a demon?" he asked.

"Small ones," Glorbad answered. "There's some the size of humans. Tend to run in packs. Nasty wee things. Claws like knives. Nothing like we just saw, though. Those things were..." He shook his head. "Well, I don't know what they were. But hey!" He slapped Vastin across the back. "You survived your first fight, didn't you? And you did all right. Your fancy shield stood up." He knocked on his own shield a few times.

"They're good shields." Vastin felt a little spike of pride.

"Made by a good man," said the soldier.

Vastin's lip curled, just a little. "I don't know." He hadn't felt like a good man. He'd been terrified.

"Don't know what? Do you not remember battering into a demon to save our great leader? That man owes you his life, son."

That was silly. Laird Aranok would have been fine without him, with the things he could do. Vastin had never seen an earth *draoidh* use magic before. He'd watched an illusionist when he was little, but actual flames coming from a man's hands, pulling the Thakhati around with his mind? What could kill a man who could do that? He was all but a god. "Nah. He'd have been fine. It's me who owes him."

"How so?" Glorbad's breathing was noticeably laboured. Vastin made a point of slowing down a little more to tell the story of how he'd met the envoy.

"That right?" Glorbad asked when he'd finished. It was starting to get murky and harder to see the others. "Well, let's hope there's a break in our marching soon, so I can show you how to use that axe properly. Next time you can see off trouble yourself."

A whistle from ahead. Vastin looked up to see Nirea waving. Her red leathers stood out better in the gathering dusk. It took them a few minutes to catch up. Aranok was standing a little farther up the road; Allandria was nowhere to be seen. Glorbad dropped his pack. "What now?"

Nirea gave him an unimpressed look. "We're getting off the road. We've been talking. Safest place to camp is going to be away from trees." She gestured to the canopy above her. "We're heading toward the coast. Allandria's scouting a route."

"Why not?" said Glorbad. "The only thing more fun than marching a road in full armour is marching the Wilds."

Vastin stifled a giggle.

———

Darginn's arse hurt. He sat up in the saddle, arching his back, trying to take pressure off the aching muscles. He'd ridden hard through the day to make Lestalric before nightfall and his old bones were not fit for it. To his surprise, he'd managed to sleep awhile on the ferry after they'd passed Dun Eidyn. But he'd made it.

The gates of Lestalric lay before him. He carefully dismounted, feeling the tingle of blood returning to deprived limbs. He rocked back and forth on his feet and heard himself groan as his legs welcomed the change of use. He was too old for messengering, but their ranks were thin. They'd lost a lot of good people in the war. Often to bloody Reivers, picking them off on the roads and cutting off their communication channels. The best fighters had survived—and the sneaky bastards like him.

Rust enveloped the gates like ivy. Surprising for one of the high houses but, like the messengers, everyone was shorthanded. Even servants were hard to find. There was no sign of anyone in the courtyard, though a couple of torches flickered against the descending gloom. An old bell hung inside the gate, its frayed rope just within reach. Darginn stretched through and pulled. It was stiff, but it worked. The bell's clang echoed off the cobblestones.

Then silence. Until Darginn noticed a shuffling noise from the left. He peered through the gates. There seemed to be a stable to that side, but there was no obvious movement.

A face appeared before him, so suddenly that he jolted backwards, nearly falling against his horse. "Ah! Sorry, son, I didn't see you coming."

The boy looked in his late teens. He had sandy hair and a thin, sallow face. For a long moment, he looked at Darginn like a curiosity, as if he'd found a frog there looking back at him.

"Is your mistress at home?" Darginn smiled agreeably.

The boy gave no answer, simply turning and limping toward the house. Hells. Things must be bad for the baroness to have a hobbled mute tending the gate.

After what seemed an age, the door opened for a second time, and a lady emerged in a deep red dress. Her light brown hair was curled up on her head—not as neatly as Darginn might have expected. The boy trailed behind her obediently, as did a girl of about six or seven.

"Good evening!" the woman said as she walked toward him. "How can we help you?"

"Darginn Argyll, king's messenger. I bring an urgent letter from the king." He'd be glad to be rid of it.

"Do you, indeed? I wonder what urgent business the king could have with me."

"Not my businesses to know, m'lady," said Darginn, now she'd confirmed his suspicion he was looking at the baroness. "I merely deliver it."

She arrived at the gate and stopped. The girl hid behind her skirt, peeking out at the strange visitor.

The boy stood beside her, still staring blankly at Darginn. It was beginning to feel unsettling.

"Don't mind Somal," the baroness said, "Took a nasty fall off a horse last year. Worked here most of his life."

Somal looked to her at the sound of his name, then back at Darginn.

"So you have a letter for me?"

She offered her white-gloved hand through the gates. Darginn reached into his coat and pulled out the parchment. She took it and folded her hands against her skirts. They regarded each other in awkward silence. Darginn realised with a rush of fear that she didn't intend to invite him in. He was probably a day's ride from Lochen. Camping outside alone at night was a terrible idea, assuming you wanted to live.

"Anything else?" The baroness smiled sweetly.

Darginn looked at his feet.

"Beg your pardon, m'lady, but it's traditional to offer a king's messenger safe haven for the night, when there's none other to be had."

She looked back at him wordlessly for a moment, as if deciding how to answer. Would she really leave him out here to die?

"Of course it is," she finally said. "What do you think, Kiana, should we have Master Argyll in for dinner?"

The girl's eyes brightened. She looked at Darginn and smiled, nodding.

"Who am I to turn away a king's messenger?" said the baroness. "Somal, open the gate."

The boy did as ordered. The gates creaked in protest, raking across dead leaves.

"Stable the horse," she said to the boy. "Master Argyll, please join us."

She turned and walked for the house. The girl crept nervously to him, reached up and gently pulled at his hand.

Darginn sighed deeply. He'd keep his head another night, thank God.

# CHAPTER 9

Nirea stretched out her arms behind her as they walked, feeling the pull through her shoulders.

"Stiff?" Allandria asked.

"A bit, yeah."

It had been a pleasantly quiet night, for a change, despite them having to camp rough. They'd gone a long way off the road, but it had been worth it. Everyone got a decent sleep and there had been no sign of the monsters that hated the light. Even Glorbad was complaining less today.

"It's funny how quickly it becomes normal, isn't it?" Allandria asked.

"What?"

"Sleeping on the ground, always being on guard, expecting a fight."

"Light sleep, I'm used to, but this lying on rocks is murder. Give me a hammock any day." Her exhaustion had put her out for the night, but it wasn't a habit she was keen to form.

"Of course," said Allandria. "I hadn't thought. This is new to you."

"It's not like I've never done it, but this isn't my element. Never has been. I don't much like forests. Too many trees. I like clean lines of sight and the space to breathe. To be able to see your enemy coming. This is messy."

"Do you miss it?" Allandria asked.

*Every day.*

Her relationship with the sea was complicated. She'd hated it at first. For years. Took her a long time to really get her sea legs. And she still had plenty of reason to hate it. She'd have given anything, then, to be back on land. Back with the family she couldn't even remember now. They were ghosts. Memories of memories. A dream of happiness.

"I do. You been at sea much?"

Allandria shook her head.

"Something about it makes you feel alive. In that moment, there is nothing else. Just the salt and the gulls, and the ends of the world. All a girl needs."

"That's funny. That's exactly how I feel here." Allandria spread her arms. "The smell of the green, the insects, the birds. It's all home."

"Home" wasn't quite how Nirea felt about the sea. She felt free on the ocean, but home? No, not truly. A sense of longing washed over her for the home she'd never had, as if it had just been taken from her all over again. Her stomach flipped; her hands trembled. She balled them into fists, willing them to steady.

"Well, you'll get your sight lines back, at least." Allandria pointed ahead. The forest was thinning as the trees gave way to a small meadow.

In the distance, Nirea could just see the first of the wheat fields. She was glad of the change of subject but took a few deep breaths to calm herself before answering. "You had any more thoughts about where you know those things from?"

"The Thakhati? No," said Allandria. "It's just a name. I must have heard it somewhere."

"You're from Lochen, right? Could it be something around there?"

"Maybe, but I've been thinking about it—trying to work out what was familiar, and it's the oddest thing…"

"Odd how?" Nirea asked.

"I think it was the smell." Allandria scrunched up her face.

"The smell?" They had stunk, right enough.

"I know," said Allandria. "It sounds mad. But they smelled familiar."

That did make some sense. Many times, a smell—baking bread, wet grass—had brought Nirea a wave of familiarity. Sometimes to things she couldn't place—just an emotion. If they sparked a pleasant feeling, it was likely from before the boat. There were plenty more that brought anger, pain and fear.

"Everyone on guard!" Aranok said from behind them. "We're about to lose cover."

"Of course," said Allandria, "the downside of being able to see your enemies coming is they can see you too."

"Good." Nirea grinned. "Then they'll be bloody terrified by the time I kill them." She'd always thought the best way to attack an enemy was to go straight at them. No sense dancing around. Hit them hard, fast and angry. Get them off-balance. But keep a few tricks up your sleeve. She was a pirate at heart, and no pirate went into battle without a few concealed weapons.

As soon as they cleared the trees, they saw the smoke. Huge swathes of crops must have been burning.

"Holy shite," said Glorbad.

Nirea was already running.

---

Aranok's feet pounded on the dirt path between fields. He'd never been the quickest, but he was also thinking. And the weight of his pack made running more difficult. What he'd have given for those horses right then as sweat lashed down his back.

"Glorbad!" he shouted to the man struggling beside him.

The soldier turned his head without speaking. Running in that armour, with the baggage, Aranok was surprised he was still upright.

"It needs time between fire bursts! Get in close and hit it right after one!" he said. He was already having to shout over the roar of the fire. The heat was intense.

Glorbad nodded ahead of them, where Vastin had easily outpaced them both. "The boy?"

Aranok shrugged. Vastin wanted to fight. "Try to keep him behind it!"

He hoped they'd keep him alive long enough for him to learn to be useful.

They rounded a corner and slowed as the demon loomed ahead.

It was at least nine feet tall, with leathery brown skin, broken where shards of bone jutted from limbs. A pair of clawed hands hung low from sinewy arms and a horse-like face was dominated by a huge pair of curled horns.

"Fuck," Glorbad panted.

Aranok stopped. The left field was almost completely ablaze. Three arrows stuck out of the thing's hide, and it had a bad wound across one flank. Allandria was on the other side of it, loosing arrows at its head. One after another bounced off. Nirea was in close. She slashed at its legs, nimbly dodging the slow, lumbering swipes of its claws.

Vastin and Glorbad came up behind it. Glorbad put a hand on the boy's shoulder and he stepped back to give the soldier room. His sword glanced off once. Twice. The demon spun, its huge hand smashing the soldier into the wheat.

"Damn it," Aranok spat. The beast inhaled deep. It was about to spit fire. Vastin charged forward, axe raised, a lamb to the brazier.

"*Gluais!*" Aranok instinctively threw the boy to the side just as flames scorched the earth black.

Allandria volleyed more arrows, but they weren't slowing it. He couldn't see Nirea now. She might be down. Hells, they were going to die in their first real fight.

The right field had caught fire. Glorbad and Vastin were in there.

He could put out the fire, but Allandria would be alone against this thing. It was much more powerful than he'd expected. His arrogance was going to kill them. Hells, what had he thought he and Allandria were going to do alone against this thing? He hadn't thought. He was just angry. Angry at feeling helpless.

*Damn it!*

Vastin appeared from the crops, pulling Glorbad away from the flames. The soldier looked bad. Once clear of the wheat, Vastin released his grip and Glorbad slipped to one knee.

Aranok ran toward the beast. His armour would protect him from its fire—theoretically—and at least he might see where Nirea was.

"Stay with him!" he shouted as he passed the men. Glorbad raised a shaky hand in acknowledgement. Aranok had been talking to the boy.

He stopped as Nirea reappeared. She sprang into the air, bringing

both scimitars down into the demon's shoulders. They barely pen-
etrated the thick hide, but the monster shrieked with rage. It could be
hurt, at least. It jerked and flailed, turning and reaching to grab at the
woman on its back. Its head reared, belching flames into the sky.

Good, another wasted blast.

Nirea fell away and he heard her land hard on the dirt. On the wrong
side of the beast. He just had to hope she was all right. Allandria was
still peppering the thing's head with arrows. They were a distraction
but were also making it angry. And she would run out soon.

The monster spotted Glorbad and, perhaps sensing easier prey,
turned its back on Allandria and lunged toward him.

Vastin stepped between them, shield raised.

"*Balla na talamh,*" Aranok roared. The earth tore skyward, forming
a protective wall before the boy. The beast turned and lunged toward
Aranok instead.

*Fuck.*

He'd been running low on energy when they arrived. He needed to
do this thing some damage, and fire would be useless. He'd only bolster the flames already engulfing the crops.

"*Clach.*" He charged his armour. The runes glowed red as he roared
and threw himself at the creature's abdomen.

The energy burst threw Aranok back and he felt his neck twist awkwardly. He landed just inside the crops. The heat. He needed to move.
He tried to get to his knees, but his head spun. He clambered back onto
the path.

*Damn it, think!*

"Soldier!" an unfamiliar voice bellowed. "Shield!"

Aranok turned to see who was sprinting toward them.

*Thank God.*

Glorbad dropped to one knee and braced his shield at an angle. The newcomer ran straight at him, put one foot on the shield, and Glorbad groaned
with the effort of pushing upwards, collapsing backwards as he did.

The figure leapt high, white armour gleaming in the firelight like a
burning angel.

The knight's sword fell, splitting the demon's head. It dropped with
a resonant thud.

Aranok shook his head. No time for questions.

"*Uisge.*"

Water sprayed from his hands. He ignored the pain in his neck, the pain in his back, the dizziness threatening to take him. One thing mattered: flooding the crops. It wasn't going to be enough. Most of it was already gone. The world lurched and he stumbled sideways. Between the energy he'd used and the head knock, he could barely stand. But he had to get this fire out. He had to save as many of the crops as he could.

And then he couldn't stand at all.

# CHAPTER 10

Samily watched the demon burn. It stank all the worse for her having to cut it open so it would catch. Its skin was almost completely resistant to fire—on the outside. It needed to be done, else the rotting carcass would poison the earth and crops wouldn't grow here for generations. Just another curse of their unnatural existence. Even their deaths brought misery.

"It's bigger than I thought it would be," the boy said.

He'd insisted on staying to help, despite there being nothing for him to do. Samily knew well how to burn a demon.

"Is it the biggest one you've killed?" he asked.

Samily thought back to her first kill. A snake-like thing, with legs and wings. Its teeth like great blunted rocks, crushing anything they got hold of—including Merrick's arm. He'd barely survived the blood loss. But he had—they both had. It was the demon that died that day, not her friend. By Heaven, it was huge. It took four of them to bring it down. Her, Merrick, Asha and...who else? She could almost see him, but every time his name was on her tongue, it slipped away. Like a blur on the edge of her vision that vanished when she turned to look at it. How could she not remember who else had been there? It would come to her later, when she wasn't thinking of it.

"On my own, yes," she finally answered the boy.

"But you weren't on your own," he said, confused.

Samily realised her error and smiled at him. "Of course, I'm sorry. I only meant without another Thorn."

"Oh, aye. Of course." The boy shifted awkwardly on his feet. He seemed uncomfortable or agitated. It was hard to tell. She wasn't as good at reading boys as she was girls. Girls were simpler; they didn't hide their emotions. When a girl was upset, it was clear, but with boys—it was like trying to read a book in a foreign language. She could work out broad bits with educated guesswork, but the details were nonsense.

"How old are you?" he finally asked.

"I'm not sure."

"What? How can you not know how old you are?"

"I am a child of God," she said plainly. "Like many White Thorns."

"A child of God?"

"I had no parents. Brother Meristan found me as a child. He brought me to the Order and raised me as a Thorn." It was a common route to joining the Order: the abandoned favoured by God to be found by a Brother or another Thorn.

"You're an orphan? Me too." He smiled weakly, as if he wanted it to be a good thing.

"Oh?" she said. "You did not know your parents?"

"Oh, no." That same watery smile. "I knew them. They were wonderful." His voice cracked on the last word.

Samily put a hand on his shoulder. "Then I am sorry for your loss."

He smiled. "Thank you. So, wait, you really don't know how old you are? You don't look much older than me."

Samily turned and walked toward the farmhouse. Why did her age matter so much to this boy? He was strange.

"No. We can ask Brother Meristan if it's important to you—he may have a better idea."

"But, how do you celebrate your birth day if you don't know your age?" he asked, following her.

"The Order does not celebrate birth days. We do not mark the passing of years. When you are old enough to fight, you wear the armour. You wear the armour until God calls you home. Every day you are given is a celebration."

The boy stopped. "But…everybody should have a birth day."
She turned back to him. "Why?"
"So you can celebrate," he said haltingly. "And get presents."
"I have everything I need," said Samily. "What would someone give me?"
"I don't know. Maybe a pretty necklace, or some nice gloves?"
"Gloves?" Why would such a functional thing be considered a gift?
"Yes," said Vastin. "You know—to protect your hands. In winter."
Samily looked down at her hands, at the sleek white metal gloves caked in dirt, ash and demon blood. She held one up to him and shrugged. The boy opened his mouth as if to say something, but closed it again.
He really was an odd boy.

---

Aranok sat bolt upright and instantly regretted it. He grabbed his neck, which had seized stiff. His head pounded. He slumped back against something soft. A bed? Hell, his vision was swimming. What happened?
"Easy, friend," came a nearby voice. "You're in no shape to be bouncing about."
Aranok's eyes focused on a large, bald man with a neat beard, smiling serenely.
"I'm Brother Meristan." He bent to pick up something from the floor. "You dropped this."
The monk placed a cold cloth on Aranok's forehead. The salve was welcome. The room spun a little less.
"Where are we?" he asked. "What happened?"
"What do you remember?" the monk asked.
*A gleaming angel, burning in the sky…*
"You're from the Order?" Aranok asked. "That was a White Thorn who saved us?"
Meristan smiled and nodded.
"Am I remembering right—did he kill it with one blow?" Aranok asked.

"I believe she did."

"Ah, sorry." Aranok winced. Of all people, he should know better. The greatest warrior he'd ever known was his lover.

"Many people have underestimated Samily," the monk said. "It has done them more harm than her, I assure you."

Aranok went to nod, but it hurt too much, so he blinked an agreement. His head was clearing a little. He looked around a sparse room with white stone walls and two small beds. An oil lamp on his bedside table. Shuttered windows. In the other bed, a mountainous shape slumbered.

"We're in a farmhouse," Meristan explained. "Dahev's. He came running when the beast went down. Insisted we come here to rest. This is his sons' room. He sent them to the next farm, to spread word of the demon's death."

Aranok smiled. "Spontaneous human kindness."

"Pardon?" the monk asked.

"Nothing. Just something a friend says." Aranok gestured to the other bed. "How's Glorbad?"

Meristan's face darkened. "Not good. He has nasty bruising to his chest. Probably some broken ribs. Says his back's killing him too. Gave him some poppy milk to let him sleep. Must have taken a nasty hit."

"Aye, he did," said Aranok. "The kind that kills a man."

"Good thing he's made of sterner stuff, then. Or at least his armour is."

"Aye," said Aranok. "But is he going to be fit to move tomorrow?"

Meristan shook his head. "Does he have to?"

"We're on a mission. From the king," Aranok said honestly. It didn't matter that he planned to subvert that mission a little along the way.

"Ah," said Meristan. "A coincidence. We're on our way to see the king ourselves."

"Are you?" That was interesting.

"Indeed. He has asked me to sit on a council," he said sheepishly. Aranok laughed.

Meristan recoiled slightly. "You don't think I belong on it?"

"I think you're on it!" Aranok reached inside his leathers and produced the Royal Envoy brooch that he never wore publicly. The monk's mouth fell open as Aranok pointed at Glorbad's snoring mass. "There's your military advisor, and I presume the naval advisor is around here somewhere. Red leathers, two swords, you can't miss her."

Meristan's eyebrows rose. "Aranok. You're the king's envoy? I thought I recognised the name. Forgive me, I don't pay as much attention to politics as I should."

"No forgiveness required," Aranok said, offering his hand. Meristan shook it firmly.

"A pleasure to meet you, Laird Envoy."

Aranok winced. "Please. You and your knight are the reason I'm alive. Call me Aranok."

"As you say." The monk put his hands back in his lap and looked thoughtfully at Glorbad. "So it's important he heals quickly?"

Aranok considered. Would it be awful if they had to leave the pair of them here? It would avoid the inevitable conflict when he told them they were going to Mournside. And he still wasn't sure he trusted the soldier—though he'd now seen the man risk his life for others twice. Still, maybe this was a blessing in disguise.

"Maybe he should rest up. Nirea can stay and keep an eye on him, take him back to Haven when he's fit to travel. Allandria, Vastin and I can carry on."

There was no chance of the boy arguing about going off mission. Meristan took a deep breath and rubbed his hand across his bald head.

"Well, then it seems to me that, assuming the king would have sent me with you anyway had I made it to Haven earlier, it is my responsibility to come with you in their place."

Aranok opened his mouth to object, but the monk spoke again.

"And Samily, of course."

Aranok stopped. After the way she'd dispatched that demon, he'd be a fool not to accept the Thorn as a companion. And they hadn't been there to hear the king forbid him from going to Mournside. This was working out well.

"Hell's arse you will!" Glorbad rolled toward them with a grunt, wincing as he did. His face was ashen and his black pupils wide. "My king sent me to do a job, and I'll damn well do it if I have to crawl to Barrock!"

*Bollocks.*

Allandria raised the spoon to her mouth. Her hand trembled. People reacted differently to battle. During a fight she was calm. Her training took hold, her mind quieted and she focused on her job.

*Breathe in, draw, aim, breathe out, release.*

Aranok said it was part of what made her such an asset—she never panicked. But afterwards, when the danger was past, that was when the tremors came, when her body coursed with lightning. She'd seen huge, scarred, battle-forged men lose their breakfasts the moment a battle was done.

"You all right?" Nirea asked, nodding to her hand.

"Yes." Allandria drew the hand toward her. "Just cold."

It was a silly lie. The fire warmed the cottage well. Dahev, the farmer who'd taken them in, stirred the pot over it. His white hair and beard were peppered with hints of the red it had once been. Despite his age, he was sturdy. His skin was dark and leathery, weather-beaten by a lifetime of hard labour. And despite all he'd seen, his eyes were kind; gentle and warm.

Nirea smiled. "I think someone's smitten." She nodded to Vastin, who was helping the Thorn out of her armour. The boy looked at her with something akin to reverence; she appeared completely oblivious. It was kind of adorable.

"Samily?"

The monk had appeared at the bottom of the stairs.

"Yes, Brother?" she replied, turning toward him and standing to attention with half her armour off.

"Are you busy?" he asked.

"I was just going to clean my armour," she answered, gesturing to the thick black demon blood that half covered it. "So it doesn't corrode."

"It will have to wait," said Meristan.

"I can do it," Vastin volunteered. "I'm a blacksmith. I can clean armour."

Samily looked at him dispassionately. "Thank you. I am in your debt."

"We're all in your debt, my lady." Nirea raised her cup in salute.

Samily nodded. "As you say."

Vastin grinned sheepishly. The knight finished removing the armour from her legs, handed it to Vastin, and stalked after Meristan. Vastin watched her until she disappeared up the steps.

Nirea leaned across the table. "Definitely smitten," she whispered with a grin.

---

"I have to ask you both not to speak of what you are about to witness."

The monk had brought Samily—the White Thorn—up to the room. She seemed less otherworldly in plain grey aketon and trousers, but still had a presence about her. The girl couldn't be more than twenty, if that, but she carried herself with the poise and confidence of a much older woman. Even if he hadn't seen her kill a demon, Aranok would have taken her seriously.

"Why?" Aranok asked.

"You'll see," Meristan replied. "Samily?"

The girl approached Glorbad's bedside and moved his armour aside to kneel. She unbuttoned and removed her aketon, to reveal a similarly grey vest beneath. Her arms were pure muscle and bore surprisingly few scars. For all that she was not large, she looked a match for any man. And Aranok knew she was a match for a lot more.

"May I?" She gestured to the soldier's shirt.

Glorbad looked uncomfortable. "Aye," he said, his eyes still glazed.

Slowly, she pushed the shirt up to reveal his bruising. It was as impressive as Meristan had suggested.

"She has training?" Aranok asked the monk. He raised two fingers in response, silently telling him to wait. Aranok's eyebrows went up instinctively. There weren't many people who shushed the king's envoy. The king himself rarely tried. He decided to let it go for the moment, more interested in seeing what was about to happen.

Samily placed her hands on the old warrior's chest and muttered something quietly. He inhaled sharply. Aranok stood up for a better look and his head spun again.

*Damn it.*

He flopped back down. That needed to stop.

As he saw the bruises disappearing before his eyes under the knight's touch, all else was gone from his mind.

"My God," he whispered, trying to marry what he knew with what he was seeing. "You're a *healer*?"

Again, Meristan raised a hand to quiet him as Samily moved her hands to his other side.

Glorbad breathed deeply, arching his back. His eyes opened wide. He looked as if about to scream but then breathed out hard. Again, the bruises melted away, and Aranok imagined he heard the crick of bones snapping into place. *Did he* imagine it?

"Can you roll onto your side?" Samily asked. Her voice sounded weak—tired.

Glorbad carefully did as asked, and she placed her hands on his back.

"Where is the pain?" she asked.

"Lower," he growled. Her hands came to rest in the small of his back. "There." Again, she closed her eyes and muttered something. There was nothing visible, but Glorbad arched at her touch, groaning with a mix of pain and pleasure. This time, Aranok definitely heard something pop. Glorbad grunted as if punched in the gut.

"Fuck," the soldier moaned, then was quiet. Samily slumped to her knees, barely holding herself up.

"Please help me, envoy." The monk moved to lift her from the floor. Aranok grabbed her other arm and they helped her onto his bed.

"She'll need to sleep." Meristan lowered her head carefully onto the pillow. "I hope you can spare the bed."

"Of course." Aranok's mind was still swimming.

Healers weren't real.

Healers were myths.

There was no such thing as healing magic.

And yet...

"It is the work of God." The monk pulled the door shut quietly. "She's a miracle."

Aranok couldn't argue. "How? How have you kept this quiet?"

"It was necessary," Meristan replied. "It takes a great toll on her, as you see. If it were public knowledge she's a healer, people would come from all over the country—perhaps the world. And they would not be swayed by the fact that healing them, or their children, might well kill the girl. There would be riots. And worse, she would try to help them all."

"All magic takes a toll." Aranok's own woozy head was evidence of that. "Is it sympathetic? Does she take on the wound?"

"No," the monk answered. "I've seen her heal a man with crushed legs. She took no injury herself but slept for near three days after. I wondered if she'd ever wake."

"My God," said Aranok. "This...this changes everything." If healing magic was real, could there be more like her? Battlefields would be transformed! Hospitals could...

"But you must please say nothing," Meristan repeated. "You understand how dangerous this information is?"

Aranok considered for a moment, then nodded. It was enough that he knew. For now. "However, I have to ask you to hold to your offer."

Meristan cocked his head curiously.

"I still want you, and her, to travel with us. I will take responsibility, but I also assume that the king would have sent you with me given the chance."

Meristan looked at him suspiciously. "You see? Even you want a healer travelling with you. Be careful, envoy. Men who think their wounds can be healed are prone to taking risks."

Aranok smiled. "I wanted her the minute she killed that demon. The fact she has a power I believed a myth is an additional gift. And I never take risks."

"As I understand it," said the monk, "you charged a demon unarmed."

"All right. Calculated risks."

———

"Not bad, wee man!" Glorbad bellowed, parrying Vastin's blow with his shield. "Hold there and let me show you something." Vastin was happy to take the break. They'd been at it for a long time and his arms were beginning to ache. He dropped his weapons, leaned on his thighs and breathed deeply. "You're no tired, are you?" the soldier asked.

Vastin glanced sideways at Nirea and Allandria. He stood up and breathed deep, pushing his shoulders back. "Course not," he lied. He already felt like spare baggage in the group. If he couldn't keep up with the old man...He looked up at the first-floor window. Just in case. No sign of movement. Maybe she wasn't up yet.

"Here," said Glorbad. "Let me show you an axe's biggest advantage over a sword. Swing that down toward me. Overhead."

Vastin took a step back and swung gently—he was extremely aware of not accidentally wounding his sparring partner, regardless of the fact that it was more likely to be him who got hurt. Glorbad lifted his shield and the axe-head caught on the top of it. "Now pull," said the soldier. Vastin yanked the weapon back toward himself, and the soldier came with it, his shield dipping as he stumbled.

"See?" he said, catching himself against Vastin. "Axes aren't just for cutting. You can grab an opponent and pull them off-balance. Useful if you're fighting an enemy with a shield wall—axes open gaps for swords and pikes."

Vastin hoped not to be seeing action against a "wall" of shields. That sounded like a very good way to get killed.

"Cheer up, lad. You've gone a horrible shade. You're not dead yet." Glorbad slapped Vastin on the back so hard that he had to take a step to keep his balance. He laughed gently, looking at the women.

"Don't let him rattle you, Vastin, you're doing fine," Nirea called. Vastin smiled weakly at her and glanced up at the window again. Was she awake? Was she watching?

Glorbad followed his gaze and, after a moment, turned back to look at him as if he'd discovered an extra pie on his plate. The soldier put an arm around Vastin's shoulders and turned him away from the farmhouse. "Let me give you some advice, son. Man to man."

"All right." He hoped this wasn't going where he suspected.

"That girl? She's not a girl. She's a Thorn. Thorns are different. They serve God before everything. I've fought beside a few and they are fierce, but devout. Just don't get your hopes up. Not for her."

Vastin felt his face warming. "I...I didn't...I haven't..."

"Come on, son," said Glorbad. "She's a pretty girl and you're a fifteen-year-old boy. I'm not so addled I can't remember what that's like. You're all cock and nerves. But she's fire, that one. She's a warrior, not a tavern girl."

A hot rush of anger washed over Vastin. Maybe for the soldier's patronising tone. Maybe for the casual way he dismissed "tavern girls" as if they were nothing. Like Amollari. Maybe for something else. "I'm not a child." He threw off the arm and stepped away.

The amusement fell from Glorbad's face. A brief flash of what Vastin thought might be hurt gave him pause. The soldier's eyes hardened, his jaw stiffened. "Fair enough. Just the weapons, then." He turned and lifted the silver flask to his mouth, walked a few paces and turned back to Vastin. "Again," he said flatly, raising his shield.

Vastin raised his axe and lunged.

---

The sound of clashing metal jolted Aranok awake. He jumped from the chair and nearly fell over when his left leg took no weight.

*Damned chair!*

Dahev looked at him curiously and, when the sound came again, put a hand on Aranok's shoulder.

"It's fine. Yer soldier's sparring with the lad. Teaching him to use that nice axe."

"Glorbad?" Aranok asked. "He's up?" He leaned heavily on his right leg and bounced the left on the ground, feeling the tingle of blood flowing back to his foot.

"Woke bright as a hare this morning. Offered to help with my rounds. I told him he'd done enough already." Dahev placed a plate in front of Aranok, with a pair of boiled eggs, a crust of bread and a lump of cheese. "I'm sorry we've no got more."

"No. Thank you," Aranok said. "This is very generous. Did your boys get home?"

"Aye, they did," the farmer answered. "Though I daresay they'd have been happy to spend the night down at Lorston's place. He's three daughters, poor bugger. Never blessed with a son could help with the heavy work. I'm lucky to have my two."

Aranok raised a wry grin. Dahev had just seen a teenage girl behead a demon but still thought she wouldn't be up to farmwork. To be fair, he'd first assumed Samily a man himself. Still, he knew better than his assumptions—Dahev might not appreciate having his questioned. And the man was hosting them. No point risking offence. "Where are the others?"

"The monk's upstairs, taking breakfast to the Thorn. She's something, eh?" Dahev nodded to her armour, which shone like new in the early sunlight. Vastin had made an excellent job of cleaning it.

"She is." Much more than the farmer imagined.

"And the women are outside, drinking tea and watching the sparring."

"Your boys?" Aranok asked.

"Been out in the fields since sunrise. Clearing the dead, seeing what they can salvage."

"I'm sorry we couldn't save it all."

"Tosh." Dahev was plating up another meal for himself. It was the same as Aranok's, but with one egg and less cheese. He was rationing himself to provide for their party. "You saved us from losing everything. What you did, with the water? I know what folks say. *Draoidhs* can't be trusted. What you can do's unnatural. Ungodly. Dangerous. Specially after Mynygogg and all, but…far as I'm concerned, you're a goddamn miracle, sire. Pardon my blasphemy."

Aranok smiled. "You need no pardon from me. But I wouldn't repeat that in front of the monk."

"No, sir." Dahev dipped his head.

Aranok moved to look out the window. Sure enough, Nirea and Allandria sat chatting on a bench, watching Glorbad parry a blow from Vastin's axe. The boy's smithing skills had stood up to their first battle. He hoped there wouldn't be another too soon.

"Dahev, you've been a wonderful host," said Aranok. "But I must ask a further favour of you. Do you have any horses to spare?"

Dahev sucked through his teeth. "To spare? No really."

"I can pay, of course." Aranok produced a pouch of coins.

"It's not that. I've only got a pair of workers," he said. "I suppose I could spare you one as a pack horse, seeing as I've got a damn sight less crops to work."

Aranok winced. "No. I'm sorry to have asked." He'd hoped it might be a way to repay the man for his hospitality. He was going to have a hard winter, minus a large chunk of his crops. And they really did need horses.

"Lorston's got a stableful, though," said Dahev. "Breeds 'em. Go see him and tell him I sent you. If the grumpy bastard doesn't do you a fair price after what you done for us yesterday, tell him I'll take it out his hide."

"I will, thank you." Aranok sat back at the table. He lifted his coin purse. Dahev looked at him strangely. "Would you... would you allow me to pay for our bed and board?"

Dahev sat up straight, his face hardening. "I need no charity, sire. I'm in your debt for saving our crops. This is the least I can do."

He'd offended a proud man—exactly what he was trying to avoid. Damn it. He needed a pretence, an excuse.

"Actually, as an agent of the king, I'm forbidden from taking free lodgings."

"What?" asked Dahev. "Why?"

*Why indeed.*

"To avoid bribes. From those who would want me to influence the king on their behalf." It sounded plausible. It actually sounded reasonable. Perhaps that should be a rule.

Dahev did not look convinced. "I'm no trying to influence anybody."

"Oh no, not you," said Aranok. "Others. Wealthy folk who want lower taxes. So, as a rule, I have to pay. It's a matter of honour really." Aranok shrugged apologetically.

Dahev looked hard at him for a moment. No doubt he needed the money. It was only a question of whether Aranok had given him enough of an excuse to accept it. The farmer glanced to the stairs.

"The brother and the Thorn are free. An offering," he said.

Aranok raised his hands. "Of course."

Silence again. Dahev took a bite of his bread and seemed to take an age to chew it.

"All right," he finally said. "If it's the law."

Aranok nodded. "Thank you. Shall we call it one mark a head, for the five of us?" It was the price of a reasonable hostel. For the same,

Aranok would have had his own bed and a more substantial breakfast, but he knew what the farmer had given them was more valuable.

Still, the man looked slightly taken aback. "Five coppers is fair."

"Eight, then?" Aranok asked, trying to put on his best earnest face.

"Aye, all right then," said Dahev. "Eight."

Aranok smiled. "Excellent, thank you." He poured four silver marks into his hand and offered them to the farmer. The old man took them carefully and poured them into a ceramic jar near the stove. The clink of the coins echoed off the sides.

"One last thing," Aranok said, tucking into his own food. "Could we keep this between you and me? King's business?"

A smile cracked the edge of the farmer's mouth. "King's business."

With horses and full bellies, they could be on their way again. From here, the road to Barrock was also the road to Mournside. Aranok's thoughts shifted to his family. He didn't see them often, but just knowing they were there—that home was there—was a comfort. A foundation. The ground his life was built on. The idea that his parents, his sister, his niece could be gone...it was too much. A stab of pain from his hand pulled his attention. The thumbnail he'd been idly worrying had torn, and a dot of blood rose under its edge. He put it in his mouth, pressing his tongue against it to relieve the sting.

Tomorrow he would be home. Then he'd know.

One way or another.

# CHAPTER 11

Samily wiped her blade clean. She hated killing people. It was not her purpose. When it had to be done, it was to be quick and painless. Decapitation was the best choice. It left the White Thorns an undeserved reputation for brutality; the grisly remains were difficult to see as a kindness. But Samily knew the dead who had been left to bleed out from a stomach wound had suffered more. She pitied them, regardless of which master they served.

"Nice cut." Nirea broke the quiet. "That's some edge."

"Indeed," Samily replied. "The Green Laird does excellent work."

"Who's the Green Laird?" asked Vastin.

"The martial instructor at Baile Airneach, and their weaponsmith," Aranok answered. "His work is legendary."

"Never heard of him." The boy seemed irritated. He kicked a stone idly into the trees.

"Brother, may I?" Samily nodded to the Reiver's body.

"Of course, child," Meristan answered.

Samily stepped off the road. If she could find some soft ground amid the trees, it would make the digging quicker and easier.

"What's she doing?" she heard Glorbad ask.

"Burying him," Meristan answered.

"What? We've no got time for that! What if the others come back with reinforcements? We need to move."

Samily turned back, pushing aside a thin branch to see the soldier. "Would you deny him a proper burial?"

Glorbad stared at her for a moment, as if trying to understand what she'd said. Which was odd. It was a simple question.

"He was trying to kill you," he finally said.

"He is still God's child," she replied. Meristan smiled approvingly.

"I can't see how murdering a White Thorn is doing God's work." He pointed at the headless corpse bleeding into the dirt. "That man was your enemy."

Samily stepped back onto the road. The soldier was so full of anger.

"He was not my enemy," she said calmly. "He only believed me his enemy."

"What?" Glorbad asked. "He tried to kill you. That makes him your enemy!"

Why did the soldier not understand the difference? She looked to Meristan, hoping he might be able to elaborate in a way the soldier would comprehend. But the monk smiled and gestured for her to continue. She took a breath and turned back to Glorbad.

"For some reason—his childhood, his king, his family—he believed I was his enemy. He believed he had to kill me, because he believed me a threat to his life. He believed he was defending himself, because someone, at some time, convinced him that he or his loved ones were threatened. That does not make him my enemy, it simply makes him wrong. I had no malice for him. God alone will judge whether his reasons were adequate to excuse his actions. My part is only to deliver him. We all deserve respect in death."

"So you don't blame him?" Glorbad asked.

"I would as soon blame his knife for its cut."

"Then who do you blame?" The soldier sounded almost aggressive.

Samily stopped for a moment, unsure how exactly to answer the question. She disliked the idea of blame. Responsibility was a better concept—one she'd been taught from a young age.

"For some reason, this man's master, whoever they may be, saw some advantage in convincing him that the people of Eidyn were his enemies. That they were 'other' than he. Less worthy of life. They taught him that Eidyn must be conquered or plundered. Perhaps it was for riches, or perhaps for power, I don't know—but those, I understand, are the usual reasons. Whatever they may be, that person, the one who made us this man's enemy—they bear the responsibility."

"So his chieftain?" Glorbad spat. "His chieftain is the only one you blame? These bastards are out here picking over the carcass of Eidyn. They've raided us for fucking years and when Mynygogg came, they only hit us harder! Now they're robbing what little we have left and murdering folk on the road! You telling me these fuckers are *innocent*?"

Nirea put a hand on his shoulder, which seemed to calm him. Why was he so agitated by Samily's words? Had he come to see all Reivers as "the enemy"? She hoped not. There was no good down that path.

"All people are born innocent. Their lives shape them. Some are selfish. Some make poor choices. Some are manipulated. It is not for me to judge them. God will do that, and they will have to answer for their lives. For me to hate them would be"—she shrugged—"pointless."

Glorbad turned to the envoy openmouthed. Still, he did not understand. God's grace was hard for some to grasp. And yet it was so wonderful. So liberating.

Aranok turned and walked past Meristan to Allandria. As he passed, he said something quietly, which made her master smile.

"He doesn't look like he worshipped God to me," Glorbad finally said.

"You cannot know a man's heart from his clothes," she replied. "But we are all God's children, whether we know it or not."

The soldier gave her a look that seemed somewhere between confusion and consternation, and turned to Aranok. He was looking down the road and seemed to be in conversation with Allandria. "Either way, we don't have time to stop," Glorbad said.

The envoy looked at the sky. The sun was getting low—not that it was visible through the clouds. "Actually, we probably do. We've ridden hard, and by my mark we're less than an hour from the inn. Let's take a breath, let Samily do what she needs to, then make for the inn and settle for the night."

Glorbad looked to Nirea. She shrugged.

"Fine," he grumbled, and turned to his horse's saddlebag.

Samily returned to the undergrowth. There had been a spongy, peaty area a few feet away. If it was big enough, she could be done within the hour.

———

"When are you planning to tell them?" Allandria nodded toward the bar, where Glorbad and Nirea were deep in conversation beneath the low-hanging dark wooden beams of Ryrie's Inn.

"When I need to." Aranok sipped his ale. It was watered down but still welcome. Times were hard; he could hardly fault an innkeeper for trying to eke out whatever profit they could.

"How is that not now?" she asked. "We'll reach the crossroads tomorrow. They're going to notice when we don't turn toward Auldun."

Aranok sighed. "Why have a fight tonight that you can put off until tomorrow?"

Allandria curled her lip at him. "It's your grave you're digging. Don't say I didn't warn you."

She was probably right. But he just didn't have the energy for an argument. And there were other things on his mind. "There's another conversation I need to have." He stood and crossed to the table where Vastin sat with Samily and Meristan. The boy was enraptured by a story the knight was telling.

"Excuse me." He put a hand on the boy's shoulder. "I'm sorry to interrupt, but may I speak with Brother Meristan?"

Samily looked to her master, who nodded and smiled.

"Of course," she said, standing. "I will retire."

They had managed to secure the last three rooms, with only a pair of beds each. His relationship with Allandria was a secret—to avoid her being a target for those who would seek leverage over the king's envoy—so there was no easy way to procure them a private room. They'd be sleeping in their own beds tonight, while Vastin slept on a bedroll between them.

The boy looked disappointed the story had been cut short, but he also rose and joined his new mentor at the bar. Hopefully he would learn to control his drinking, as well as his axe—unlike the soldier, who was already swaying gently. He would certainly have more stories to share.

"What can I do for you, Envoy?" The monk sat back and placed his hands across his stomach.

"Whisky drinker." Aranok gestured to Meristan's glass.

"Indeed," he answered. "I've always found it more to my taste than ale. Though I admit, it does less to quench a man's thirst than it does to dull his wits."

Aranok laughed. "I don't know about that." He glanced at the bar again. The smile faded as he turned back to the monk. "Brother Meristan, you know a great deal about demons?"

"I suppose I do. As much as any man who's never actually battled one." The monk gestured to his robes.

"Of course," Aranok replied. "But you've studied them."

"I have. Though no two are the same, they do seem to have common traits."

"Like what?"

"Well, they prefer the dark. They're largely mindless—driven by instinct to destroy. And they are vulnerable to Green blades."

"Right." That largely tallied with what he thought. "So would you say it was unusual that we should encounter a demon during the day? A demon that burned crops, but didn't kill a single man, woman or child? Who never set fire to a building over several days of rampaging?"

Meristan sat back thoughtfully. "That is unusual."

"Isn't it?" The smell of food drew Aranok's attention, and his stomach reminded him he hadn't eaten since breakfast. Ryrie's Inn was known for the quality of its roast lamb, and being both the son of a wealthy merchant and the envoy to the king, Aranok had no shortage of coin. Paying for a good meal was a fine way to get any company on your side. Perhaps it would help when he told them the truth tomorrow. Perhaps not.

"Another thing…" He turned back to his companion. "Have you ever heard of a beast shaped like a man, that comes out of a cocoon?"

Meristan recoiled. "No. What kind of cocoon?"

"Big ones."

"How 'like a man'?" Meristan asked.

"They have extra limbs, and their skin is like slatted armour. But they burn in sunlight."

Meristan breathed deep and shook his head. "I have never heard of such a thing. It sounds monstrous."

"They hunt in packs," Aranok added.

"What do you think they are?"

"Allandria thinks she's heard of them. Perhaps from childhood." Though how she would not remember them seemed…unlikely. "She called them Thakhati."

"From childhood?" The monk furrowed his brow. "Where did she grow up that they have such monsters?"

"Long story. Mostly Lochen, but before that the southern Reiver Lands. Her parents were nomadic. Settled in Lochen for her benefit."

The monk rubbed his hand over his bald head. "It's not a name I know. But then, they don't sound like demons. Demons are summoned by *draoidhs*, as you know. They do not grow in cocoons."

"No," Aranok agreed. "But where have they come from? And why now?"

"I honestly don't know. You should ask Samily. She has more direct experience with the monsters than I do."

"Well, that's the thing," said Aranok. "I don't think she has. I think they're new. And I'm worried about why."

"You think it could be related to Mynygogg?"

Glorbad laughed heartily. The others, including Allandria, who had moved across, joined him. Nirea waved her arm in the air, brandishing an invisible sword. Vastin stood engrossed in another tale. It was good to see the boy smile. He deserved to smile. The bloody irony that Aranok had had to put his life in danger to bring it to him was not lost.

"I don't know. It may be. Something is not right."

The monk looked at him thoughtfully. For the size and build of him, he was unexpectedly pensive. He had the frame to be a great warrior, had he been so inclined—and yet he'd chosen the life of a brother, allowing others to do the fighting. Aranok wondered what childhood had put him on that path, and how different it must have been from his own.

"I have something to show you." Meristan sat forward almost conspiratorially. "I don't know what it means—if it means anything."

He reached into a pouch on his belt and produced a scrap of cloth. It was stained and spattered with blood, but Aranok could still see what it was. "Where did you get this?"

"Two nights ago, a wounded Reiver stumbled into our camp. He was badly injured—he died in the night, despite our efforts."

"Did Samily...?" Aranok asked.

"No. She wanted to, but I would not allow it."

*Interesting.*

"So you don't agree with her about the Reivers? About them not being our enemies?"

"No, about that she is right," the monk said. "But to heal a wound that severe—she'd have been completely drained, and we would have been defenceless, in the Wilds, at night. Regrettably, I am not a fighting man, Envoy. And had I known about the creatures you describe..."

*He may not even have left Baile Airneach.*

Aranok nodded and picked up the scrap of cloth. "Why would they do this? What purpose would it serve for a Reiver to wear a crest like this? We've never been in alliance with them."

"I don't know, but I took this from the man Samily killed today." Meristan tossed another scrap onto the table. It was blood-soaked, but Aranok could make out enough to see it was the same pair of crests. Why in Hell would Reivers be wearing false crests?

He put his hands on his head and stretched back in his chair. "Put those away. I don't know what that's about, but it's not likely anything to do with Mynygogg, so it's not our first concern."

"Could it be a message?" Meristan asked. "I've been thinking—what if this is an attempt to make peace? An overture from the Reiver council?"

Could it be? Peace with the Reivers would be a massive boon. They could stop focusing on repairing the Malcanmore Wall and rebuild houses instead. Trade routes could flow more easily within Eidyn without fear of raids. Access to land routes could be negotiated, allowing Eidyn to trade with other countries without having to rely on their seaports—especially while Leet was under siege.

Peace with the Reivers would change everything. Still, it didn't make sense. "They have a funny way of delivering messages—at the point of a sword."

"Aha! Food!" Glorbad bellowed. Ryrie herself carried large platters from the kitchen. Aranok's stomach growled as the smell reached him.

"I'll fetch Samily back," Meristan said, standing.

"Wait." Aranok put a hand on his arm. "There is one more thing." He'd left this for last. He'd rather not have to tell the monk about it, but he deserved to know.

Meristan cocked his head and sat again.

"How many Thorns are there?" Aranok asked.

Meristan frowned. "We numbered about fifty at our height. After the war—more like thirty, I believe. Though some are out in the country, helping where they can. It's hard to know an exact number."

"Well, reduce that number by one," Aranok said. "I'm sorry. We found a set of white armour on the road to Mutton Hole."

Meristan raised his hands to his lips. "The body? What did they look like? Man or woman?"

"Neither," said Aranok. "There was no body—just the armour. Completely clean—no sign of what happened to your knight. But male by the size of the armour, unless you have a giant woman Thorn? About your size?"

Meristan shook his head solemnly. "There are a few men who fit that description. Good men."

"I'm sorry," said Aranok again. "We have no idea what happened to him. But it was near where we encountered the Thakhati…"

"You think…? By God, if these creatures can kill a Thorn and leave nothing behind…"

"I know. Which is why we travel by day. But can I ask you…Glorbad assured me no Thorn would abandon their armour. I just wondered…"

"No," Meristan interrupted. "Glorbad is right. No Thorn would give up their armour but with their life. They forfeit their soul if they abandon their calling. It would be worse than suicide."

The two looked at each other silently across the table. This likely meant they had something else to worry about, or the Thakhati were even more lethal than they had seemed. Or, a worse thought—there were enough of them to overcome a Thorn.

"Are you two not hungry?" Allandria sat with her dinner.

"I'll have yours!" Glorbad offered, stuffing a potato into his mouth.

"Between you and me?" Aranok asked quietly as he stood.

"As you say," Meristan replied.

# CHAPTER 12

A bsolutely fucking not!" Glorbad raged. "Hell's arse, man, who do you think you are?"

It was exactly the reaction Allandria had expected. She resisted the urge to point this out to Aranok. Even so, he gave her a black look. He knew—which was a little satisfying, if she was honest.

Glorbad all but vaulted off his horse. If anything, he seemed nimbler since recovering from his injuries.

"Glorbad, for fuck's sake…" Nirea scrambled to get off her own mount.

"Quiet, woman! I'm not having it!"

Nirea stopped with a venomous look.

"The king clearly said no, Envoy." Glorbad pointed up at him. Aranok's horse whinnied in protest, stepping away from the soldier. "It was his only condition."

"He also clearly said I'm in charge." Aranok calmly dismounted to face the soldier.

Glorbad fumed up at him. "Unacceptable! I'll not be party to defying a direct order from the king!"

"You're not. I am. And I will take the consequences. You are following my direct order."

That was easy for him to say. He knew fine well there would be no consequences. Well, nothing significant anyway. Janaeus might have to make a show of some kind of punishment after this, but nothing Aranok would fret over. It would blow over quickly. But Glorbad did not know that, nor did he have the luxury of a close friendship with his regent.

"I am not!" Glorbad leaned in. That was enough. He was over the line, regardless of being arguably in the right.

"Step back," Allandria said flatly. This could end badly. She needed to pour some water on the fire.

"Or what?" Glorbad growled.

*Oh good.*

"Or I'll make you." Allandria gently touched her bow. She really hoped she wouldn't have to say more.

"Janaeus rescued this country from Hofnag, then Mynygogg, and you'd treat him like a common laird!" Spittle flecked Glorbad's lips. But he did step back. Just a little. Enough.

But what he'd said was a problem. Aranok grew an inch with indignation. "Oh, Janaeus saved the country, did he? All on his own? I must have missed that while I was standing next to him! Good thing he didn't need any help, isn't it?" His voice rose as he spoke.

Meristan dismounted. "Perhaps we could all take a moment and calm down? I'm sure we can talk this through sensibly."

"Aye, right!" said Glorbad. "This idiot's trying to get us all hanged for treason."

Before Allandria could react, the soldier brought his arms up to shove Aranok in the chest—but was flung backwards onto his arse with a spark of red. Good God, he'd actually charged his armour before the conversation. He knew it might go this way and he'd done it anyway, the infuriating bastard.

Allandria leapt from her horse. Aranok stood still, staring defiantly down at Glorbad—as if that would help. Why were men so damned stupid?

"Fucking magic armour, is it?" Glorbad cursed from the floor. He brought himself to one knee, hand on his sword.

*Shit.*

"Glorbad!" Nirea barked. "Don't be a fucking idiot!"

He glowered over his shoulder at her.

"You can't undraw that sword," she said tersely, her eyes dark.

"No, you can't." Allandria reached for an arrow, just in case.

Nirea pointed at her. "That goes for you too. Put your hand down!"

Allandria froze. The sailor was probably right. She didn't lower her hand, but she stopped. "I won't draw if he doesn't."

"Now, Envoy," Nirea said, as Glorbad got to his feet, hand still on the hilt of his sword. "Why the Hell should we go to Mournside, as the king expressly told us not to, rather than go straight to Barrock?"

Aranok spread his hands wide. He looked like the most reasonable man alive.

"Look, we have to take shelter for the night. We either stay here at the Cross Keys"—he gestured to the inn across the road—"or we make use of the last of the daylight to get to Mournside and check it out. We can stay there tonight instead."

"You want to see if the walls have been breached by the Blackened!" Glorbad growled. "Hardly somewhere to stay the night if they have, is it? You could be walking us all into a death trap!"

Aranok almost smiled. They were debating it now. He had what he wanted: the chink in the armour. "The Blackened can only harm you if they touch your skin. We're all well covered—you're wearing armour, for God's sake! If they have breached the walls, we can help, and we can surely manage to find a building secure enough to let us all get some sleep. We can ride cross-country to meet the Auld Road in the morning and lose no time."

"Excuse me," Samily said, still astride her horse. "Brother Meristan is not well covered, as you say. It would be dangerous for him to be amongst the Blackened."

Meristan demurred with a raised hand. "Please, make no decisions for my sake." It was true, his robes were much less protective than the armour the others wore. The Blackened's disease spread skin to skin. He would be the most vulnerable.

Aranok sighed. "I just want to check on my family."

"We've all had family!" bawled Glorbad. "But some of us know how to follow orders. We know what duty means. And honour. And loyalty."

*Oh shit.*

Aranok's face turned dark. She needed to do something before this exploded.

"Samily's right." Allandria stepped forward. All heads turned toward her. "Brother Meristan is not equipped for the Blackened. He shouldn't go. If Glorbad feels strongly about it, he should stay here too. In fact, everyone should stay here." She turned to Aranok. "You're asking people to defy an order from their king. You want to do that, that's fine. We'll go."

Glorbad snarled and turned away.

Aranok looked at her intently for a moment. "Fine." He was either furious or grateful, and it was disturbingly hard to tell which. "We'll meet the rest of you on the Auld Road tomorrow—at the edge of the Black Hills. We'll make the White Hart tomorrow night."

"We ride in the morning. You're welcome to catch up." Glorbad led his horse toward the stables.

Meristan did the same, placing a hand on Aranok's shoulder as he passed. "I will pray for your family." Aranok nodded a silent thanks. Samily followed her master.

"Well done. I was worried how that would end." Nirea had paused beside Allandria, leading her own mount.

"Two wild boars butting heads?" she replied. "What could go wrong?"

Nirea didn't smile. "Seriously."

"I know." It could have been a lot worse. It almost was.

"I'm sorry for snapping at you."

"No, it's fine," said Allandria. "You were probably right."

"Oh, I was right," Nirea said flatly, "but I'm still sorry." She reached out a gloved hand, and Allandria took it.

"Fair enough."

Nirea nodded and followed the others.

"Master Aranok?" Vastin stood looking up at Aranok, who had remounted his horse.

The *draoidh* winced. "I'm nobody's master, Vastin, least of all yours."

"Sorry. It's just..." The boy hesitated. Aranok looked down at him, a shadow across his face. "I'll come."

Aranok drew a deep breath. When he let it out, he finally smiled.

*God bless you, boy.*

"I've put you in enough danger, Vastin," he said, "without risking getting you hanged too." He knew fine there was no risk of that, but he probably thought it would explain why he was turning down the boy's offer. In truth, keeping the boy safe would have been an extra burden they could do without. But he had spine, that one.

"No, sir," the boy protested. "The king didn't order me to do anything. He was going to take my business; it was you stopped him. Far as I'm concerned, my debt's to you, not him."

"Don't let anyone else hear you say that," Aranok said. "You'll get yourself flogged, proclaiming loyalty to a *draoidh* over Great King Janaeus."

"Yes, sir." The boy grinned.

Aranok leaned down and placed a hand on his shoulder. "Stay here for the night and make sure they meet us on the Auld Road tomorrow. All right?"

Vastin nodded. "If that's what you want." The boy's voice wavered. He was probably terrified at the thought of riding into a pack of Blackened, but he was willing to do it. As much as he might be disappointed, he was almost certainly relieved.

"It is. Here. Take this." Aranok's coin pouch jingled as it dropped into Vastin's waiting hands. "If you've any concerns, speak to Brother Meristan. He'll keep you right."

"Aye, sir." Vastin tied the pouch to his belt. His horse whinnied as the boy led it and the pack horse toward the stables.

Allandria pulled herself back onto her horse. She breathed deeply and looked up at the sun dipping toward the horizon. It was calming, reassuring. The promise of rest and of another day.

Aranok rode slowly past.

"Thank you," he said quietly.

She nudged her horse to follow him. "You're angry at me."

"No." He was lying, but did he even know it? Did he know why?

"I told you this would be a problem," she said.

*Damn it.* She wasn't going to say that.

"I know you did," he said without looking back. "You were right. I just wish you'd backed me."

Allandria pulled up. "What? I did back you. I'm coming with you!"

"I mean with the rest. We could have convinced them, together," he said.

She kicked her horse into a trot and rode in front of his, blocking his path. He pulled up with a start.

"You petulant prick!" she said, seething. "I just stopped you causing an actual fight with our allies, and you think *I* let *you* down? Maybe you should go on your own, see how far you get."

Aranok looked at her blankly. "I...No. Please. I'm sorry."

"Damned right you're sorry." She was still fuming. "Don't take it out on me that you didn't get your own way." She pointed at the inn. "They don't know you. They don't know what you've done—what you can do. They don't know what you can get away with because Janaeus owes you what they think they owe him."

Aranok nodded.

"Don't forget who's at your back, Laird Aranok." She turned her horse and kicked it into a canter without another word. They would need to ride hard to make Mournside before dark.

———◦———

"What the fucking Hell did you think you were going to do, kill him?" Nirea closed the door behind her. Glorbad sat on the edge of his bed, removing the last of his armour. The room was small. A simple wooden bed, a wooden table, and just about enough space for the discarded armour on the floor.

"No..." Glorbad replied with a whine. It was pitiful. Like a child caught with his hand in the bread bin. For all his bluster and noise, he was usually harmless. Tonight he'd been dangerous.

She needed to know why. "Then what?"

"I don't know!" He lifted a silver flask from the table and took a swig. "He needed to be told."

"Told what? That he was wrong? You could have done that without the sword!"

"Aye, all right, but...fuck. The boy just pisses me off, all right?" he answered.

"Why?"

"Never had to work for anything, has he? Fucking son of a laird. Envoy to the king. Moves things with his fucking mind! Never gets his hands dirty. Never risks himself. And he prances about like some fucking hero. I've heard stories about him. All shite."

"So what?" Nirea asked.

"I've seen real heroes. I've seen folk run headfirst into a battle they've no chance of winning, just to protect their families. And I've seen their broken, bloody corpses. That boy is no hero. And no leader."

"He literally threw himself at a demon to protect Vastin," said Nirea. "I know you missed that, but it happened."

Glorbad pursed his mouth a moment, as if maybe the fire was burning down.

No such luck.

"Look at Janaeus! Farming family. Worked his way up. Grafted. Got a laird to sponsor him for the university because of his brains. Served in the army. Actually served! Built a rebellion from nothing! Because it was the right thing to do. *That's* a man. *That's* a leader."

Nirea sighed and sat down on the bed next to him. She understood why the old goat was so loyal to the king. He had to be. Because siding with Janaeus had cost him. Everything. And if Janaeus wasn't the man Glorbad chose to ally with—he'd sacrificed for nothing. For a promise of a future his son would never see.

She put out her hand, and he gave her the flask. She raised it in salute and drank. The whisky warmed her tongue and nipped at the back of her throat as she breathed in before swallowing. It was good. She preferred the sweetness of rum, but whisky was a fine alternative.

"We've both seen enough death," she said. "And I've heard the stories about the envoy too. But d'you know what I haven't heard?"

Glorbad looked at her blankly.

"I've never heard him claim to be a hero. In fact, I'd never heard him say anything about himself before today, when you pressed him."

"You can see it in his face," said the soldier. "Fucking privilege, every ounce of him."

"He's a *draoidh*, man. He grew up a *draoidh*. That was practically illegal for years under Hofnag." She left that a moment to sink in and took another swig of whisky. "He probably grew up terrified. Scared of being caught. Afraid to tell anyone what he was. Did his parents know? Did they accept him? Imagine knowing people would hate him just for existing. What does that do to a child? Does he start hating himself too? Maybe wishing he wasn't a *draoidh*? Maybe wishing he didn't exist?"

Glorbad grumbled. "Ach, we all had difficult childhoods, I mean..."

"Don't," Nirea interrupted. "Don't fucking dare." He knew better than to complain about his upbringing. Not to her. His eyes changed—softened—and he closed his mouth.

"Way I see it, he risked everything when he stood with Janaeus—for people who would have shunned him. Some still would, still do."

"That's not what...Look, I've no problem with *draoidhs*, but...ah, fuck." He seemed to know there was no good way to finish that sentence. At least that was something. He took back the flask and emptied the last of it down his throat, then stood and looked out the window. The sun was setting. Revelry echoed from the bar downstairs: laughter, chatter, tankards banged on tables. The smell of food.

"I hope they find shelter," the soldier said quietly.

---

"Fetch us some more drinks, lad?" said Meristan.

"Of course." Vastin smiled at Samily. He seemed pleased to do so. She wondered why. Was it his age? He stood grinning at the bar, waiting for the innkeeper's attention. She caught his eye and he smiled even wider, raising his eyebrows at her before looking away. He smiled at her a lot.

"Something bothering you, Samily?" Meristan asked.

"The boy keeps looking at me. What's wrong with him?"

Meristan snorted. "There's nothing wrong with him. He's just a boy. And you're a girl."

It took Samily a moment to realise what he meant. "Oh. Oh, no. No."

Meristan gave her a puzzled look. "Is that so bad? I mean, you're a pretty girl, and he's not that much younger than you."

*Pretty? Ugh.*

Samily had no desire to be "pretty." It was as useless to her as this ridiculous boy's attention. The look on her face must have made that obvious.

"What's wrong?" her master asked.

Samily frowned. It bothered her that Meristan had to ask. "I am a White Thorn. I am a warrior. I serve God and God's children. I am not 'pretty.'"

"I'm sorry." Meristan leaned back. "I meant it as a compliment. Why can't you be all of those things?"

"I'm not a doll." She could feel her anger rising. But this was Meristan. She knew he meant her no insult. But still. "Compliment my skill, my strength, my sword even—but not my face. It is an accident of birth, a gift from parents I never knew. I have no claim to it and I take no pride in it."

Meristan contemplated her silently.

"And anyway," she said. "I have no interest in boys."

"Ah," said Meristan awkwardly. "I'm sorry; I didn't know. You prefer girls?"

"What? No. I just don't feel that way...about people."

Meristan looked confused. "Are you sure? Perhaps you just haven't met the right person?"

"No, not like that." Frustration crept into her voice. "I just don't have that...desire. You must understand, Brother. You're a monk."

Meristan blinked at her. "Samily, we take a vow of celibacy, of course. But that doesn't stop us being men. We still have desires."

Her master looked extremely uncomfortable now, raising his almost empty drink and looking away.

"So what do you do?" Samily asked.

Meristan choked on the last of his ale. Coughing, he put down the tankard.

"Well...that's...Vastin!"

The boy returned to the table with two fresh tankards and a glass. He proudly placed them on the table.

"M'lord and lady." He effected an elaborate bow.

Samily sighed. She had no patience for this. "Excuse me. I need to pee."

She passed Glorbad at the bottom of the stairs. He nodded, reeking of whisky already. His mouth opened, but Samily stopped him with a raised hand. "Peeing."

Whatever words he'd planned caught in his throat as she swung open the door and stepped outside.

———◦———

"What happened?" Vastin asked. Samily had seemed angry about something, but it couldn't be him, could it? He'd just bought drinks.

The old monk screwed up his mouth and looked at him oddly. "I think we need to have a chat."

"About what?" Had he done something wrong? Or said something he shouldn't have?

"I think I've made a mistake, and I might owe you an apology," said Meristan. That didn't sound good. But at least it wasn't something Vastin had done.

"Samily is quite different. You might have noticed." He had. He felt happy just being around her. Whenever a door opened, he looked for her.

"Well," the monk said, "she sees the world differently from you and me. More black and white, I suppose. And amongst those things . . . are boys."

Vastin felt a shiver run across his neck. Not this again. He'd had this from Glorbad already. A desire to get up and walk away seized him— but where would he go? And he sort of needed to know why the monk wanted to apologise. He needed to know what had happened, what had been said. "All right." He tried to look calmer than he felt.

"I've only just learned this myself, you see," said Meristan. "It seems that Samily is not interested in boys. Any boys."

"Oh." Vastin hoped he didn't sound as disappointed as he felt. "She likes girls?"

"Well, no. It seems she's just not interested either way."

"Oh." That was an end to that, then. It was probably silly anyway, to imagine a warrior like her might see him as . . . as what? It didn't matter. The door was closed. Still, he needed a way out of this conversation without making a fool of himself. "Why are you telling me?"

Meristan opened his hands. "That's where I might owe you an apology. You see, I was somewhat overenthusiastic in playing matchmaker, and suggested to Samily that you and she…" He gestured with his hands. The meaning was clear.

"Oh!" Vastin laughed nervously. "I…I hadn't thought. She didn't think I was…did she?" He really, really hoped not.

"No, of course not," said Meristan. "It's nothing you've done. Entirely my fault, I'm afraid. I hope I haven't embarrassed you."

Vastin felt his face flushing. He gulped back a mouthful of ale. "No. Not at all." It came out shriller than he intended. "I mean, of course, she's very pretty, but, you know, she's a Thorn, right? First duty to God." He shrugged as if it were the most meaningless thing in the world.

"Indeed." Meristan lifted his glass and clinked it against Vastin's tankard. "I'm so glad you understand. I'm sorry if I was presumptuous on your behalf."

"No," said Vastin. "No harm done."

The monk smiled. "Besides, I'm sure a lad like you, with his own business, has a few girls at home with their eyes on you."

Not as far as he knew. But he returned the smile anyway. As long as Samily didn't think he liked her, it would be fine. He lifted his tankard and drank deeply. When he put it down, he looked back at the bar. The knight had come back and was talking to Nirea. He caught Glorbad's eye. The soldier raised an eyebrow and nodded at him. Vastin raised his tankard in return and gave him a shaky smile. The soldier looked momentarily confused, then brightened and raised his own drink in return.

Vastin turned back to the monk. He really, really wanted to change the conversation now. "So tell me about the Green Laird."

———

They slowed the horses as the walls of Mournside came into sight. The animals breathed heavily; they had pushed them hard. The sky was almost completely dark. They hadn't encountered anything on the run: no Blackened, no Reivers, no Thakhati.

"Hood up, gloves on," Aranok said quietly, pulling his dark red scarf up to cover all but his eyes. "If there are Blackened here, let's be ready."

Allandria showed him her already gloved hands. She did pull up her hood, though. They hadn't spoken since the crossroads. He probably deserved that. He hadn't handled things well—though he still couldn't see any point in having had that conversation earlier. It would have gone the same way. But Allandria's solution was the right one, and he should have told her so. He would tell her. Later. When the silence had passed.

They slowly walked the horses closer. The main gate looked intact. But the town was three miles wide. The walls could have been breached anywhere—most likely on the opposite side, facing the Black Hills. Something moved near the gate. Aranok raised a hand and they stopped, climbed quietly off their horses and tethered them to a sturdy bush. Steam rose from the animals' bodies like smoke in the twilight. Allandria nocked an arrow, and they crept forward. There were two ways to stop a Blackened. Damage the brain or damage the heart. Anything else would just slow them down. Aranok had come across a group once, during the war. He'd set them on fire, thinking it a good way to take them all out at once. They'd kept going too long, and nearly burned down the cottage he was protecting. Allandria's way was better.

He felt a hand on his shoulder and stopped. Allandria pointed. Something was burning, just behind the wall, out of sight. The glow cast a long, distended shadow. But there was little doubt—it was human. Well, it had been human. Aranok breathed deep and moved sideways, trying to see in far enough to find out what, and how many, they were dealing with.

Something split the air in front of him and thunked into the earth. Allandria barrelled into him, rolling him away as another landed where he'd been.

Hells, arrows! Reivers?

He rolled onto his chest and pushed up, when a voice stopped him. "Who goes there?"

He looked at Allandria. Her face reflected his own shock. They looked up to see a sentry looming over the edge of the wall.

"Aranok," he called back. "Son of Dorann!"

There was a long silence. Neither of them moved. A large bolt slid open, and the gates swung out. A man dressed in the navy blue uniform of the town guard walked toward them, flanked by two others.

The guard was still intact? As he drew closer, Aranok could see he had dark, receding hair and an impressive moustache. He didn't recognise the man, but he hadn't been home in a long time. The two picked themselves up off the ground. Aranok wiped the dirt from his hands and lowered his hood.

"Laird Aranok," the man said, pushing a hand toward him. "Bak, captain of the guard. Welcome home."

Aranok offered his hand in return. "What's the damage? How much of the town have you been able to secure?"

Bak looked confused. "From what?"

"From the Blackened. We heard the walls were breached. How bad is it?" Allandria asked.

"I'm sorry, m'lady, you've been misinformed," said Bak. "The walls are intact. Mournside stands."

# CHAPTER 13

Aranok's legs threatened to either collapse beneath him or break into a run. His heart pounded like a blacksmith's hammer. For everything he'd expected, prepared himself for, feared, he had not considered this possibility. That Mournside would be...fine.

They walked up the cobbled street toward the town centre. It was much as Aranok remembered. The large sandstone houses lining the roads were the envy of most of Eidyn. Some had window boxes with flowers. Creeping ivy reached for a few slate roofs. The wealthiest were set back from the road by small gardens, bursting with life. Fir trees dotted the lanes, and torches sent shadows dancing in alleys. Above it all, the great white tower of commerce loomed over the town. It was beautiful.

The grin on his face was almost uncomfortable, but he had no desire to stifle it. His home, his family, were safe. Surely, at any moment, he'd wake from this wonderful dream and find himself camped in the forest. But Allandria's face reflected his own surprise and delight. Dread had weighed them down like pack horses, growing heavier each day they bore it. And now, suddenly, unexpectedly, it was lifted. Her hand found his for a surreptitious squeeze.

"I apologise for my woman firing on you," said the captain. "We received reports of the Blackened crossing the Black Hills. With that to the east, and the threat of Reivers on the roads to the west, we've closed the gates and doubled our watch. No sign of the Blackened so far, but the guard are jumpy—and tired."

"I understand," said Aranok. "So you've had the reports of the Blackened. The king believes the town has fallen. He'll be glad to hear otherwise."

Bak stopped and turned back to them both.

"Pardon?"

Aranok looked at him, confused. Why was that odd?

The captain cocked his head curiously. "The king can't believe the town has fallen. We received a king's messenger this afternoon."

"What?" That made no sense. Why would Janaeus send a messenger to an overrun town? A town he'd forbidden Aranok from visiting?

"He must have received new information after we left," said Allandria. "If she left as much as a day after us, she could have beaten us here, coming direct."

That was true. But a little convenient.

"Possibly," Aranok said. "Where is she staying?"

"The Canny Man, I expect," said Bak. "That's where they usually stay."

Aranok looked at Allandria. She nodded.

"Thank you, Bak. You can leave us here," he said. "I know my way."

"Of course, m'laird." Bak bowed slightly and walked back the way they'd come. "We're all delighted to hear the kingdom's flourishing again!"

Allandria looked at him quizzically. Aranok ran.

"Wait." He put a hand on Bak's shoulder.

"M'lord?" Bak asked.

"What do you mean 'the kingdom is flourishing'?"

"Only that the kingdom is recovering so well, after the war," said Bak.

"Who told you that?"

"The messenger," the captain said, as if it was the most obvious thing in the world.

Aranok turned to Allandria as she reached them. "The king's messenger reported that the kingdom is recovering well after the war."

"Did she?" the archer asked. "Well, that's lovely to hear!"

"What, specifically, did she report?" Aranok asked.

"Surely you know better than me." Bak's face was contorted in confusion now.

"Indulge me." This was important.

"Well, Haven has been set up as the capital, until it can be decided what to do with Mynygogg. Leet is back under our control and commencing merchant shipments again soon. Mutton Hole is secured and the harvest prospects are good. Repairs are going well, and things should be back to normal within eighteen months."

Aranok breathed deep. Not a word of that was true—at least, not as far as he knew.

Bak stood silently, seemingly waiting for a cue that he should say more.

"All right, thank you, Bak." Aranok shook the man's hand again. "I appreciate it."

"My laird." With a blank look, Bak turned and continued his walk back to the gate, the click of boots on cobbles echoing off the surrounding houses.

"What the Hell?" Allandria asked when he was out of earshot.

"Indeed," said Aranok. "Either Janaeus got a lot of news after we left, or..."

Allandria finished his thought. "Or that woman is no king's messenger."

"Or worse," said Aranok. "If someone is feeding the king false information, we could be in the midst of a coup."

Every ounce of him was desperate to go home—to see his family. But they were likely fine. And he had responsibilities.

"Canny Man?" Allandria asked.

"Aye. Canny Man."

---

The inside of the Canny Man was oddly laid out. Instead of a tavern's usual open space, with wooden tables and benches scattered around, it was separated into smaller nooks with tables sheltered in almost private, walled sections. Many were hidden entirely from the centre of the room. The original builder had, legend said, planned it with the local merchant community in mind. He'd understood their desire for privacy when discussing business. It had been a roaring success—not just with the merchants, but with gamblers and those conducting other affairs they didn't want on display. The Merchant's Arms, an older pub across the square, had originally lost most of its custom to the newcomer. However, several friends of the owner were prominent members of the Merchants Guild, and he had convinced them to designate it their official meeting place. Merchants from out of town were then obliged to take a room, and all public meetings of the guild were held there. Half the crowd still poured out across the square afterwards.

The Canny Man had become so popular that the innkeeper had started throwing out anyone he considered underdressed, unkempt, or just too drunk. And so the Merchant's Arms fed off its scraps, usually finding its business picking up later in the evening.

Aranok's runic armour drew the usual suspicious stares—though fewer than usual here, in Mournside, where esteem for his father and his title gained him some respect.

Of course, his position as king's envoy meant he could have walked in buck naked had he chosen to, and the innkeeper, Calador, wouldn't have dared throw him out. It would have made him unpopular, though. More unpopular.

There were a few faces he recognised at the bar. One man nodded in what seemed like a respectful manner—some would recognise him, though he had longer hair than the last time he'd been here. He nodded back. It was strange. This was his home, but his childhood here had been difficult. Many of these people had shunned him when his abilities became public, only to welcome him home like a conquering hero after the rebellion and his appointment as envoy. He wished he could believe it was his actions, rather than his station, that brought the respect.

"That's not young Laird Aranok, is it?"

Aranok turned to the bar. Calador's belly had got rounder. The ginger of his remaining hair and beard was whitening, but there was no mistaking those red cheeks.

"Calador!" He offered his hand across the bar. A few of the nearest patrons had heard the name and turned to see the newcomers. Some gave the same respectful nods. One lady smiled earnestly.

"How are you, young man?" the innkeeper asked. "I hear you and His Majesty are doing a fine job of running the country."

Aranok raised an eyebrow. "We do our best." No point tipping their hand to the messenger if she was in earshot.

"What can I get for you and your lady friend?" he asked. "Are you joining Dorann?"

*Oh Hells.*

His father was there? That was a complication he didn't need. Anything other than going directly to see him would be considered a slight, especially in public.

"Where is he?" Aranok asked.

Calador pointed to the back right corner. A few heads turned to look. His father was more famous than him here.

"Sorry," Aranok said, "I must introduce you to Lady Allandria." He looked her right in the eye as he said it and watched her lips pucker as her eyes sparkled. "Let me present Calador, keeper of this fine hostelry."

With a sly grin, Allandria offered her hand.

Calador took it gently. "M'lady. It's an honour."

She gently slapped Aranok's arm as she retracted it.

"So...?" Calador asked.

Allandria played up to the role. "Wine, if you please."

Calador looked at Aranok.

"The same," he said. "Oh, Calador, did I hear you've got a king's messenger here?" He hoped it sounded casual. An afterthought.

"We do. First in a while."

"I need a word with her."

Calador nodded to a table off to the left side of the tavern. Aranok could just see the shoulder and part of the back of a woman's head. She seemed to be eating.

The landlord filled two goblets and passed them across. Aranok handed him a coin in return. More than they cost, but the innkeeper's good graces were worth the extra. It was common here to overpay—in public. A show of wealth. A demonstration of status.

"So," Allandria asked when Calador had moved on to another customer. "Family or business?"

Business, preferably. Hang public opinion. If they could just get to the messenger's table without being noticed by...

"Laird Aranok. You grace us."

*Fuck.*

He knew that voice. It was not one he'd looked forward to. He turned to find the condescending smile of his sister's husband.

"Hello, Pol."

———◆———

"Hello, Father."

The old man looked up from his papers. Dorann had aged noticeably since Allandria last saw him. He was a good ten years older than Aranok's mother, Sumara, and he really looked it now. His face was tight and grey. Dark circles hung below his pale green eyes. The same circles she often saw on her lover. He was well-dressed, as he had to be. Couldn't have the purveyor of the finest clothes in Mournside looking shabby. His red doublet and trousers were lined with gold. Pol, on the other hand, wore royal blue—the most expensive colour, of course. Only in his thirties, like Ikara, he'd been born into farming but had a knack for selling that caught Dorann's attention.

Once it was clear Aranok wasn't going to take over the business, Pol had become the heir apparent. Marrying him to Ikara had been the crowning achievement in Dorann's eyes. Pol was a proud man—just like his father-in-law and mentor. He all but made a display of placing the two drinks he'd bought on the table and taking his place next to Aranok's father.

"Well..." Dorann sat back and casually picked up his pipe. "It's good to see you, boy. How have you been?"

*How had he been?* Allandria had never understood their relationship.

"I'm well, thank you," Aranok answered.

"You look well." Dorann tapped his pipe on the table and filled it from his pouch. "Though you might have cleaned up." He waved a vague hand in their direction.

Allandria bristled. Once, she might have been uncomfortable with his scorn, but she'd long since realised that her service to the country, and to Aranok, far outweighed any approval she might wish from her lover's father.

Aranok opened his hands. "Unfortunately, war is a messy business."

"Hmph." Dorann lit the pipe.

"May we?" Aranok gestured at the chairs in front of them. Dorann waved at them as he sucked on the pipe. Aranok pulled out a seat and looked at her. It took her a moment to realise it was meant for her. She sat as gracefully as she could and smiled. "Dorann."

Pol gave her the same dead smile.

Dorann blew out a puff of smoke. "Allandria. You still looking after my boy?"

"He looks after himself pretty well, sir. I'm just backup."

"I'm sure he does. What brings you to see us?"

Aranok drummed his fingers lightly on the table. "We had reports the Blackened had breached the walls."

"The Blackened? Inside the walls? Nonsense. I don't know where you're getting your reports from, son, but you need to get back and see your king more often!"

"Well, that's just…" Allandria started, but Aranok cut across her.

"Yes, we think Janaeus may have newer information. We'll get back to Haven as soon as we can."

"What's keeping you away?" Dorann asked.

"I can't say," Aranok replied.

Pol snorted a burst of air. Allandria glowered at him. She'd forgotten how much she disliked him. Just sitting near him made her skin itch.

"Can't be much secret business in peacetime, surely?" Dorann said dismissively. "Especially if you've got time to stop in for a drink with your family."

Aranok laughed uncomfortably. He held his own with kings and generals, but his own father… Maybe it was just like that for sons. She wouldn't know, as an only child. She had wonderful relationships with both her parents.

"Speaking of which, your boy's doing a good job running the country," Dorann said. "Looks like you made the right bet. Lucky Hofnag didn't kill you both, of course."

"Wasn't a bet," said Aranok. "Hofnag was a corrupt, greedy prick. I'm glad you can see how much better Janaeus is."

Dorann shrugged. "S'made very little difference to my life, son. People need clothes, whoever's on the throne."

*Ugh.*

It wasn't him they'd fought for. It wasn't Mournside, and its legion of merchant lairds. It was villages like Lochen and Mutton Hole, where people scraped a living. Where volunteers rose from poverty and gave their lives for their children's futures. Like Vastin's parents.

"Mynygogg is imprisoned in Dun Eidyn?" Pol's face showed contempt, disdain, but there was a quaver of fear in his voice. Allandria found that a little gratifying.

Aranok turned to him. "Aye."

Dorann's mouth curled. "Shame."

*Shame?* What the fuck shame was there in it? Aranok looked as confused as she felt.

The old man breathed out a cloud of smoke. "I just mean . . . Hofnag exiled, Mynygogg imprisoned—problems left unfinished come back to bite you."

"Mynygogg's like no other *draoidh*," Allandria said defensively. "No *draoidh*'s ever had more than one skill, and he got the two worst. It's a miracle we stopped him at all. Without Aranok, we wouldn't have."

Pol snorted again. That was enough.

"You have something to say?" Allandria snapped at him.

Pol raised his hands in mock defence. "I didn't say anything."

"Now, now." Dorann raised his hands. "We're all friends here. I'm sure Aranok did very well. I doubt anyone could have done better. Just saying—would have been better if you'd killed him is all."

Aranok put a hand on Allandria's arm. She sat back, opened her fist and picked up her wine. Dorann sucked on his pipe again. "You know what they call you here, son?"

"I know what they used to call me," Aranok said darkly.

"'The good *draoidh*.' You're liked, Aranok. Loved even. You know that?"

"I didn't," he answered. "But it shouldn't be like that."

"Why not?" asked Dorann. "You've earned it."

"The way you say it, as if the other *draoidhs* are bad. You know they're not."

"Most are." Pol crossed his arms. He likely intended it to look commanding. All Allandria saw was fear. "Never seen many do anything except for themselves. Once you can do things others can't, I reckon it changes you. Think you're better. Get ideas above your station." It was a pointed comment. Allandria leaned forward, smiling politely, as if she was at afternoon tea with highborn ladies.

"The only station above his"—Allandria gestured to Aranok—"is king."

"Indeed." Pol looked at Aranok.

"You think I want to be king?" Aranok asked him flatly.

Pol grinned. "Seems you're next in line since Janaeus has no wife or heir. Something happens to him..."

Aranok laughed quietly. "Janaeus gave me this role. I didn't want it."

"Why not?" his father asked. "You're more than good enough." Allandria couldn't tell if Dorann's defence was of Aranok or of *his son*. The man could be cutting and kind in the same breath.

Aranok didn't seem to register the ambiguity. "Selfish, I suppose. And the people would never accept a *draoidh* as king."

Dorann shrugged. "Maybe. Would we be better off—as people, I mean—if there were no *draoidhs*? I mean, it's not like you chose this life, is it?"

Allandria stood abruptly. "I'm sorry." She'd had enough. If she couldn't punch someone, she was going to have to get away from this conversation. "I need some air. There's something rank in here." She registered Dorann's mock surprise, as if he couldn't imagine what had upset her, and it only made her want to punch him harder. She dared not look at Aranok.

She placed her cup on the bar on the way past. "Again." Calador nodded and lifted a bottle as she bristled outside. The evening air was heavy with lavender and nightstock. Only in Mournside was the town square lined with such luxuries. Still, it was pleasant and relaxing. Stars sparkled in the murky black through a few gaps in the clouds, but mostly it was the usual grey Eidyn sky. She leaned against a pillar and breathed deeply. Pol was an arsehole, and she could generally handle that, but Dorann—the way he needled his son was cruel. The old man never seemed to have got over Aranok being a *draoidh*, and though he professed to have accepted it, every word, every action, said otherwise.

It was easier when she could shoot people.

The door opened behind her. She thought it might be Aranok coming to fetch her back in, but when she looked it was a small, skinny man with a hunted look. He stopped a moment when he saw her, almost startled, then raised the hood of his cloak against the wind and scurried off across the square. Plenty of secrets were kept within the walls of the Canny Man. He likely didn't want his wife finding out about his vice, whether gambling or women.

Across the square, an old woman carrying a bundle of flowers whistled happily. A wood-carver closing the shutters at the front of his workshop waved to her. It was bizarre to find life so normal here. Completely shut off from the outside—unaware of the horrors they'd gone through to get here. As if the war had never happened. For a moment, she allowed herself to pretend it hadn't—that it had all been a savage, bloody dream.

A dream of fire and rot. Of rain and little sleep. Of marching men to their deaths against nightmare beasts and legions of Dead. Of the Reivers, taking advantage of the chaos to increase their raids—picking off soldiers on the road. Killing the wounded, robbing the dead. Carrion birds. Vermin. In many ways, she resented them more than Mynygogg himself. The *draoidh* was evil, but he wasn't sneaky. He came straight at them, with his demons and his corpses. The Reivers could have helped. They could have stood by their fellow human beings against the monsters. Instead, their chieftains pressed their advantage while Eidyn was weak and distracted. It was vile and cowardly. It was inhuman—and she would never forget it.

Killing Reivers was, in some ways, even easier than killing monsters. Samily was wrong. They had a choice. They weren't mindless beasts controlled by their chieftains. They were men and women who chose to attack a country that was already on fire.

She couldn't imagine there ever being peace between them now, no matter how much she wished for it. The Reivers were irredeemable, unforgivable.

Allandria breathed deeply. She needed to calm down before she went back in. Frustrated tears formed and she dabbed them away. Wouldn't do to have Pol and Dorann think she'd been out here crying. They'd think it a weakness, and she had no intention of giving them an inch.

There was rain in the air. She could feel it, like needles in her skin. A storm was coming.

A clatter from inside the pub shook her from her thoughts.

A scream.

Allandria burst back through the door. But there was no fight, just a small crowd forming around a table. A drunken argument most likely.

Calador came round the end of the bar. Allandria stepped aside for him and picked up the full cup of wine he'd left for her.

"Move aside, move aside!" he called. Two men stepped back to reveal what they had been attending to. A woman's pallid, grey face stared lifelessly from the floor. It took her a moment to recognise where she was lying. Who she was.

The messenger's eyes rolled back in her head and vomit trailed from her mouth. Now she'd seen it, the smell hit Allandria. She gagged, covering her nose with her hand.

"What the fuck happened?" Aranok had arrived from the back of the room. Several others were tentatively making their way into the main area.

Allandria shrugged. She pointed over her shoulder, indicating the door she'd just come in.

Calador leaned over the woman's body. He sniffed at her, then at the goblet beside her.

"Bloody Hell. Poison."

There were several gasps and the muttering increased.

"What?" Aranok asked.

"By who?" asked a red-faced man in a decorative green overcoat.

Allandria dropped her cup, turned and ran back out the door.

Which way had he gone? The alley beside the butcher? Or was it the other, in the corner? The door of the inn opened behind her, footsteps following. She reached the corner—no sign of him. The butcher. Also nothing. She stopped, tried to slow her breathing, quiet her heartbeat and listen. Listen for the sound of a footstep, or a door—something. But the rain was starting. All she could hear was the *pit pit pit* of drops hitting dirt and stone—meaning there would soon be nothing to track, even if she had the light.

"What?" Aranok arrived behind her. "What is it?"

"God damn it!" She slapped the stone wall. "I saw him. I looked right at him!"

"What? Who?"

"The sleekit bastard who did that!" She pointed back at the inn.

"How do you know?"

Because she had seen it. In his eyes. The guilt. The surprise. The fear of being caught. She just hadn't known why.

"It was him. Trust me."

"Shite," said Aranok. "Come on, let's get back in out of the rain."

Several people had come out of the inn. Possibly to escape the smell, possibly to see why the two of them had run out.

"Well, there's one thing we can take from this," she said.

"What?"

"You were right."

"Yeah," Aranok answered solemnly.

Killing her was treason. Nobody risked that without damned good cause. Somebody didn't want Aranok talking to the king's messenger.

# CHAPTER 14

Ugly little bastard he was." Calador stood with his hands behind his head, his thick arms framing his head like wings. The crowd had quickly dissipated once the stench of murder permeated the bar. Aranok suspected the last thing many of them wanted was to be there while the guard were sniffing about. The Merchant's Arms would do good business tonight.

"Never seen him before, far as I can remember," the innkeeper said.

Bak frowned. "Would you remember what he ordered? Where he sat? Who did he talk to?"

Calador shook his head. "A couple of ales. He was quiet. Sat by himself over there..." He pointed to a table two along from where the messenger had been sitting. Aranok moved to sit there. Not only could he see the victim's table clearly, but he was close enough to the bar to hear conversation—close enough to have heard Aranok ask about her.

He should have been more careful. He would be. Bak looked at him, eyebrows raised.

"Good vantage point," said Aranok. "He could see her and the door. Easy to slip something in her drink on the way past if he knew what he was doing."

"Mmm," Bak agreed.

"Little shite," said Calador. "I'll wring the bastard's neck if I see him."

"You won't," said Aranok. Whoever he was working for had clearly decided to burn any rope that led back to them. But there were still too many questions.

What was the point of lying to the town? Who benefitted? Was the messenger involved, or an unwitting pawn doing her duty?

"What are you thinking?" Allandria asked.

Aranok tilted his head. "I don't know. Honestly, more questions than answers."

"How do you want to deal with this, sir?" Bak asked.

"What do you mean?"

"Would you prefer we handled it quietly or put up 'wanted' posters? We could have an artist sit with Lady Allandria and Calador—attempt to draw him from their descriptions?"

"We're leaving in the morning. Calador, you can describe him?"

"I reckon I can," the big man said. "But tomorrow. Tonight, I've got to clean up this mess, or the whole bar's going to stink to Hell in the morning." He poured himself a nip of whisky, breathing in the scent before sipping it and sighing deeply.

"All right," said Bak. "We've got a wagon coming for the body. Once we move her, it's all yours."

Calador nodded gravely.

Bak sat down opposite Aranok, and Allandria excused herself to the bar. The captain was usually the highest authority in the town. But Aranok had no desire to lead the case for him. The fewer people knew he'd been here, the better. Though how much he could keep that quiet from the Mournside gossip circles was questionable. If there was some conspiracy behind this, some plot to undermine Janaeus, he'd rather they not know he was onto them—which meant staying out of this investigation. And they had to meet the others on the Auld Road tomorrow anyway.

"Please, handle this as you normally would." Aranok answered his earlier question. "It's an unpleasant coincidence that I was here."

"Beg your pardon, Envoy, but I disagree," said the captain.

*Interesting.* "How so?"

"Seems to me you were very interested in what news the messenger had brought us. As if there was something odd about it. And then she gets killed while you're ten yards away? That seems like a bit more than coincidence to me."

Aranok smiled. He was sharp.

"All right. Maybe it wasn't a coincidence."

"Had you spoken to her?" Bak asked quietly.

Aranok shook his head.

"But you intended to?"

He nodded.

"Do I need to know what about?"

Aranok considered. He'd said too much before and probably got the woman killed. Bak seemed reasonable, and as the captain of the guard, he must have proven himself. And he seemed genuinely interested in catching the murderer.

"All right," Aranok finally said. "Some of what she reported was inaccurate."

"How much?" Bak asked.

"Definitely some, possibly all."

Bak sat back. "Why?" When Aranok didn't reply, he answered his own question. "That's what you wanted to speak to her about."

He nodded.

"Well, she was genuine. Had all the right credentials—but more than that, she's been here before," said Bak.

"Right." That ruled out one theory. She wasn't an impostor.

Bak stood. "I'd best go and have a look round her room, then."

Aranok nodded. "We're going to leave you to your work, Captain. But one thing…" He grabbed Bak's arm. "If you catch him, keep him here and send for me, please? I'll be away for about a month, but I'll come as soon as I can."

"Of course, sir. I'll send word to Greytoun if we find him."

"Wait, no." Aranok almost surprised himself. "There's a blacksmith's on Grey Square. Closed up. Leave a note for me there. I'll get it."

He couldn't shake the feeling there might be someone in the castle working against them, undermining Janaeus. Someone had told him Mournside was compromised. Aranok's first thoughts might have been for the new council Janaeus had just formed, but he knew exactly where all of them were, and they weren't in a position to be plotting a coup right now. The head messenger, however… her Aranok was going to visit.

Bak gave him a curious scowl but didn't press the matter. "As you say, sir. Calador! Could you please show me to the messenger's room?"

Calador nodded at the stairs, gesturing for Bak to go first. Aranok moved to Allandria. It was still raining. They were going to get wet.

"Well?" she asked.

"He seems competent. And we need to leave in the morning. We shouldn't even be here."

"Janaeus will have you flogged when we get back."

Aranok smiled. "He'd like to, sometimes. Can I escort you home, m'lady?" He made a grand gesture of offering his arm.

"You can." She hooked her arm in his. They stepped outside and pulled up their hoods. They weren't going far—they'd walked a lot farther through a lot worse.

"What was her name?" Allandria asked as they stepped out from the cover of the doorway.

"What?" Aranok asked.

"Her name?"

"God, I don't know. I didn't ask."

"Why not?" she asked, surprised.

"It honestly didn't occur to me."

She was quiet for a moment. "It should have. She was a person. Whatever else is happening, she was a person. She might have been innocent. And now she's dead. Remember what you said to me when Janaeus asked you to be envoy? 'People who are responsible for everyone eventually feel responsibility for no one.'"

She was right. And this had been exactly what he meant. It was hard to feel all the little tragedies that made up the big ones. He'd seen so many people die without knowing their names.

"I should have asked."

The rain got heavier.

———※———

They stopped in front of the dark wooden door. Aranok made no move either to knock or to open it. It was one of the grandest houses in town. The small walled garden at the front dripped with life. Allandria hadn't been here in years—since before the war. Neither had Aranok, as far as she knew. "Well?"

Aranok turned his head slightly. "Give me a moment. I thought she was…"

"I know." Allandria put a hand on his arm. She realised how much this had been weighing on him—on both of them—and chastised herself a little for being so hard on him earlier. "But she's not. So let's see her."

The door flew open and a flurry of magenta dress wrapped itself around Aranok.

"My boy!" the woman squealed.

After a moment's pause, he wrapped his arms about her tightly and pulled her head to his shoulder. "Mother."

Allandria smiled. "Hello, Sumara."

Sumara looked up at her, tears in her eyes. "Allandria. You brought him back to me." She reached out and cupped Allandria's cheek. "You good girl, you brought him back to me."

Allandria nodded and felt her own eyes dampening. Sumara released her son and pulled Allandria into a similar hug. She had incredible strength for a woman of her age and size. She nearly pulled Allandria off her feet.

"I knew you would," she said. "I knew you would."

When she finally released her grip, it was only to whip them in out of the rain.

"Come in, come in! Are you hungry? Have you eaten? How long can you stay? We've got sausage casserole. Take off your boots, relax!"

Aranok laughed, as happily as she'd heard him in a long time. "We'd love some sausages, Mum." He sat down on a chair by the hearth and removed his boots. Allandria sat on the bench at the table and did the same. She wiggled her toes and sighed.

No sign of Dorann. He and Pol had made themselves scarce rather quickly at the Canny Man. They'd likely done the same as most of the crowd—crossed the square to the Merchant's Arms to gossip about the murder, carefully ensuring they weren't associated with it. She imagined Dorann humbly boasting about how important his son would be to the investigation.

Sumara crossed to the kitchen door. She was over sixty but still moved like a dancer. Her years working for Aranok's father as a seamstress before they married had made her tough, but the lines on her face only accentuated her contagious smile. "Cressida? Would you serve up two bowls of casserole, please?"

Cressida had cooked for Aranok's family for as long as Allandria had known him. The idea of paying someone else simply to cook meals for them had seemed bizarre to Allandria at first, when so many she knew from home were lucky just to be able to afford food. If she was honest, it had seemed almost obscene, and she'd felt guilty about eating the food Cressida cooked the first time she'd visited. But over time, and with the experience of living in an actual castle, she'd become used to it—especially once Janaeus had started his work to improve the lives of the poor in Eidyn. Their work. It was as much Aranok's dream as the king's.

"Let me look at you." Sumara grabbed Aranok's face with both hands. "You look tired. Are you sleeping?" She turned to Allandria with a mischievous grin. "Are you keeping him awake all night?"

Allandria felt her face reddening and her eyes widen. Which, it seemed, was exactly the reaction Sumara wanted, and she laughed heartily.

"I'm sorry, I'm just teasing. Seriously, how are you both? Ah! My boy!" She put a hand on Aranok's thigh, seeming reluctant to be out of contact with him.

"Tired is fair, I suppose," said Aranok.

"Yes," said Allandria. "Plenty tired."

Sumara "hmmed" to herself. "And how is Janaeus, now things are getting back to normal? I always liked him, he's a good boy."

Aranok looked at Allandria and back at his mother. "Well, it's interesting you should ask, actually." He rubbed his thumb and middle finger together absentmindedly, as he often did when worrying over something. "Things aren't as well as you might have heard."

Sumara sat up. "Really? How so?"

Aranok appeared to think for a moment, before continuing. "Things are bad. Haven is overcrowded. We've had to squeeze the population of Auldun—what's left of it—in with the locals. Mutton Hole's been under attack by a demon, which has meant a shortfall in crop deliveries. You must have noticed..."

Sumara frowned and shook her head. Mournside would always be well stocked with reserves, as the home of so many of the country's wealthiest merchants, but even they should have felt a little pain.

"You'll know about the reports of the Blackened crossing the Hills, though?" Aranok asked.

"Yes," she answered darkly. "We've been told to shut the whole town against them. Hardly anyone in or out. Not that we go anywhere much these days anyway. But your father's garments are stuck in our warehouse for now. Luckily, we have more than enough to make do, and plenty of customers in town willing to pay well for good clothes—especially when they can't go anywhere else for them."

Allandria realised her feet were really throbbing—probably grateful to get a full complement of blood after several days of riding. She brought her left leg across her right and rubbed at her sole.

"Right," said Aranok. "Well, reports also tell us Leet is overrun with pirates. Gardille is in disarray, and we're woefully short of soldiers. It's a lot worse than you've heard."

Sumara raised a finger to her mouth. "But we had a messenger just today."

Aranok raised an eyebrow. "Yes. We know... She was murdered. Poisoned."

Sumara all but threw up her hands in shock. "What? When? Where?"

"At the Canny Man. We... stopped in there on the way here. Saw Dad. And Pol."

"And a woman was murdered? My God, Ari." Sumara moved even closer to him. "That must have been awful."

"Yes. It was horrible." But there was no horror in Aranok's tone. He'd seen worse. Much worse.

"You think it was related?" Sumara asked.

Aranok sighed and stretched. "Maybe. Maybe not."

Of course, it was possible Janaeus had received new information after they left. It was possible the country was in better shape than they believed. And it was possible that the messenger's murder was an unfortunate coincidence. But that was a lot of "possibles" and "coincidences" for her liking.

Cressida placed steaming bowls in front of each of them, breaking the dour mood. Allandria breathed in the hearty aroma. It smelled of childhood and safety. "Thank you."

Cressida smiled and nodded. "Good to see you, Lady Allandria, Laird Aranok."

Aranok stood and drew the woman into a bear hug, much to her apparent surprise, judging by the little squeak she let out.

"It's lovely to see you, Cressida." He smiled broadly. "I've missed your cooking."

"Don't be daft!" Cressida turned back toward the kitchen. She was older than Sumara, and the stiffness of her movements made the age gap seem even wider. "You've got the best cooks in the kingdom to feed you."

"Not one of them can do a roast suckling pig like you!" Aranok called after her. Cressida's appreciative laugh echoed from the next room, as Aranok retook his seat and lifted a spoon.

"You were saying...?" Sumara asked. "About the messenger?"

"There are a few options." Aranok looked pointedly at Allandria as she spooned casserole into her mouth. "The messenger is lying; the head messenger is lying to her people; someone is lying to Janaeus; or Janaeus is lying."

Allandria choked on her food. "Janaeus? You think Janaeus is lying? *To you?*"

"Of course not. He might be lying to them." He nodded to his mother. "If he knows the town is in danger from the Blackened, he might tell them everything's all right outside to discourage anyone from venturing out. One less thing for him to worry about."

"Oh," Allandria said. That sort of made sense. But why not tell Aranok about it? Why tell him Mournside had fallen? Unless he really had only heard after they left. It all sounded a bit convenient and she doubted that was the truth of it.

"We know he's not lying to us," said Aranok. "Even if I didn't trust him completely, he told us there was a demon at Mutton Hole, and there it was."

"You saw a demon?" Sumara asked, horrified.

"We killed a demon," Allandria said, as if they did it every day.

Aranok shrugged. "We fought a demon. A White Thorn killed it."

"My God, Aranok, I know you're special," said Sumara, "but you're not a god! You can't go fighting demons—you'll get yourselves killed!"

"It's not…" Allandria started, but a dark look from Aranok made her stop. There was no good in telling his mother this wasn't the first demon they'd fought. "It's not as bad as it sounds."

Sumara looked at her with deep, soulful eyes. It felt as though she looked straight through her. After a moment that felt like an eternity, she patted Aranok's leg and stood up. As she turned away, she might have dabbed at her eyes. "You should go and see your sister while you're here."

Aranok picked up his spoon. "I'd love to, but we have to leave at first light."

Sumara turned to face him, her face almost stern. "Go tonight, then." She paused a moment, considering something. "Where did your father and Pol go? After the…" She waved her hand, indicating an unpleasantness she clearly didn't want to give voice again.

Aranok shrugged. "I assume the Merchant's."

"Good. Fine. Go see her while Pol's still at the pub."

Aranok's face changed. "Why? What's wrong? Is he…?"

"No, no," Sumara interrupted. "Nothing like that. Pol's a dolt, but he's harmless. But you should see her. She'll appreciate it."

Aranok looked at Allandria. She nodded. Why not? It would be good to see Ikara too.

"All right," he said. "We'll go after we've eaten."

"And then you'll come back. You're staying here tonight, yes?"

Aranok smiled at her. "I suppose we are."

# CHAPTER 15

Ikara's house was smaller than their parents'. Pol had only been working for their father when she married him. They'd bought this cottage soon after, with help from the family. When Pol took over running the business, they stayed out of habit more than desire, Aranok thought. They could certainly have afforded a larger house now. But this was home.

This time he knocked without hesitation. The door swung open quickly and a young girl stood in the arch. For a moment it was as if he was looking through a window into the past, at his six-year-old little sister beaming up at him.

"Who are you?" the girl asked suspiciously.

Aranok crouched down to nearer her height.

"Hello, Emelina. Don't recognise your uncle Aranok?"

The girl's eyes opened wide. She turned and ran inside.

"Mummy!" they heard her cry. "It's Uncle Aranok and a warrior!"

Allandria giggled. "I suppose it's a few years since you were here."

Footsteps banged down the stairs.

"Ari!" Ikara threw her arms around him.

"Hey, kid." He hugged her back.

She held him there for a long time, her face buried in his chest.

"We thought..." she started. "We didn't know..."

"I know, I know." He held her tight. It was so good to see her, he could barely believe he'd considered not coming.

When she finally released him, they moved inside. Emelina stood half-hidden behind a chair, watching them intently.

"Have you eaten?" Ikara asked.

Aranok smiled. Like mother, like daughter. "We've been to Mum's."

Ikara laughed. "Of course you have. Can I offer you some wine, then?"

Wine might be good for his nerves. He was still struggling to accept that his family were fine. He felt light-headed. With relief. With joy. With exhaustion.

"Yes, please."

Ikara held out a goblet questioningly to Allandria, who nodded. She poured three.

"So how is everything?" Aranok asked as Ikara joined them by the fire.

"Well enough, I suppose." But her smile was tired.

Allandria ran a hand down his back, just reminding him she was there. His skin tingled, even through his leathers. It felt good. Sitting by the fire with his family. Like it was before the war. Before the rebellion. Before everything.

But they were older now. Slower. Greyer.

"Really?" He looked his sister in the eye this time.

Ikara looked away—to Emelina playing on the floor. She held a little wooden doll, walking it around and chattering to herself as if there was nobody in the room but her and her tiny friend.

"Mum sent you?" Ikara asked quietly.

"Yes."

*Wait.*

He looked closer at Emelina. She was pale. Paler than she should be.

*Oh God, no, please...*

Ikara looked back at him.

"I'm sorry." She glanced at Allandria and back to her brother. "I don't know how to ask this, but..." She looked pleadingly back at Allandria.

"Oh!" Allandria stood abruptly. "Hey, Emelina, can you show me your room?"

The girl jumped to her feet and ran toward the stairs. Ikara raised a hand. "No, wait," she said with unexpected urgency. Her daughter froze, seemingly unsure how to react to her mother's tone.

"Oh," Allandria said. "I'm sorry, I didn't..."

"It's all right; it's not your fault." Ikara held out her hands to Emelina, who ran to her.

"Should I...?" Allandria gestured to the door.

Aranok put up a hand. "Hey, kid," he said gently, trying to keep his voice even. "Whatever you need, it's yours. From both of us. I promise."

Ikara raised her head to look questioningly at Allandria. She smiled and nodded. "Anything."

Ikara took a deep, trembling breath. "Bolt the door."

Once Allandria sat back down, Ikara released Emelina and held her firmly by the shoulders.

"You know what I said, about never showing anyone except Grandma and me?"

The girl's eyes widened. She nodded silently.

"Well, it's all right to show Uncle Aranok and Allandria too."

Emelina looked round at them shyly. She rubbed her hands together as if washing them in the air.

What was wrong with her? If she was sick, they could ride back to the inn tonight. Bring back the Thorn in the morning. He wasn't sure how her power worked, if she could heal sickness the way she could a broken rib, but...

Emelina turned toward them and held out her hand. Aranok scanned it for a sign, discolouration, scarring—anything to indicate what was wrong. His face must have given away his concern; she withdrew her hand nervously.

"It's all right, sweetheart," Allandria said. "What do you want to show us?"

Thank God for her composure.

Emelina moved her arm forward again. There was no sign of anything Aranok could see. Just the small, grubby hand of a child.

Aranok sucked in a breath as a tiny, barely visible light appeared above her palm. It grew a little brighter, twisted and stretched, until two flat edges spread from the sides. They grew and flattened more, splitting almost into four, then rippling until they began to gently flap. The centre had condensed, become tighter and brighter. Aranok was looking at a butterfly made of pure light.

"Wonderful!" Allandria clapped.

The girl's mouth turned into a nervous smile and the butterfly glowed a little brighter. Still, she looked tentatively up at her uncle. He didn't know why until he realised he was crying.

Overcome, he scooped her up in his arms. "You beautiful, brilliant girl!"

She squealed and giggled with delight as the butterfly dissipated.

Ikara sobbed, more with relief, it seemed, than anything else. Allandria put an arm around her. "It's all right. It's all right."

Aranok rained kisses on his niece's cheek and she squealed even louder.

---

"Does Pol know?" Aranok asked.

Allandria had taken Emelina upstairs to see her room after all.

Ikara shook her head.

"Father? Anyone else?"

"No. Just Mum."

"How long?"

"About a year." She looked into the fire as she spoke. "Thank God, Pol was working. She came running down the stairs, laughing. I turned around to see what was making her so happy, and she was surrounded by dancing lights. I don't even know what I said, but she startled and... Ari, I just wanted to keep her safe. You know I love her—and you! But, people..."

People did not like *draoidhs*. Even children. Even six-year-olds. They were suspicious and scared and ignorant. And hateful. When Janaeus had first offered to make him envoy, he'd refused—told him nobody would accept a *draoidh* as the king's closest advisor. But the new king had insisted that was exactly why it had to be him. He'd been crucial to the rebellion that overthrew Hofnag, and Janaeus wanted people to know that. His support for *draoidhs* was one of the reasons Aranok had been drawn to him. That, and his vision for the country. And the man knew how to speak. God, he'd never met a man who could capture a room the way Janaeus did. He was inspiring, but more than that, he was earnest. You could tell he meant every word he said. He cared, passionately, for everyone. But that passion had not reached all of Eidyn's people yet.

"I understand." He put a hand on his sister's knee. "It must have been hard. I'm glad you had Mum."

She nodded. "I knew, if you came back…" She stopped, apparently realising the weight of that *if.* "I mean…"

"I know. Ikara—does she know?" He lowered his voice. "About her father?"

His sister's face paled. "No. She was too young, and once this happened—how could I tell her, Ari? After what happened to him?"

Aranok sighed. She was right. Why terrify the child? And why tell her the idiot who'd raised her wasn't her father, just the man her grandfather had chosen for his pregnant, unmarried daughter? In return, his business stayed in the family after his own son had been such a disappointment.

"All right. She needs a teacher. It can't be me, as much as I'd love that. I can't be here all the time and she needs someone who can."

Ikara nodded in silent agreement, idly stroking the bench. He would make sure his niece had someone. The person he should have had.

"I'll find someone. In Traverlyn. I'll hire a tutor for her. You can tell Pol and Father it was my idea—tell them I felt guilty about not being around." That was truer than he'd realised until he said it out loud. "They can come during the day, when it's just the two of you."

"All right." She smiled. "Ari, thank you. Thank you so much. For everything."

"It's going to be all right."

It might not. He knew everything that could go wrong; everything that would be heartbreakingly, crushingly hard. But if Emelina was going to have a chance, she needed people who believed in her. She needed an army until she could stand for herself.

And she'd have one.

---

"Wheeeeeeee!" Emelina screamed as Allandria spun her around. "Uncle Aranok! I'm flying!"

Aranok laughed. "Look at you, little bird!"

Allandria put her down and slumped dramatically onto the bed. "I'm afraid I'm too tired for any more flying tonight. Why don't you ask Uncle Aranok if he'll help you?"

Emelina looked up at him, her eyes sparkling.

"All right, all right. But can we have a little chat first?" The girl nodded enthusiastically.

Allandria stood and drank her wine. "I'll just go downstairs and refill this."

As she was closing the door, Emelina shouted, "Thank you, Auntie Allandria!"

She paused without looking around. Their relationship was known to his family, but it had never been "official"—for many reasons. That fact felt very heavy in the moment. Aranok held his breath, not knowing how to react without making it more awkward. Allandria turned her head, smiled and said, "You're welcome, sweetheart," then closed the door behind her.

They could deal with that later. Or, preferably, not at all.

Aranok sat on the bed where Allandria had been. "Your powers are really pretty, aren't they?"

Emelina smiled and nodded.

"Do you know what they mean?"

She shrugged.

"They mean you're a *draoidh*. Do you know what that is?"

"A magic person?" she asked quietly.

"That's right! And do you know any other magic people?"

She shrugged again. "You?"

Aranok beamed at her. "That's right, me. So we're not just family, we're also members of a very special group. We can do things most people can't. And that's wonderful and amazing, but it can also be scary for people who don't understand. Sometimes people are afraid of things that are different. If they can't do something, or they don't understand it, they're scared of how it will affect them. Do you understand?"

His heart pounded in his chest as childhood emotions boiled up.

"I don't know," she said. "I won't hurt anybody. I just have pretty lights."

Aranok's shoulders slumped. The innocence of youth.

He pulled her toward him. "I know you wouldn't, sweetheart. I know you wouldn't. But other people who don't know what a brilliant girl you are, they might not know that. So that's why it's important that only people who know you really, really well know about your lights until you're older, all right?"

She curled her mouth in thought, then nodded. "What about Daddy?"

Her real father would be overjoyed. It wasn't often *draoidhs* passed their abilities to their children, but there were stories. Aranok had never met anyone like it before but, well, now he had.

"Your daddy knows how kind and special you are, darling, but he's also a bit scared of how your magic works. He doesn't understand it like Mummy and I do. And Grandma."

"And Auntie Allandria." She smiled.

Looked like that was sticking.

"Yes, and Allandria. But listen"—he lifted her onto his knee—"I need you to know something, all right? It's something I wish I had known when I was your age. You are amazing. What you can do and who you are is wonderful. There is nothing wrong with you—don't ever let anyone make you think so. The world just isn't quite ready for you yet. You might hear people saying bad things about *draoidhs*. Those people are scared, or jealous, because they can't do what we can do. If you ever start to think bad things about *draoidhs*, just you remember, your uncle tells the king what to do!"

Her eyes widened and she gasped. "Really?"

"Really. But don't tell anybody else, all right? That's our secret too." He winked at her. She concentrated hard and winked back. He pulled her into a hug and, typically for a six-year-old, she let him but did little to reciprocate. It was enough.

"Uncle Aranok?" she asked. "Can I fly now?"

Aranok put her back on her feet, grinning widely.

"*Gluais.*"

———◦———

"So things are still bad?" Ikara leaned forward, her goblet clasped between her hands. The warmth of the fire matched the heat of the wine as it reached Allandria's stomach.

"Very bad. It's good that you're safe, though."

"But shouldn't we be doing something?"

"Like what?"

"I don't know. Offering supplies...help...just...something. It doesn't feel right that we're sitting here behind walls when others are in need." She rubbed her fingers together, just like her brother did when he was agitated. Allandria hadn't noticed that before.

"Ikara, you're no fighter. The Blackened really are a threat. So are the Reivers. And other things. Running supply wagons around the country—you'd be a target. You'd need a small army to protect you—and they'd have to be taken away from defending Mournside."

"Well, money, then!" she said, exasperated. "Surely if the kingdom needs money, we have it. We should donate it to the treasury."

"That would be very useful, I'm sure. But it's a drop in the well. You could send every penny you have, and it still wouldn't make a real dent."

Ikara stood and paced. "It just seems wrong. There must be something useful we can do."

"Well, unless you can convince everyone in Mournside to donate to the treasury, above and beyond their normal taxes, I think you're buggered."

Ikara's eyes widened. Allandria had forgotten she wasn't camped on the road with a bunch of soldiers. "Sorry."

"Ha!" Ikara laughed. "It's fine, honestly. Just not what you usually hear. But thank you for your honesty. People need to know what's really happening." She emptied her goblet and reached for the bottle. "More?"

Allandria looked toward the stairs. The sound of happy giggling made her smile. It was good they had come. This was important. Family was important. But she could feel the weight of the day pulling at her eyelids. And they had a hard ride in the morning. For all Aranok had asked Vastin to make sure they waited, there wasn't a lot the boy could do if Glorbad convinced the rest to carry on because they were late.

"Better not. We're up early and it's been a long day. But we'll get back again soon." She looked up the stairs. "I'll make sure of it."

# CHAPTER 16

Mournside's dark streets were an unexpected salve. That morning, Aranok had woken knowing he was likely to find his family dead by evening. He'd been preparing himself for it for days—not consciously, but looking back he could see he'd been shutting himself off from his emotions.

But now, seeing them all safe, it was like a fire had burned back into life. The world felt real. He smelled the torches burning on the roadsides, felt their warmth and heard the crunch of their feet as they walked. The world was no longer some flat thing he observed, but a tangible, rich existence he was immersed in. They walked in a work of art painted from his memories. It felt good.

Allandria looked as soothed as he felt. There was something glowing about her. And that was something, since he always found light in her, even when the rest of the world was darkness. Was it just because he could see it now? She turned to him and her broad smile answered. "Can I ask you something?"

"Of course."

"What kind of magic was that?"

"Illusion. Visual magic."

"So it's different from yours? I mean, you can make light too."

"Mine is earth magic. It's real light. Just like it's real fire and real water. Hers is only real in the minds of those who see it. But I can't make butterflies." To be fair, he'd never tried. But he wouldn't know where to start.

"What else will she be able to do?"

*So much.*

"With training, she'll be able to create complex illusions. I've seen an illusionist hide a building. I've seen him change his appearance for an entire evening. That's called a *masg*. Once it's in place, it stays until he removes it—or loses consciousness, if he exhausts his energy reserves."

"He?" she asked. "As in Korvin?"

The name was like a dagger. It still hurt. For some reason, he could talk about him in the abstract without really feeling it, but his name... his name made him real.

He tried not to remember his friend's broken, bloody body in the wreckage of the stage. But it was an image that would never leave him. He tried not to remember what he'd done. He tried to pretend he regretted it.

"Yes." His voice caught. "He was incredible. His shows were breathtaking."

"I really wish I could have seen one."

"Well"—he looked back over his shoulder—"maybe you will, one day."

She smiled a moment, before her face turned serious. "Listen, there's something else I wanted to ask..."

"It's all right," he interrupted. "I know it was awkward when she called you aunt. You don't have to feel...well, obliged or anything. I mean, our thing—it is what it is. It doesn't change anything."

"Oh," she said awkwardly. "Erm, that's...that's not what I was going to say, but..."

"Oh, sorry," he said quickly. "I thought..."

"No, that...that was all right. I mean, she's just a girl. It was cute. I liked it. But, yeah, it doesn't mean anything; it's fine."

Excellent. He'd definitely made that better.

"Oh, good, all right. So what did you...?"

"Oh, right, yes, I just wanted to ask, well...it seems like you really trust the monk, and I was just wondering why."

"Meristan?" He hadn't really thought about it. The man was sharp and insightful. "You don't think I should?"

"No, it's just that you don't trust anybody. Glorbad, Nirea...but him, it seemed like you accepted him very easily. Do you know him?"

"No. I don't know." He didn't, in honesty. "He just felt safe, I suppose. He shared something with me, and that...maybe that was why. I mean, isn't it pretty much his job to be trustworthy? He's a monk."

Allandria laughed gently. "I know that, but you don't believe in God, so why should you believe in him?"

"I don't need to believe in God. He believes in God."

"What does that mean?"

"It means I believe he'll act morally, because he believes God wants that from him. Whether I believe it is irrelevant."

"Hmm." She stopped. "So what if he's a fraud? What if he's just passing himself off as a believer?"

Aranok frowned. "I don't think you get to be the head of the Order if you're a fraud. Someone would have noticed."

Allandria snorted. "You'd be surprised."

"Well, all right. But you've seen how Samily is. Do you think she was raised by a nonbeliever? Do you think she'd tolerate him running the Order if she didn't absolutely believe in him?"

Allandria looked quietly up the road for a moment. His parents' house was just ahead. "I suppose not."

"You don't trust him?" It seemed odd that she wouldn't. After all, she did believe, and she was always telling him to be less paranoid.

"Oh, no. I feel the same way. I think he seems like a good man. I just couldn't understand why you did."

"Oh, well, there you go." He smiled. "I definitely trust you."

———◦———

"It doesn't make any bloody sense, boy!" Dorann sat by the fire, smoking his pipe. He'd waited up for them coming back from Ikara's and was several sheets to the wind now. Allandria had gone straight upstairs to get out of her leathers but found Aranok still in his boots when she returned, sitting opposite his father. "Why would anyone lie to us about the state of the kingdom? It would be pointless. We'd find out the truth as soon as someone left the town walls!"

"But you're not leaving the town walls, are you?" Aranok answered from the opposite chair.

"Ach! You know what I mean." The old man waved his hand dismissively. Too often, she'd seen him dismiss his son. "What purpose does it serve?"

"I don't know yet."

"Listen, what makes more sense," said Dorann, "that there's some mad conspiracy to convince the people of Mournside that all's well in the kingdom, and that a king's messenger was murdered specifically to prevent you from finding out about it, or that Janaeus has better information than you, and her being killed was a coincidence? Most likely a jealous husband or a jilted lover!"

Aranok leaned forward, elbows on knees and hands clasped in front of his mouth.

"She spent the evening eating alone, at a table that looked directly at her killer. Would she have sat there calmly while her 'jilted lover' stared back at her?"

"Are they always like this?" Allandria whispered to Sumara, who had changed into a nightgown and was sipping a cup of warm milk.

"Yes." There was a resigned tone in her voice. Allandria could well understand it, after a lifetime of seeing her husband and son butt heads. Sumara was so peaceful, so kind. She obviously disliked conflict.

Dorann stood abruptly.

"Ach, it's all nonsense, boy. Pol was right, you've got your head in the clouds! Nobody's hiding anything from you—what would be the point?"

Allandria took a step forward, but Sumara's hand on her arm stopped her. She looked back, silently pleading with Aranok's mother to do something, say something to make this stop. She only shook her head.

"Why?" Allandria whispered.

Aranok sat back in the chair. "Maybe you're right. Maybe it's nothing."

The fire went out of Dorann. "Of course it's nothing." There was a long, quiet pause as the two looked at each other. "Right, I'm going up to bed. We'll see you in the morning?"

"Maybe," said Aranok.

Dorann grunted, turned and walked up the stairs. Sumara crossed to her son and gently placed a hand on his cheek. He put his hand over hers, without looking up, and she kissed him on the head.

"Good night, Mum."

She followed her husband.

Allandria took the seat Dorann had vacated. "You really think it might be nothing?"

"No," he answered. "I'm certain it's not. And he's just told me why." He nodded at the ceiling. "Somebody wants the people of Mournside to stay in the city walls, to believe there's no reason to leave."

"Why?"

"Think about it. There were reports of the Blackened here—meaning nobody would come here and nobody would try to leave. Except we didn't see a single Blackened on the road. We also didn't encounter any Reivers—maybe they've also heard about the Blackened. We get inside to find out they've been told there's a threat outside the walls, so they need to stay safe, but everyone else is fine. They're being cut off from the rest of the country."

"My God." It was staggering, but it made sense. "If we had obeyed Janaeus's orders and not come here…"

"Nobody would have known there was anything wrong."

"But why?" Allandria asked.

"Taxes? The kingdom needs money. Janaeus can't collect taxes from a dead town. But somebody will have to keep collecting them or the town's going to start wondering why not."

"So whoever's collecting the taxes…"

"Is probably working for the person behind this."

"What do they want?"

"Good question." Aranok sat back and locked his hands behind his head. "Money? Destabilise the kingdom? The Reivers would want that. Overthrow Janaeus? Maybe some old allies of Hofnag trying to take advantage of the war? Or there's the worst possibility."

"Mynygogg?" Allandria could barely believe she was saying it.

"He could have allies we didn't know about. If he does…"

*Then maybe the war's not over after all.* That was a dark, depressing thought. "What do we do? Should we tell someone?"

Aranok frowned. "I've been thinking about that. The problem is we don't know who we can trust. Bak seems decent, but...the captain of the city guard would be in a good position to control the flow of information—and people—in and out of Mournside."

"You think it might be him?" She knew Aranok had told him a lot about his suspicions. If he was involved...

"My instinct is no. Everything about him said he wanted to get to the bottom of that murder. Unless he's an exceptional actor, I think we can trust him. But I can't be certain. So for now, we sleep. Tomorrow, we meet up with the others to collect Taneitheia from Barrock. Then we take her back to Haven and put her on a boat."

Allandria looked at him, waiting for the coin to drop.

"And while we're there, maybe we visit a few people."

# CHAPTER 17

N irea's head pounded. It was as if she'd been cracked across the
head with a rock in her sleep. In truth, it was a wine bottle. It
had also been a long while since she'd spent so much time on a horse.

The Auld Road began with the Royal Mile running through Auldun, but the cobbles and grandeur ended at the city gates. Out here in
the country it was little more than a wide clearing through the trees,
rutted by wagon wheels and trampled by hooves. In some places, the
foliage cleared and you could see for miles across rolling farmlands and
heath, but here, as they approached the shadow of the Black Hills, the
trees were so thick that in places the canopy formed a tunnel of green
and amber.

It had been a strange, quiet day. Glorbad still seemed grumpy about
his argument with the envoy, and the fact that Aranok and Allandria
were not there hung over the group like a fat black cloud. Even the boy,
who had been hanging off Samily like a puppy since she arrived, was
sullen. While Samily rode at the head of the group alongside Nirea,
he'd fallen back beside Glorbad at the rear, leaving Meristan to guide
the pack horse. She'd heard very little from any of them all day, and the
silence was becoming painful.

Maybe conversation would take her mind off the pain. "Vastin tells
me you're an orphan too."

"I am a child of God," the knight replied.

"Hmph. I suppose that's a nicer way to look at it. Aren't we all supposed to be children of God?"

Samily looked at her curiously. "You don't believe?"

"I've never seen anything in my life to make me believe in a god, I'm afraid."

*Quite the opposite.*

"I'm sorry for you," the Thorn said. "But I believe everyone's life has God in it."

Of course she did. "Well, you grew up surrounded by it."

"And you did not?"

No, she did not. "I don't even remember my parents. I assume they were murdered by the bastards that took me, but not one of them ever had the decency to tell me either way. First thing I remember is cleaning. Scrubbing the deck. Washing the blood out of dead men's shirts. Sometimes, they'd get drunk and use me for target practice, promising worse with rotten, rum-soaked breath. If there's a god who planned my childhood, I prefer not to believe in them."

*Damn it.* The headache got worse; her vision took a spin. Why did she have to go digging in that dirt?

Samily had turned a sickly shade of grey and her eyes were wide. It had probably seemed an innocuous conversation until Nirea blurted out her childhood trauma. What had she done that for? "I'm sorry. I had no idea. How did you survive?"

"By being harder than those drunken old cunts." Nirea could feel her heart beating faster, nausea rising in her guts. She took a deep breath. "I learned how to use a knife. Then a sword. And one day, when I had the captain alone, I slit his bastard throat. Some of the crew were unhappy when I gave them his head, but once I sent them after him, the rest fell in line. The only way to become a pirate captain is to kill the previous one."

"You were a pirate?" The shock was apparent in Samily's voice.

"I was a pirate captain." She was feeling bolder now. Stronger. "But when you're a woman, there's always some dull ox thinks he can take you."

"So you left?" Before Nirea could answer, the Thorn put up a hand, looking ahead down the Auld Road. They were approaching the foothills where they were to meet Aranok and Allandria. Was it them?

They stopped and Glorbad rode up alongside Nirea. "What's wrong? Why are we stopping?"

"I heard something," said Samily.

Then so did Nirea, and despite the fading light, she saw something too. A man, maybe two, running toward them. She vaulted from her horse and drew her swords. Glorbad joined her on the ground.

Samily turned her horse sideways, blocking off the rest of the path. "Stay behind me."

As the men drew closer, she could see they wore Reiver colours. All right then. It had been a quiet day. Maybe this was just what she needed to get her blood pumping. She heard Glorbad draw his sword and prepared to run.

"Wait." Samily raised her hand again.

"Why?" It wouldn't do to have the Reivers crash upon them—they would have the momentum.

"Something's wrong," the knight said.

"What the fuck are you talking about?" asked Glorbad.

Nirea looked again. The men had no obvious weapons—and they weren't charging, they were running. As they drew close enough to see Nirea and the others, they faltered for a few steps, looked back and kept running. One of them shouted something, but Nirea couldn't make out what. "What did he say?"

Samily muttered something in reply, and when the Reiver shouted again, she heard it clear as glass.

"Blackened!"

"Dear God," said Samily, "horses!" Nirea sheathed her swords and leapt back on her mount. Glorbad took longer—his armour slowing him.

"Come on!" she screamed at him. A distant rumble. The Reivers drew level and barely slowed to skirt around them. Vastin raised his axe as the smaller one passed close by, but the Reiver didn't even look up at the boy.

"Run, you idiots!" the larger one panted.

Then she saw them. A shambling mess of broken humanity. The withered, sickly remains of victims of the worst plague ever known to man. The Blackened. Hundreds, maybe thousands of them.

She pulled alongside Glorbad's horse and helped yank him up into his seat.

"Come on!" Samily screamed, kicking her horse into action. She took the pack horse's lead from Meristan, and he prodded his animal into life. Nirea could feel her horse's nerves. The Blackening didn't affect animals, but it bloody unsettled them.

She dug in her heels and the animal gladly took flight.

They rode hard. But the pack horse was slowing them down. It whinnied in fear, steam pouring from its skin. Samily rode with it at the back. But they had to keep going. The Blackened didn't tire. They might not be able to outrun the horses, but they could keep running forever—unlike them.

"What in Hell's arse are they doing this far north?" Glorbad yelled.

Nirea shrugged. How should she know? They were supposed to be at Mournside, across the Black Hills—not here.

"What do we do?" shouted Vastin from the front.

Nirea drew her horse up. "Stop!"

"What?" Glorbad's horse almost barrelled into hers. "Are you touched, woman?"

But they stopped.

"We can't just run like this. Now they're chasing us, they'll keep going until they find others to infect—and this road leads straight to the White Hart." They'd passed the inn not long ago, at the junction to Auldun. It would never withstand an onslaught like this. Everyone there would be infected by morning. "We need to draw them off the road!"

"And then what?" asked Glorbad.

She ignored him. She didn't have an answer. "Meristan, Vastin, take the pack horse and ride for the inn. Tell them to bar every door and window and stay inside! Samily, Glorbad, we're taking them south!"

"Why south?" the soldier asked.

"Because Mournside has walls!" And if it wasn't already overrun, it was probably the only place outside Haven that could survive. Plus, they might run into the envoy—and they could do with some magic right now.

"No." Samily sat proud in her saddle. "I stay with Meristan."

"No!" It was the loudest she'd ever heard the monk. "You go with them, Samily. That is an order."

"Yes, Brother." The knight's tone was solemn, but with a hint of defiance Nirea hadn't heard before.

"It's all right." Vastin tried to smile bravely. "I'll protect him. I promise."

"Go!" Nirea pulled her horse around. They didn't have long before the horde caught up. The Reivers must have got off the road, knowing the Blackened would follow the last prey they'd seen.

Meristan gave Samily a final nod as he took the reins of the pack horse and set off with Vastin. Once they were out of sight, Glorbad spoke. "We'll never make Mournside. It's almost a day's ride cross-country. The horses are already fucked."

He was right. She could feel the heat coming off her mount. They might well have to ride the horses into the ground. And even then, they'd have a long way to run on foot.

"I know." She pulled up her hood. "Have you got a better idea?"

He stared for a moment, then shook his head. The ground rumbled again.

"How are they this far north?" Samily asked. "I have never known of them straying from the Black Meadows."

*Because they haven't.* "If we survive the night, we'll figure that out."

The first of them came into view. It was relatively unwasted. Must have been fresh. That explained her speed, poor bitch. She was well ahead of the rest. As she drew closer, Nirea made out the telltale black handprint on her face. The touch that had killed her—and gave the Blackened their name. The woman screamed as she saw them, and bloodlust took her. She ran even faster.

"Hold!" Nirea held up a hand. They needed to wait for the rest of the horde. If they didn't change tack here, they'd eventually catch the others.

Samily moved her horse in front and drew her sword. But as the Blackened barrelled toward them, the Thorn's horse whinnied an objection, shying away. Samily raised her blade—and the horse stumbled. A rock, a divot in the road, and it went over. Nirea heard the sickening crack as its leg snapped, then the thud as Samily landed, one leg still underneath it.

*Fuck!*

Nirea leapt down and drew her scimitars. Samily's helm lay next to her head. The Blackened was nearly on top of her, scrambling over the horse. Nirea swung her blade and split the back of its head. It slumped forward on the horse, which was desperately trying to get back up, but with only three legs it was going nowhere.

"Nirea!" Glorbad bellowed.

She didn't need to look. The horde was coming.

"Come on!" she shouted, dragging Samily to her feet. The knight shook her head, trying to regain her focus. Nirea picked up her helm and put it in her hands. "Come on, get on my horse!" The rumble was becoming deafening. She turned to see Glorbad getting down from his own mount. "What are you doing?"

"It's too late." Glorbad closed his visor and turned as the first of the Blackened barrelled toward him.

He swung his giant sword and nearly split it in half. It had been a young boy once. He crumpled like a broken sail. Nirea pulled her scarf up over her face. The three of them against God knew how many Blackened. Here on the Auld Road.

She breathed deep, and they were upon them.

Nirea swung for the first to reach her, a man with red hair. The first blow took his jaw off, but he didn't even flinch. She brought up the other blade and drove it through the soft, exposed flesh of his mouth. He dropped before her. Another came from the side—she swung instinctively, knocking it back. A girl maybe. She couldn't tell. Her hood blocked her side vision. Another lunged, tripping over the first she'd killed. Glorbad and Samily were both swinging. Their armour should protect them. Her leathers suddenly felt like satin.

"Behind the horse!" Glorbad shouted, stepping back beside Samily. He slit the animal's throat as he passed. Its body was a barrier now, giving them space to swing as the Blackened kept coming. Nirea took the head off a woman in front of her and flinched away as blood splattered across her face.

*Damn it!*

She wiped the blood with the back of her hand, and suddenly she was down. She kicked and wriggled, trying to get the Blackened off—could feel its hands clawing at her chest, reaching for her face, for her only exposed skin.

She screamed.

A blade took the top of its head off as it knelt above her. She pushed it away and rolled to the side, then pushed up, forcing herself toward the horse, near the others.

"This isn't working!" screamed Samily as she dispatched another one. "There are too many!"

She was right. They needed another option. But the horses were gone. They must have bolted.

Nirea slashed at another, taking out both eyes—still it reached for her, until the next blow went deeper and it dropped on the horse's carcass. Another came, then another. She was almost swinging blind now.

*Aim for the head. Just aim for the head.*

She heard a scream. Blackened maybe. Hopefully. She couldn't even see the others anymore. The horse was lost under a pile of bodies. She looked up at the sky and gulped air.

*Keep swinging. The head. The head.*

The trees. Blackened couldn't climb. She slammed a scimitar into an ear and ran. Leaping, she buried both blades in a massive tree trunk and pulled herself up. Her shoulders screamed, her back ached, but she reached the lowest branch and retrieved her swords. She could see the white of Samily's armour, but she was surrounded. Her blade, though. It cut through the Blackened like butter. Three, four, six Blackened gathered below the tree branch, reaching for her. Her heart pounded in her ears.

"Samily!" she bellowed. "Tree!"

If the knight heard, she made no reply. She swung, and swung, and swung again. Where was Glorbad? She caught her breath, felt her heart stop beating against her ribs, and looked down. One at a time, she split the skulls of the Blackened below her. One. Two. Three. The fourth didn't go down the first time, or the second. She was weakening. Four. Five.

The rest had given her up and gone back for Samily. They'd killed the fittest—the newest. These were older now. More withered. Slower. Maybe now they could run.

Next to the horse, an arm appeared.

*Glorbad!*

She dropped down from the branch and charged. Still Samily stood. Still Samily swung. The Blackened were struggling even to reach her over the pile of bodies.

Nirea sliced her way through three more Blackened—one could barely stand—and reached Glorbad's hand. She pulled, and the two Blackened on top of him rolled away. They were both finished—and his armour was intact.

*Thank God!*

"Fuck me!" he bellowed. Another came at them. Nirea speared it through the face, but her blade stuck as it fell, leaving her only one.

She tossed it from her weaker left hand to her right. Glorbad recovered his sword from the ground, panting heavily.

Still they came.

Suddenly, Nirea was on the ground again. Two of them on her, crawling up her back, clawing at her head. She heard a crash as Glorbad went down again beside her. A grunt as the air battered out of his lungs.

*Shite.*

She was facedown. She couldn't lift an arm. The weight on her was only getting worse—crushing her lungs. Forcing her face into the mud. She felt the panic rising. The writhing on her back. If she didn't move, she was going to suffocate. Glorbad roared next to her.

She couldn't move. She couldn't breathe.

The weight lessened. Again, and again. She rolled onto her back and sucked in precious air.

And saw the Blackened, floating above her.

*What the fuck?*

An arrow thunked through the skull of a Blackened. She forced herself back onto her feet and looked into the trees. The *draoidh* sat on his horse, gesturing at the Blackened, throwing them back—giving her time to breathe, to pause, to think.

She found one sword. The other stuck proud out the back of the Blackened head it speared. She kicked the body over, put her boot against the withered neck and wrenched the weapon free. Glorbad was up again. Samily still stood. The girl was incredible. She must have taken out twice as many as Nirea and Glorbad together, and was still going. An arrow went straight in the temple of what was once an old man. Allandria had circled behind them and fired from her horse, picking off the strays that got past Aranok's magic.

Samily and Glorbad stepped back, away from the piles of corpses. Another rumble, louder than before, and the earth rose before her eyes. With a burst of stones, a wall of mud grew in front of them, cutting them off from the Blackened.

And then there were flames. Aranok had dismounted and come closer, throwing fire from his hands at the other side of the wall. She saw the Blackened catching, heard the screeching as they burned.

"Are you all right?" It was Allandria, behind her. She turned.

"Were you touched?" the archer yelled over the screaming.

Nirea felt her face. She pulled her hood and scarf down, feeling for any sign she'd been infected. There was blood and dirt, but... Allandria leapt down from her horse and grabbed her face with gloved hands. She wiped at it, clearing away the gore, held her cheeks and examined her, and then, satisfied, let her go with a relieved smile.

Nirea collapsed to her knees, her heart pounding. She loosened her leathers. She needed to breathe. Allandria nocked another arrow and fired over her head. One of the Blackened must have cleared the wall. She heard it crackling as it landed behind her.

Glorbad's helm dropped to the ground, his breath laboured. "Well, that was fun!"

Nirea felt herself laugh. She didn't know why.

"Samily!" she said. "Where's Samily?"

"Here." The girl's blade was slick with dark red blood. There was hardly any white visible on her armour. She looked like she'd been turned inside out.

Nirea forced herself to her feet. Her thighs screamed in objection.

"I may have been wrong," she said to the Thorn.

"About what?" Samily removed her helm. Her face was red and her slick hair stuck to her head.

"Watching you fight, maybe there is a god."

# CHAPTER 18

Allandria kept an arrow nocked, listening, watching for any sign of movement. Blackened lay piled like grotesque logs, some still alight. Ideally, they would burn them all, but the threat wasn't done, just contained. For the moment. Aranok's wall of earth had cut them off, and without line of sight, the Blackened became confused, milling, searching for new prey. The fading light would help, but Allandria watched the shadows. They'd find their way through the trees soon enough.

God, but she was tired of death. Every day. For as long as she could remember. Surely, eventually, it had to be enough. How much blood could Eidyn spill before it drowned? The circle of violence, like this disease, feeding on itself, devouring the country. What she would give some days for a quiet life in the country. Or maybe to travel, like her parents. See something of the world.

Aranok leaned heavily against his horse. He would be exhausted after the magic he'd used. They all were. "We need to move." Suddenly, he stood, his eyes searching urgently. "Wait. Where are Vastin and Meristan?"

Nirea raised a placating hand. "We sent them to the White Hart with the pack horse."

"And you stayed here?" Allandria asked. "Why?"

"We were going to lead them off the road, but Samily's horse fell and…"

*Hell.* They'd be dead if she and Aranok had arrived much later.

The *draoidh* put a hand on Nirea's shoulder. "Well done."

She nodded a silent thank-you.

"Should have bloody been here," Glorbad grumbled.

Aranok looked up. "Maybe."

They could have been. Would have been, if he'd known Mournside was safe. But this was not the time for revisiting their argument. "We are here," Allandria said. "More importantly, what are the Blackened doing here?"

"Chasing a pair of Reivers," said Nirea. "God knows where they started, but those two were running like the mouth of Hell was about to swallow them. Can't have come far at that pace—even with this lot behind them."

A Blackened came out of the woods. Allandria took it down. Burning Blackened screamed beyond the wall. It was more rage than pain. She'd be worried about them setting the forest ablaze, but the ground was still damp from the afternoon's rain. Fire wouldn't catch easy. More likely to spread to other Blackened—and that would be a blessing. She quickly went about retrieving the arrows she could salvage.

"We've five riders and two horses." Glorbad said it flatly, as if dropping the problem at Aranok's feet, daring him to pick it up.

"I can walk," said Allandria. She was probably the fittest of the lot at that point, considering.

"As can I," said Samily.

"I'm afraid I'll need mine." Aranok wouldn't be able to walk at any decent pace. He'd used a lot of energy.

"Glorbad, you take it." Nirea gestured at Allandria's horse. "Your armour will slow you."

The old soldier looked at Aranok climbing back onto his horse and grumbled. He likely considered it an indignity, but he at least had the sense to recognise his pride was not worth dying for. "Aye, all right."

Allandria picked off another two that had skirted Aranok's wall. They really did need to move.

"Mournside?" Nirea asked.

"It's fine," said Aranok. "The walls stand."

He wouldn't bother to explain the rest, Allandria knew. Glorbad looked hard at him but softened after a moment. "Good."

Then they ran.

It was pitch-black by the time they came upon the White Hart. As Aranok had hoped, it was boarded up tight. That was a good sign. The boy and the monk had made it.

"Now what?" asked Glorbad. He rode level with Aranok, just behind the women. They'd encountered three more Blackened on the road, but those were the last they'd seen. Samily had easily taken care of them all, sparing Allandria's arrows. Hopefully they'd contained the spread. For now.

"I don't know," Aranok answered. The Blackened had never made it this far north. The nature of the disease meant they withered and weakened too soon. But something had changed. Or someone.

"Why do you think they're here?" the soldier asked.

"There's one obvious answer." Aranok dismounted. The Auld Road was the main road to Auldun—and Dun Eidyn. "Mynygogg."

"Aye, I wondered about that." Glorbad climbed down too. "Is it possible?"

"That they're being drawn to him? Or that he's somehow summoning them? I don't know," said Aranok. "I don't know enough about necromancy."

"What do you think?"

Aranok looked across at him. "I think we're going to have to deal with Mynygogg permanently. Maybe sooner than we'd like."

"Aye," said the soldier gravely. "I thought that too."

Nirea banged on the inn door. "Hey! Open up! We're alive out here!"

The silence in the White Hart was eerie. Its white stone walls danced with shadows from the candles. Besides the seven of them, there were about twenty other people scattered around the bar. A family sat together at a table near Aranok and Meristan, the father trying to entertain his son, who looked about seven, with a little wooden puppet. It made a *clack clack* noise as its red feet danced on the table. The boy smiled faintly. His mother stared blankly into the distance, gripping a cup she never drank from.

A pair of merchants sat in a corner, smoking, largely ignoring the ales in front of them. They'd said maybe ten words to each other since Aranok sat down. The older one, who had a thick blond beard, caught his eye, held it for a moment, and looked down as if he'd never seen him.

*Clack clack.*

Nirea, Allandria and Samily had gone through to the back bar. Samily's gruesome armour had been disturbing—and not just for the children. He might have thought the sight of Blackened blood would be heartening, knowing she was there to protect them. But when it came to the grisly details of their protection, it seemed people preferred to know it was there without having to see it. Perhaps it was easier to forget what was out there, what might be coming.

"It was worse before you arrived." Meristan leaned in toward him. "A lot of people packed up and ran. I told them they'd be safer here, but..." He opened his hands on the table. Fear does strange things to people. They run when they should hide. They hide when they should run. They wait to die when they should fight with every breath.

Someone was sobbing. A girl, nearly a woman, sitting by the fire. An older woman, maybe her mother, held her.

The innkeeper, Ardene, pottered behind the bar. Her auburn hair, streaked with grey, was tied back tightly and would have made her look severe, but for her kind blue eyes. When she'd let them in, the look of genuine relief, of hope, had been... pleasing, despite the circumstances. It was nice to be welcome.

*Clack clack.*

Glorbad and Vastin returned from the bar with four ales.

"So," said the monk. "What now?"

Indeed. What now? The road to Barrock was blocked. The Blackened were an immediate threat. Then there were the Thakhati, which were God knew what. And Mournside, the messenger, her murder. Where to begin?

"We finish the job," said Glorbad.

*Clack clack.*

Aranok raised an eyebrow. "How?"

"Way I see it, if we know where the Blackened are, we know where they're not," he said.

"What do you mean?" asked Meristan.

"He means if they're on the Auld Road, they're not in the Black Meadows," Aranok answered for him. That wasn't a terrible idea. It was a very bad idea, but it wasn't terrible.

*Clack clack.*

"For fuck's sake, shut that thing up!"

It was the blond merchant. The father turned to look at him, wide-eyed. "Sorry." He put down the puppet. Tears welled in his son's eyes. He pulled the boy in against his chest. The mother stood and crossed to the merchants' table.

She leaned on the edge and growled, "You leave my son alone, y'hear me?"

The merchant snorted. "Tell your man to keep the fucking noise down, and we'll be fine."

The woman straightened and walked back to her family. She picked up the puppet and, staring straight at the merchant, banged it down on the table. Again. Again.

*Damn it.*

The merchant slammed down his tankard and stood. He strode toward the other table.

Aranok and Glorbad both moved, but before they could stand, the merchant juddered to a halt as an arrow thudded into the wood at his feet. Aranok turned to see Allandria next to the bar, another arrow nocked—this one aimed higher.

The merchant glowered venomously at her.

"Sit," she said. When he didn't move, she stepped toward him. "Do I need to ask again?"

With a grunt, he walked back to his table and sat down. His companion leaned in and whispered something to him. He nodded, looking sideways at the archer.

The boy was crying, sobbing into his father's chest. The mother put down the toy but kept the merchant fixed with a stare that would have wilted cabbage. He pretended not to notice.

Allandria came to the table. "You need to say something, or this is going to get worse." She retrieved her arrow from the floor in silence and returned to the back bar.

She was probably right. But he was no great speaker. And he was a *draoidh*. Whatever else these people might think of him, he was always a *draoidh* first.

"Listen, please, all of you." It was Meristan. The monk stood and nodded gently to Aranok. "I am not a brave man. You are all scared—understandably. But let me tell you why I am not."

The room quieted as all eyes turned to him.

"You might think I would say that it's because I'm a man of God, and that is true. I do have faith in God. But more than that, I have faith in people. You all know of the White Thorns. That woman"—he pointed toward the back room—"her name is Samily. I've known her since she was younger than you." He pointed to the boy, who had stopped crying enough to listen.

"She is a miracle. I have seen her face things that would make great men weep. I owe her my life, many times over, and so do countless others. Just days ago, she killed a demon at Mutton Hole with one strike!" He held up a finger. "And she is here with you.

"And this soldier here." He pointed at Glorbad, who sat up a little straighter. "Glorbad and his companion, Nirea, faced down an entire horde of Blackened, just today—and here they are to tell the tale! When we were in danger, when the Blackened were on the road here, they sent the boy and me on to safety, and they stayed to stop that horde reaching us. And they are here with you.

"And this man." He pointed to Aranok. "This is Aranok, envoy to the King of Eidyn." He nodded at the crowd. "Yes, you've heard the stories. Janaeus's right hand. Hofnag's demise. The *draoidh* who faced down Mynygogg! You may fear his magic. But I believe that, like everything, magic flows from God, and each person chooses how to use it. This man, Aranok, chooses to defend you."

He turned to Glorbad. "Tell the people, Glorbad, when you were almost overrun by the Blackened, what did he do?"

Glorbad bristled. He looked Aranok dead in the eye, then turned to Meristan. "He made a wall of mud."

"He pulled a wall of earth from the ground to protect them!" Meristan swept his arms upwards. There were a few gasps from the room. "And then what?" He turned back to Glorbad.

"He burned them."

"He burned them, with fire from his own hands!"

More gasps. The girl who had been weeping by the fire was staring at Aranok in what could have been either awe or disbelief.

"And this man, this man who can do wondrous things is here with you.

"Then there's his bodyguard, Allandria. You've just seen her skill with a bow. She can take down Blackened quicker than they rise. Never has there been a more remarkable archer. Imagine, when the king was faced with the task of providing a man such as Aranok with a guard, of all the warriors in Eidyn, he chose her. And she is here with you.

"And if yet you find your courage fails you, let me introduce you to Vastin."

Vastin looked confused but managed an awkward half smile.

"At just fifteen years old, the greatest blacksmith in Eidyn!" Now Vastin's smile reached his eyes. "This young man's weapons and armour are legendary. His blades sharp enough to split hair! His shields harder than stone, but light as wood. These, your guardians, bear his weapons. Today, I entrusted myself to his care, and he delivered me safely here, to you. And now we are both here. We are with you."

Vastin was now beaming from ear to ear, blushing. He picked up his ale and supped it, hiding behind the tankard.

"Tonight, we are all companions. We are all friends. And we are lucky. Because tonight, we are in the safest place in all of Eidyn. So eat, drink and sleep soundly. I promise you, we will all see the dawn."

The monk smiled broadly and returned to his seat.

It started with one tankard. The merchant banged it on his table. Then another. The father's hand. The weeping girl's mother banged on the bench beside her, until it became a cacophony of approval.

Aranok looked round to see Allandria standing in the passage next to the bar. She cocked her head at him with a frown that said "not bad." He nodded in return, and she disappeared again.

"Nice speech," said Glorbad as the banging died down to be replaced with a more normal level of chatter.

"Words are easy weapons when fear is the enemy," said Meristan.

"I think you may have started a few new legends," said Aranok. He didn't mind this one.

"Legends make people happy. They make them feel safe."

A bottle of whisky thunked onto the table. Aranok looked up at Ardene.

"Thank you." She nodded to each of them. "Closest inn to Auldun used to be a good thing. But since… well, you know. Good to have you here."

Aranok nodded thanks and she moved on to another table, collecting empty tankards and cups. It would be a long night.

———◦———

"What, never?" Nirea was asking as Allandria rejoined them.

"No." Samily shrugged. She was still cleaning her armour using the rags Ardene had given her. She'd already changed the water twice.

"Not even, you know… by yourself?" Nirea asked.

Samily stopped working and looked at her in horror. "What? No!"

Allandria sat down. This sounded interesting. "What are we talking about?"

Samily blushed furiously. It was odd to see this powerful girl look so young.

"Sex," Nirea said casually.

"Oh! All right then." Allandria put her feet up on the table. "Where are we?"

"I'm in favour," said Nirea.

Samily looked up silently, then back at her armour.

"Oh," said Allandria. "And you're not?"

"I don't see why it's so important. I just don't feel that way," said the knight. "It is such an odd thing to do. Like putting your foot in someone's mouth."

Nirea frowned and raised both eyebrows. "Well, as long as you've bathed first…"

"What?" Samily was clearly scandalised by the notion. "You would… you would actually…"

Nirea raised her cup and shrugged. "It's nicer than it sounds."

The Thorn was wide-eyed, bless her. But she was starting to look uncomfortable. Allandria decided to step in. "In fairness, it probably is an odd thing to do, if you think too hard about it."

"Thinking about it has rarely been my problem." Nirea grinned.

Allandria batted her arm. "You're not helping."

"I've been told that before too."

Allandria snorted despite herself. "No, seriously." She turned back to Samily. "Sex is a wonderful thing between two people who want to do it. If you don't want to, then absolutely don't. And don't feel pressured to." Samily looked as if she'd warned her not to fall over in a light wind. As if anyone could push that girl into anything against her will. "But honestly, with the right person, it's much more than it sounds. It can be wonderful."

Nirea's eyes lit with devilry. "It can be pretty good with the wrong person if you've got a decent imagination."

Allandria couldn't help but smile. "Nirea..."

She waved her hands apologetically. "I know, I'm being an arse. Sorry. I'm used to saltier company." She turned to the knight. "Allandria's right. If you're not interested, then you're not. But if you're ever curious, I heartily recommend it."

"Oh, me too," Allandria added, perhaps a little too enthusiastically.

Nirea's eyebrows rose again and she gestured to the main room. "You do, do you?"

Allandria felt her face flush before she could stifle it. Her relationship with Aranok was a secret, for several reasons. But apparently not so well concealed as she liked to think. She widened her eyes at the sailor, begging her not to continue.

Nirea smiled conspiratorially and winked. "I need more wine." She emptied the contents of her cup and walked toward the front bar, but stopped when Aranok appeared in the doorway.

"Envoy?" she said playfully.

Aranok drew closer before speaking quietly. "We have a plan. With the Blackened on the Auld Road, the Meadows are probably clear."

Allandria did not like where this was going.

"Tomorrow, we're going over the Black Hills. We'll cross the Black Meadows to Lepertoun."

Yep. That was exactly what she didn't want to do.

# CHAPTER 19

The Black Meadows. The first time Aranok had come here, it was golden fields of wheat and barley as far as he could see. The Blackening had ended that. The verdant farmlands had become a grey-brown wasteland once all the farmers either were infected or had fled. At first, unharvested crops rotted in the fields, drawing insects. Over winter, pests and fungus had taken root in the crop detritus, meaning all that grew from their husks in the spring were the hardiest weeds.

The living stayed away, except for the medics. Lepertoun Tower had been set up as a hospital, but little word had ever come from them. Janaeus had decided their best hope was to keep people away and hope the plague burned itself out—with no new victims to infect, the spread would end. Aranok had reluctantly agreed. That hope died on the Auld Road. They needed a new plan.

It had taken a full day to cross the Black Hills. None of them had looked forward to sleeping outside in the foothills. But their watches had passed almost completely uneventfully. Glorbad had taken down one Blackened—a boy whose legs had withered so badly he could barely stand. Whatever drove the horde north, he had been too far gone to follow.

With no trees and little vegetation in the Meadows, there was nowhere for the Thakhati to take cover during the day, so they didn't need to worry about them. And there was nothing out here for demons to attack. Ironically, this was probably one of the safest places in Eidyn now.

All the same, Aranok was glad to see the walls of Lepertoun Tower in the distance. There had been odd stragglers throughout the day—an old, hobbled woman and a child of no more than five, so withered Aranok hadn't even been able to tell if it was a boy or a girl. The child's lank hair covered most of its face. The huge black handprint on its shoulder had rattled him. What that child must have gone through—terrified, as an adult, possibly its own parent, had come shambling toward them. Did they know what was happening? That they were going to die? He shook his head, trying to clear it of the macabre image.

"Why are we really here?" asked Allandria. The two of them were on foot, along with Meristan, while the others rode.

"We can take shelter for the night," Aranok answered.

"Mm-hmm. But are we still going to Barrock?"

Aranok smiled. He was rarely successful at keeping anything from her. He looked up to see that the riders were far enough ahead. "Maybe, maybe not."

"Uh-huh," she replied.

Meristan stepped closer. "You don't intend to go on to Barrock?"

"It depends what we find. We haven't had any news out of Lepertoun in over six months. We don't know what the disease is. Our best chance of finding out"—Aranok pointed ahead to the sandstone tower—"is right there."

"And the Blackened are an immediate threat now that they've moved north," said Allandria.

"And the others?" Meristan nodded ahead.

"This was Glorbad's plan," said Aranok. "I just agreed with it." Whether the soldier would still agree with him tomorrow was another question.

"Try not to be an arsehole when you tell him," said Allandria.

"Me?" Aranok placed an affronted hand against his chest. "I'll be the consummate diplomat."

---

Vastin looked around, trying to take in the scale of the place. The Tower of Lepertoun was a huge sandstone cube dominating the rest of the building. It formed one corner of a square built over a river. The other three corners were much smaller towers, and the buildings running between them had ornate, colourful roofs, with balconies on the inside. The inner courtyard was dominated by the river, which fed the trees and vegetation growing there. It was the first life they'd seen since the Black Hills. He couldn't believe this grand place had once been home to just one family. Dozens, maybe hundreds, could live here. Though he supposed there would have been servants. He couldn't imagine being able to pay someone simply to cook for him, or clean or stable horses. He couldn't imagine owning horses! It was like a different world. And yet, for all its opulence, it was dead.

He drew up his horse next to the river, climbed down and encouraged it to drink. Glorbad drew alongside him and dismounted. "Fine beasts. Go on, get your nose in that." He drew his mount's head down and the horse eagerly sucked at the water. The soldier unbuckled his vambraces. "Be good to get some of this weight off and cool down, eh?"

"Oh, yeah," said Vastin, as if he'd been thinking the same. He loosened his own straps and slipped his arms out of their armour. The light breeze tingled on his skin as he rolled up his sleeves. Glorbad knelt at the water's edge, cupped the water in his hands and splashed it over his face, then drank a handful.

"Ah! Get some of this in you, lad. Nowt more refreshing than water straight from the source."

Vastin knelt beside him. He was right; it was wonderful—quenching his thirst like no beer ever had. He looked down and realised his arms were filthy. His face felt the same. Reaching back into the river, he splashed the cold water over his face and rubbed to clear some of the dust. He dipped his arms in and rubbed at them too, watching the dirt come away.

"Oi." Glorbad nudged him. Vastin looked round to see him grinning. "D'you mind not having a bath in my drinking water?"

Vastin laughed with him.

"How you doing, lad? You all right?"

"How do you mean?" Vastin heard the defensiveness in his own voice. He really didn't want to talk about the thing again.

"Just in general." Glorbad was washing his own face now. "You've been quiet."

"Have I?" It was awkward talking to anyone. Maybe especially Glorbad, after he'd snapped at him. How many of them had noticed he liked Samily? Had they laughed about it? He hated them thinking of him as a child. A naïve child.

"Aye, a bit," said Glorbad. "Then again, I suppose maybe we all have. The Blackened—that was something."

"Well, yeah. I kind of missed it." Vastin had run when the rest stood and fought. He'd never been in any danger. Not really.

Glorbad looked up at him with a curious expression. "Listen, lad, you followed orders. That's what good soldiers do. It's up to the leaders, the ones with experience, the ones who can see the whole picture—they make the decisions. Our job is to do what we're told."

"S'pose," said Vastin. "I didn't really do anything, though, did I?"

"You kidding? Imagine you'd stayed with us. Imagine Laird Envoy hadn't shown up when he did, and we'd all gone down. Including you. What would have happened to the folk in the White Hart?"

"Meristan could have gone," he answered quietly.

Glorbad flicked his shoulder. "And what if he'd come across some Blackened himself? On his own? With his bare-arse legs and his flimsy robes. You think the monk would have fought his way through?"

"Well, no, but…"

"But what?"

"We didn't see any Blackened." They'd had a completely clear run to the White Hart.

"But what if he had?" Glorbad looked him hard in the eye. "We had to allow for that. Someone had to get to the White Hart and warn them. Someone had to protect the monk. We might not have survived, Vastin. We bloody nearly didn't. I'm not kidding. We were in trouble. If we'd failed, and that horde had kept coming…You've got to see the whole picture, son. Your mission was to save lives. The monk, and everybody in that inn. We were lucky, but we won't always be lucky. That's why we do what we do. We follow orders or people die."

Vastin smiled. He was pretty sure the soldier was comforting him, but it did make sense. It hadn't felt important, but maybe, if things hadn't gone as they did…maybe.

"And even if none of that was true"—Glorbad pointed to the shield hanging off his horse—"that, right there. That shield kept me alive. Never been able to move so freely with a shield. And that edge took a few heads off. So even if you don't think you saved anyone else, you saved me. I find that pretty fucking important." The soldier put a hand on Vastin's shoulder. "You're doing grand, lad. Your father'd be proud."

Vastin felt his lip tremble. He nodded, biting down to stop the tears welling in his eyes.

Glorbad stood. "Clean up your gear and we'll get some more sparring in later, aye?"

Vastin nodded. "Definitely."

The soldier smiled and walked toward Laird Aranok. Vastin turned back to the river as the tears spilled.

---

Nirea knelt, took off a glove and let the river flow over her fingers. It was cold but calming, soothing. With the gurgle of the water, she could feel her shoulders relaxing, her jaw loosening.

She scooped up a handful and splashed her face. She must have gasped with delight, because when she opened her eyes, Samily looked at her curiously. She'd brought her horse to drink.

"This'll do nicely." Glorbad surveyed the courtyard as if he'd just purchased the place. "Just need to search the buildings—make sure they're clear, before dark."

Nirea closed her eyes and leaned her head back. "You do that. I'm going to sit right here and listen to this river."

"How d'you want to do this?" the soldier asked Aranok.

"Your shout," he answered.

Glorbad pointed to the main tower. "Right, then. You and Samily take the north tower, Allandria and I will take the south. One close combat and one ranged in each group. Work your way through the tower, then move east. We'll do the same and work west. Meet back here when we've cleared the lot. Shout if you need help."

Aranok nodded. "Makes sense."

"Brother, would you close the gates?" Glorbad asked.

"Of course." Meristan smiled. "Would you assist me, Vastin?"

The boy jumped up to join him, wiping at his face, where he'd also obviously splashed water.

"I'll mind the horses," Nirea said. Meaning she'd sit exactly where she was. For a little while anyway.

Once the animals had drunk their fill, she stabled them, checking for cocoons first. She always would now. The memory of that Thakhati tearing into the horse at the Starbank wasn't going away.

The sun was setting as she returned to the courtyard. Meristan sat quietly, cross-legged on the floor. Vastin had removed his armour and was cleaning it in the river. The boy was holding up well. Since the demon, they'd managed to keep him out of any more fights—more by luck than intent. The two groups had cleared a tower each and moved to the next ones. Nirea looked up at the darkening sky. They should build a fire soon. She started clearing a space.

"You seem at peace here."

Nirea jumped. She hadn't realised Meristan had opened his eyes.

"How long have you been watching me?" she asked, half playfully.

The monk shook his head. "I was merely listening."

"It is peaceful, don't you think?"

"I do," he answered. "I'm happy that you do too. God's presence feels clearer here. It is comforting."

Everything led back to God with these two. She supposed it shouldn't be a surprise. A monk and a holy knight were going to be big on God. But she'd never been around anyone for whom God loomed so large in their lives. "What made you become a monk?"

Meristan looked up at her with a benevolent smile. "Some would say it was a calling, I suppose. Some destiny. I prefer to think I chose this life."

"Were you raised in the Order?"

"No. Well, not like Samily anyway. My mother was a devout woman. Her faith sustained us when my father passed away. I was very young. Five or six. We worked the farm together."

A farmer? That explained his physique. "So why did you leave?"

Meristan's smile turned melancholy. "My mother passed when I was"—he looked over his shoulder toward Vastin—"about his age, I suppose. A parasite in her lungs. From the fertiliser, most likely. We thought so, anyway."

"I'm sorry. That must have been hard." It was difficult for her to relate to the loss of a parent. She'd never known any. But she knew loss.

"She is with God." Meristan smiled again. "Her faith drove me to the Order. I was too old to train as a Thorn. Probably for the best. But they took me in."

"What about the farm?"

"Sold to our neighbours. They were glad of the extra land. The money got me where I was going—and swelled the Order's coffers when I arrived."

"You gave them the money?" Nirea instantly regretted her sceptical tone. She jolted as a loud splash echoed across the courtyard. Meristan jumped to his feet. Where Vastin had been squatting next to the river there was only wet armour and a few lines in the dirt.

"I'll get him." The monk chuckled. He walked to the river, near one of the biggest trees, and bent over.

"Wait! Don't touch him!"

Nirea drew her blades and spun to face the source of the voice. A woman in black with a bright red streak in her dark hair leapt from the northwest balcony and ran toward Meristan. Nirea moved to cut her off, but she wasn't carrying a weapon. What was she doing?

"Stop!" she pleaded. "Don't touch him!"

*Oh Hells.*

She turned to warn Meristan. Vastin's hand reached up out of the water and grasped the monk's forearm. He yelped and yanked his arm away.

He looked at Nirea curiously, then down at the vivid black handprint. Nirea screamed.

The woman passed as if she weren't there, running at Meristan. She grabbed and bound his wrists with rope from her belt, tying him to the lowest tree branch. He didn't resist, seemed lost in a haze.

"Stay back!" the woman called. Nirea's heart pounded in her chest like a drum. Vastin was scrambling up out of the water, the same mindless, driven look in his eyes she'd seen on the Auld Road.

"Careful!" she tried to shout, but her throat seized. Nothing came out. The boy reached for the woman and, inexplicably, she took his hand and helped him onto land.

*What the Hell?*

The woman held Vastin's face, forcing him to look directly at her. He quieted, and the frenzy left him. She allowed him to reach up and touch her face. When he was entirely docile, she took another length of rope and bound his wrists too, tying him to the same branch as Meristan. The monk, conversely, was becoming agitated, head darting about like a hungry animal with the scent of carrion in its nostrils. The woman touched his cheek with her hand and met his eyes. The blood-lust drained from him too.

She turned to Nirea, who could hardly see through watery eyes. "I'm sorry. They're gone."

Nirea's legs collapsed beneath her. It had only been seconds.

Seconds. But Vastin and Meristan were dead.

---

Allandria burst through the door back into the courtyard, bow raised. Nirea's scream had been like a bolt of lightning. It wasn't a sound Allandria expected to hear from the sailor. Her heart pounded as she scanned the area. Nirea knelt on the ground near the river. She had a hand over her mouth and was looking at... Vastin and Meristan. Were they tied to the tree? A woman stood near them. There was something unsettling about her. It was almost hard to look at her. She seemed to be stroking the monk's face.

"Hey! Step away!" she called. The woman looked up at her and slowly stepped back, hands raised.

"Wait, wait." Nirea's voice cracked. "It's not what you think!"

"Your friend's right; I'm not your enemy," said the woman.

"Then what the Hell is it?" Glorbad followed her out of the tower and stalked toward the woman, sword levelled at her.

"Just wait, for fuck's sake!" said Nirea.

Glorbad ignored her and kept walking toward their friends.

"You don't want to do that." The woman was calm but firm.

"Glorbad, no!" shouted Nirea. "They're Blackened!"

Allandria's blood froze.

"No!" Samily ran from the opposite tower. Aranok followed close behind. She threw off her helm and dropped her sword as she crossed toward her master.

"Samily, no!" shouted the *draoidh*. She couldn't hear him.

"You need to stop her." The woman stepped out of her path.

Glorbad moved to intercept her. "Wait, girl." But she barrelled straight into him and they tumbled to the ground together.

*Damn it.*

Allandria dropped her bow and ran toward them. Vastin and Meristan were becoming agitated. They struggled against their ropes—trying to reach the pair wrestling on the ground. Glorbad was no match for Samily, but he was doing enough to keep her from getting past him.

"Samily, stop!" Aranok shouted again, but still she struggled and pushed against Glorbad. Meristan groaned and she only struggled harder. She rolled away from Glorbad, kicking him in the face with a crunch. The soldier fell back, holding his nose.

She got to one knee and stopped, struggling as if she were too heavy for her own legs.

"Envoy," she growled, "release me!"

Allandria looked up to see Aranok struggling to hold her in place. His arms shook and his face reddened. Samily was strong.

"Calm down!" Allandria pleaded with her. They couldn't lose her too.

Nirea crouched in front of the girl and placed her hands on her face. Samily glowered back.

"Sweetheart," the sailor said. "I'm so sorry."

"No!" Samily barked back at her. "No!"

"Yes, honey." Nirea gently put her arms around the girl's neck and took her head on her shoulder.

"No!" Samily stopped struggling. Nirea looked up at Aranok and waved him off. He relaxed with a sigh.

The girl crumpled into Nirea, giving up the fight completely, heaving with huge, racking sobs. Vastin and Meristan jerked at their bonds, desperate to be free and reach the women.

"My ducking gose!" Glorbad complained, sitting up. Blood poured through his fingers.

"What happened?" Aranok demanded in a tone of urgency and panic she didn't often hear from him.

Nirea looked up from Samily and shrugged.

"Your friend was cleaning his armour." The new woman had deathly pale skin and deep black hair with a stripe of red. Again, Allandria realised there was something wrong about her, but she couldn't put her finger on it. A smell?

"I didn't see until it was too late. There's a Blackened at the edge of the river—caught in the tree roots. If I'd known it was there…"

Allandria moved to the river. She was right. Tangled in the roots, held tight against the riverbank and covered in mud, what was once a baby looked piteously up at her, a black handprint just discernible on its tiny, skeletal head. She could have stood right there and completely missed it. Just like Vastin.

A baby, for God's sake.

When it saw her, it struggled, trying to free itself from its cage, to reach her. She closed her eyes. The things she'd seen, and yet this… this was still too much. She drew her short sword and carefully slid it through the roots into the baby's skull. It went limp, like a doll. When she withdrew her blade, a dark red trickle swirled into the river. She slumped onto the earth, watching the red ribbon weave and dance in the water.

Glorbad had pulled a handkerchief from somewhere to stem the flow of blood from his nose and moved well away from Meristan and Vastin.

Allandria looked up at Aranok and saw the same devastation in his eyes that she felt. How had this happened? Why?

"Who are you?" Aranok asked the woman.

"My name is Morienne. May I?" She gestured at Vastin and Meristan. "I can make them calm."

Aranok looked to Nirea, who now had Samily's head in her lap, stroking the girl's hair as she cried. She nodded.

"All right," he said.

Morienne took a strip of black cloth from her belt and approached Meristan. The monk increased his fervour as she approached, but as she touched his face he calmed again. She reached up and gently tied the cloth over his eyes. She lifted another strip to do the same with Vastin, and they were both docile. Still, Allandria found it hard to look directly at her.

"They hunt by sight," said Morienne. "If they can't see, they don't hunt."

"Why aren't you infected?" asked Allandria. Surely, if there was a cure, they'd have heard something.

"Are you immune to the plague?" Aranok's tone was desperate.

Morienne released the ropes tying each man's hands to the branch and used them like reins to lead them toward the largest tower. "Let's make your friends comfortable—then we can talk."

# CHAPTER 20

**A**ranok gasped despite himself. They'd climbed six floors of Lepertoun Tower. When Morienne pushed open the heavy oak door, a burst of stale air buffeted him. He raised his hand to cover his nose and mouth.

"Sorry." Morienne led the two men—he couldn't yet think of them as Blackened—into the room.

What had once probably been a dining room now held about twenty makeshift beds. Some were actual beds that must have been dragged from other rooms—others were simply sheets laid on straw. On about a dozen of the beds lay what Aranok would have assumed were patients—except that every one of them had both hands tied to something by the bed and wore cloth blindfolds.

"Don't touch them." Morienne picked her way skillfully amongst the human detritus. "They won't attack you, but any skin-on-skin contact will pass it on."

"Understood." Aranok was even more careful to give them a lot of space. They all looked frail, like they'd been here a long time already. One boy was so thin, so still, Aranok assumed he was dead until he twitched like an upturned insect.

"Fuck," Allandria whispered behind him.

"I know."

"You don't have to whisper," Morienne called back. "They really only hunt on sight." She stopped at one of the beds, left Meristan to stand placidly alone, and guided Vastin first to sit, then lie on the bed. She tied his hands to a bedpost. Aranok had barely been able to look at him, but he had little choice as he passed the bed. Fifteen years old. And Aranok had done exactly what he was trying to avoid. He'd killed him.

Of course.

Allandria put a hand on his shoulder. "It's not your fault."

He knew better.

Vastin's head lolled like a newborn's, trying to take in the world. He shuffled on the bed, as though trying to understand it by touch.

"It's all right. They won't suffer, I promise." Morienne finished tying Meristan to the next bed, then moved to the end of the room and sat on a stone dais that might once have been a stage for dinner entertainment— a bard or a jester. Now it was laden with blankets and ropes.

"What is this?" Allandria gestured to the room.

"I try to make them comfortable," said Morienne. "They only get agitated when they see an uninfected. As long as they don't..." Her voice trailed off. She was an odd woman, and Aranok could only now think about her. She had an aura of animosity... It was difficult to keep looking at her for any length of time. When he did, he found himself wanting to look away. Only when he did could he think clearly again.

"But wouldn't it be more merciful to...?"

"Kill them?" Morienne finished for him. "I don't know. But it feels wrong. They're not monsters, they're victims."

"How long have you been doing this?" Allandria still paced the room, looking at the Blackened. Maybe she felt the same thing and being farther from Morienne was easier—even if looking at the horrors of this disease was the alternative.

"Eight months?" she answered. "I've lost track. When I arrived, I was passing through. Not everyone knew about the Blackening then. I came across a few of them." She nodded to a living corpse. "I wasn't affected. I came to see if I could help. See if maybe I could be... a cure."

"Why?" asked Aranok. "Are you a healer?"

Morienne paused. "No. It was just the right thing to do. There were people here, trying to help. Trying to understand what was happening."

Yes, there were. "What happened to them?"

Morienne walked to one of the beds. She pointed at the woman who lay bound there. She was skin and bone. "This is Amaru. She was the last one to fall. It's hard to keep them under control. Until the other day, new Blackened wandered in all the time."

"The other day?" Allandria took a seat, perched on a stone window-sill between two beds.

"Three, four days ago. They all stopped coming. I went up to the roof of the tower. Normally, they're aimless unless they see an uninfected—then they frenzy until they catch and turn them. Three days ago, they all went north. Like herded sheep. Even the ones in here tried to go. If they hadn't been tied up... I've never seen anything like it. It was as if something called them."

A sudden growling turned their heads. A man, down near the door, had worked his blindfold off and was trying to get to Allandria. He strained at his rope, pulling and jerking to be free. Allandria leaned back into the window. He was at least twenty feet away, but it was still disconcerting. Like watching a crazed animal trying to tear itself free of a trap. There was so little of him, his wrists looked as though they might snap, his hands tear right off.

Morienne casually walked to him, picking her way amongst the beds as if they held sleeping babies, not these things. Some of the others were becoming agitated by the noise.

She knelt on the floor next to him and touched his face, as she'd done before. He looked in her eyes and calmed, almost as if there was some recognition there, some trace of what he had been. Morienne gently replaced the blindfold and guided his head down.

"How do you do this?" Allandria asked. "Isn't it... awful?"

Morienne shrugged. "It is what it is."

Allandria looked at the floor as Morienne passed her. As she came closer to him, Aranok again felt the urge to move away—to leave. What was that?

"Do you know why you're immune?" he asked.

"I don't." Morienne sat again. "Sorry. They were trying to under-stand it when..." She opened her hands toward the room.

Aranok nodded.

"Such a cruel disease," she said. "You know, they only die because they stop eating? They waste away—and yet the Blackening keeps them alive. Their only purpose seems to be to spread the disease, and when they're so broken that they can't do that anymore—they finally die."

"That's so sad," said Allandria. "If they would eat, they could survive?"

Aranok was starting to feel light-headed. "I need to get some air." He moved carefully toward the door. He didn't dare look back at Meristan and Vastin. The thought made him feel sick.

"I understand," said Morienne. "It's difficult for people to be near me."

Aranok stopped with a hand on the doorframe. She knew about that? He turned and looked up at her, forcing himself to fight the repulsion. She wasn't ugly. She wasn't evil. And yet his eyes were beginning to water.

Then he realised.

"Morienne, are you *damainte*?" He looked away and wiped the tears from his eyes.

"I am," she answered.

"What's *damainte*?" asked Allandria.

"It's a *draoidh* word for 'cursed.'" Aranok could barely stand still as his brain raced.

*My God, could it be? Is it that simple?*

Could this strange, cursed woman be the end of the Blackening?

———◦———

"A ducking gagy." Glorbad dabbed at his nose with a bloody handkerchief as he looked down at the tree roots. "Hell's arse. A gagy. Of all the ducking thigs."

"I know," said Nirea. Samily had stopped crying but still lay with her head on Nirea's lap. She stroked the girl's fine blonde hair, silk under her fingers.

If only Vastin had been a foot farther from the tree. If only he'd had his armour on. If only the baby hadn't been caught in the roots. How the Hell did it even get there? If only, if only…all the little things that could have been different, and their friends would be alive. Odd that she thought of them as friends. She'd only known them both a few days. And yet she felt their loss like an open wound.

*Damn this infernal plague!*

"I'm sorry," a tiny voice said. She looked down to see Samily had opened her eyes.

"Sorry?" Nirea asked.

Samily sat up. Her eyes were red and puffy, her cheeks streaked with tears in the dust. She looked at Glorbad. "I'm sorry. About your nose."

Glorbad's shoulders slumped. "Ah've 'ad wuss. An' you had cause."

"No, you were protecting me. I understand."

Glorbad nodded. Samily slowly climbed to her feet and crossed to him, by the water. She looked down. "Poor child. Barely even started its life. I trust she's with God now. We should bury her."

Nirea got to her feet slowly. Her calves tingled as blood returned to them. Even in grief, Samily's first thoughts were for others. The girl was unique. Nirea had never seen compassion like it.

The knight turned to Glorbad. "May I see?"

He looked at her curiously. She met his gaze without flinching. Eventually, he lowered the handkerchief. "S'not as bad as't loogs," he said with a grin of bravado. He was lying. His swollen nose was squashed against his face, which was caked in blood around his mouth. Samily gasped.

"Please, let me." She lifted her hand to his face. He flinched away. "It's all right. I've done this for you before, remember?"

*What the Hell was she talking about?*

Glorbad looked suspicious but didn't protest any further. The knight gently placed one fingertip against the end of his shattered nose and said, *"Air ais."*

Nirea's mouth fell open as the soldier's shattered nose moved. It cracked and clicked itself back into shape and the gash on his nose sealed itself before her eyes.

"Demon's balls!" Glorbad blinked away tears.

Nirea knew what she'd done. "Good God, girl. You're a healer? You're full of surprises, aren't you?"

Samily sighed, and her mouth twitched with the hint of a smile. She looked pale. Tired. She sat down with her back against the tree and crossed her hands on her lap. "I am."

Glorbad poked and prodded at his nose. "Ha ha! What about that?"

Nirea shushed him. He'd forgotten where they were. What had just happened.

"Oh. Aye," he said quietly.

"Meristan told me to keep it secret." Samily's voice was small again. "It makes me tired."

She looked every inch an angel, leaning peacefully against the tree. And after what she'd just done, Nirea found herself wondering if maybe there was more to this girl than she was prepared to admit.

"We can save them!" came a shout from across the courtyard.

Samily jerked and opened her eyes. "What?"

Aranok ran toward them. Allandria and Morienne appeared from the door behind him.

"We can save them!" he repeated.

Samily's eyes widened. She burst to her feet and met him, grabbing his shoulders. "Meristan? We can save him?"

"And the boy?" demanded Glorbad.

"All of them," said Aranok. "If I'm right, we can save all of the Blackened. Every one."

------

"How?" asked Nirea.

Aranok's heart was pounding hard. Could it really be this easy? Could he really have stumbled into the answer? "Morienne is *damainte*—cursed." He pointed at the woman, who bowed her head slightly. "It's why we find it difficult to be near her."

Morienne flinched away from Allandria. The archer put a hand on her arm. "No. It's all right."

A faint, bittersweet smile crossed Morienne's lips.

"She's immune to the Blackening!" said Aranok.

"So?" asked Glorbad. "You think her curse made her immune?"

"A *mollachd*—curse—is a particular kind of magic." Aranok was struggling to get the words out coherently—they wanted to pour from him. "They're not limited by a *draoidh*'s talent. Any *draoidh* can cast them. But they're dangerous. And difficult. Most *draoidhs* stay away from them. But the important thing is this: A person can only bear one curse at a time."

He paused, giving them all a moment to catch up. He'd barely been able to contain the idea himself.

Nirea spoke first. "So, wait, you think Morienne is immune because..."

"Because the Blackening isn't a disease; it's a *mollachd*. And a *mollachd* can be lifted!"

"You think my curse is what makes me immune?" asked Morienne.

"I do." He was all but certain of it.

Samily dropped to her knees. "Thank you, thank you."

Aranok shifted uncomfortably, unsure how to respond.

"She doesn't mean you, she means..." Nirea pointed upwards.

"Oh, of course," said Aranok. That was much less awkward.

"Right!" Glorbad rubbed his hands together cheerily. "So how do we lift a curse?"

Aranok noticed his nose was fixed. Interesting that Samily had revealed her ability. Glorbad might not have remembered it from Mutton Hole; he was deep in an opium haze that first time. But he must surely know what she had done here. Nirea too. In fact, everyone there would eventually wonder how the soldier's shattered nose had repaired itself. As soon as she thought her master was gone, she'd freely displayed her skill. Was it only his order keeping her in check? Or was it the shock and the grief that had slipped her guard? Perhaps she'd not really considered her actions—or what they would mean. Either way, she'd exposed her power, and that wasn't a trick she could put back in its box. The existence of a healer was a fundamental change in the understanding of magic.

One thing at a time, though. For now. "Well, that's the difficult part. We'll have to go to Traverlyn. There are books I need in the university."

As well as someone he needed to consult and ask a favour of—but they didn't need to know either of those things.

"Hang on," said the soldier. "Traverlyn's north. We're going east. Right?"

Incredible. Surely the idiot wasn't still focused on the bloody mission?

"Technically, it's northeast," said Aranok. "It'll cost us a day, maybe two. And we'll be back on the Auld Road after we're done."

"Or we go to Barrock first, as we were ordered to do," said Glorbad, "and stop at Traverlyn on the way back with Queen Taneitheia."

"No." To everyone's surprise, it was Samily. She stood and turned to face Glorbad. "If going to Traverlyn cures the Blackened, we go to Traverlyn."

Good to know she was on his side. Allandria would be, obviously. That just left... "Nirea?"

The sailor stood, arms crossed, looking at Glorbad, then Aranok, and back again. "Well, fuck. You really think this is what Meristan would want you to do?" she asked Samily. "Prioritise him over the king's orders?"

The knight didn't flinch. "White Thorns serve three masters: God, God's children and the king—in that order. God wants this curse lifted. God brought us here to do it. And even if I was not absolutely sure of that fact, God's children are suffering. The king waits."

Nirea nodded and turned to Aranok. "You can cure the Blackening? You're certain?"

"Of course I'm not certain. Until a moment ago I thought it was an incurable plague. Now I believe it's a curse. But I know a curse can be lifted. And I'm going to try."

"Fuck." Nirea's face drained of colour. Aranok suspected she'd realised what he'd been trying hard not to think about. "If they can be cured, then...all those people..." She put a trembling hand to her mouth.

"I know." They had killed hundreds. Slaughtered them. Samily in particular. And him. Hundreds of innocent victims who might have been saved. The baby. "We didn't know." Allandria's face was ashen. Samily closed her eyes.

After a long silence, Nirea turned to Glorbad. "He's right. If there's even a chance we can cure the Blackening—save all those people—we have to try. How could we live with ourselves if we don't? Surely you can't want to leave Meristan and Vastin to...?"

Samily put a hand on Glorbad's shoulder. "I understand. I know what you've seen. I know what it means to you. When we follow orders, people still die. Sometimes, we have to weigh the good we can do. This would be such a good, Glorbad."

It was the first time Aranok could recall her addressing him by name. Or anyone, come to think of it.

"What if he's wrong?" The soldier's voice now echoed with uncertainty. "What if we do this, and he's wrong?"

"Never be afraid to hope," said the knight. "Hope is the only thing no one can take from you. Hope is life. Without it, we are nothing."

After a long pause, Glorbad nodded. "What about the Auld Road? We have to cross it to get to Traverlyn. As soon as the Blackened see us, they're going to come for us. Then what?"

Aranok breathed out in relief. He was thinking like a strategist again. "You're right. That's a problem." He turned to Morienne. "A problem I hope you can help with."

"Me?" Morienne's surprise was palpable, as if he'd stirred her from slumber. "What can I do?"

"If they can't see us, they don't come for us, right?" He asked the question of Morienne, but he was looking at Glorbad.

"Yes," the woman answered.

"It'll take us a day to get back to the Auld Road. So if we leave in the morning, we'll reach it by nightfall. We'll cross in the dark. And Morienne"—he turned to her—"will be our scout."

"Scout?" she asked. "I'm no scout."

"That's brilliant," said Allandria. "You scout ahead, take one horse with you to carry rope and rags. Any Blackened you come across, you calm and bind them before we even get there."

"But..." Morienne objected.

"It's fine," Allandria assured her. "You're a natural. None of us saw you when we arrived. And nobody's calmer around Blackened."

"And that way," said Aranok, "we don't kill them. We can save them."

Glorbad breathed deeply. "All right. That's not a bad plan." He looked to Morienne. "You in?" She nodded hesitantly.

"All right. Traverlyn," the soldier said flatly.

"Excellent." Aranok smiled and put out a hand.

Glorbad looked at him impassively, his eyes like glass. "I told you, Envoy. I said you'd get him killed."

Aranok lowered the hand. "I know."

Glorbad nodded and turned away toward the river. Aranok would need to keep an eye on that. The soldier wasn't all right. The drinking, the melancholy, the outbursts—he recognised it after what Samily had said. Sometimes people come back from war incomplete. Every time a broken thing is put back together, pieces are lost. Glorbad was broken. At least he understood why now. It could easily have been him. Sometimes he wondered if it wasn't.

"Laird Aranok?" Morienne said quietly.

He turned toward her and did his best to look her in the eye. It took great concentration. She looked down, her right hand held protectively across her stomach.

"Please, just Aranok."

"Aranok." Her voice trembled. Her hands were shaking. "You...you can really...lift a curse?" The words were tiny. Scared.

Hopeful.

*Of course.* How had he been so thoughtless? Fighting every instinct, he took her cold hands. "Morienne, come with us to Traverlyn. Whatever else happens, if it can be done, I will lift your curse."

# CHAPTER 21

Through the dancing flames of the campfire, Samily watched
Glorbad lift the flask from his belt, unscrew the lid and drink
deeply. In some ways, he reminded her of Meristan, another man who
bore a heavy sadness she did not understand.

He proffered the drink. "Whisky?"

*Very like Meristan.*

"No. Thank you," she answered. "I prefer to be alert on watch."

He shrugged and took another drink. Aranok believed it unlikely
they would be bothered by more Blackened, or by the insect-like things
he had described, but Reivers were always a concern—unlikely as it was
that they would venture into the Black Meadows. Samily was happy
to volunteer for the mid-night watch. She hadn't slept well anyway—
couldn't stop thinking about Meristan. He'd been lost to her. And then
there was hope from nothing. She had to trust that God would watch
over him—over both of them.

Glorbad sighed.

"What troubles you, soldier?" she asked.

"I just…I don't know." He threw a stone into the dirt. "Dunno what
to do."

"About what?"

"All of it. What's it for? What's the bloody point?" He looked up at
the sky.

That was a bigger question than she had expected.

"Is that why you drink?" she asked. "Because you are lost?"

"Lost?" Glorbad laughed. "I don't know that I've ever thought myself lost, girl. Temporarily confused, maybe."

"Hmm."

"What does that mean?" He looked at her suspiciously, as if expecting a slight from her next words.

"I asked you a serious question, and you made a joke."

"And?"

"You didn't like the question?"

He was quiet for a moment. His eyes ran over her, examining her. It was uncomfortable.

"How many men have you known, girl?"

Samily felt heat rise from her neck as she blushed furiously.

He raised his hands defensively. "No, not like that. I mean how many men have you known well? Other than Brother Meristan."

*Oh. Good.*

She thought about it. She knew Tull quite well. They'd grown up together at Baile Airneach. And Merrick. Though the way he looked at her sometimes made her uncomfortable. Like he was hungry and she was a hare. A few of the other brothers maybe—Caparth and Habersin. "A few." The words came out more defensively than she'd intended.

"I'll tell you something about men. All men wrestle with a dark heart. All of them. Some win. Some lose. Some embrace it. And some"—he held up the flask—"drown it."

He took another small mouthful and spat it at the fire, which flared, crackled and spat back at him. He looked at her through the flames with a maudlin half smile.

"What does your heart want?" Samily asked.

Glorbad looked up thoughtfully, frowning. "I honestly don't know. Can't remember the last time I slept well, the last time I woke up rested. I'm so fucking tired."

"Perhaps less whisky...?"

Glorbad snorted. He held up the flask. "Without this, I wouldn't sleep at all."

Samily interlocked her fingers and leaned forward, elbows on her knees. "You have nightmares?" She'd known many who did. The scars of war were not only on the skin.

He looked up at her, and then away. "Aye. Sometimes."

"Bad memories?"

"Some memories, aye. Faces of the dead. The men I failed. The women. The children."

Something about the way he said "children" was odd. "You have a family?"

Glorbad stared at the fire for a long time, gently tapping his finger against the metal flask. For a moment, Samily wondered if he had heard her and opened her mouth to ask again, but the words did not come. Instead, she watched in silence as the soldier drained the flask, stood and walked out of the firelight.

Maybe she was wrong about him. Maybe he wasn't like Meristan.

Or maybe he was.

And that was worse.

---

The sun was barely up when Allandria opened the gates to let Morienne out of Lepertoun. She sucked in a nervous, tight breath at the sight of her companions. The woman led the horse by its reins, its back a pile of rope and cloth. But it was the others who carved a nauseating hole in her gut. Meristan and Vastin were each attached to the horse's side by a length of rope binding their wrists. It was best that Samily slept now. She wouldn't enjoy this. Morienne had fashioned hoods from pillowcases—more reliable than blindfolds, less likely to come undone or fall and send them into a frenzy. Not that Morienne would be in any danger, but they might attract unwanted attention.

"You all right with this?" Allandria asked. She could feel the hairs on the back of her neck rising as Morienne came closer. A tingle ran down her arms and goose bumps rose on her flesh. She clenched her fists against the instinct to back away.

"I think so. I mean, it's fairly simple. I lead them to within sight of the Auld Road, stop and wait for you. You definitely want to take these two with us?" Morienne nodded at the hooded pair.

"Yes. They're strong enough to travel, and the sooner we can lift their curse the less damage they'll bear," said Allandria. "But anyway, I don't think Samily would let us leave Meristan behind."

Morienne nodded. "Then I'll see you tonight."

"You don't want company? It's a long day."

Morienne shrugged. "You're kind, but it would be hard for you. And you're not immune. I'm used to being alone. It is what it is."

That was true, but it didn't make her feel any better about it. Morienne had assured them she could look after herself. She wore a short wooden jaegerstock strapped to her back, with dark blades at each end, and several knives strapped to her belt. She certainly looked like she knew what she was doing.

"Be safe." Allandria closed the gate behind her. It felt wrong, letting her go alone. Aranok had said the chance of Reivers being out there was tiny—and in their current state, Meristan and Vastin would likely ward them off anyway. Thakhati wouldn't be out during daylight. Demons were uncommon and preferred the dark—and there was little prey out here to draw them. But still. She didn't like it.

Back at the dwindling fire, Allandria pulled strips of dried meat from the rations bag. It was tough, salty, and brought back memories of sleeping rough in the war. They'd been lucky to have beds recently.

Even if things were bad, they were better than they had been. That was something.

---

"There's another one." Allandria pointed ahead. Aranok squinted. Her eyesight was better than his—one of the many things that made her a better scout. Plus, she was sneaky, which was usually a good thing.

He could just make out the solitary Blackened. As they drew closer, it became clear Morienne had taken care of her already. The teenage girl was blindfolded and her wrists bound, just like the other three they'd seen through the day.

"She looks fresh," said Nirea, from horseback. She did, which meant the girl had probably been cursed since the horde came north. It was already spreading. They needed to find a way to lift the curse quickly when they reached Traverlyn. Who knew how much time they had before the spread became uncontrollable? Hell, what if it had already reached Traverlyn?

"Do you think they know?" asked Samily. "Do you think they suffer?"

"God, I hope not." Glorbad had insisted on leading the pack horse this evening. "Hells, I'd rather be dead."

Allandria slapped his shoulder and nodded silently to Samily. The knight was watching the young girl intently. She'd all but stopped walking. She didn't need a reason to think of Meristan suffering.

Glorbad shrugged. "I would," he mouthed at Allandria.

"Shut up," she mouthed back.

Aranok understood how she felt. Yesterday, the Blackened had been all but walking corpses. Today, they knew they were more. That the people, the thinking, feeling people, were still in there. Maybe. Today, they were victims of an insidious, evil *mollachd*. Tomorrow, maybe they could be whole again. In the meantime, they were a danger to everyone else. It was all but overwhelming to think on for too long. Who could have imagined such an awful curse? What darkness must live in them to cause such widespread, random pain? He hoped it was Mynygogg. At least that would mean there wasn't another *draoidh* out there this evil, this cruel.

"I pray they are not aware," said Samily. "I pray God walks with them."

And there, she lost him. Aranok had never understood how the faithful maintained their unshakable belief in a benevolent god in the face of such misery. Truthfully, he didn't care either way whether God existed or not.

He'd certainly seen no evidence of it today.

———◦———

The moss-caked dry stane dyke snaked its way north, winding through scattered copses. Allandria's steps crunched in the carpet of dead leaves. The wreckage of infested, mouldering crops did not reach the wall, offering surer footing for the horses. The western side of the wall must have been grazing land, as a sea of wild grass rolled away from the tree line. What had happened to the animals that fed there? Without farmers to care for them, did they starve? Wander off? Fall to predators? The Blackened unsettled the horses—they likely terrified the agricultural beasts too. One break in the wall and they'd all find their way free. As Allandria was considering it, a gap in the trees revealed the rotting husk of a sheep carcass.

Predators, then.

"Land ahoy." Nirea pointed ahead.

Allandria squinted in the gathering dark to see the outline of the pack horse. As they got closer, she could see the horse was tied to a gatepost, with the huge figure of Meristan standing idly in front of it. She assumed Vastin was still on the other side. Seeing them again made her heart skip. Through the day's travelling, she had managed to forget—or at least not think about them. Morienne sat cross-legged a few feet from the horse, eating.

Nobody spoke. They were too close to the Auld Road. They needed to be quiet here and wait for total dark. Samily walked almost to within touching distance of Meristan and watched him silently.

"We have a problem," Morienne said quietly, before even a hello had passed between them.

"Are you all right?" Allandria asked.

"Fine." Morienne dismissed her, as if it were an odd question to ask. "But we can't cross easily."

"Damn it," whispered Aranok. "Too many Blackened?"

"Just one. But she's right in our path. I tied the horse here and went up to the road—to see if it was clear. There's a break in the trees near the junction to Traverlyn, where we can walk the horses through. But there's a woman at the crossroads."

"Right," said Aranok. "Can't you just…?" He raised his hands, held together as if bound.

"I can," said Morienne, "but as soon as she sees me, she'll frenzy until I reach her. And there's a large pack of them about a hundred yards that way." She pointed west, the direction they'd run into the horde a few days ago. God, was it only a few days?

"I thought they only hunted on sight," said Glorbad. "Wait until it's dark, right…?"

"Well, yes, but if she starts screaming she'll attract the others," Morienne explained. "If they get close enough to see us..."

"They'll follow us straight to Traverlyn," Aranok finished. Morienne nodded. "Shite."

Unlike Mournside, Traverlyn was not a walled city. It could be overrun.

"All right." Glorbad opened his hands. "So we kill it, right? We've got an archer." He nodded to Allandria. She flinched instinctively. The thought of killing another Blackened was...God, after the baby?

"No. We're not killing her." Aranok obviously agreed. Of course.

"Look, I appreciate the sentiment, lad, but..."

Aranok cut him off. "I said no."

Glorbad bristled, shook his head and walked a few paces away.

"What are our other options?" Nirea asked.

"I'll move her," said Aranok. He could use *gluais* from a distance.

"And what if she sees you first?" the sailor countered.

"She won't." Aranok sounded confident, but she knew he couldn't be sure. He could be sneaky, quiet as Hell for a man of his size, but it wasn't that simple. He would need to see the Blackened to use his magic. It was already pretty dark. He'd have to get close, and then with the gestures and speaking the word...

"Aranok," she said. "It's too risky. If she sees you before you can move her. And what if she screams when she's moved? We're only going to get one shot to do this right. If we don't..."

Aranok glowered at her. "I can do it."

"There's another thing," said Morienne. They all turned to face her. "I'm not sure she'd survive anyway."

There was a horrible moment of silence.

"See?" Glorbad had turned back to them. "It's probably a mercy." Samily snapped her head around at him. He looked back, then turned away. "It's the right decision. We can't save everybody."

Aranok bristled. "We're not even fucking close to saving everybody."

Allandria took his arm and pulled him away from the others. "Let Morienne and me go. If there's a way to do it without killing her, we'll come back. All right?"

"I can do it," he said firmly.

"I know. But think about it. If something goes wrong. If there's another one nearby...Let me go. Trust me."

She brushed his hand with hers. His finger stroked the back of her hand. "All right. I trust you."

Minutes later, Allandria and Morienne had crept to the edge of the road. She was impressed with the woman's stealth. The sad fact was it probably came from a necessity to go unseen in order to survive. Slowly, Allandria pressed down the leaves of the bush she crouched behind.

"Can you see her?" Morienne had been keeping herself a good distance away, so as not to affect Allandria's eyesight or concentration.

It wasn't good. The Blackened woman must have been in her thirties, maybe younger. Her fair hair was matted over hollow, dark eyes. What might once have been a pretty summer dress was now streaked brown and green. She knelt on her right leg, struggling to stand, and failing—but she kept trying, like a weathervane spinning in the wind. Her left leg was the problem. At the knee, it made an ugly break sideways, like a branch snapped in a storm. Her muscles were too weak to support her weight—her bones brittle from lack of food. She must have been one of those that migrated up from the Meadows. It was surprising she'd even made it this far. She'd probably been Blackened for months, to be so scrawny. Unless she'd been starving before she was turned. God, that was a horrible thought.

A shiver ran down Allandria's back. She stretched her shoulders and shook it off.

"You see what I mean?" Morienne asked.

She'd been sugaring it. The poor thing had no chance. She was already dead, she just didn't know it. The minute her curse was lifted, she'd die of malnutrition. The curse was all that was keeping her going.

Allandria nocked an arrow. Quietly, she took aim.

*Breathe in.*

But she couldn't release. Now that she knew about these people—that they were cursed, that they could be saved—killing one wasn't easy. They weren't monsters. They weren't vermin. They were people. Innocent people.

This woman had a life. A childhood. She'd played and laughed and loved—if she was lucky. She'd had dreams. Would there be anyone left to miss her? To even know she was gone? To remember her name?

Allandria felt a tear run down her cheek. "I'll remember you." She breathed out and released.

The woman stopped her endless attempts to stand and slumped forward onto her own knee before toppling over to the left. What remained of her broken leg made a sickening crunch as she landed on it. She looked like a bag of bones, discarded in a back alley. Allandria closed her eyes, but it was too late. That image was with her now. Always.

Allandria was pale when she and Morienne returned. Nirea didn't bother to ask what had happened. Aranok exchanged quiet words with the archer, while Morienne prepared the horse and their hooded friends. He looked angry, or upset; it was hard to tell. He could be difficult to read.

Quietly, the archer waved them all on. It was as dark as it would get, and they needed to move as soon as possible. Nirea's hips ached. All this walking was no good for her. She wanted a boat beneath her feet and a sea to swim in. Closing her eyes, she imagined seawater on her skin—the cool, clean embrace of the ocean. It felt like years since she'd been there, tasted the salt in the air and felt completely alive.

They slowed as they approached the gap in the trees. Morienne raised her hand and waved them forward. They walked slowly—especially Glorbad, who was aware his armour made more noise than the rest of them. Vastin moved only as quickly as the pack horse, and Samily's armour was as oddly quiet as it was light.

Aranok, Allandria and she wore leathers, which were as quiet as needed, while Morienne's black clothing and Meristan's robes were as good as silent.

The horses were a worry. Another reason they had to stay quiet. The sound of hooves wouldn't necessarily attract the Blackened, if they were as sight-driven as Morienne said, but Nirea still felt every click of their hooves like a cannonball hitting the deck.

Ahead of her, Morienne led her horse, with their friends attached, followed by Aranok and Allandria with another horse, then Samily. Nirea was next, leading her horse, with Glorbad last. She stepped slowly out into the road. The dark made it difficult to see more than about twenty feet away. But she didn't need to see—she could hear the murmur of the Blackened Morienne had described. There was a low hum, and the shuffling of dozens, maybe hundreds of feet. She peered up the road, but the darkness gave her nothing. The trees lining the Auld Road disappeared into blackness. The air picked up and she was hit with the stink of the unwashed. She gagged and put a hand to her nose. Normally, she'd have been glad to be downwind of something hunting her, but since that didn't matter here she would have much preferred it the other way around.

With a start, her horse whinnied a protest.

Nirea snapped her head around. What was it? A Blackened they'd missed? Reivers?

She looked down to see an arm across her path. She'd been so distracted with the remaining Blackened, she'd nearly stepped on the one Allandria had killed. Hells, there was practically nothing left of her. Poor bitch. Looked like she hadn't eaten in months. Nirea soothed the horse and guided it around the corpse. Shame they couldn't even stop and give the girl the dignity of a burial. Samily would have wanted that. There wasn't a lot of dignity around these days.

She reached the other side of the road and joined the others, out of sight of the Blackened, on the road to Traverlyn. She waved Glorbad across. But he wasn't looking. His head was tilted up, toward the trees. Suddenly, he started walking—quicker than he should. He looked awkward, like a man trying to hurry and be slow at the same time.

"What's he doing?" Samily whispered. Nirea shrugged. She had no idea what the idiot was up to. She waved her hands at him to slow him down, but he glanced over his shoulder and continued clanking across the road. Oh Hells, he wasn't looking down at all, but scanning the trees instead, so when he reached the dead Blackened on the road, he kicked her leg and stumbled with a loud clunk.

Nirea stopped breathing. She listened intently, trying to tune out the sounds of the night and focus on whether there were footsteps charging down the road toward them. She didn't think so.

Glorbad continued his odd stagger across the road and practically ran into Nirea, waiting for him.

"What the fuck are you doing?" she whispered.

His white eyes were wide in the dark. "Cocoons. In the trees!"

# CHAPTER 22

They'd quickly walked a few hundred yards away from the junction to talk. Samily hadn't grasped the significance of "cocoons" until she heard the word *Thakhati* and remembered the stories of bug-like monsters in the night.

They needed to move quickly. Morienne untied Meristan and Vastin, and Aranok used his abilities to lift them both onto the back of a horse. Morienne looped the ropes under the horse and tied them to their feet. Clever. They'd be secure that way.

Glorbad, the least mobile of the party, was given the other horse. The rest would be on foot.

Samily took the reins of the pack horse. Morienne led the horse with Brother Meristan and the boy.

And they ran.

Allandria, bow in hand, and Nirea, swords drawn, ran at the front to set the pace. Aranok followed, just ahead of Glorbad on his mount, while Samily and Morienne led the horses at the back. It was only a trot for the animals. Samily kept her sword sheathed. She could draw it quickly enough, and the weight would unbalance her running. She thanked God for the light weight of her armour.

Traverlyn was only five miles away, but they were all tired. They wouldn't be able to keep up this pace.

Samily pounded on, trying not to think about the ache in her legs, the pain in her feet, the twinge in her shoulder from pulling the horse.

*Run. Run. Run.*

After a few miles, Allandria pulled up and raised a hand. They stopped. Samily's heart pounded in her chest and all she could hear was her own heavy breathing.

As it slowed, she heard something else.

Rustling. Movement.

Even in the dark, she could see the trees were alive. For a long, silent moment, nobody moved.

They'd run into an ambush.

"Aim for the face or the slats! Cut up!" Allandria cried, and suddenly there was chaos as dark shapes dropped from branches.

A deep thud behind Samily. She turned to see the hulking shadow rear up: an unholy mix of man and insect—exactly as they'd described. She drew her sword and brought it down in one movement, taking off two arms. Thank God, the Green blade was as effective against these things as against demons. The monster screamed in rage, baring its awful teeth. It turned and tried to run but, unbalanced, tumbled to the side.

A clash of metal from behind the horse. A shout from Nirea she couldn't understand. Two more shapes crawled down trees. They fell on the wounded one, tearing, shredding until there was little left but blood and gristle.

They reared up and stalked toward her, dripping gore from their eight hands. More cautious than the first. They'd seen what she could do.

A cry behind her. She looked round to see Morienne on the ground, a Thakhati looming over her. Her jaegerstock was jammed between its scales. The beast was stuck, but its four dark arms thrashed violently, frantically trying to reach her. The woman's clothes were no armour.

Samily stepped back, turned and brought her sword up, decapitating it. The head landed with a dull thud and rolled away as she turned back to face the other two.

"Thank you," Morienne gasped, throwing off the thing's body.

More fighting behind them, beyond the horses. A cry of pain. She needed to finish these two quickly—to help their friends. The pack horse whinnied and jerked nervously, steam rising from its nostrils.

"Above you!" Morienne called. Samily looked up. Another, hanging from a branch. Another, over Morienne's horse. Like spiders, these things! She swiped at the nearest. It recoiled, dodging the cut.

The other slashed at Meristan and Vastin. She lunged and stabbed it through the back. It dropped, screaming, to the ground. Samily stabbed her blade into the earth, grabbed two arms and heaved it toward the other two, now stalking Morienne. They quickly eviscerated it, giving her a moment to think.

"Get the horses in the middle!" she said to Morienne. The woman pulled both reins to bring the horses in from the edges, to where the branches were thinner. Samily glanced over her shoulder. Glorbad had dismounted and was using his shield to force the Thakhati back. Aranok pushed them back with his magic. Pushing them back would not be enough. They needed to kill them.

The two facing her crept forward again. Samily pulled Morienne in behind her protectively.

"I tied the reins together," the woman said.

"Good. Stay there."

A third, from the tree, dropped to the ground, landing on all six limbs. It cocked its head at her curiously, and she felt a shiver. It felt like evil; cold, dark evil. But worse, it looked intelligent. No mindless demons these.

She swiped her blade wide and held it high, her empty hand out in warning.

"Allandria!" A panicked cry. She hoped the archer was all right.

Samily lowered her sword. She needed them closer.

"Watch above," she said to Morienne.

The three drew in slowly, chattering. A warning intended to take her courage. She backed away, allowing them to get almost within reach, and slapped the pack horse's side. It kicked out, catching one Thakhati in the chest and knocking it back into the trees. She lunged forward and slashed at the left one, catching it across the chest. It screamed in surprise and anger.

Something hit her from the right, and she was facedown. The third must have attacked. S'grace, they were quick!

Her right arm was pinned above her head, holding her sword. She felt the thing scrabbling and stabbing at her armour, looking for a way into her flesh. She released the sword from her right hand and reached for it with her left. The other Thakhati leapt over them. Morienne screamed—not in pain; it was a cry of war.

Samily twisted and thrust the sword back over her shoulder, poking the monster in the face. It recoiled and, off-balance, fell away as Samily rolled. She came up onto one knee as it lunged again, only to impale itself on her sword. She stood, lifting sword and monster with her. Its own weight split it from gut to skull and it dropped like a side of hog.

She turned to Morienne. The woman pulled her jaegerstock's blade from the chest wound Samily had opened on the other. It twitched but stayed down.

"Well done." Samily nodded.

Still the sounds of battle from beyond the horses. She prayed her allies stood. She prayed for all of them.

The Thakhati kicked by the horse reappeared from the dark. It looked angry. Rearing back, it unleashed a shriek so piercing that Samily tried to cover her ears even through her helm.

Silence. She looked up.

The trees trembled with life.

Dark, metallic arms and legs appeared as if from everywhere. They dropped to the road, skittered down trunks, appeared through gaps in the trees as far ahead as she could see. The screamer cocked its head at her. Bravado. A challenge.

Samily might survive this—but not all of them would. Morienne and Meristan wore no armour. And she was starting to feel the dizzying effects of being too close to the cursed woman.

She shook her head to clear it. There were ten, a dozen, more, closing in on them. That was just those she could see. She backed against the horse. They were running out of space. She reached her arm across Morienne, pulling her close behind her.

A swipe from the left. She batted it away. Two crawled toward her like giant tailless scorpions. She took the head off one to her right. Another fell on it, all claws and teeth.

"To me!"

Samily quickly glanced round. It was the envoy. He'd mounted

Glorbad's horse. What was he doing? There was nowhere to run. They were surrounded.

"Let them close!" he shouted.

"Are you mad?" Glorbad bellowed. Samily found herself agreeing with the soldier.

"Just do it!" shouted Allandria.

Samily swiped again, keeping the nearest out of reach. If the *draoidh* wanted them close, he must have a plan. Morienne stabbed at the face of one on the ground. It paused but kept coming.

It was getting difficult to see through them. Another clawed at her. She swiped, and it recoiled. Closer, closer. Samily darted forward, stabbed the nearest through the gut and danced back into position. This time, the others ignored it when it fell. They eyed bigger prey now. The nearest to her sniffed the air hungrily. Was it the one that screamed? Maybe. It was hard to tell.

Closer.

She could all but feel the things' breath. Soon there wouldn't be room to swing her sword. They were about to be overrun.

"Whatever you're going to do, Envoy, do it now!" she called.

"Close your eyes!" he shouted back.

Close her eyes? Was he mad? She scanned the monsters. If she closed her eyes now, she wouldn't open them again. Maybe it was already too late.

But Brother Meristan trusted this man. She would do the same.

The Thakhati directly in front of her drew back its top two arms, poised to strike. Samily held her sword upright before her, closed her eyes and prayed.

"*Gal!*" the envoy cried.

And suddenly it was day.

---

Nirea pushed the sizzling corpse off her and hesitantly opened her eyes. She blinked, waiting for her sight to return. Her chest ached. Her back too.

"What the fuck was that?" asked Glorbad.

"A sunstone," said Aranok.

She was beginning to see shapes again. Silhouettes moving in the inky blackness. She pushed herself to her feet.

"Everyone all right?" Aranok called urgently.

"Fit as a fiddle," said Glorbad, though he breathed heavily.

"Fine!" reported Allandria.

"Yes, all right," said Morienne.

"I'm fine." Nirea felt her side. Her leathers had taken a beating, but nothing had got through. She'd have some bruised ribs tomorrow, though.

"Fine, yes," said Samily. "Well played, Envoy."

Nirea's sight finally cleared enough to make out her surroundings. It was mostly smoking Thakhati. She counted at least twenty, but she knew there were more around the other side of the horses. They'd been as good as dead. Thank all the Hells for Aranok's trick. She'd never been happier to be with a *draoidh*.

"Why the fuck did you wait so long to do that?" Glorbad asked.

Aranok climbed down from the horse. "I could only do it once." He staggered slightly as he reached the ground. "I had to get them all." He held out a stone. It looked like an ordinary rock.

"How did that work?" Nirea asked.

"I've had it soaking up sun since Mutton Hole. I released it all."

Glorbad laughed. "Well, that's a damn fine trick, lad! I wish I'd known you could do that."

"If everyone knows what you can do, your enemies can plan to beat you," said Aranok.

Glorbad nodded in appreciation. Nirea might have called it respect. It wasn't something she'd seen from him on this trip, other than for Samily.

"How many of them you got?" Glorbad asked.

"That was it. While it's soaking, it drains me. I can't do more than one at a time. I'll start it again tomorrow." Aranok put the stone back inside a little metal cage that hung around his neck. Nirea remembered seeing it and wondering what it was for. She'd taken it for an affectation—not a mistake she'd make again.

"Thank you." Nirea offered her hand.

Aranok looked at her oddly for a moment, then took it. "Of course." Samily screamed.

They both jumped and turned to find her frantically scrabbling at the horse carrying Meristan and Vastin.

"Blood!" she called. She was right. Nirea could see it dripping off the animal's belly.

"Don't touch him!" Aranok barked.

Samily caught herself with her hand outstretched. She turned to Morienne. "Please..."

Morienne ran her hands over Meristan, looking for the wound. Not on his legs, his back, his head. She felt under his neck and slid her hands under him as much as she could.

"Need him down," she said to Aranok. The *draoidh* nodded. She untied his feet and Aranok lifted him onto the ground. Samily paced like a trapped animal. Nirea put a hand on her arm, and the knight stopped. She looked up at her, lips trembling.

"He'll be all right." Nirea tried to sound soothing. She hoped it was true.

"Allandria, Glorbad—keep watch." Aranok pointed to the trees. Of course. They couldn't get caught unawares now. The pair took a side of the road each and scanned the foliage.

"Nothing," said Morienne. "I can't find where it's coming from. He's wet with it, but..."

"Fuck." Aranok's face was grim. "It's the boy."

Samily shook, partly with relief and partly with shock, Nirea imagined. She looked at Glorbad. The soldier didn't turn.

Morienne dived back to the horse and ran her hands over Vastin, until she yelped.

"Here! His armpit!" She untied him and Aranok lowered him carefully to the ground. Morienne removed his armour as quickly as she could. The boy was bleeding heavily from a nasty slash under his arm. He wasn't moving.

"Is he alive?" Nirea asked.

"Yes. But I need to stop the bleeding. Get me some rags."

Nirea grabbed a handful from the packhorse and rejected the top ones as too dirty. She handed the cleanest she could find to Morienne, who bundled them up to pack the wound and tied them as tight as she could. "All right. I think I've stopped it."

"Will he live?" asked Aranok.

Morienne frowned. "Ironically, the curse is protecting him. He's fine for now, but..."

She didn't need to finish. Lifting the Blackening would kill him.

"I can heal him!" Samily was still jittery—nervous. "I will heal him."

"You can't touch him," Aranok said quietly.

"Once he's cured," Samily pleaded.

Aranok tilted his head. "That might take days. By then..."

By then, it might be too late.

"Then for fuck's sake let's get moving!" Glorbad marched toward his mount. "Let's not lose the boy for lack of bloody trying!"

# CHAPTER 23

Aranok's legs had all but given up when the first buildings of Traverlyn finally came into sight.

Nestled in the shadow of the dormant volcano, Archer's Hill, and its smaller, craggy companion, Crow Hill, Traverlyn was Eidyn's nexus of learning and culture. Legend had it that the whole town had grown from one inn, the Sheep's Heid, where travellers from across the world would meet to swap stories, trade goods and share music and art. The Sheep's Heid was still at the heart of the town, both physically and culturally. Musicians played nightly and philosophical debates were hosted regularly. The town's motto was "all welcome" and it functioned as a sanctuary for those otherwise on the edges of society. That the country's university and largest hospital had both been established here was only natural, and they had enhanced the town's reputation.

Magic was all but synonymous with Traverlyn, where any *draoidh* was entitled to a place in the university regardless of wealth or status. It was a hodgepodge of vastly different buildings, some constructed by artisan hands, others with magical assistance. The elegant sandstone buildings of the university campus were interspersed with serene garden quadrangles, growing plants unseen anywhere else in Eidyn. The great redbrick hospital with its majestic spires sat amongst modest cottages, extravagant homes splashed with glorious art, dwellings that looked to have grown organically from the earth, and at least one house

Aranok knew that was entirely constructed around an ancient tree, its canopy spreading over the roof like a shade. Piercing the sky above it all, the spire of ancient Traverlyn kirk, its golden orb like a welcoming sun.

Traverlyn was the only place Aranok had never experienced the sting of a dark look or been refused service because of who he was. That happened less since he'd become envoy, but they were not experiences one forgot—or forgave. In Traverlyn, he felt truly at home—more so than in Mournside, Haven or even Dun Eidyn. Coming here felt like breathing again, like the sun on his face.

But not tonight. Tonight it just felt like relief.

"Identify yourselves!" came a shout. A pair of torches moved toward them. The town guard posted on the road. They had no idea what danger they were in.

"King's Envoy!" he called back between breaths, stopping and putting his hands on his thighs. Blood pounded in his ears.

"Laird Aranok?" One of the torches moved toward him and by its light he made out a blond boy, no more than twenty. "You shouldn't be out here after dark. There are things in the Wilds."

"We know," said Glorbad from his horse. "We killed them."

"That flash," said the boy. "That was you?"

Glorbad nodded to Aranok. "It was him."

Aranok looked round. Morienne had collapsed to the ground, breathing heavily. Samily leaned on the pack horse. Allandria also sat on the ground; Nirea crouched beside her. They were all shattered.

Glorbad dismounted. He was the only one in a fit state to speak to the guards.

"Right, boys, here's what we need." He pointed to the horse carrying Vastin and Meristan.

"Ahem." The other guard cleared her throat. Now she was closer, Aranok could see she was a powerfully built, redheaded woman. And she carried a bow, of course. Allandria's adopted hometown of Lochen was the other side of Archer's Hill. Many of the archers trained there came to work in Traverlyn.

Glorbad glanced at her and carried on. "These two need to go straight to the hospital—but don't let anyone touch them—they're contagious.

Only this woman"—he pointed to Morienne—"can have any direct contact with them, understood?"

The boy nodded.

"Stable these horses. Where can we get rooms?"

"Sheep's Heid's your best bet," said the archer. "S'got the most rooms."

The boy nodded in agreement. "I'll take the horses. Tabera, will you lead them to the hospital?"

"Aye." The archer offered Morienne a hand to get up.

"I'm coming with you." Aranok needed to explain to the medics. And possibly use some of his authority to make sure they didn't execute Vastin and Meristan as soon as they realised what they were. And he needed to find Conifax.

"As am I," said Samily.

"Fine," said Glorbad. "The rest of us will find beds."

---

Traverlyn hospital was a beautiful, sprawling red sandstone building. It had been constructed through a combination of engineering and magical skill and was one of the most impressive structures in the kingdom. Perhaps only the university and Dun Eidyn itself rivalled it.

Aranok hammered on the large oak doors. After a short wait, an elderly woman dressed in blue robes opened one, scowling. Aranok didn't recognise her.

"What do you think you're doing, making such a racket at this time of night?"

"I'm Aranok, king's envoy. Our friends are in urgent need of help." He gestured behind him. They must have looked a sight. A *draoidh* in runic leathers, a White Thorn in full armour, and a cursed woman in black leading a pair of bound and hooded men behind her. The lot of them bedraggled and stinking.

"Well." The woman cocked her head and opened the doors wide. "You'd better come in."

"Before we enter," said Aranok, "the men are contagious. Only Morienne can touch them."

The woman raised a sceptical eyebrow. "Contagious with what?"

"That's a long story. I will explain, but they need private rooms. Locked."

The woman frowned. "You're right. You will explain."

Aranok turned to the guard. "Thank you for the escort. May I ask a favour?"

Tabera nodded.

"Do you know Master Conifax?"

"I know of him."

"We need him. Could you have someone fetch him, please?"

"Tonight?" she asked.

"Yes. Wake him if necessary. Tell him Aranok needs him at the hospital urgently."

He knew Conifax would come. He hoped he'd be in a good mood. And he hoped he'd forgive him for bringing a pair of Blackened into the heart of Traverlyn.

When they'd moved to a secure room and settled the pair, Aranok finally said the word he'd been carefully avoiding until that moment.

"Blackened."

"And you brought them here? Are you mad?" Egretta, the woman who'd greeted them, bellowed at him. He'd been hearing that a lot recently. Morienne was carefully stitching Vastin's wound under another medic's instruction. The medic, a grey-haired, slender man, looked up at Aranok, then at Morienne, and took a step back. His eyes asked the same question of Aranok's sanity.

It wasn't going well. Once they'd got Vastin's armour off, they could see the wound was even worse than it had appeared in the dark. His arm had nearly come off.

"Are you trying to get us killed?" Egretta demanded.

Aranok put up his hands in defence. "Of course not. I'm trying to save us."

"And how the Hell is this doing that?" she demanded through gritted teeth. It seemed she'd abandoned her earlier concern for quiet. "Hell, boy, we need to put these two down before they infect the whole hospital!"

Egretta turned as if to leave, but Aranok grabbed her arm. She looked back at him murderously. "What?"

"If I'm right," he said calmly, "it's not a plague. It's a curse."

"A curse?" The anger faded from her like a wave. She turned away to look at Meristan, tied against the wall. "That's why you want Conifax."

"It is."

"If it's a curse..." Egretta trailed off. Aranok nodded. She understood.

*Good.*

"I'm sorry, what does that mean?" asked the medic, who had backed as far from Vastin as the room allowed.

"If it's true," Egretta said gravely, "if it's a curse—then perhaps it can be lifted. Right?"

The last was directed at Aranok. He nodded.

"I trust that all the shouting is down to my former student?" Aranok's shoulders relaxed as he heard the voice down the corridor. He looked past Egretta to see his old master coming toward them. His round glasses and shaggy grey beard were even more comforting than the sight of Traverlyn had been.

"Conifax!" Aranok greeted him with open arms. The old man embraced him enthusiastically. He felt thin under the robes. It had been a long time since Aranok had seen him, but still, the change was shocking.

"You've lost weight," he said, holding the man at arm's length.

"I've gained years!" Conifax answered with a cheeky grin. "Never mind that, what's so important you had me raised in the middle of the night, boy?" The old man peeked curiously into the room.

Aranok turned to Egretta. "Is there somewhere we can talk? And, actually, eat?" His stomach was growling, and he felt a little light-headed.

"The kitchens are closed. But I'm sure we can find something. Coben," she said to the medic, "don't touch them. Either of them. Do not leave this room without locking it behind you. She can handle them?" she asked Aranok.

"She can."

Conifax's expression turned serious. "What's going on?"

"I'll explain everything," Aranok said.

"Do a better job than you did with me." Egretta turned and walked down the corridor. Conifax followed. Aranok gestured to Samily to come with them, but she didn't move.

*Of course.*

"It's all right," Aranok said. "Meristan is secured. He can't hurt himself or anyone else. Morienne is with them. Morienne, you're all right?"

The woman looked up from her task only to nod, and continued tending the boy's wound.

The knight stared at her master for a moment, turned and placed a gentle hand on Morienne's shoulder, then followed him.

———

Samily was extremely grateful for the bread and cheese, and the mead to wash it down. As the warm drink reached her stomach, she felt a wave of tiredness land. It had been a very long day—and it wasn't over.

"Why do you think it's a curse?" Conifax leaned back in his chair. The old man had Meristan's authority and a similar bright wisdom in his eyes. The four of them sat around a table in the kitchen. Based on the cuts and stains, Samily assumed the worktop was commonly used for preparing food, not eating it. The scarred wood smelled of garlic, onion and fish.

"Our companion, Morienne, is immune," Aranok answered.

"There's something not right about that girl," Egretta said, bristling. "I don't like her."

Aranok looked at Egretta, smiled, and raised his eyebrows at Conifax.

"You don't," the old man said, "because she's cursed?" The envoy nodded. "And if she's immune, that's most likely why?"

"Most likely," said the envoy.

"Oh." Egretta almost crumpled. "Oh, that poor girl. I should apologise. I'm sure I was terribly rude to her."

"She's used to it," said Aranok sadly.

Judging by Egretta's face, that did not make it better. Samily understood. It must feel like kicking a wounded dog. She would pray for Morienne tonight, along with Meristan and the boy.

"So who's going around throwing curses?" Conifax stroked his chin. "That's a hanging offence. Curses have been outlawed for generations."

They had. Under Hofnag, all magic had been outlawed outside of Traverlyn for a long time. The university earned itself an exception. When Janaeus took control, curses remained punishable by death. It was one magic ban the king had kept—for good reason it seemed. For this reason.

"Since the Blackening began just before the war, I'd guess Mynygogg—or an ally," said Aranok.

"You think he had an ally we don't know about?" Conifax's eyebrows rose.

"I don't know. But it's possible. We've encountered...things."

Conifax breathed deeply. He seemed particularly bothered by that possibility. "And the woman?"

"Morienne? No idea. She says it's a family curse," said Aranok.

"Oof, a bloodline curse. That's powerful, dark magic. How far back?" Conifax asked.

"She doesn't know. Her parents, her grandparents, all had it. They've been nomads for generations." Aranok shook his head and took a bite of bread. He looked tired—drawn, the way Samily felt.

"Nobody wants them settling in their town. What kind of bastard does that to a family? To unborn children?" Conifax pointed at Aranok. "It's things like this that make people hate us."

Aranok nodded solemnly.

"Listen, even if the Blackening is a curse and you can lift it," said Egretta, "you've got another problem. That boy's lost too much blood. He'd be dead if he was"—she searched for the word—"normal."

"That's why I wanted Samily here." The *draoidh* turned to look at her expectantly. He raised his eyebrows. "May I?"

This was exactly what Meristan had warned her about. Once one person knew, it would be impossible to keep it a secret. And then...

But wasn't that what she wanted? And wasn't it surely what God wanted her to do with the ability? She had faith God would not ask more of her than she could do. And if so, truthfully, she would gladly give her life in service to God's children. God had brought her here, now, to this place, with these people. Perhaps they could cure a plague that had seemed unstoppable. She nodded her permission to Aranok and he turned back to the others.

"Strictly between the four of us," he said in a hushed voice, "Samily is a healer."

Egretta spat out a breath of air.

"Rubbish," said Conifax. "Healers don't exist, boy. I taught you that when you were twelve years old."

Aranok sighed and looked at his old teacher. "I've seen her do it. Twice. I wouldn't be sitting here telling you if I wasn't certain. She's a healer."

"Have you, now?" Conifax stroked his beard and looked intently at Samily. It was uncomfortable, as if she were a rat in a cage.

"My God, girl." Egretta became agitated, as if she could barely sit still. "Do you know what this means? The people you can help?"

"No," said Aranok. "It drains her. Like no magic I've seen. She can only do so much."

"But...but there are children..." the medic pleaded.

Samily felt her heart sink. Sick children. Surely this was what her powers were for? "I would like to help. What can I do?"

Egretta stood and paced. "My God. My God. I don't know where to start!"

"Start by sitting down," said Conifax. "There's more to discuss."

Egretta sat down, still twitching.

Conifax looked at Samily over steepled fingers. "Tell me, Lady Thorn, how does your ability work?"

"I don't know. It just does. I say some prayer words for them to heal, put my hands on their wound, and..." Samily opened her palms and shrugged.

"Interesting," said the old man. "How did you learn to use the power?"

"I don't know." She was aware she was repeating herself. She'd always known how. Meristan often told the story of how she'd seen a nasty bruise on his shoulder when she was four years old. She'd pestered him to let her touch it, and when he did, it healed. It was the moment he said he knew she was truly a gift from God.

"You don't know?" Conifax asked.

"I have always known," said Samily. "Like breathing."

"Like breathing," he echoed. "And you find it exhausting?"

"Yes," Aranok answered for her. "I've said that."

"I'd like to hear it from her." Conifax's admonishing tone reminded Samily again of Meristan. The envoy seemed disgruntled but didn't argue.

"Yes," Samily answered.

"Do you take on the wounds yourself? Is it a sympathetic healing?" he asked.

Samily was starting to feel a little irritated by the questioning. As if she had done something wrong. It must have been evident from her face, because the old man quickly interjected before she could answer.

"Sorry, sorry, it's late, and I am less diplomatic than I should be. Forgive me."

Samily took a drink of her mead and again felt it warm her stomach. He was right, it was late, and she felt it more every passing moment.

Conifax turned back to Aranok. "So what is your plan, Envoy?" He said the title with a hint of humour that Samily found disrespectful. Aranok may have been this man's student once, but he was the king's envoy now. The old man's words were improper.

"You remove the curse; Samily heals the wound," Aranok said plainly.

"Can she put blood back in him?" asked Conifax. "Egretta has just told you that's his biggest problem."

"I have healed those who have lost blood before," said Samily. "It should be fine."

Aranok gestured to her. "It should be fine."

Conifax took a deep breath. He looked back and forth between them. "All right. We'll do it your way. I'll need a day or two to do some reading. Contagious curses are nasty, tricky things. Easy to get wrong and end up cursed yourself. Bloodline curses—even worse. That one will take a while."

"All right," said Aranok. "We'll focus on the Blackening first?"

Conifax tipped his head. "Of course. That is most urgent."

"Is there nothing we can do now?" Samily hated the idea of Meristan suffering alone in a cell for days.

"Yes!" said Egretta. "There are people who need…"

"I'm sorry," Aranok interrupted. "But no. Not until Meristan is back. He knows what she can take. He knows how to care for her."

Samily bristled. She disliked being spoken for, even by the envoy, and in her interest.

"I can help." She tried not to sound angry. "And I will."

"What happens if that costs Vastin his life?" Aranok asked.

*What?* "Why should it cost the boy anything?"

"The Blackening is both killing him and keeping him alive. At the moment. Without food and water, his body will decay. With his injury, it could happen quicker." He looked at Egretta, who nodded. "We need you ready to heal him the moment Conifax lifts the curse. And what if you've put yourself into a deep sleep when that happens? What if the delay costs Vastin his life? Can you live with that?"

Samily flushed. It wasn't a fair question. "You're asking me to put Vastin's life before others because I know him. All of God's children are equal."

"So why doesn't Meristan have you here all the time, healing?" Aranok asked.

He was right about that. Meristan had always warned her to keep quiet. Not take on too much. But then, he'd been questioning himself recently. Was that one of the reasons?

"I don't know," she answered honestly.

"So can we at least agree that you wait until Meristan is cured and discuss it with him?"

"You don't have to listen to him, you know." Egretta pointed at Aranok. "You're your own person. You choose what to do with your gift."

There was something desperate about her. Heaven, how many people must she have watched die, helpless to save them. Samily must seem like a gift from God to her too. But that desperation was also unnerving. It reminded her of Meristan's warnings. "Everyone will want a piece of you," he'd said. "You'll be torn apart."

"No," she said sadly. "The envoy is right. I will wait for Brother Meristan's advice. I'm sorry." She said the last words looking Egretta in the eye—as she deserved. The woman tutted, stood and bustled out of the room.

"Well, that could have gone better," said Conifax, who'd watched in silence.

"You weren't much help," said Aranok.

"Oh, I learned a long time ago, boy, if you want a swift kick in the stones, tell a woman what to do!" Conifax leaned back in his chair. "Now, if you'll excuse me, I'm going back to my bed. These old bones need rest. As for you two, I'd find yourselves beds. And a bath. You look like Hell."

The sky was lightening when Allandria half woke to Aranok sliding into bed behind her. He smelled terrible—but only because she'd had a chance to bathe. She turned her head sleepily.

"How'd it go?"

"They're alive," he said quietly.

"Can they save them?" She could already feel herself drifting off again.

"Maybe." He snuggled in against her and draped an arm over her waist.

"Huh," she mumbled as sleep overcame her again.

# CHAPTER 24

Nirea banged on the door of Samily's room. She'd apparently come in early that morning and would have needed sleep, but she was on the verge of missing lunch. The girl answered the door half dressed in her grubby aketon and trousers. The front of her top hung open, revealing more than Nirea would have expected, but the knight appeared entirely comfortable.

"Yes?" she asked sleepily.

Nirea looked her up and down. "You should wear something else today. Have that washed. We're not going anywhere. The inn will do it for you."

Samily looked down at herself. "I don't have anything else."

It took Nirea a moment to process this information. "Nothing? What do you do when you need to wash it?"

"If I'm not at Baile Airneach, I take it in the river with me."

"And what about when it's drying?"

Samily shrugged. "I have a blanket."

"So you just sit around naked under a blanket while your clothes dry?"

"If it's cold," the knight answered.

Again, it took Nirea a moment. "And if it's not...?"

Samily shrugged.

Right, she was taking her to a tailor. Nirea was not having Samily sitting around naked in the Wilds. Besides, she found it pleasant to be out of her leathers and into a comfortable shirt and trousers—Samily deserved the same. "Get your boots on, come and eat, then we're going shopping."

"What for?" Samily asked.

"My peace of mind," Nirea shouted back from the stairs.

---

Aranok loved coming to the university library. It was huge, with vaulted wooden arches holding up a ceiling covered in intricate frescos of Eidyn's history. Each side of the three floors was lined with dark wooden shelves, holding the vast majority of human knowledge from the known world. History, magic, medicine—if it was known, it was in this room. On the ground floor were dozens of study desks—large round tables quartered by wooden screens atop them. Students referred to studying in the library as being "in quarters."

He'd found it intimidating as a child, but now he felt a little smarter just breathing in the oak, vanilla and almond. He wore the black doublet and trousers his mother had given him. The greatest likelihood of a fight was after dark, and it was a pleasant change to blend in amongst a crowd in which he felt entirely comfortable. Being a *draoidh* would not make him stand out here, but being recognised as the king's envoy certainly would. There were plenty of well-dressed lairds and ladies sent to the university by their wealthy parents, so even his clothing was unexceptional.

He could almost imagine himself a student here again—his only responsibilities learning to control his magic and deciding which room he and his friends would drink in that night. Much of it was a blur, but there were days and nights he could remember as if he were standing in them now. He breathed deep and closed his eyes, feeling his shoulders drop an inch.

When he opened them, it was to search for his old teacher. Conifax would be here somewhere and he needed to speak to him, away from the others. There were about forty or fifty students milling around already. He finally discovered the old man on the third floor, his nose buried in a book and a stack of six more beside him. Across the table from him, Aranok recognised the owlish figure of Master Balaban, similarly engrossed in a heavy tome. Aranok approached quietly and put a light hand on Conifax's shoulder.

The master held up the index finger of his left hand while he finished reading something, then placed his right index finger on a line before turning around. Balaban looked up and smiled over his round glasses. "Envoy. Nice to see you."

Aranok wasn't surprised Conifax had asked for Balaban's assistance. He wasn't a *draoidh*, but Aranok remembered now that the man had a voracious interest in the history of curses. The opportunity to put that knowledge to practical use was likely exciting for him, if disturbing.

"And you, Master. Thank you for"—Aranok gestured to the books—"this."

"Oh, thank *you*. If you're right about this, about what we can do…" Balaban puffed out his cheeks and blew out air. "There'll be a book in here about you before long."

Aranok smiled. He'd never sought fame, but the idea of being part of this place—forever—gave him more pleasure than he'd have thought. "About us, maybe. How goes it?"

"As expected," Conifax answered. "It would be a great deal more straightforward if we knew who had cast the curse, and how…But I am confident."

"Contagious curses are rare but not unheard-of." Balaban patted the pile of books affectionately. "We'll find the answer in here."

"Good." Aranok waited, not entirely sure how to ask the next question. "Um, Master Balaban, I'm sorry to ask, but would it be possible to have a moment alone with Master Conifax? There's a personal matter…"

Conifax furrowed his brow. "Now? I thought this was urgent, boy."

"Oh, it is, of course. This will only take a moment…" he stammered.

Balaban sat up tall. "Do you know, I find myself in need of a stretch and a cup of tea." He stood, and Aranok noticed that he too was more slight. His grey hair had thinned and his skin hung loosely on his face. Balaban looked like a frail old man, not the wiry, towering presence he had been when Aranok studied here. Time had stolen from them all. "I'll be back in a bit." He nodded to Conifax and placed a hand on Aranok's arm as he passed.

Aranok drew a chair from the next quarter and sat beside Conifax. What he needed seemed trivial in comparison. But he did need it. "Can I ask you another favour?"

The old man's eyebrows rose. He slowly sat back and turned his head to Aranok. "Aside from curing the Blackening, saving your friends and lifting a bloodline curse, you mean?"

And that was why he felt awkward. Aranok nodded.

"Go on..." said Conifax wryly.

Aranok looked around. There were only two other students on the top floor: one in a quarter on the opposite side of the balcony; one about thirty feet away, standing at a shelf, reading a book in her hands. He spoke quietly, aware of the acoustics of the building and the otherwise silent atmosphere. "My niece is a *draoidh*."

"Fabulous!" Conifax beamed. "What skill?"

Aranok held up a hand, asking his teacher to speak more quietly. The master looked puzzled.

"Illusion," said Aranok.

Conifax's face lit up. "Wonderful!" he whispered. "We haven't had an illusionist in the university since..." He trailed off, and his face changed to a tired sadness. "She's his daughter?"

Aranok nodded. The man had always been perceptive. It had been impossible to hide anything from him as a student. The moment Conifax looked hard at him, it was as if the truth appeared written across his face.

"He and your sister were not married when he died?"

"When he was murdered." Aranok's jaw clenched as he said it.

Conifax nodded and placed a hand on Aranok's. He knew what Korvin's death had done to him. He knew what he had done because of it. "Some old scars never stop itching," the old man said, "but scratch too hard and they bleed."

Aranok realised he had an iron grip on the chair arm. He breathed in deep and released his fingers as he exhaled in the way his master had taught him. Conifax gave him a moment before speaking again. "Your sister did marry, I recall."

"Yes. He's an idiot," said Aranok. "Works for my father. Well, runs the business these days."

Conifax nodded. "And he would not appreciate people knowing that your niece is not his daughter."

"He doesn't know she's a *draoidh*. Ikara's too scared to tell him. Or my father."

"Hmph!" Conifax snorted. He and Aranok's father had never seen eye to eye. "Of course not. So you want a tutor for her? One who can pass as mundane?"

Aranok nodded. Given the option, he'd have had Emelina brought here to study with Conifax. But that would require a full explanation.

Conifax looked around the room. He stood and walked to the balcony, scanning the other floors. Appearing to find what he was looking for, he shouted, "Rasa!" A young woman with pale skin and jet-black hair appeared at the second-floor balcony, as half the students in the library looked to see who had broken the silence, returning to their studies when they realised it was a master. He beckoned her to join them, and she ascended the ornate spiral staircase.

As she approached, Aranok found himself engrossed in her beauty. Up close, her striking colouring was accentuated by large emerald eyes, high cheekbones and deep red lips. Despite her plain cream dress, she resembled a painting. Conifax was smiling at him. Presumably his appreciation was evident.

"Yes, Master Conifax?" she asked, in a deeper voice than her delicacy suggested.

"Rasa, would you join us?" he asked, indicating a chair at an adjacent table. Rasa pulled it over and sat. "Rasa, this is Laird Aranok, the king's envoy."

"My laird." She smiled and nodded at Aranok. "It's an honour."

Conifax turned to him. "Aranok, Rasa recently graduated with highest honours. She has expressed an interest in joining the staff here. I believe she would make an excellent tutor."

Rasa smiled. "Thank you, Master."

"Congratulations," said Aranok. She nodded her thanks. "Can you keep a secret, Rasa?"

She smiled at him in an odd, knowing way and glanced at Conifax. "I can."

*What was that about?*

Aranok looked to Conifax for confirmation. He blinked slowly in agreement. Aranok looked around again. The student nearest them had gone. Only the one across the balcony was in sight. He leaned toward Rasa.

"My niece is six. She's a *draoidh* and needs a tutor. But it must appear she is being educated in the arts and sciences. Not magic."

"Why?" Rasa looked almost offended.

"It's complicated," said Aranok. "It will make life harder for her, and my family, if it's known. Only my sister and mother know."

Now Rasa looked for Conifax's confirmation. Again, the old man simply nodded.

"All right," she said. "It would be my honour."

"Can I trust you to keep this secret?" he asked.

"You can," she said seriously. "It is each person's right to choose how the world knows them."

It seemed a more philosophical answer than his question invited, but it would do. And if Conifax vouched for her, that was already enough.

"Can I ask, what is your skill?" said Aranok.

She grinned. "Metamorphosis."

"A metamorph?" Aranok nearly choked on his own surprise. He looked round at Conifax, who was also smiling. A metamorph was perfect! She could come and go unnoticed, as a cat or some other animal. She could even change into a different person entirely, should the need arise. "That's...brilliant!"

"Indeed," said Conifax. "Would you say it is almost as if I chose her because she is ideal for the job?"

Aranok smiled at his teacher. "As you say, Master."

"When should I begin?" Rasa asked.

"Well, the envoy will need to make arrangements for your pay, and give you a letter of introduction, I assume?" said Conifax.

Aranok nodded. "I'll arrange for funds to be transferred to the university, to cover the first year. And I will provide you with a letter for my sister. She will be expecting you, but she will behave as though she is not. Her husband may be suspicious. Do you understand?"

"I do. But you may be surprised how uncommon it is for men to distrust me."

He could understand that. Most men probably never saw past her beauty to suspect her of anything. Women, perhaps…

"Excellent, Rasa. How long will it take you to prepare to travel to Mournside?" Conifax asked.

"Mournside?" she asked. "Lovely. May I have until the end of the week?"

"Ah. Actually, that's a good point." Aranok hadn't thought about how she'd actually get to Mournside. The road out of Traverlyn might still be infested with Thakhati and the Auld Road was impassable to humans. "You'll have to travel by day. The road is unsafe at night. And you'll need to travel the Auld Road in animal form—it's overrun with Blackened."

"Is it, now?" asked Conifax. "How did that happen?"

"We don't know," said Aranok conspiratorially. "We suspect Mynygogg—somehow."

"Hmm," was all the old man said.

"And you'll need somewhere safe to stay overnight. It's over a hundred miles to Mournside," said Aranok.

Rasa smiled. "It's only about sixty, as the crow flies."

*Of course.*

She had no need to worry about any of it. She could simply fly above it all.

"How fast can you fly?" asked Aranok excitedly.

The woman pursed her mouth. "As a falcon, I could make Mournside in about an hour."

It was beginning to come together.

"I assume, when you transform back to your human form, you lack…" Aranok wasn't quite sure how to ask the question.

"I am in need of clothing," she finished for him.

"Right. So if I could arrange for clothing to be waiting for you at the other end…?"

"Then I suppose I could simply stay here and travel to Mournside each day. That would be extremely agreeable, Laird Aranok."

"Indeed it would," said Conifax. "And it would allow me to keep in touch with your niece's progress."

"Excellent," said Aranok. "I'll write a note for you to take to my sister. My family owns a clothing business. She'll find you something fitting."

Rasa smiled. "Well, how nicely that all works out!"

"It does," said Conifax. "Now, Rasa, if you'll excuse us..."

"Of course, Master, I just wanted to ask"—she turned to Aranok—"what is your niece's skill?"

"Illusion," he answered quietly.

"How marvellous!" Rasa looked delighted. "I can't wait to meet her!" She curtseyed to Aranok and headed back toward the stairs.

He turned back to his mentor. "She's perfect."

"Indeed." Conifax raised an eyebrow. "But...?"

Of course his mentor saw his concern. Was she too perfect? Aranok rarely found an unexpected gift to come without a price. "What do I need to know?"

Conifax leaned back and crossed his arms. "Nothing. Rasa is as entitled to her privacy as you or me, Laird Envoy. You can take my recommendation and trust me, or not."

In theory, that was all well and good, but he needed to be certain. This was too fragile, too dangerous to leave anything to chance. "I understand. But this is my family. Is there anything I should know?"

"Unless you're planning to ask for her hand, I'd say it's none of your damned business—and maybe not even then," Conifax answered.

"Very well, but..."

The master raised a hand to interrupt. "Rasa's privacy has no bearing on her ability to tutor your niece, nor is it anything that should cause you concern. Fair enough?"

"Fair enough." That was all he needed.

"Now, tell me why you suggested Rasa travel by day. What don't I know about?"

Aranok found himself looking around again. Still nobody close. "Have you heard the name *Thakhati*?"

Conifax considered for a moment. "Don't think so. Should I have?"

Aranok briefly told him the story of the Starbank Inn and how they'd encountered so many of them on the road into Traverlyn.

"A sunstone?" said Conifax. "That's a fine usage, my boy. I might not have thought of that."

Sunstones were usually used for light, with the stored energy released slowly so as to last. Bursting it the way Aranok had was unusual. He felt a little twinge of pride at Conifax's praise. Being respected by someone who understood what he'd done was different from the thanks of someone who thought everything he could do was in itself miraculous.

"Where did you get the name?" the master asked.

"Thakhati? Allandria remembers it from somewhere. Maybe her childhood."

"Oh? Where was she raised?" Conifax asked.

"Well, mostly Lochen. But she wasn't born there. Her parents migrated from the south when she was young."

"You think maybe she knows the name from there?"

"I think it's possible," said Aranok. "But truthfully, I've no idea. She could be remembering some fairy tale, and we've just given the name to these things for something to call them."

"Hmm. Yes. Either way, now we know what they are, and when they are dangerous. I'll arrange a proclamation that nobody is to travel the road at night, and to stay off the Auld Road. Anyone travelling east will have to go the long way round or go cross-country."

"Do you think there might be anything in there?" Aranok nodded at the metal door at the end of the landing. The one with three bolts and three locks. The one all students knew to stay away from on pain of expulsion. The *caibineat puinnsean*: the home of every "dangerous" and banned text in Eidyn.

Conifax looked over his shoulder at the door and back at Aranok. "What's your obsession with getting in there, boy? What do you think you need?"

"You know what I think," said Aranok. "Knowledge shouldn't be kept for the elite."

"You still think all information should be free to anyone who wants it?" said Conifax.

"In theory. Yes."

"And what if that information leads to harm? What then?" he asked.

"Who decides what is and isn't harmful?" asked Aranok.

"We do," said Conifax. "Literally the most well-informed people in the country. You challenge our ability to make that judgement?"

Aranok breathed deep. They'd had this argument before. "Not your ability. Your right."

Conifax nodded. "What if the only book with the Blackening curse was in there, and we could have prevented it?"

"What if the cure is in there, and we're missing it?" Aranok countered.

"You feel left out," he said. "Don't you? The problem is that *you're* not allowed in there, isn't it?"

"Not just me. Everyone." Though the statement did sting a little and he wondered with a twinge of shame if there wasn't some truth in it.

"Let me ask you, Aranok: Let's say there was a book in there that argued that, for the sake of the greater society, all *draoidhs* should be put to death. Is that a book you would want in circulation? Where it could convince people to hate you?"

"Plenty don't need any convincing," he said pointedly.

"Indeed they do not. And what if there was one suggesting that all women should be held as property by their husbands and fathers? Would that be acceptable to you? If it was well written and presented a logical, coherent argument?"

"Well…" The concept was abhorrent, but was it acceptable to withhold an idea? "Why keep it, then? Why let the book exist at all?"

"Because understanding your opponent's argument prepares you to answer it when it is made. Because being able to read an opposing opinion and understand why it is wrong sharpens the mind. Because remembering the mistakes of the past helps prevent us making them again."

"So why keep that from the students?" he asked. "These are the best and brightest, aren't they?"

"They are," Conifax agreed. "But even the most intelligent students can be swayed by a well-made argument. And, frankly, you'd be surprised how disappointing people can be if you give them just enough information to feed their ignorance."

That was hard to argue. He'd experienced it often enough. "All right. So what if the answer to our problem is in there? Then what?"

Conifax smiled widely and patted the stack of books on the table.

"My dear boy, where do you think we got these from?"

"What is the purpose of this?" Samily was running her hand along the ruffled edge of a blouse. "Doesn't it irritate your chest?"

Allandria stifled a smile. The knight saw simplicity in everything. "It's just pretty. It doesn't really have a purpose. It makes you feel nice."

Samily looked at her as if she'd spoken a foreign language. "I feel fine."

One side of the modest tailor shop they'd found was adorned with examples of blouses, dresses, shawls and some simple skirts. The other was all shirts, trousers and jackets. In a third section, beside the counter at the rear, black robes of the university hung like spectres.

"What Allandria means is that some women enjoy feeling like they look pretty," said Nirea.

Samily looked at her blankly. "Why?"

*Eesh.* It really was a foreign language. This wasn't going anywhere. Allandria decided to try another tack. "What makes you feel good?"

Samily shrugged. "Serving God. Pleasing Brother Meristan. Praying. Nature."

"But what makes you feel good about yourself?" asked Nirea.

"Should I not?" asked the knight, as if she'd said something particularly vicious. "Am I not a good person?"

"I..." Allandria stumbled over a response. It seemed so ridiculously obvious to her. "Of course you are."

"Maybe we're going about this wrong," said Nirea. "Is there anything here you do like?"

Samily looked around the shop and crossed to a wooden dummy wearing a relatively plain white doublet. "This is 'nice.'" She shrugged.

The tailor coughed behind the counter. He was a wiry old man, with a pale bald head framed by two shocks of white hair jutting out above his ears. "Ah, that is a gentleman's item, m'lady."

Samily turned to face him, with the same confused look she'd worn since entering the shop. "Why?"

"Ah, well, um, it just...is," he said. God knew what he thought of Nirea's black leather trousers. Allandria wore her usual "off duty" outfit—a relatively plain beige dress, which Sumara had insisted on embroidering with delicate blue flowers along the hem. It was comfortable and allowed her to move freely. And she liked the flowers. They were pretty.

Samily looked at Allandria and Nirea blankly. She shrugged and shook her head. "I don't understand."

"No," said Nirea. "And actually, you shouldn't have to." She walked over to the counter. "What's your name?"

"Alexin," the man said deferentially. Allandria couldn't decide if he was being respectful or just oily. Merchants could be like that. Hard to read. It made her defensive.

"Alexin, this lady is Samily of the White Thorns." Nirea made a slightly dramatic sweeping gesture toward the knight.

"My lady." Alexin bowed. "I apologise, I did not recognise you out of armour."

In fact, he'd turned up his nose at her grubby grey aketon when they'd come in. Allandria realised she'd taken an instant dislike to the man and wondered if it was because a tailor put her in mind of Dorann and Pol. Perhaps. Or perhaps he was equally overstuffed with his own importance.

Samily nodded in acknowledgement of the "apology." The girl was pure confidence in some ways and utterly fragile in others.

"No reason why you should," said Nirea. "However, now that you know, wouldn't you say that a White Thorn should wear whatever the Hell they please?"

"I... Well... I suppose so?" stammered Alexin.

"So if she chooses to wear a doublet and breeches, you would happily sell them to her and adjust them to fit?"

Alexin looked at Samily and back at Nirea. "Yes...?" he said, almost fearfully. The oiliness was gone now. There was something very satisfying about his discomfort.

"Excellent." Nirea put a hand on Samily's shoulder. "Now, how about you measure her up, so you can make the necessary adjustments, and we'll come back for it this evening?"

"This evening...?" the tailor spluttered. He looked piteously at Allandria, as if for assistance. She smiled pleasantly. "I require several days to make amendments. And I have other customers who..."

"Are any of your other customers White Thorns who need to get back on the road and kill demons?" Allandria filled her voice with faux innocence.

He stared for a moment. "Not that I know of."

"Then you can make an exception?" Nirea asked.

"Of course," Alexin finally said. "If m'lady would care to follow me through to the back room"—he pulled back a curtain behind him—"we can take your measurements."

Samily looked at Nirea, who nodded; she followed the man's invitation and the two disappeared behind the curtain.

"She's not exactly going to blend in—a young woman dressed in men's clothes," said Allandria.

"You know what?" Nirea crossed her arms and leaned against the counter. "I think that girl is going to stand out wherever she goes."

# CHAPTER 25

As soon as Aranok stepped into the Sheep's Heid, the smell of food made his stomach rumble. He'd spent the day in quarters with Conifax and Balaban and had completely forgotten to have lunch. The smell of roast lamb and lentil soup, he surmised, was extremely welcome.

The inn was busy, as he expected at dinnertime. He scanned the room, looking for familiar faces, and found Glorbad sitting in a booth, with a couple of men rapt by one of the old goat's stories.

He caught the soldier's eye and waved. Glorbad raised his mug in reply. Aranok mimed eating and got a raised thumb in response. He gestured to the serving girl behind the bar.

"Two lambs," he mouthed, and pointed to Glorbad. She craned her neck past the crowds at the bar and also pointed. Aranok nodded, tossed her a coin and made his way through the crowd to join Glorbad.

"Welcome back!" the soldier roared in his orotund tenor. "Allow me to introduce..." He pointed at his first companion, a portly, ginger-bearded man in fine clothes. "Warum?"

"Indeed!" The man offered Aranok his hand. He shook it politely.

"And Skellit." Glorbad pointed to the second man, who was younger, thinner and darker than his friend, with a nasty-looking scar above his ear that cut into his hair. The kind of scar most don't live to show off. He also offered his hand. It was cold and clammy.

"This is Aranok," Glorbad said, a little louder than he would have liked. A flicker of panic crossed Warum's eyes.

"Not…the Aranok," he sputtered.

"No," Aranok said quickly, before Glorbad could answer. The soldier was well in his cups but still caught the hint and kept quiet.

The smile returned to Warum's eyes. "Ah. Must be a pest, sharing a name with someone so famous."

Aranok shrugged. "It's not so bad. We move in different circles."

"These gentlemen have been plying me with drink in return for war stories!" Glorbad grinned widely. "Have I told you about the time wee Salvyn nearly got himself killed taking a piss on a boar? Thought it was a bush in the dark! Bastard thing went berserk when it woke up to a stream of warm pish in its face! Good thing he already had his cock out, or he'd have soiled his breeks!" Glorbad roared and the two men laughed with him.

"Well, gentlemen, I'm sorry to cut short your session, but Glorbad and I have some business to discuss," said Aranok.

Warum looked at Skellit. "Oh, of course." The thinner man shrugged, and they both slid off the end of the bench. Aranok put one hand on his purse and ushered them away with the other.

"Been a pleasure." Glorbad saluted them with his mug.

"All ours, of course," said Warum, backing away. He turned and followed Skellit straight out the door. Aranok sat.

"What business? We got the cure?" Glorbad asked in a voice he probably considered hushed.

"No," said Aranok. "I just thought I'd save you the indignity of being robbed."

"What?" Glorbad sat back with a jerk and put his hand on his own purse.

"Did you see them hand over any money for your drinks?" Aranok asked.

"Well…no," said Glorbad after a moment's drunken consideration.

"I'd wager they intended to get you stinking drunk, steal your purse and settle the bill with your own coins."

"What? Why?"

"They looked worried when you gave them my name. The quiet one had a nasty scar on his head from the kind of wound you only survive because there's a medic on hand—like in Auldun gaol. And the two of them were drinking water."

Aranok shoved the mug in front of him across the table to Glorbad, who sipped from it and scowled distastefully. "Devious bastards! I'll fillet them!"

Aranok put a hand on his arm to stop him standing. "They're long gone. But in future, be careful who you let buy you a drink."

Glorbad raised an eyebrow at him. "Why did you say you weren't... you?" He swayed slightly in his seat.

"I told you, I don't like people knowing where I am. Especially cutpurses."

The soldier sat back and looked at him as if appraising a horse. "I didn't trust you, you know."

"I know." Aranok was growing concerned about where this conversation was going. Two drunks could have a perfectly unintelligible conversation and come away enlightened. One drunk meant the sober one was going to spend the evening nodding and agreeing repeatedly to the same point dressed in different clothes. It was tedious. He should have ordered beer too.

"What you did, with the boy..." said Glorbad. "What you did with the boy was good. He told me. What you did. It was good." The soldier pointed at him with an unsteady hand. "You're a difficult man, Envoy."

Aranok raised his hands and gestured for him to be quiet. Glorbad mimicked the gesture and nodded, shushing himself.

"You're a good man, but you're difficult to like. Paying the boy's debt was a good thing. He appreciated that. A lot."

"I know," said Aranok.

"And I know... I understand why you brought him. You shouldn't have brought him. I understand why you did. It's not your fault. What happened. It's... it's nobody's fault. Well, the cunt that cast the curse..." He half laughed to himself. "That was fun to say. 'The cunt that cashed the curse.'" A huge burp ripped itself free from his chest.

"Thank you," Aranok said seriously.

"For what?" The soldier's eyes were glazed.

With a clunk, the serving girl placed two steaming plates of roast lamb, carrots and potatoes in front of them. Aranok had never been more glad to see food.

"That's exactly what I need!" Glorbad took a deep, dramatic sniff at the plate.

It certainly was.

"Hey!" Aranok turned to find Allandria beside the table. His heart jumped. He hadn't realised he'd missed her until she stood in front of him. "Any news?"

"Nothing solid. But Conifax is confident." More confident than Aranok, after a long day of finding nothing of use.

"Good," she said. "We need some money."

"Oh, all right." He grabbed for his purse. "For dinner?"

"For Samily. She needs clothes."

Aranok paused. "Why am I buying Samily clothes? I mean, not that I object, I suppose..."

"Then don't object." Allandria smiled sweetly at him. His curiosity lost out to his hunger; he fished a couple of gold crowns from his purse and handed them over.

"Thank you!" she chirped, putting them in her own purse.

"Have you eaten?" he asked.

"We'll get something when we come back." She waved as she walked away.

"Women." Glorbad shrugged, stuffing a carrot into his mouth lengthwise, so it caught on his lips and had to bend. Gravy spattered onto the table as it sprang in.

"Women..." Aranok agreed, lifting his cutlery.

———————

"Is Samily wearing a doublet?" Glorbad asked quietly.

Aranok smelled the remnants of last night's beer on his breath and leaned back a little. "It would appear so."

In fact, it seemed he had bought Samily a rather elegant white doublet and breeches, which oddly suited her. She looked knightly, even without her armour. It was fitting, so to speak.

The girl paced nervously outside the door to Meristan's room. Conifax had summoned them all here at noon for his first attempt to lift the monk's curse. They had agreed it made sense to cure him first—to be sure it worked—before Vastin, who would need immediate attention from Samily.

Glorbad, Aranok, Allandria and Nirea sat on a bench opposite the door, watching Samily fidget.

When Aranok had all but given up hope of Conifax arriving, the old man came round a corner with Morienne and Balaban trailing behind him. She looked tired, from what Aranok could make out before he had to look away.

"Right!" Conifax wiped his eyes clear. "Shall we?"

Allandria touched Morienne's arm. "How are you?"

"I'm fine." Morienne sounded a little surprised. She wasn't used to people being concerned about her, Aranok supposed. "Just tired."

She followed Conifax and Balaban into the room, and the rest filed in. Meristan sat in a wooden chair, each of his arms bound to it. He still wore a hood over his head. It was a small room, no more than twelve feet square, and Conifax waved everyone back to the walls. The masters knelt on the ground in front of Meristan. Conifax inscribed an intricate rune in chalk, while Balaban held open the book he was referring to. They repeated this for another three runes at equal distances, so that Meristan sat in the middle of what looked like a giant magical sundial.

"All right." Conifax looked to Morienne. "Would you expose the black mark?"

Balaban handed Conifax the open book and stepped back against the wall with the rest of them. Morienne moved forward and untied Meristan's right arm. He made no show of resistance as she turned it over and drew back the sleeve of his robe, revealing the black handprint where Vastin had grabbed him.

Samily drew a sharp breath. Nirea took her hand.

Conifax knelt before the first rune and lay the thick red-leather tome on the floor. He looked up at the other master questioningly. Balaban nodded solemnly. "It will work."

Conifax took a deep breath and read:

"*Anam na gaoth*
*Cridhe na tabh*
*Dìoghras an teine*
*Neart na talamh*
*Claist*
*Saor an anam seo*
*Dùisg an cridhe seo*
*Árd-loisg e glan*
*Dèan e làidir*"

Conifax looked up at Meristan. Every eye in the room was on the black mark on his arm. Aranok could feel his heart racing in his chest. Was this it? Was he right? Could they cure the Blackening? Could they save their friends? There was no sound but eight souls silently praying for a miracle, and one whose life depended on it.

Meristan lurched in his seat and roared like a wounded bear. He threw out his huge arm, knocking Morienne to the ground. Aranok raised his hands, ready to take control of the monk, but Conifax waved him down.

"No, no! I think it's working!"

"Meristan!" Samily screamed as though he would hear her in the dark and come home. "Meristan!"

The monk stood and slammed himself onto the ground, shattering the chair beneath him. Hells, he was free!

"Everybody, out!" bellowed Aranok, making the gestures for *gluais*.

Nirea reacted first, pulling Samily with her. "No!" the knight objected, but Nirea pulled harder. Allandria and Glorbad followed. Conifax did not move. He remained kneeling in front of the great bear of a man as he picked himself up out of the wreckage of the chair. Instead of fleeing, Conifax stood and, with the book still in one hand, placed the other on Meristan's arm as the monk rested on one knee.

"No!" Aranok bellowed. "What are you doing?" His concentration broken, he made a mess of the final gesture and had to start again.

"It's all right!" Balaban grabbed his arm and pulled him toward the door. "It will work!"

Conifax read, louder this time.

*"Anam na gaoth*
*Cridhe na tabh*
*Dìoghras an teine*
*Neart na talamh*
*Claist*
*Saor an anam seo*
*Dùisg an cridhe seo*
*Árd-loisg e glan*
*Dèan e làidir"*

Meristan roared. His skin almost glowed red. Aranok allowed Balaban to pull him to the doorway but no farther. Meristan threw his arms into the air, screaming as if he were being murdered.

"No!" he heard Samily scream again, vaguely aware of her trying to jostle past him. "Meristan!"

As suddenly as he had begun thrashing, the monk dropped to the floor and was silent. Conifax stood over him, panting.

"Conifax?" Aranok asked tentatively. If his teacher had been Blackened, they were in trouble. Conifax turned slowly toward him and held out his hand—the one he'd put on Meristan. It was burned. But not black.

"I think it worked." Conifax collapsed forward into Aranok's arms. He dragged the old man out of the room, keen to get clear and close the door before Meristan woke. If he woke. Aranok looked down at the prone figure of the monk. He was a mess, but one thing caught his eye amongst the chaos. His right arm, outstretched as if reaching for the wall, with a fresh, hand-shaped burn.

---

Egretta came charging down the corridor. "What in all Hells was that?" She paused when she saw Conifax slumped in Aranok's arms. "What happened?"

"I'm not sure," said Aranok. "He said it worked, then..."

"It worked," said Balaban. "We knew it might be...violent. Now we must wait."

"For what?" Samily demanded.

"For what comes next," the master answered calmly.

Egretta helped him get Conifax onto the bench and sit him up. She produced some herbs from a pouch on her apron and held them under his nose.

After a moment, he jerked awake. "How long was I out?"

"Just a moment," Balaban answered.

"Right, let's get a look at our patient." Conifax put his hand on the arm of the bench, yelped and pulled it away again. He looked at it as if he'd forgotten what it was for a moment. "Ah yes, I seem to have burned myself. Egretta, would you...?"

Egretta stalked off back down the corridor with an indignant "hmph."

"Bring some water, and porridge!" Balaban shouted after her. "He hasn't eaten in days," he said, turning to the group.

"You think...you think it worked?" Samily struggled to catch her breath. Nirea still held her hand. The girl was in pieces.

Conifax looked at Balaban. "We do. We just can't guarantee he survived it."

Samily turned grey. She pulled her hand free of Nirea's and pushed open the door before Aranok could open his mouth. She fell into the room, next to Meristan's body, and turned him over. Aranok and Nirea followed her in. She pulled off his hood and cradled him in her arms. He was deathly pale. Samily looked up at them, her eyes begging for help.

"Well, he's not Blackened," said Conifax, entering the room. "Now, is he alive? Check his heart, girl."

Samily bent her head to the huge man's chest, her face a mask of fear. But it quickly changed to relief and joy. "He's alive! He's alive!"

Egretta returned and handed Samily a small wooden cup. "Here, give him this. Just sips now. He'll only bring it straight back up if you rush."

Samily nodded and carefully placed the cup to his cracked lips, dribbling a tiny amount into the gap between them. After a moment, Meristan's lips drew slowly apart and made a smacking sound, moving as if he were chewing overcooked toffee. Samily poured a little more in and he smacked even louder. After a few moments, his eyes flickered open.

"Sam...ly?" he rasped, with a throat dry as sand.

"Yes, Brother, yes. It's me! You're back. God has brought you back to me!" Tears streamed down the girl's face.

"Ha." Conifax turned to Balaban. "We do all the work and God gets the credit."

"Such is the way of things." Balaban shrugged, but he smiled widely, watching the knight hug Meristan to her chest.

"My God, old man, you did it!" Aranok grabbed Conifax by the shoulders. "You cured the Blackening!"

"We cured it," said Conifax. "You realised it was a *mollachd*..."

"You cured it together!" Glorbad slapped each of them on the shoulder. "Let's celebrate!"

"First things first," said Conifax. "This man needs a bed, food and water. Then we need to see to your other friend, who will be somewhat more complicated. And"—he turned to Egretta—"my hand really bloody hurts!"

---

They moved Meristan to a bed and he fell asleep immediately, which Egretta considered a good thing. His body would be exhausted after days without sleep, and he would wake naturally when his hunger overtook his fatigue.

Only when he was completely settled, and Samily had been assured that someone would be with him at all times, did they move to Vastin's room.

After the unexpected excitement of the first attempt, it was decided that the number of people in the room should be kept to a minimum, and that Vastin should be thoroughly strapped to the bed. Facedown, hooded and stripped to the waist, he had leather straps across his wrists, ankles, neck, upper arms (though carefully placed not too near his wound), back and thighs. Aranok wondered who these restraints were usually needed for and was momentarily grateful for his relatively good health.

Those deemed essential to the process were Conifax, obviously; Egretta, for tending to the wound if necessary; Samily, to heal the wound; Morienne, who could touch him before the curse was lifted; and Aranok as backup—and he had refused to not be in the room in case something else went wrong. Balaban wanted to be there, but Conifax assured him he could handle it himself, now they knew it worked, and the fewer bodies in the room the better.

Ideally, they'd have given the boy a large dose of poppy milk first, for the pain he was about to be in, but since they had no way to make him swallow, they just had to hope Samily's ability worked quickly enough to spare him the worst of it.

Egretta wore gloves and a mask to protect her face, as she would in surgery. Just in case.

Aranok drew the last of the runes on the floor. They were well described in the book, and Conifax's writing hand was currently wrapped in bandages soaked with healing balm. He stood and stepped back when he'd finished, comparing each with the examples.

"They're fine. Stop worrying about perfection." Conifax took a breath before starting again. "Morienne, I need you to hold his shoulder down as firmly as you can, please. If he thrashes around the way Meristan did, he could tear his arm off. Let go if it starts to burn. Samily, the moment I give the word, you…do what you do." He smiled at her. The old man was probably more excited to see Samily's healing ability than about the fact that he'd cured the worst plague in history. Aranok understood. He remembered the euphoria.

Samily nodded silently. She'd had a rough few days, but she was holding together. The girl was tough.

"Aranok and Egretta, please stand back," said his old master. "You'll know if you're needed."

He looked down at his book again, sighed, and looked up.

"All right. Here we go again:

*Anam na gaoth*
*Cridhe na tabh*
*Dìoghras an teine*
*Neart na talamh*
*Claist*
*Saor an anam seo*

*Dùisg an cridhe seo
Àrd-loisg e glan
Dèan e làidir"*

This time, the reaction was immediate. Vastin strained against his bonds, growling like a cornered animal. Morienne leaned forward, pressing down on the top of his shoulder, trying to keep it in place. Vastin was a lot smaller than Meristan, so between her and the straps, he kept relatively still. He was also weak from blood loss. All the same, Aranok could see the stitches in his shoulder straining. He realised he was grinding his teeth and clenching his fists as if his own force of will could keep the stitches together.

The boy's skin began to turn pink as his grunting intensified. The tiny black handprint on his arm glowed red.

"Aaah!" Morienne jerked back and pulled her hands off the boy. He thrashed a little harder and Aranok winced as two of the stitches burst, leaving an angry red rip in his armpit. The sight of the wounds shook Aranok from his trance. *"Gluais."* He focused everything he had on keeping the boy's shoulder still. Vastin thrashed violently, like a fish caught in a net. Thick red liquid oozed from the gap, but the remaining stitches held.

Conifax spoke again, though he'd clearly learned the lesson of his first attempt and kept his hands clear this time.

*"Anam na gaoth
Cridhe na tabh
Dìoghras an teine
Neart na talamh
Claist
Saor an anam seo
Dùisg an cridhe seo
Àrd-loisg e glan
Dèan e làidir"*

As he spoke the last word, Vastin released an agonised scream and collapsed like an empty sack against the bed.

"Now!" Conifax said to Samily.

The knight stepped forward and put her hands on the boy's wound. She closed her eyes and said, *"Air ais."*

Aranok held his breath and stared at the jagged red-and-black mess, waiting for it to knit back together.

"Wait." A quiet voice. It was Conifax. Aranok turned to look at him. He seemed confused. The old man looked at Aranok. "You've seen this?" Aranok nodded. Why did he look so worried?

Vastin made an odd groan, and something caught the edge of Aranok's vision. He followed it to Vastin's arm. The other arm. The one with the newly burnt baby handprint.

It was black again.

"Stop!" he bellowed at Samily. "Stop!" He went to reach for her, but Conifax batted his arm down. Samily lifted her hands off Vastin and groggily turned to face him. As she turned, he saw both palms were black as soot.

Samily lunged for him, and he instinctively fell backwards, arms raised. He caught both forearms as they reached for him, thankful for the arms of the doublet he'd bought her protecting his skin.

She leaned over him, her full weight bearing down on him. Her face was contorted with venom. Holy Hells, she was so strong! Aranok pulled his right leg up and got his knee between them to take some pressure off his arms. If she'd been in control of her senses, she'd have overpowered him already.

"Morienne!" he heard a voice call. And suddenly, the woman was also above him, her arms wrapped around Samily's chest and head, pulling her back. She covered the knight's eyes with one hand, which disorientated her. The knight shook her head, trying to throw Morienne off. Finally, she lashed backwards and they fell to the ground in a tangle.

"Get out!" Morienne shouted. "I'll calm her! Get out!"

Aranok scrambled to his feet. Conifax already had the door open, ushering Egretta out. Samily roared in frustration, and Aranok could hear Morienne whispering something. He half fell out of the door and pulled it closed behind him.

Allandria caught him as he lurched against the opposite wall, his chest heaving. "What happened?" There was panic in her voice.

Aranok looked at Conifax. "I don't know!"

Balaban stood with his hands outstretched, his mouth hanging open.

"You fool! You complete idiot!" Conifax barked at him. "You said you'd seen her do it!"

*What?*

Aranok sat on the bench, catching his breath. "I have!"

"You said she was a healer!" Conifax said. "You said you'd seen her heal!"

"I have!" Aranok was completely confused. Why was he so angry?

"*Air ais!*" he shouted. "*Air ais!*"

"Oh God," said Balaban. "Those were her 'prayer words'?"

"What is it?" Aranok stood, frustrated now with his teacher's behaviour.

"*Air ais* means 'back,' boy!"

"Oh shit." Aranok sat again, his legs shaking as the ramifications of that one lack of understanding sank in.

"What does that mean?" Allandria asked. Aranok looked up. Seven pairs of eyes were fixed on him—five begging for an answer, two anticipating it.

"It means Samily's not a healer. She's a time *draoidh*."

# CHAPTER 26

Allandria stared at Aranok, trying to take in what he had said—and what it meant. "A time *draoidh*? I've never heard of that."

Aranok shrugged. "I've never known one. It's possibly the rarest skill."

"If you'd done your bloody studying, you'd have recognised the words!" Conifax grumbled. He glowered at Aranok for a moment, shook his head and turned away.

Aranok said something quietly that Allandria couldn't make out.

"What?" snapped Conifax.

Aranok stared at the floor. "I never heard the words. Even if I'd known them, I never heard her speak them."

"Then who did you see her 'heal'?" the old man demanded.

Aranok nodded at Glorbad. "My nose!" The soldier was touching it as if to confirm it was still there.

"And your back," said Aranok. "At Mutton Hole." That explained his miraculous recovery after the demon fight. Allandria had assumed he had some sort of magic potion in his silver flask.

"Right enough." Glorbad put his hands on his lower back and rotated his hips. "I've not had this little back pain for years."

"Hang on," said Nirea. "What actually happened? Where's Samily? And Morienne?"

Aranok's answer was still quiet. Subdued. "After Conifax cured Vastin, Samily tried to heal him, but instead..."

"Instead," interrupted Conifax, "her time skills took him back to being Blackened again. And since her hands were on him…"

Nirea gasped. "Oh fuck! She's Blackened?"

"Don't panic." Balaban's voice was gentle, which Allandria appreciated. The conversation needed some calming waters. "We know we can return her. She won't remember anything and she won't suffer any damage over such a short term. This isn't a disaster. And we've learned something new."

"It could have been avoided!" Conifax pointed at Aranok. "If he'd paid attention!"

"Master Conifax, one could equally argue that as a master you might have asked for a demonstration yourself before this experiment," said Balaban. "Or enquired as to exactly what Samily's 'prayer words' were. Perhaps we were all a little carried away with ourselves."

Conifax fumed back at him, but it seemed to Allandria that at least some of the heat was gone from the fire. Good. If it wasn't for Aranok, they wouldn't even be here, trying this.

The door squeaked open and Morienne stepped out. "I had to improvise." She indicated her missing sleeves. "She's calm now."

Nirea lurched to the door and looked in. She put a hand to her mouth.

"Did she say anything when she did this?" Conifax pointed at Glorbad's nose.

"Can't remember." Glorbad touched his face again, pressing his nose first one way, then the other. "Maybe? I was in a fair bit of pain, mind."

"Yes." Nirea turned back to them. "Yes. She said those words. What you said."

Conifax nodded.

"So pardon me for interrupting," said Egretta. "But would I not be right in thinking the next course of action should be to cure Lady Samily as soon as possible?"

"Yes, yes." Conifax was much calmer now. "Quite right, Egretta. We'll use the same runes. Just need to move the boy." He turned to Glorbad. "Let's put your young back to good use."

"I can move him." Aranok went to stand but paused when Conifax cut him off.

"You can stay here." The master didn't even look at him. "I'll let you know if you're needed."

Aranok slowly sat again. Short of his father, Allandria had never seen anyone talk to him that way. Conifax bustled into the room with Glorbad and Morienne in tow. Egretta followed them in and closed the door behind her.

"It's not your fault," said Allandria.

Nirea's head whipped round to look at her. "Why would it be his fault?"

"It is. He's right," said Aranok quietly. "I should have got her to show me how she did it. I should have made sure." He put his head in his hands.

"Why didn't you?" Nirea's tone was challenging. Demanding, almost. Balaban frowned and crossed his arms but said nothing.

Aranok shrugged. "I don't know. I saw her do it. I didn't hear her say anything. There were no gestures."

Allandria had had enough of this examination. It was becoming cruel. Kicking a wounded man. She was going to take control. "When, exactly?"

"Mutton Hole. Upstairs."

"After you'd been knocked out?" Allandria looked at Nirea as she asked.

"Yes," he answered flatly.

Nirea visibly softened. "Fuck. Don't fret about it." She put a hand on his shoulder. "It's actually good to know you're human, Aranok. I was beginning to wonder."

*Good.* That was better.

"Aranok, you are no more perfect than the rest of us," said Balaban. "If, indeed, you were unconscious just before this happened, you may well have suffered an injury to your brain that prevented you from thinking clearly. I'm sure Egretta would confirm that."

Aranok looked up at him sadly and nodded. Allandria nudged him. "Your brain's broken."

A hint of a smile.

Balaban was kind, but Allandria knew it wouldn't really help. Nobody held the king's envoy to higher standards than the man himself.

They sat in silence as the now familiar screaming and banging permeated the door. After an age, it opened again. Conifax swept out, book in his good hand, followed by Glorbad, who had the self-awareness to look slightly uncomfortable.

"She's fine," he said to Aranok. "Just rattled."

"Thank you," he answered.

When nobody else came out, Nirea went in. Allandria followed her.

Samily sat in a chair with Egretta wrapping her hands in the same balm-soaked bandages. Morienne was doing something with Vastin's wound.

"Are you all right?" Nirea asked Samily.

The knight looked up, slightly dazed. "I am. I just…What happened?"

The women looked at each other. Allandria certainly wasn't about to be the one to tell the White Thorn that her God-given miraculous healing ability…wasn't.

"Conifax will explain it." Nirea obviously felt the same way.

At that, the old man stuck his head around the door. "Lady Thorn, are you feeling well enough to join us? We have a great deal to discuss. And I feel we could all do with some lunch. And a stiff drink."

---

The group sat around a large wooden table laden with soup, bread and beer.

Samily was finding it slightly awkward handling the spoon with the bandages on her hands, but they didn't hurt, which was somewhat surprising considering how they had looked. But the food was welcome, as was the beer.

Morienne had considerately taken a place at the far end of the large table, at a distance that minimised her curse's effect on the rest.

Everyone sat silently, and Samily had the notion that there was something they were all reluctant to say. Her wits had seemingly all returned. She couldn't remember anything after trying to heal Vastin, and nobody had yet offered her an explanation. "Could someone please tell me what happened?"

"Tell me, Lady Thorn, where did you learn those words?" Conifax asked between mouthfuls.

"What words?"

*"Air ais."*

"I don't know." She'd always known them. They were the prayer that made her healing power work. Meristan had said he thought she must have heard them a lot as a child, and she had liked to think they were from her mother, though she had no memory of her.

"Have you always been able to do this? Has anyone trained you?" Balaban asked.

"Yes, always. Brother Meristan told me of a bruise when I was small. When I saw, I put my hands on him, said the words and it was healed."

"Hmm." Conifax looked at her intently. "Have you ever used your power on something other than a person? An object?"

*What?* Why would she try to heal a thing?

"A broken plate, perhaps," Conifax suggested, "or a weapon?"

"No." She was somewhat irritated at the oddity of the question.

"Have you ever tried it with any other words, child?" asked Balaban. "Have you heard the words *air adhart*, for example?"

"No." Samily felt her face tightening as the irritation rose.

"Conifax...?" Aranok's tone was almost pleading. She turned to look at him. His face was difficult to read and he avoided meeting her eyes.

The old man put down his spoon and looked directly at her. "You're not a healer, Lady Samily. But you are certainly something rare and wonderful. Something we've not seen in at least three generations."

What did he mean she wasn't a healer? She'd been a healer her whole life! The envoy had seen her do it! She turned to him, hoping he'd offer some explanation, but his face was sad, almost stern.

"The words *air ais* are *draoidh*," he said. "They mean 'back.' You're not a healer, Samily. You're a *draoidh*. Like me. Like us."

———

Samily's face was a mix of confusion and what Aranok would have considered fear in anyone else. He'd hated having to say the words. He knew the tempest they'd cause in her. Meristan should have been here. The monk would have known how to do this gently, with dignity.

"What do you mean, I'm a *draoidh*?" she asked, as if he'd told her she was a tree.

"You are not healing a wound," Balaban explained. "You are taking the body part back in time to a point before the wound existed."

"What difference does it make?" the knight asked. "Surely healing is healing?"

"A very great deal," said Conifax. "For a start, there's your friend upstairs. When you tried to heal him, you were trying to take his wound back to a point in time before it was injured. Since he was wounded while he was Blackened, that meant the area was first returned to its cursed state. Since your hands were on him when that happened..."

Samily's mouth fell open. "I was Blackened?"

Conifax nodded.

"Only briefly," Aranok said. "We..." His eyes flitted to his master. "Conifax cured you quickly. No one else was hurt, thanks to Morienne." He nodded to the woman, who he thought smiled back at him.

Conifax leaned forward. "Let me ask you, have you noticed that the wounds that drain your energy the most are not the biggest, but the oldest?"

Samily closed her mouth and looked about her as if she'd just walked into the wrong room. "I felt nothing. I remember nothing. Thank God." Conifax looked at her curiously, but Aranok knew it wasn't herself she was grateful for. It was Meristan. And Vastin. And all of them.

"It's not the wound that matters," Conifax continued, "it's how far back you have to take the person to heal it. And if you've never had any training in focusing your *draoidh* energy..."

"Ohhh," Aranok groaned. "Of course!" That was why it was so draining. When he'd first learned to use his own powers, he'd found them completely exhausting until Conifax taught him how to only give the magic as much energy as it required—and no more.

"I don't understand," said Samily. "Are you saying my ability is not a gift from God?"

Conifax laughed, which made the knight scowl. The master realised his mistake and checked himself. "I'm sorry. In truth, it's no more or less a gift from God than any other *draoidh*'s abilities. I suppose it's only a matter of belief. If yours are a gift from God, then so are mine; so are Aranok's."

Samily looked shaken. Aranok put a hand on her arm. He hoped it was reassuring. He wished again that Meristan were here. "Welcome to the ranks."

She didn't look up, but she didn't withdraw her arm either.

Egretta cleared her throat, and the room turned to her. "So now what? What do we do for the boy?"

*Hells.* He'd almost forgotten.

"Well, it occurs to me that if the only reason the Blackened decay is because they stop eating, then we must simply feed him!" said Conifax.

Balaban raised his eyebrows. "Indeed. If we can do that, he should heal naturally. Well, as naturally as possible under the circumstances."

"How?" asked Nirea. "You can't force him to chew, to swallow."

"Actually, we can," said Egretta. "We have a system for feeding those who are not able to eat. He won't like it, but it appears he won't remember it." She gestured to Samily as evidence.

"Eurgh." Allandria grimaced.

Egretta gave her a reproachful look. "It's distasteful, but it'll keep him alive."

"How long will it take? For him to heal?" asked Glorbad.

"I've no idea," said Egretta. "It should have killed him. If the Blackening keeps him alive and we can get food and water in him, if it heals like a normal wound—months, at least." There was a general groan from the group. "He's lucky he didn't lose his arm."

Glorbad crossed his arms and sat back. "Bollocks. We can't spend months here."

"We can't and we won't," said Aranok. "If Egretta can heal him enough to survive the wound—you can cure him, Conifax?"

"I can."

Aranok looked back to Egretta. "Then we'll leave him here in your care, if that's all right?"

"Well, there is one significant problem." The medic's gaze was directed at the other end of the table.

At Morienne. "You need me. And my curse."

"We do," the medic agreed.

*Damn it.* Another promise Aranok was going to have to break. "Morienne..."

"It's fine," she interrupted him. "I've lived with this my whole life. I can live with it some more. They're not even sure they can lift it."

Aranok looked to his teacher, who closed his eyes.

"Morienne, you don't have to do this." Allandria stood and walked to her end of the table. Her eyes seemed to twitch as she approached.

"I've been doing it alone for months." Morienne shrugged. "I'll have company."

"Thank you, Morienne," said Aranok. "I owe you a debt. The kingdom owes you a debt. We won't forget it."

"A debt that will be repaid." Allandria took a seat near Morienne. She obviously had a connection with the woman. Maybe their shared nomadic heritage? Maybe she saw something of herself in her.

"There may be something we can do," said Balaban. "I have some thoughts."

"Like what?" Aranok whipped his head round to the master.

Balaban raised a hand. "I don't know for certain yet, but we may be able to mitigate the curse, if we can't cure it."

"What does that mean?" Aranok asked.

"I don't know yet. But there is reason to hope." Balaban smiled at Morienne as the room fell silent.

Hope. They needed hope.

"So now what?" Nirea asked.

It was a good question.

"Now we get to Barrock, right?" There was an edge in Glorbad's voice that almost dared anyone to disagree with him.

"Surely, we must cure the Blackened first?" As always, Samily's first thought was for others. Never for herself. When Meristan said she was a miracle, he might have been right.

"It's more complicated than that," said Conifax.

"We can cure one at a time," said Aranok, "but to cure all of them..."

"Even if you could cure them all—many of them are past saving," said Egretta. "Curing them would be cruel. They'd come back only to die. Painfully."

Allandria raised a hand to her mouth. Aranok had been thinking about little else for days. How to cure everyone, when missing even one would keep the curse alive, and many of those cured would suffer and die. The room settled into a cold silence.

"There might be a way," said Conifax finally. All heads turned to him. He looked directly at Aranok. "There is a book in the *caibineat puinnsean*. Stories of a powerful item. With it, a *draoidh* can cast their power wider."

*Hells.* That would change everything!

"How wide?" Aranok asked eagerly.

"Wide enough," the old man answered. "If the stories are accurate. If we summon the magic to lift the curse from the item itself, it could reflect the effect outwards for a hundred miles in every direction. Maybe more."

Aranok's mind raced. "That's enough to cover almost the entire country."

"Indeed," said Conifax. "And since we know where most of the Blackened are anyway..."

"Then what?" It was Nirea. "You just said curing them all would be cruel."

"If we knew when, we could be ready," said Egretta. "There are a lot of medics here. And others. We could be ready with food, water, medical supplies. We could treat them as soon as they're cured. With help, maybe we could transport them back here—if we had enough wagons..."

"I can get you wagons." Aranok knew his sister had wanted to help. Rasa could deliver a message. It could work.

"But some would still suffer, and die?" asked Samily.

Nobody answered.

"Sometimes, Samily, you cannot save everyone."

Aranok turned to find the source of the voice. It was weak, but it was distinctly...

"Meristan!" Samily leapt from her seat and grabbed her master in a great hug.

"Careful, girl." He laughed gently. "I'm just out of my hospital bed."

"You should still be in it." Egretta crossed to him and grabbed his wrist. "A man your size without food or sleep for days..."

"I'm fine. Honestly. I've had some porridge." The monk held Samily away from him.

"Sit down." The knight offered her seat. He took it, his legs trembling slightly as he sat.

"It's good to see you again, Brother." Nirea slapped him on the shoulder.

There was a general chorus of agreement, and the mood in the room warmed for the first time. It was good to see the fruits of their victory after taking so many hits.

"It's a pleasure to meet you, Brother Meristan." Conifax stood and offered his hand across the table. "I am Conifax, a master here at the university."

"As I hear it, you're also the man to whom I owe my life." The monk clasped his hand firmly. "I cannot thank you enough."

"I can't take all the credit. My colleague Master Balaban was instrumental." Conifax gestured to the man, who simply nodded.

"Thank you." Meristan smiled at him.

"It was my absolute pleasure, I assure you," said the master. "It is a rare treat to see one's academic studies put to such beneficial use."

"Aranok worked out it was a curse," said Allandria. "Morienne kept you safe."

Meristan turned to look at Morienne and squinted. "I...Oh." He raised a hand to his head. "I'm sorry, I'm...a bit dizzy. Perhaps I should still be in bed."

"It's her curse," Samily explained. "It is why she was immune to the Blackening."

"Is that right?" asked Meristan, wide-eyed. "Then your curse makes you our blessing. I am grateful to meet you, Lady Morienne."

Morienne half laughed. It was the happiest noise Aranok had heard from her.

"As for you, Envoy, I expect no less." The monk smiled broadly at Aranok. "God has blessed me with your companionship." He looked up at Egretta, who was fussing at his throat. "And may I ask your name?"

"Egretta," she said plainly. "Keep your head still, please, I need your heartbeat."

Meristan smiled and nodded, like an amused child. "I'm sorry; I interrupted. You have a plan for the rest of the Blackened?"

"Maybe." Aranok looked to Conifax. "What's the item?"

Conifax leaned back and stroked his beard with his good hand. "Well, that's the thing. It doesn't say."

"What?" asked Glorbad. "That's about as much use as shite on a log!" Nirea snorted a laugh. "Surely you've got more than that, Master."

"Very little," said Conifax. "Except where it could be."

"Well, you could've started with that!" said Glorbad. "Where is it?"

"Caer Amon."

The soldier let out a long sigh. "Fuck."

Caer Amon was the oldest known settlement in Eidyn, founded using upturned boats from the north hundreds of years ago. At the mouth of the River Amon, it had been the heart of the new country, from where the population spread east and north. Legend had it that the priest from the nearby kirk, Crostorfyn, had travelled into the village after seeing nobody at the kirk in several days. He found no trace of life, nor death, and every structure devastated, as if it had been in ruins for decades. Most who visited Caer Amon never returned, and those who did raved about ghosts and living buildings. Nobody went there without good reason. Yet here they were, with the best reason possible.

"We are not going to Caer Amon." Glorbad looked pointedly at Aranok. "That's fucking suicide."

"What's the alternative? You tell me." Aranok hoped it was evident there wasn't one.

"We do what we were sent to do! We get to Barrock and…" The soldier looked around the room, seeming to realise not everyone was supposed to know what their mission entailed. "You know…"

"And how are you getting to Haven, with the Auld Road blocked? You planning to go over the Black Hills with your cargo?" Aranok asked.

Glorbad sat up defiantly. "We'll go the long way. Cross-country to Lochen, pick up the Easter Road and take the ferry across the Nor Loch."

"The ferry?" Allandria was clearly appalled. The Nor Loch ferry was not fit for royalty of any country. Nirea frowned and shook her head at Glorbad.

He threw his arms up. "All right, then we'll follow the Easter Road to Leet, and come back up the Wester Road."

"Leet is overrun with pirates," said Allandria.

"I can handle Leet," said Nirea testily.

"Surely you see this is more important?" Samily gestured to Meristan.

"With respect, that's not our decision to make," said Glorbad.

Conifax stood. "All right, clearly you're all dancing around some secret we're not meant to know. Egretta, Balaban, Morienne, would you be kind enough to join me in making arrangements for our young patient?"

They silently followed Conifax out of the room, Egretta with a look of disapproval that would have shrivelled the hardiest man. The moment the door closed, the silence was over.

"You can't take the queen of Gaulle through Leet!" said Allandria. And suddenly everyone was talking at once. Allandria and Nirea argued over the safety of Leet, Samily and Glorbad over which took precedence, their orders or the Blackening. Meristan sat looking around at them as if he were surrounded by lunatics.

"All right!" Aranok called. It made no difference. "Hey!" Still nothing.

Meristan stood and raised a hand. Samily stopped speaking immediately and sat back in her chair, which disarmed Glorbad, who also stopped talking.

"I know Leet inside out!" bawled Nirea. "We'll be fine!"

"But you can't guarantee that!" said Allandria.

"Ladies, if I may?" asked Meristan. Both turned to face him. "Perhaps we should all remember that we are the king's council, but Aranok is the envoy. And we haven't heard anything from him yet."

Everyone turned to face him. Which would have been a lot easier if he'd known the right thing to do.

"I realise Caer Amon is dangerous." He was working out his answer as he spoke.

"And a week's ride back the way we came," said Glorbad.

"That too. But the Blackening has spread beyond the Meadows. We have to stop it before it spreads to the whole kingdom. One Blackened in Haven and the whole population would be turned in days. Our obligation is to protect the kingdom."

Glorbad stood. "Damn it, man, that is for the king to decide, not you! This 'item' could be a myth. Then what? Your job is to do the king's work. We take Taneitheia back to Haven, tell Janaeus what we know and let him decide what to do next!"

Aranok sighed and shook his head.

"All right," said Meristan calmly. "May I propose a third solution? There are six of us. It seems we have more than enough to be in two places at the same time. Aranok, Allandria and Samily can go to Caer Amon; the rest of us can go to Barrock."

Again, the room fell into silence. It wasn't a bad idea.

"Won't work," Glorbad grumbled. "The queen won't listen to us without the envoy. She has no idea who we are!"

"Meristan is head of the Order," said Allandria. "Gaulle is a faithful country. She'll listen."

"She's right," said Aranok. "And I've never met her."

"So can we consider that a plan?" The monk's calm was infectious.

"Fine." Glorbad sat again. "It's your head, Envoy."

Allandria nodded. Samily sat quietly with her head bowed. She didn't look happy, but she didn't speak.

Nirea leaned back and put her boots on the table. "All right then."

Aranok stood. "Well then, I suppose we can call this meeting of the king's council to a close."

# CHAPTER 27

I'm sorry."

Aranok sat in the ornate chair at the front of Conifax's office desk. The entire wall behind the master and the one to their right were lined with shelves, overflowing with books. One section was behind glass and seemed devoted to what Allandria would have called trinkets in any other place, but here they were most likely items of some magical significance. The opposite wall was almost all window and, facing south, allowed a huge amount of light to spill into the room.

The old man raised his eyes from the book, without lifting his head. "I'm sure you are."

Allandria bristled. They'd sat here in silence for an age. He wasn't being fair. And even if Aranok would resent her for it, she, at least, wasn't keeping quiet any longer. "What's wrong with you?" She wasn't entirely sure which one of them she was addressing.

They both turned to look at her.

"You've just figured out how to cure the worst plague this country's ever seen. You've saved at least one life already and probably two. You've got a plan to save everybody. Would you both please get over this…" She gestured to them both, generally.

Aranok looked disapprovingly at her, but she didn't care. It was long past time these two had a good hard shake. She should just bang their heads together. Nirea probably would have.

"It's not quite that simple…" Conifax began, but Allandria's tail was up.

"It is! It's extremely simple! You're angry because he made a mistake at a point when he'd taken a massive blow to the head. And do you know why? Because he'd headbutted a bloody demon! Have you ever headbutted a demon? Because I can tell you, they're pretty fucking solid!"

She stood, breathing heavily. Both men looked at her wide-eyed, in stunned silence.

Conifax roared with laughter and looked at Aranok. "You did what? Are you insane?"

Aranok shrugged with a smile. "It was a complicated situation."

"So you thought you'd throw your head at it?" Conifax laughed even harder, and Aranok joined him.

"I've had better ideas." He rubbed the back of his head.

"All right." Allandria took the chair next to Aranok. "That's better."

"She's fearsome," said Conifax. "I see why you keep her around."

"She's right here, and she can hear you." Allandria was in no mood for tolerating anything else today. There were more than enough slaps to go round.

Conifax put up his hands. "I meant no disrespect; I'm sorry."

Aranok smiled sidelong at her. Good.

"So any more idea what we're looking for?" Aranok asked.

Conifax looked down at the book, shaking his head. "It doesn't say. It talks about a relic from the 'heart of devastation.' From what I can glean, I think perhaps there was a powerful item in Caer Amon that could amplify the power of a *draoidh*. It may have played a part in the destruction. I think what you're looking for may be that—or what's left of it."

"The 'heart of devastation.' Well, that sounds lovely," said Allandria.

"It's not much to go on," said Aranok. "But I suppose it's something."

"I'm sorry I can't give you more." Conifax looked away, at the floor.

"What else?" Aranok shifted in his seat.

"Pardon?" said Conifax.

"What else? What aren't you telling me?"

The old man sat back and steepled his fingers against his lips.

"Clever boy. I forgot how well you read people. Close the door," he said to Allandria.

She cocked her head at him and raised an eyebrow.

"Would you mind closing the door, please?" he rephrased.

Allandria nodded and did as he asked, staying by the door to prevent anyone coming in unannounced.

"I found more books. In the *caibineat puinnsean*. Books I've never seen before. Books I didn't know existed." Conifax spoke in barely more than a whisper.

"What's in them?" asked Aranok.

"I don't know yet. But they don't seem like *draoidh* texts. They look like... histories. Of Eidyn."

"Histories?" Aranok asked. "That doesn't make sense. Who would want to ban the reading of history?"

"That is the question I've been asking myself," said Conifax. "Who, and why. And how."

"Who has access to the *caibineat*?" Allandria asked.

"That's the thing," said Conifax. "Only the senior masters. That's a dozen people. All of whom I believed I could trust. And now I'm having trouble trusting any of them."

"Could it be an error?" asked Aranok.

"Nothing goes in the *caibineat puinnsean* in error. But I do have a concern about..." Conifax trailed off.

"What?" asked Aranok.

"Mynygogg. I noticed his name as I flicked through one of the books."

"You think someone is trying to hide Mynygogg's history?" asked Aranok. "To what end?"

"I don't know," said Conifax.

"But wait—does that mean Mynygogg has an ally amongst the senior masters?" Allandria asked.

"That, my dear, is exactly why you're guarding that door," said Conifax.

"Hells." Aranok covered his mouth. "That makes sense."

"In what way?" Conifax asked.

Aranok looked over his shoulder at Allandria and back to his old teacher. "We've come across some oddities."

Aranok covered everything they'd encountered since leaving Haven: the Thakhati, the king's messenger in Mournside, the Blackened moving to the Auld Road. He also mentioned something Meristan had told him about Reivers wearing odd crests.

"Don't forget the armour," Allandria reminded him.

"Of course. We found an empty suit of White Thorn armour. Abandoned on the road to Mutton Hole."

Conifax had sat back, arms crossed, in silence through the whole retelling. When Aranok finished, he remained quiet for a long time. Allandria could hear the footsteps of students scraping past outside the door. The low murmur of their everyday chatter. She wondered how much these children knew of what was going on outside Traverlyn. How much their lives were even affected by it. They lived a sheltered existence here—some of them with *draoidh* abilities. Surrounded by art and academia, were they even conscious of the horrors outside the town? Part of her hoped not. Maybe it was good to have this untouched haven, where the young could be young and sleep soundly at night. Eventually, they would need to know the truth. For their sake and the country's.

"Well," Conifax finally said. "That's all bloody odd, isn't it? What do you make of it?"

"Hard to know," said Aranok. "My best guess is that Mynygogg is trying to undermine Janaeus somehow."

"Undermine the whole kingdom, more like!" said Conifax. "But what does he gain?"

"That, I don't know," said Aranok. "Yet. But in addition to at least one ally here, I suspect he may have some control over the head messenger. And at least one assassin—likely more."

"How's he commanding them?" Conifax furrowed his brow.

"I'm not sure he is," said Aranok. "I think, maybe, someone else is. Maybe your senior master." That was a horrible thought—especially if it was one of the *draoidh* masters.

"Hmm. That is troubling," said Conifax. "Who do you trust when your allies are suspect?"

"You have to tell them," Allandria said.

Aranok turned to her. "Who?"

"Glorbad. Nirea. You can't send them off without knowing all this."
Aranok leaned his head to the side. His neck cracked like a branch breaking. "I'm still not sure I trust them. Not completely."

Allandria sat, took his hands and looked him in the eye. "You're wrong. He's a pain in the arse, and she can be reckless, but they've both risked their lives for us. There comes a point where keeping secrets works against you. They're allies. Tell them the truth."

Aranok looked round at Conifax, who shrugged.

"All right." He looked back at her. "All right. We'll tell them everything."

---

Samily sat cross-legged on the floor beside Meristan's bed. He'd been sleeping most of the afternoon. She'd spent the time in prayer and contemplation. Mostly, she was trying to take control of her fear. She'd lost Meristan by leaving him alone in Lepertoun. She didn't want to do it again. She'd never feared for him when she left him in Baile Airneach. Why was that?

Perhaps because it was home. Where she'd always been safe. Where he'd kept her safe. Maybe that was it. She was used to him being her protector. She'd assumed him immortal. Like a rock she could always lean on. And now he was terrifyingly, dangerously mortal. As fragile as any other human. And that scared her.

Perhaps that realisation of his own mortality had been what was preying on his mind too. Had something happened that made him feel vulnerable? The war maybe?

"What's troubling you, child?"

Samily opened her eyes to see her master looking down from his bed. "Brother?"

"The way you're contorting your face, I imagine you're trying to solve a particularly difficult puzzle." He sat up and took a drink of water from the cup beside him. "Did you win?"

"Brother, I..." She didn't know where to start.

"Speak freely, Samily."

She still wasn't entirely accustomed to this new arrangement—no matter how many times he said it.

"Please don't go!" she blurted out.

"To Barrock?"

"Yes. Stay here."

Meristan reached down and touched her cheek. "My child. I understand."

Samily stood up and took his hand in hers.

"You died. You were gone. And now I have you back."

Meristan smiled. "Exactly. I am back. Because you saved me. All of you. Why do you think that is?"

"What do you mean?"

"Why do you think I was Blackened and then saved?" he asked.

"I don't know. Because God willed it?"

"And why would God will that?"

She shrugged.

"Well, as a result, we may be able to cure the Blackening. Because we were there, because Aranok and the others were there, because we were close enough to Traverlyn to reach Conifax and Balaban. It was the right place and time, and I was the right person. Don't you think that's a great honour? That God chose me to be the instrument of ending the plague?"

She hadn't seen it that way. She'd been too absorbed in trying to save her master. But he had a point. Even Morienne being there, being cursed, so that Aranok could work it out—even the baby, bless its tiny soul. Everything had happened just as it needed to, to bring them here.

"I see."

"When you were little, Samily, there was a woman in Dail Ruigh, whose children played in the fields while she worked the market. She said that it gave her such joy, but at the same time, a terrible, crushing fear. Letting her children out of her care was like letting her heart run free outside of her chest. When it was gone, she felt a tightness, a hole, an empty longing for it to return. But it came back bigger, wiser, happier. That is what it is to have a child, Samily. That is what it is to love. We all have to learn to live with the hole in our chest, so our hearts can be free. Do you understand?"

Samily realised she was trembling. "I think so."

Meristan opened his arms wide, and she fell on him, hugging him tight and breathing in the smell of him. She never wanted to let him go again. But she would. And she would pray to God every day to keep him safe.

"Do you think you could do me a favour?" he asked.

She nodded on his shoulder.

"Could you find some whisky in this place?"

Samily's shoulders trembled with laughter.

---

"Why the Hell didn't you tell us sooner?" Glorbad was not taking the news well. He stood, fuming in the tight space between the two beds in Aranok and Allandria's room at the Sheep's Heid.

"Keep your voice down," Allandria said. "We came up here to prevent anyone overhearing us." The last thing they needed was someone eavesdropping in the hall and spreading rumours based on a half-heard story.

"Honestly?" Aranok asked. "I didn't know if I could trust you. There were Reivers on the road we should have taken out of Haven."

"Told you," Nirea said to Glorbad. The soldier shook his head reproachfully, as if this was a discussion they'd had already. Interesting.

"There are Reivers everywhere. I check my fucking soup for Reivers before I eat!" he hissed. "That means nothing!"

"Surely it means something that we're telling you now." Allandria really just wanted this to be over. Anger was inevitable, but it was important they cauterise this wound. The sooner the flames burned out, the better for everyone.

"He's right," said Nirea. "You should have told us before."

Allandria sighed, exasperated. She felt more like a schoolteacher today than a bodyguard. "For God's sake, can everybody please get over their wounded pride and see the bigger picture? We need to work together. Can we all be bloody grown-ups?"

Glorbad flumped down onto the bed beside Nirea. "So there's a load of weird bollocks going on, and your best guess is Mynygogg's allies are trying to overthrow the kingdom by stealth; is that about it?"

"Yes," Aranok said after a moment of consideration.

"All right then," said Glorbad. "Now we know. What about the others?"

"Meristan knows. And Conifax," said Aranok. "We can tell Samily en route to Caer Amon."

Nirea looked at Glorbad, who was still seething but had at least stopped complaining. "Well, I suggest we all get some food and get a decent night's sleep, then, if we're leaving in the morning," she said.

"Egretta and Conifax think Meristan needs at least another day to recover, before he'll be well enough to travel," said Aranok.

Allandria thought it was a fair estimate. Ideally, he'd probably take a week, but...

"All right?" Nirea asked Glorbad.

"Aye, fine," said the soldier. "He deserves a rest. I can manage another day here on your coin, Envoy."

"Then I'm happy to buy back your good graces, soldier," said Aranok.

"One other thing," said Nirea. "The monk needs leathers. Whether he fights or not, he's a liability in those robes. If we encounter more Blackened..."

Aranok nodded. "Good idea. I'll speak to him."

"Right, then," said Glorbad. "If we're done, I hear the distinctive sound of your beer calling my name."

"Are we good?" Aranok offered his hand to the soldier. Glorbad looked at it a moment, then broke into a grin and grasped it firmly.

"We're good. As long as there's nothing else you're keeping quiet."

"You know what I know," Aranok answered.

"Nirea?" Aranok offered her the same hand. She took it and pulled herself up to stand facing him.

"It took you too long to realise we're on the same side. Don't make that mistake again. As long as you've got my back, I've got yours. Deal?"

"Deal." He nodded.

*Thank God for that.*

⸺◦⸺

Rasa sat in quarters, as elegant and beautiful as Aranok remembered her. She was engrossed in a book about natural herbs, a subject for which Aranok had never managed to muster up much enthusiasm. He knew how useful they could be, but learning to tell one leaf from another had been beyond his patience. He had liked to think that he was focused on bigger things, but with age he realised it was simply his lack of patience for anything that didn't excite him.

"Hello, Rasa," he said quietly. "May I interrupt you?"

Rasa looked up from the book and smiled when she saw him. That was a good sign. "Laird Aranok." She made to stand, but Aranok gestured to her to remain seated.

"May I?" He gestured to the chair beside her.

"Of course. What can I do for you?"

"You delivered the note of introduction to my sister?" he asked.

"I did. She has a lovely home. And Emelina is delightful."

Good. The thought of them warmed him. The thought of Emelina receiving the direction she needed, even more so.

"Ikara asked me to thank you again when I next saw you. Which I suppose is now!" She smiled. "She took my measurements and said she'd have a few outfits ready for me in three days."

"Ideal," said Aranok. "May I ask something else of you in the meantime?"

"If it is within my power." She closed the book before her.

Aranok took out two pieces of paper and placed them in front of her on the table. He touched the first, smaller one. "This is another note for my sister. I'd be incredibly grateful if you could please deliver it to her tomorrow. It's not in relation to you, I just need her to know that I'll be arriving there myself in a few days."

"Oh?" Rasa raised an eyebrow.

"Just passing through. Which is the second thing." He moved his hand to the other, larger piece of paper, unfolding the map and laying it out before her. "Since we're already sharing secrets, this is a plan of where we should be for the next five days or so. I don't share this kind of information with anyone usually, but Conifax vouched for you, and he's one of the few I trust. Can I trust you?"

Rasa's face turned earnestly serious. "You can. But why are you showing me this?"

"Because I may need a second favour. Things are happening at the moment, and Conifax may need to get word to me quickly. If he does…"

"You want me to be able to find you. Of course."

"I've arranged with Conifax that you'll be paid a bonus, should that be necessary."

"Thank you." Rasa looked down at the map. Her face changed as she examined it. "You're going to Caer Amon?"

"We are." Aranok looked over his shoulder. There was a boy lurking closer than he'd have liked. He reached over and folded the map in half. "But I really don't want anyone else knowing that."

Rasa nodded, folded the map again, and slipped it into her shirt. "Nobody sees this but me. I understand. Can I ask why?"

Aranok could count the number of people he trusted completely on one hand: Allandria, Janaeus, Conifax, Ikara and Sumara. But Conifax swore Rasa was an ally, and as he'd learned very recently, sometimes a little trust could be helpful.

"We have a cure for the Blackening," he whispered. "And there may be something in Caer Amon that will help."

Rasa's eyes opened wide.

"At the moment, we can cure one person at a time," he continued. "But if we get this item, we might be able to cure everyone."

Rasa put her hand to her chest, where the map lay. "I'll protect this with my life. If there is anything I can do, you need only ask. I need no payment."

Aranok smiled. "Thank you. I appreciate that very much." He looked down at the book. "You're interested in herbs?"

"A little. I am interested in the healing properties. I was once caught outside…injured. It would have been useful to know which plants would have helped."

"Have Ikara introduce you to my mother. She's fascinated with herbs. She gave me this." He lifted his bottle of rejuvenating oils and opened it for Rasa to smell. She leaned toward it and gently breathed in, then sprang back.

"Wow! What's that?"

"Basil, mint and rosemary," he said. "It keeps me awake."

"I could have done with that when I was studying. It has a real kick."

"It certainly does. But fair warning, it can take hours to come down. Take it at the start of your watch, or else you'll be awake all night."

"I'll wager you would." She smiled.

"Where are you from, Rasa?" The smile disappeared. Damn. He'd pushed too far. "I'm sorry; I didn't mean to…"

"It's all right," she said. "I just don't like to talk about my past. Traverlyn is my home."

"I understand," he said, backing off. He knew what it was like to have a difficult childhood, and his was more privileged than most. Being a young metamorph could have been awful. He should have known better. "And I'm very sorry."

"It's fine." Half of her smile returned. "You didn't know."

"Gracious and talented. I see why Conifax likes you." He stood and put out a hand. Rasa placed hers in it delicately. "Thank you again."

She stood too. "Please, it's my pleasure. And I mean it. Anything I can do to help."

"I'll take you up on that." Aranok nodded politely and turned away.

He was very glad Rasa was on his side. She'd be a formidable enemy. And an excellent tutor for Emelina. Conifax had chosen well.

Of course.

# CHAPTER 28

H ey there." Allandria stroked the nose of the big black beast before her. It whinnied and nudged her hand, gently stamping its front feet. With the speed they'd be travelling, they needed strong, fast mounts. There was no time for a pack horse or using roads—not that they could take the Auld Road anyway. Most horses wouldn't be fit for this journey—each carrying a passenger and camping provisions, travelling cross-country over the Black Hills. It was a lot to ask of an animal. But there were no better horses than Calladells. Used as war horses by the army, the magnificent animals stood seven foot high at least. A combination of breeding and rearing meant they were built for both strength and speed.

"What's your name?" she asked the animal.

"Midnight," came a voice from behind her. She spun and reached for her quiver before she realised it wasn't there. But the "enemy" who had snuck up on her was a stable boy, standing with his hands raised in defence. "Sorry, m'lady."

"No, I'm sorry." Allandria lowered her arms. She hadn't realised how jumpy she'd become. But then, they'd been surprised a little too often lately. "Midnight?"

"Aye." The boy moved to stroke the horse himself. His slight limp made him lean to the left. A riding accident, perhaps? He also had a faint scar on his grubby cheek. But under the grime, and despite his height, he looked no more than a young teenager. "She's a beauty, i'nt she?"

The horse cocked her head at the boy affectionately.

"She certainly is. I promise to take good care of her."

"Thank you." The boy looked at her earnestly. "Like to see her again." He untied her lead from the post. "Best get you outside—sun's coming up."

Allandria followed him out into the paddock. Samily was already on her horse, a brown stallion with white hooves. The knight looked a million miles away. She was unhappy about leaving Meristan. Allandria understood. If Aranok had been through what Meristan had…

"We need to get going," said the *draoidh*, throwing his pack across his own horse. She rolled her eyes. Good of him to bring her back to reality.

"All right," she said. "Hold your horses."

Aranok groaned, but smiled.

The boy finished saddling her mount, and she threw her own pack across it.

"What are their names?" She nodded to the other animals.

"That yin's Dancer," he said, pointing to Aranok's brown-and-white-dappled mare. "And that yin's Bear. Biggest beast I ever seen."

He wasn't wrong. Even for a Calladell, Samily's horse was huge.

Once the sun was fully visible above the horizon, they set off. First, the short ride to the edge of town, warming up the horses, before the run ahead.

"How are you going to cope when we come across the Blackened?" Allandria asked. It had been playing on her mind, and she knew it would be bothering Aranok. He'd memorised the runes and the incantations for lifting the curse the night before, but only for using on the relic, he said.

"We ride on," he said in a flat tone. "We can't cure them one at a time."

"I know that. But are you going to be all right with that?"

He didn't answer for a long time.

"I have to be," he finally said.

Indeed. In part, she'd asked because she knew they'd all be feeling it—Samily especially. Better to get it out in the open now than deal with it later. They rode on in silence for a while. The tension was enough to make her squirm. Had she made it better or worse?

"Dancer," she said to Aranok. He turned to look at her curiously. She nodded at the horse.

"Oh, right." He patted her neck. "Hello, Dancer. What about yours?"

"Midnight."

Aranok snorted. "Not very imaginative, is it?"

Allandria leaned forward and pretended to cover the horse's ears. "Don't listen to him, Midnight. You're a beautiful girl."

"What's mine called?" Samily asked from behind them.

"Bear!" Allandria called back. The horse reared its head a little at the sound of its name.

Samily nodded. "Good. I like it."

"So you got all the horses' names, did you?" Aranok asked.

"I did." She smiled.

"Interesting," he said. "What was the boy's name?"

She hadn't asked. *Damn it.* And after chastising him for not getting the name of the messenger. Which, of course, was why he was asking. The git.

"I don't know," she said quietly. Aranok smiled and looked ahead. "All right then, smartarse, what was his name?"

"Tobin," Aranok said without looking at her.

She scowled. "You made that up!"

"You can ask him when we get back." He laughed and kicked his horse into action.

They'd cleared the town. It was time to run.

---

It had taken all day for the armourer to come up with an outfit that would fit Meristan—but they had explained it had to be today. They were leaving tomorrow, or else Glorbad might just go on his own. Nirea was keen to get going too. The longer she spent away from the water, the more she regretted joining the king's council. When the summons had arrived in Leet, she'd half considered jumping on the next boat and pretending she'd never received it. Nirea only knew one way to lead—the pirate way. She gave orders; people followed them or died. There were no "councils." But she'd had to learn to adapt when she'd agreed to join the rebellion against Hofnag. The bastard's corruption was the reason half her crew had turned to piracy. His taxes made it nigh impossible to make a decent, legal living on a boat. The bribes his shore porters extorted from merchants just to "protect" their goods crippled the profit on a journey. And Hofnag took a taste to allow it. So, aye, she'd been happy to unseat the old cunt. Only regret was that he'd escaped before they could be rid of him for good.

And she'd been surprised at how her new life suited her, running a navy boat on the right side of the law. Made a difference that the law was fair. Just. But Nirea had no taste for diplomacy. Hopefully, once they got Taneitheia back to Haven, she could persuade Janaeus to pick someone else for the job.

Meristan emerged from the back room, looking slightly awkward in his new leathers. Dylar, the armourer, stood with his arms crossed, silently watching.

"Well," Nirea said appreciatively. "I had no idea there was so much man under all those robes!"

He blushed slightly. But she wasn't wrong. All that bulk under his monk's attire had turned out to be a lot more muscle than flab. With leathers on, he looked a more formidable foe than either Glorbad or her. That might be useful. If only he could actually fight...

"What do they feed you in Baile Airneach?" She enjoyed Meristan's discomfort a little more than she probably should. Glorbad gave her a disapproving look.

"God blessed me with a healthy body," Meristan said.

"Still, though," said Nirea. "You must do something to stay in that condition?"

"There is physical labour to be done. We do God's work."

"God does good work." She smiled.

"How does it feel?" Glorbad asked, glancing sideways at her.

The dark brown leathers creaked as Meristan stretched his shoulders. It must have been odd to wear them for the first time. Nirea couldn't remember when she'd first put on leathers. A long time ago. Another life.

"A little odd. A little constricting," the monk said. "But overall, it seems fine, I think. I just feel a little foolish, if I'm honest."

"Why?" asked Glorbad.

"I'm no warrior, my friend. It seems wrong."

"It's not like you're wearing the White." Glorbad clapped the monk on the shoulder. "Leathers are just leathers. They're for defence. That's all. You look fine."

Nirea had to agree. He looked fine. "How are you feeling?" She reminded herself he was still a monk, despite appearances.

"Still a little weak." He put a hand to his head. "Like I've been drinking whisky for a week on an empty stomach."

"Aye." Glorbad nodded knowingly.

"I'm sure I'll be fine tomorrow," said Meristan. "I would, however, like to get back to the hospital now, if we could? I think I'm in need of a rest."

"Of course," said Glorbad. "Can I carry anything for you?"

"Well, I'd quite like to bring my robes..." He nodded toward Dylar.

"I'll get them." The armourer disappeared into the back room.

Glorbad poked around at the back of the leathers, making little "hmm" and other appreciative noises. "You know, we could easily attach a sword back here. Even just a short sword."

"I've never held a sword, I'm afraid," he said. "Never felt comfortable with it."

"Ever chopped wood?" Nirea asked.

"Often." The monk looked puzzled.

"Oh, that's a fine idea," said Glorbad. "We'll strap wee Vastin's axe to your back. He won't miss it—and at least you'll have something to protect yourself with, just in case."

Meristan seemed to lose a little more colour at that, but he didn't object. It seemed ironic to Nirea that such a powerful man would be so against any sort of violence.

Then again, maybe it was a good thing. Either way, she found herself ruing the loss of their White Thorn and resident "healer." It was something of a comfort knowing you were travelling with someone who was not only the greatest fighter you've ever seen, but who could reattach your leg if you were careless enough to lose it. Hopefully they wouldn't need her. Barrock wasn't far—only two days' ride southeast. And they were travelling away from the Blackened and Dun Eidyn. With a little luck, they might just get a bit of peace and quiet.

———※———

Samily lay on her back. The sky was unusually clear, and since they had opted not to build a fire for fear of attracting any stray Blackened, she could see the stars clearly. The deep, dark black was lit up with a dancing array of lights, twinkling down on her. It felt like a vast ocean. She wanted to dive in and swim amongst the beautiful little fires. It was at times like this, in silence and solitude, alone with nature, that she felt closest to God. It was peaceful and gentle and good.

"You're not asleep, are you?"

She bolted upright and looked round at the envoy, who was sitting up a few feet away. She'd thought he and Allandria both asleep.

"No," she whispered back.

"What were you doing?" he asked, then jumped slightly as Allandria grunted in her sleep.

"Appreciating God's beauty." Samily looked up again.

Aranok looked up too. "I suppose that is beautiful. Whether God has anything to do with it..."

It was becoming slightly irksome that everybody seemed to want to challenge her faith recently. She was unaccustomed to being around the faithless. Or, at least, faithless who were prepared to speak so to a White Thorn.

"If you do not believe in God, then where do you imagine your powers come from?"

"Our powers, you mean?" Aranok corrected her, irritatingly.

Samily nodded slowly. She was not yet accustomed to thinking of herself in the same way as the *draoidh*.

"Why do they have to come from anywhere?" he asked. "Does a fire ask where its heat comes from? Does the ocean ask why it's wet? Why can't it just be a part of us?"

"And you think something so wondrous just happened by accident?" she asked. "Why, if you can see magic for yourself and can control things others cannot, why should you find it so hard to believe in God?"

"Oh, I didn't say I don't believe there could be a god," he answered. "I'm just not convinced by yours."

That wasn't a response she'd heard before. "What do you mean?"

"You believe God has a benevolent plan, yes? That God is guiding all things, directing our lives toward the better?"

"Well, that is simplistic, but yes," she answered. "In general."

"Look around. You see stars; I see a barren wasteland where once there was an abundance of life. You see beauty; I see decay. You see good; I see suffering. I see no sign of a benevolent plan here."

Samily lifted a stick and scraped it along the ground, drawing lines in the dirt as she thought about how best to respond. "We see what we choose to see. I choose to see the good. God did not make the Blackening, Envoy. A human did. Have you considered that maybe, for all your lack of faith, you are God's instrument in curing it?"

"Pssh," said the *draoidh*. "Why is everything bad that happens the fault of humans, but when humans do good, they're God's instruments?"

She cocked her head. "I am sorry for you, Envoy. I am sorry that you have not felt God's presence. I feel it around me every day, and it is warmth, and love, and peace. I wish I could share it with you. I'm sure you would choose to believe."

"I don't think you can choose to believe anything, Samily." The envoy's face had turned serious. "You're either convinced of something, or you're not. You believe it, or you don't. There's no choosing."

"Still," she said. "I am sorry for you. I will pray for you."

Aranok looked around as if searching for the right answer. "Thank you?"

Samily did not respond. There was nothing more to say.

The envoy left a long silence before speaking again. "More importantly, since we're both up..."

"You should be asleep," she said, cutting him off. "This is my watch. You need to rest."

He shook his head as if shooing away a fly. "I'm awake now. I'll sleep later. I want to show you something."

He handed her a leaf from the ground. She took it and turned it over in her hand. "What am I missing?"

"When you use your power. How does it feel?"

"Like God flowing through me," she said honestly. Despite leaving her exhausted, using her powers felt wonderful.

Aranok raised an eyebrow. "I know that's what you think it is. But what does it actually feel like?"

She thought. It was hard to describe. She turned the leaf over in her hand, feeling it tickle her palm. Why had he given it to her? What was he doing?

"I suppose it feels like a warmth, rising and then flowing from me."

"Yes." Aranok nodded. "That's the energy that feeds your magic. But you have to learn to ration it. To only give it as much energy as it needs."

"How?" She couldn't tell whether it was the breeze or her own discomfort with this conversation that made the hairs rise on her arms.

"Imagine you are watering flowers," said the envoy. "You have an entire garden to feed. You wouldn't upend a bucket on the first flower, would you?"

Samily shrugged. "Of course not."

"You are the bucket. Your energy is water. You need energy for everything you do, but you're emptying the bucket every time you use your power."

It was an interesting metaphor, but Samily had no idea what to do with it. "How do I do that?"

He cradled a leaf in his own hands, holding it out reverentially. "Focus on your leaf."

Samily adjusted herself to sit cross-legged. The leaf was a dark orange with brown edges. Brittle. She could crush it with a gentle twist of her hand.

"Now, close your eyes and think about using your power," he said.

"To do what?"

"Heal the leaf."

"What? It's a leaf!" she said, confused.

"All right, you're not 'healing' it," he said. "I was just using the word you're familiar with. Take it back in time."

"But that is such a waste of my gift. It will only wither again."

Aranok took a deep breath. "Please?"

With a grimace, Samily closed her eyes. She focused on the leaf and thought about using her power. She felt the warmth rising inside her, from her core. It radiated out to her extremities. Pulsing. Throbbing. Itching to be released.

"You feel it?" asked Aranok. Samily nodded. "Good. Now, picture a funnel. Instead of letting all that energy burst out of you, you're just going to release a little bit of it into the leaf, turn it green again, then close the funnel. Remember, it's all in your mind. It's yours to control."

Samily opened her eyes and looked at her hands. At the dry, brittle thing in them. She pictured it as it once was—verdant and strong. She felt the energy rising within her like a cresting wave, but she held on to it.

*"Air ais."* She focused on the power in her. Focused on controlling it. Not letting it wash over her.

Nothing happened.

"Hmm. I think we've overdone it." Aranok smiled. "You have to let some out!"

Samily didn't like his tone. He spoke to her like a young child. She looked down again.

*"Air ais."* She gasped as the energy burst from her hands, pushing her back as if caught in a sudden wind. She put her hands down to catch herself. "S'grace, what was that?"

"It's all right." Aranok leaned toward her and offered a hand. "That can happen."

Samily took the hand and allowed him to pull her upright. She had dropped the leaf, and it was near impossible to see it in the dark. She felt around, but there was no sign of it.

"Ahem." Aranok cleared his throat. She looked up. He was holding something out to her. Something small. She put out a hand and he dropped it into her palm. It was a tiny little green thing, like a pod or...

"It's a leaf bud," he said. "You turned it back into a bud."

"But..." That would have meant taking it back months. She'd never really thought of it in those terms, but with healing, she'd only ever...

Aranok's eyes flitted to something behind her.

She jerked her head around to see the girl lurch toward her. Samily raised an arm instinctively to block the Blackened's hand, but it never landed. Instead, the girl was thrown backwards, away from the knight. She jumped to her feet, joining Aranok.

Allandria jolted awake, rolled to one knee and brandished a dagger. "What is it?"

"Blackened," said Aranok. "Stay there. I can hold her. We can turn her," he said to Samily.

Samily slipped on her gloves and helmet. Aranok nodded, and she moved forward, looking to see where the girl had landed. She took small steps in the dark, careful not to stumble. She couldn't have gone far, and she'd be frantically trying to get back to them, unless...

She found the girl scrabbling at the dirt, desperately trying to push herself to her feet. But she would never stand again. Her back buckled at an ugly angle where she'd hit the rock. Her legs lay, useless, sprawled behind her. She swung an arm at Samily, just brushing the front of her greaves. Poor child. She did not deserve this. Samily drew her sword and raised it above her head.

"Did you find her?" Aranok called from the dark.

Samily didn't answer. She brought down her blade and gave the girl peace.

Aranok was digging in his pack when Samily returned to the camp. Allandria stood protectively over him.

"Did you find her?" Aranok asked urgently. "I have the runes."

"I'm sorry," said Samily. "Her back was broken."

Aranok's face fell. "What?" His voice was smaller than she'd ever heard it.

"She hit a boulder. She was thin. Weak."

"Ah Hells." Allandria rubbed her face.

Aranok looked at Samily, trembling slightly. "What did you do?"

"She is with God."

For a moment, he was still. "God damn it!" He threw the sack on the ground.

Allandria leapt to her feet. "Hey. Quiet," she said softly.

He turned to Samily. "This is your God, is it? Working through me? To kill little girls?" He hissed the last words.

Samily stepped back. She did not like him like this. "Envoy, she would not have survived."

Allandria put a hand on his shoulder, but he shrugged it off with a harsh "No." He stalked toward Samily. She instinctively put up her hand, but he passed her as if she wasn't there. His footsteps disappeared into the dark.

"What happened?" Samily asked Allandria.

The archer rubbed the back of her neck. "He's angry."

"At me?" That seemed unwarranted. She'd only done the kind thing.

"No, no. At everything." Allandria gestured around her. "But right now, at himself, I think."

"Why? He did nothing wrong. He was protecting me." She hated the thought that somehow that had led to this.

Allandria sat and stretched her neck. Samily remembered she'd been asleep only minutes before. "He expects a lot of himself. He thinks, because of what he can do..." She opened her hands.

"That he should be able to do anything?" Samily asked.

"I suppose," Allandria answered. "Or, at least, never make mistakes. He expects perfection."

"But no one could live up to that. Why would he put such a burden on himself?" Samily asked.

"I don't think he can help it. I don't think he knows how not to."

Samily sat down again, happy that whatever threat she imagined from the envoy had passed. But she was alert this time—more so than when the girl had managed to creep up on them. She should have been paying attention, not playing with leaves. "Does he often lose his temper like that?"

Allandria sighed. "Truthfully? Between us, I think he's angry all the time."

"What an awful way to live," said Samily. "Why is he angry at God?"

The archer smiled ruefully. "I suppose because God is the easiest thing to blame when you can't hold anyone else responsible. Sometimes I think he sees his whole life as a struggle between him and God, and the rest of us are just players."

Samily was even more confused. This man made no sense. "But I thought he didn't believe in God?"

"He doesn't," Allandria answered. "Until he needs someone to blame."

# CHAPTER 29

Nirea disliked hospitals. The stale smell of blood and rot lingered underneath the pungent soap they used to scrub the corridors. She didn't much like medics either. Most she'd met had an arrogance about them that they didn't deserve. She'd seen too many people go to the ship's medic and come back dead. But Egretta seemed different. For all her caustic bluster, she cared deeply for her patients—and that meant something.

It was no real surprise when Nirea pushed open the door to Vastin's room and found Egretta already there, despite the early hour. What was surprising was finding Glorbad there too. The soldier stood mournfully next to the bed. He seemed to be saying something, but it was so quiet she could only make out the sibilant hisses. Egretta looked up from the table of instruments she was fussing over.

"Good morning," she said officiously, but with that underlying warmth Nirea could now see.

"Morning," Nirea answered.

Glorbad jerked around to look at her. "What are you doing here?"

"I just felt like I should say goodbye to the boy. It seemed wrong to leave him without...you know." She couldn't really explain it. She'd been there when he was turned. And somehow, that mattered. But more, she was an adult and he was a child. And they'd failed him. They'd failed to keep him safe. Even though there was nothing she should or could have done differently, looking back, she still felt the nagging sting of guilt. He was a boy, and they'd let him down. And now, they were leaving him—and that was worse. So she needed to say goodbye. Goodbye and sorry.

"Aye." Glorbad nodded. "Aye." He placed a gloved hand on the boy's good shoulder, then stepped away to allow Nirea closer. She looked down at his naked back, with the ugly purple mess blooming from his shoulder. He looked so small, so frail. Even younger than his fifteen years. She felt a terrible urge to stroke him, to soothe his pain. But for all the horror of his situation, at least now they knew—thanks to Meristan and Samily—that he wouldn't remember any of it.

"Horses are ready," said Glorbad.

Nirea looked at him and nodded. "Looks dry." She gestured to the small window. The white sky was pierced by a few hopeful patches of pale blue. Traverlyn felt muffled beneath the blanket, its bright colours and vivid skyline somehow mundane. Was it just familiarity from their days spent here, or perhaps her own melancholy reflected back? "Hopefully the rain will stay off."

"Mmm," he agreed.

"Oh, sorry," came a voice from the door. "I wasn't expecting anyone to be here."

"Nonsense, come in, Morienne," said Egretta. "You're right on time. Here." She held out a long tube, which Morienne took.

"What are you going to do with that?" Glorbad blinked.

Egretta paused and looked at them both. "We have to feed him."

"Hell, how does that work?" Though, being honest, Nirea had an idea.

"You both care for the boy?" Egretta asked as she continued fussing with metal things. One of them looked like a small bucket.

Nirea shrugged. "Yes."

"Then you should leave now," she said.

"Fair enough." Glorbad's eyes were starting to water. Probably Morienne's curse. He turned away and walked out the door. "I'll see you at the stable."

"Do you need a minute?" Egretta asked.

"No, not really." He wouldn't hear anything Nirea said anyway. She just needed to set eyes on him. And she'd done that.

"We'll look after him," said Morienne from the corner.

Nirea took her hands, despite the overwhelming urge to get away. Heart racing, eyes watering, gooseflesh spreading up her back, Nirea forced herself to look Morienne in the face. "I know you will. What you're doing…what you're sacrificing…I won't forget it." She squeezed the woman's hands before releasing them and, with a nod to Egretta, quickly followed Glorbad into the corridor.

---

"Two visits in such a short time. We are blessed." Pol's manner was convivial, but Aranok knew him well enough to feel the sneer beneath his words. He was that kind of man, who would insult you with a smile, knowing fine well you understood, and that he could deny it if confronted. Devious. Nasty.

Pol stood in the doorway like a sentry, blocking Aranok from entering. It had been a long day. First picking their way across the Black Hills with the horses, then riding hard to get to Mournside before dark. It hadn't helped that his outburst in the night had left a cloud hanging over them all day. He'd apologised to Samily. It wasn't the girl's fault. Her naivety just rubbed him the wrong way sometimes. Still, it had been a largely silent journey.

They'd settled into rooms at the Canny Man this time, but Aranok had been keen to see his sister and niece as soon as possible. It was also a good excuse to get away for a bit and let the air clear. He'd hoped his brother-in-law would be out.

"Hello, Pol. You're not going to leave the king's envoy standing in the street, are you?"

Pol's smile was oily and thin. "Of course not, my laird." He bowed deeply and swept an arm into the house. "Do come in."

Aranok resisted the urge to knee the shitbag in the face while he was down there, and walked past him.

"Uncle Aranok!" Emelina came running toward him, arms outstretched. He swept her up.

"How's my favourite princess?" He kissed her on the neck. She giggled with delight.

"Well, look at that." Pol's hostility was barely disguised. "It only takes the wealth to buy your niece a tutor and you're her favourite uncle!" Aranok smiled at him, enjoying the knowledge that his connection with his niece was much deeper than that. Deeper, in many ways, than her connection with the man she believed her father.

"Hello, Ari." Ikara came down the stairs. "We got your letter." She put a hand on his shoulder and kissed him on the cheek. "Are you staying with us?"

"No, I can't this time," he answered. "I have others with me, and we have to set off at first light."

"Uncle Aranok, can I fly?" Emelina asked as he put her down. Pol looked darkly at Ikara.

"Maybe not today." He crouched down. "But I brought you a present."

"What is it, what is it?" she asked eagerly.

He pulled the small wooden falcon he'd bought in Traverlyn from his pouch and put it in her hands.

"I love it! Just like…" But she caught Aranok's warning look and stopped.

"Just like you, flying in the sky," Aranok finished for her. She smiled conspiratorially and nodded.

"Come, sit." Ikara ushered him toward a seat by the fire. "What news do you bring?"

How much could he tell her with Pol here? Emelina sat on the hearth rug, flying her falcon around above her head.

"The Blackened have moved north. To the Auld Road."

"What? Why?" Pol took the seat opposite him. "Why would they do that?"

Aranok looked at Ikara. "Our best guess is that Mynygogg summoned them. Or an ally did."

"An ally?" Pol waved dismissively. "Mynygogg had no allies."

"Well, there's evidence to suggest that maybe he does now. Maybe did all along."

"Pssh," Pol sneered. "We'd have known if he had accomplices. The whole country was allied against him, for God's sake!"

"Pol, remember who you're speaking to," Ikara said gently. "And who's listening." She nodded to Emelina, who carried on playing, hopefully oblivious to her father. Pol rolled his eyes, stood and crossed to the sideboard, where he poured himself a tumbler of whisky.

"So what does that mean for us?" Ikara asked.

"For now, it means you're even less likely to come across any Blackened near the city. But in the long term…" He hesitated. Was this really information he wanted Pol to have? On the other hand, it might be useful for people to know. To have hope. For Emelina.

"We can cure it."

Ikara gasped and put a hand to her mouth. "What?"

"We can cure it. We figured it out. Conifax and Master Balaban. It's not a plague; it's a curse. We can lift it."

"A curse?" Pol spat. "Are you telling me the Blackening is some damned *draoidh*'s doing? Again? God, these unnatural bastards are the plague."

*Damn it.* He should have seen that coming. Aranok looked down at his niece. She'd heard. She held the falcon on her knees sullenly.

"Pol!" Ikara snapped at him. "If nothing else, mind your language."

He glowered at her for a moment, turned and walked out of the room. Aranok had a feeling Ikara might suffer for that. Pol was not a violent man—at least, he knew well enough that abusing his benefactor's daughter would see his privileged life end quickly. Paternal devotion aside, Dorann would never be seen to tolerate his child's mistreatment. But Pol was a snide little prick who cut with words. The thought was a splinter in Aranok's side.

"I'm sorry," he said.

"Don't be daft." She sat in the chair Pol had left and put her hand on his knee. "Tell me more. Can you really cure the Blackening?"

He told the story of their last week: visiting Lepertoun, Meristan and Vastin turning, meeting Morienne, the journey to Traverlyn, Conifax's cure and their mission to Caer Amon. He left out the Thakhati attack. He was already worried about Emelina's dreams.

"My God, Aranok," Ikara said when he finally finished. "You really can cure it."

"Maybe. If we can find the relic, the 'heart of devastation.'"

"And get it back to Conifax?"

"Yes." He didn't bother explaining that since he and Conifax were both earth *draoidhs*, the ritual would work for him too. He hadn't actually tried it yet and was more comfortable with his old master doing it, with all the lives at stake. "Ikara, you know you asked about helping?"

"Of course." She nodded enthusiastically and sat forward. "What can I do?"

"We're going to need wagons. As many as we can get. Ready to go when we lift the curse. People will need..."

"Medics, supplies, transport. Of course!" she interrupted. "I can do that. I'll speak to people. We'll make sure as many as we can find are ready to go at your signal, Ari. Just say the word."

He'd known she would say yes, but it still raised the hairs on his neck to see just how keen she was, how compassionate. There weren't many better people in Eidyn than his little sister.

"Uncle Aranok?" Emelina had stopped playing some time ago and had been listening intently. "You can kill the monsters?"

"They're not monsters, angel. They're people, just like you and me. But they've had a spell put on them. It makes them attack other people and hurt themselves. They're not evil; they're victims. And they need our help."

"Oh," she said. Then, hesitantly, "Is Daddy right? Did a bad *draoidh* do it?"

He looked up at Ikara, hoping she would have a perfect answer, but she only raised her eyebrows and shrugged.

"We think so." He desperately hoped the next words would come to him before he opened his mouth again. "It's...Well..."

"Come here, sweetheart," Ikara interrupted, lifting the girl onto her knee. "What Uncle Aranok is trying to say, but he's a little bit shy, is that there are good *draoidhs* and bad *draoidhs*. Now, you know Uncle Aranok is a very good *draoidh*, don't you?"

The girl nodded enthusiastically. "He fights monsters." Aranok couldn't help but smile.

"That's right!" said Ikara. "But just like there are some bad people..."

"Like strangers?" Emelina asked.

"Well, not all strangers are bad people," Ikara said. "But some are, and so are some *draoidhs*. Being a *draoidh* doesn't make someone good or bad. They each have to decide for themselves what they want to be. Do you understand?"

Emelina nodded again. She jumped down from her mother's knee, hesitantly crossed to Aranok and leaned up to his ear. "I'm good," she whispered.

He grabbed her into a tight hug. "I know you are," he whispered back.

"You've heard about the murder, I assume?" Aranok jumped. He hadn't heard Pol come back, but there he was in the doorway. He couldn't have heard what Emelina said, and even if he had, it wasn't clear what she meant—unless he knew.

"Oh, of course!" Ikara said. "You won't know! They caught the man who murdered that messenger."

"They did?" Aranok really hadn't expected a result this quickly. In fact, once he had got here and sat face-to-face with Ikara, it had very nearly slipped his mind.

"Indeed." There was a slight slur in Pol's voice. Aranok suspected he'd been tapping another source of whisky while he'd been talking with Ikara and Em. "Turns out he was her husband after all. Nothing more devious about it than that. Not so important after all, eh, Envoy?"

"Pol..." Ikara said gently.

"What?" he spat back.

Aranok felt his teeth clench. He stretched his jaw to release them. "Ikara, could you give Pol and me a minute please?"

She looked him straight in the eye. It was hard to tell if it was fear or a warning. Either way, he understood.

"All right," she said. "Come on, Emelina, let's find a nice home for your new bird."

"It's a falcon, Mummy." The girl took her mother's hand and followed her up the stairs.

"Well, a falcon is a kind of bird," he heard his sister say as they disappeared onto the upper landing.

As soon as they were out of sight, Aranok stood and crossed quickly to Pol. It had the effect of making him step back into the dining room. Good.

"What do you want?" There was fear beneath Pol's arrogance.

"It seems like you've forgotten something." Aranok took another step toward him. Pol stepped back again.

"What?" He backed into the table. His tumbler clunked down.

"Your importance," Aranok said. Pol looked confused. "You're important to my father. You're my sister's husband and my niece's father. They're under your protection. So that makes you important."

He was backed right up against the table now, and leaning back, away from Aranok.

"But let's be absolutely clear about one thing. There are exactly two people I care about in this house, and you are neither of them. I tolerate your acidic little knives for them; do not make the mistake of thinking yourself immune. As much as they are under your protection, you are under theirs. If I have any reason to believe they are unhappy, I will be unhappy. And bugger my father's happiness either way. Do we understand each other?"

Pol nodded silently.

"Then say it."

Pol swallowed. "I understand."

Aranok smiled slightly. "I think you've forgotten whom you're addressing."

"I understand, Laird Envoy." Pol said the last words through gritted teeth. If he hadn't hated Aranok before, he certainly did now. Which was fine. It was mutual.

"Excellent. We have an understanding." He clapped Pol on the shoulder like an old friend. "Now, if you'll excuse me, I'm going to say goodbye to my niece and sister." He turned and walked away without a backwards glance. For now, Pol had been reminded of his place in things. Rasa would keep an eye on them for him. He probably should have warned her more about Pol, but Ikara would keep her right. For the moment, he had a more pressing matter.

He needed to see a man about a murder.

———⊰⊱———

"Are you trying to kill me?" Meristan laughed as he stepped back, lowering Vastin's axe.

"Ha!" Glorbad lowered his sword. "You'd know if I'd been trying to kill you."

Nirea laughed.

It had been slow going, travelling cross-country. They might have made Barrock by nightfall if they'd been able to take the Auld Road, but they couldn't risk a horde of Blackened following them to the gates. As it was, they'd made it more than halfway before the sun went down and they decided that making camp for the night was the safest option. They'd found a sheltered area, carved into the side of a cliff, which hid them from view. On the one hand, it let them light a fire in relative safety; on the other, they wouldn't see Thakhati coming until they were on top of them. When the fire burned down, they'd post a guard at the entrance.

Once they had settled into camp for the night and eaten, Glorbad had convinced the monk to accept some training, so at least he wouldn't accidentally cut off his own leg. Meristan had reluctantly agreed. But Nirea had been surprised at how naturally he moved. He was fit, as she'd seen, but he was also nimble. And for all his protestations, he handled the axe like he'd had a lot more training than he suggested. In fact, in his new leathers, he looked every inch the warrior.

"Are you sure you've had no training?" she asked.

Meristan reddened slightly and looked down. "Only a little, as a boy. Same as most." He sat next to the fire, placing the axe on the ground in front of him.

"Hells, don't leave that there!" Glorbad said. "That's a wooden handle under that leather. It'll burn like a torch if the fire gets at it!"

"Oh!" Meristan jerked forward and lifted the axe away, putting it behind him instead. "I'm sorry; I'm not used to handling weapons."

"Don't apologise to me!" The soldier sat down. "It's the boy who'll want answers if you burn his favourite axe to cinders!"

"True, true." Nirea smiled. "Seriously, though, no training? You look like you were born with a weapon in your hand."

Meristan shrugged.

"Did your father no give you lessons?" Glorbad asked.

Meristan looked down. "Ah well. My father was not in my life. It was just my mother and me."

"Oh, right." Glorbad was suddenly awkward. "Sorry."

"No, no," said Meristan. "You didn't know."

"Looks like she did a fine job of raising you by herself." Nirea hoped to lift the mood. Her two companions had suddenly become morbid. She opened her flask and swigged back some rum, then offered it to the monk.

"Thank you." Meristan took the offer. "She was a kind woman. Strong. She had absolute faith in God." He drank from the flask and handed it back. She considered offering it to Glorbad too, but he had already reached for his own.

"Well, she raised a kind, brave man." Nirea toasted him with the rum.

Meristan flushed.

"Need a pish." The soldier stood abruptly and walked out of the light.

"Thank you," said the monk after a moment. "But I wouldn't say brave. I haven't earned that."

"You're here, aren't you?" She lay back against a grassy mound.

"What do you mean?"

"Well, you nearly died, you sent your guardian angel away, and you're out here with us on a dangerous mission to rescue a queen. Seems pretty damn brave to me."

"You're too kind. But the truth is, I'm no less safe with you two than I was with Samily. You are the brave ones. I'm useful only for my position."

She wasn't having that. "Was your mother brave?"

"I...I think so," said Meristan.

"Was she a fighter?"

"Well, no. A farmer."

"A farmer? That's hard labour. Not easy for a woman on her own."

"No," he answered. "I helped when I was old enough. But you're right, it was hard."

"And didn't you raise Samily?"

"Well, not alone," said the monk. "I had the brotherhood."

"Oh, the brotherhood that you run? That brotherhood?" she asked playfully.

"I...Well, yes. But I..."

"So despite having that responsibility, you also raised an orphaned girl and trained her to be a White Thorn, who... Hang on, aren't you also in charge of them?"

Meristan opened his mouth to speak, but nothing came out. He turned over his hands in a sort of surrender. Good.

"And you were their strategic commander during the war?" Nirea hammered her point home.

"Yes," Meristan agreed quietly.

"So your mother was brave for raising you on her own and running a farm, but you're not brave because you raised a daughter, ran an Order and were the architect of our defence against Mynygogg?"

Meristan was silent, simply staring into the fire. "One of the architects. Maybe."

The more men she spent time with, the more she was convinced of their innate stupidity.

Meristan looked back over his shoulder and leaned in closer, as if to share a secret.

"Can I ask, what happened to him?" He was changing the subject. That was all right. She'd allow it. She'd made her point, for now.

"Glorbad? Why?"

"It's just—he drinks a lot." The monk looked down again. "I mean, I suppose Samily might say the same about me, but..."

"No, that's fair." Nirea carefully looked over his shoulder to make sure she saw the soldier when he returned. She knew from painful experience he didn't enjoy being talked about. Who did, really?

"And he seems to be sensitive about family. Did something...?"

Of course. Nirea was accustomed to Glorbad's quirks. She knew where they came from. Many maudlin nights he'd drunkenly revealed more than he intended. He likely didn't remember most of it, probably had no idea just how much Nirea knew. "It's not a nice story. You sure you want to hear it?

Meristan reflected for a moment. "I have heard many sad histories. I have never found them other than enlightening to my understanding of people, or helpful in my relations with them. They also help to avoid missteps." He nodded into the dark, where Glorbad had walked off.

"All right." Nirea slid farther round toward the monk and gestured for him to do the same. That way they could talk quietly and see Glorbad approaching.

"He was a commander in Hofnag's army. He was respected, liked. His family lived well in Auldun."

"Family," Meristan repeated, as if confirming his belief.

"Wife and son. Younger than Vastin. Twelve, maybe. Glorbad split his time between Gardille and Auldun—until the uprising. Until the rebellion."

"He took Janaeus's side?" Meristan asked.

"Not at first. He did what a commander in Eidyn's army did—he fought the rebels. Very effectively. Rarely lost a skirmish, to hear him tell it. Had he stayed where he was...Well. It might be too much to say the rebellion would have failed, but it would have been a longer, bloodier war, I suspect.

"Anyway, he didn't. Like most of us, he had reservations about old Hofnag. I imagine fighting farmers and blacksmiths who just wanted to keep enough coin to feed their families wasn't as glorious as a soldier's dreams. Whatever you think of the man, he knows right from wrong."

Meristan nodded. The fire crackled and a branch split, making Nirea jump. She instinctively looked to where Glorbad had gone and waited a moment in the silence.

Nothing but the evening breeze bristling the grass. They'd avoided trees. She might never look at trees the same way again.

"Janaeus got to him," she continued. "I don't know when. They met. Whatever was said between them, Glorbad was convinced. He was on the wrong side. When he turned, he took half his soldiers with him."

"Impressive," said Meristan.

"Only half. He tried to let the rest go. Practically begged them. They were loyal to Hofnag. They fought. His own soldiers. Men and women who had followed him into battle more times than he could remember, trying to kill him. He won, but I don't know that he ever recovered. I think that fight—I think that's what he sees when he closes his eyes. His soldiers slaughtering one another, on his orders."

Meristan interlocked his fingers and pressed both fists to his mouth. "The poor man." After a long silence, he looked up. "His family?"

"After the war—after we won—he went back to Auldun. It was chaos. Ordinary people's lives were upturned, houses ransacked, whole streets burned from running battles as Janaeus fought through to Dun Eidyn. It was a mess. When Glorbad got home…"

"Dead?" Meristan asked.

"Gone. Just gone. As if they'd never been there."

Meristan "tched" and shook his head slowly. "He never found them?"

"Thousands were lost in the rebellion. Never seen again. Glorbad's family were known. His betrayal was known to the king. And Hofnag was just the kind of bastard who would've…"

"Killed his family," Meristan finished. "As a warning to others."

"No. Just out of fucking spite." Hofnag was an absolute cunt of a man. "Most likely, they're at the bottom of the Nor Loch. I just hope they died quick."

*Footsteps.*

Glorbad walked back into the light, stopped and looked down at them both. They must have looked guilty, because he furrowed his brow as he sat. "What?"

"Nothing." Nirea smiled.

Meristan was looking at Glorbad with a mix of sadness and respect, which the soldier clearly found uncomfortable, judging by the way he leaned slightly away from the monk as he reached for his flask. "What did I miss?"

"Nothing much, my friend," Meristan answered, after a momentary pause. "Just a philosophical discussion on the nature of bravery."

"Fuck!" Glorbad laughed. "Good time for a pish, then!" He slugged back another mouthful from his flask.

# CHAPTER 30

Even the gaol in Mournside was nicer than anywhere else in the country. It was relatively small, housed underneath the town guard's garrison, but it had been built such that the main floor was slightly raised, allowing for small, barred windows to be added along the tops of the cell walls. There was very little crime here—well, crime that was punished. Many blind eyes were turned to the indiscretions of the wealthy, something Aranok had always found distasteful. Mournside's glittering reputation cast a dark shadow. But the cells were most commonly used for allowing drunk merchants to dry out after a heavy night. Any serious prisoners kept here were usually only awaiting transport to Auldun, where the real gaol lay. It was much less hospitable.

These days, of course, the burden of the central gaol had to be shared across the country, with Auldun overrun by the Dead. Haven's gaol was a decent size, but not big enough to replace Auldun's. So the regional gaols had become more permanent than they were intended to be. Aranok had argued that they should stop imprisoning lesser offenders, like those delinquent with their taxes, but Janaeus had worried that the treasury would quickly empty if there was no consequence for withholding taxes, and the army would starve. In the end, it seemed, he'd opted for pressing criminals into his service instead.

That was going to end badly.

"Laird Envoy!" Bak sounded genuinely pleased to see Aranok escorted into his office. "Welcome back. You've heard we caught the murderer." He stood and offered his hand. Aranok took it with a smile.

"I did. I'm sorry to come so late, but I'm only here for the night, and I need to speak to him."

Bak looked confused. "The criminal?" Aranok nodded. "Why?"

This might be awkward. But it needed to be done and he didn't have a lot of time, so tact and diplomacy were going to suffer.

Aranok took the seat in front of the desk. "It doesn't make sense."

"I'm sorry?" the captain asked.

"How did you catch him?"

"Stroke of luck." Bak also sat. "An informant—a boy—came forward. Said he'd seen a man looked like the drawing leaving the Canny Man that night. We announced we were temporarily opening the western gate, and had the boy posted there, watching everyone who tried to leave. Not many did—and we turned them back. But sure enough, he rolled up two days ago with a cart full of wheat."

"Wheat?" said Aranok. "Where was he going?"

"Got quite agitated when we stopped him, right enough. Claimed he was making an urgent delivery to Haven. For the crown. You mind?" He held up a pipe.

Aranok waved his approval and Bak used a taper to light it from the fireplace. "He claims to be her husband?"

"Claims? You doubt it?" There was a hint of a smile as Bak asked.

"Does it make sense to you that her husband sat at a table only feet from her and she didn't notice? Or did they choose to ignore each other? Or that he killed her in a room full of people—including me—where he was more likely to be caught?"

Bak's smile spread. He took a deep puff from his pipe and blew smoke into the air. "I'll do you better than that. According to Calador and half a dozen other regulars who've drunk with her before, Evenna never mentioned a husband or family. One young man claims to have bedded her six months ago."

"Evenna?" At least now he could answer Allandria's question. A little late, but...

"Aye," said Bak. "And her 'husband' calls himself Tilbark."

"Well, that doesn't necessarily help," said Aranok. "If she was bedding other men on her travels, and her husband suspected..."

"Still doesn't answer your questions, though, does it?"

"It does not." It was also irritating that Aranok's father's speculation about the murder turned out to be accurate. Irritating and a little obvious.

"You've a suspicious mind, Envoy. You'd have made a fine guard," said Bak.

"Ha! I don't think so. I've never been very good with rules." Aranok stood and gestured to the door. "Can we...?"

"Of course." Bak picked up a large ring of keys.

The heavy iron door at the top of the stairs screeched in protest as Bak pulled it open. They plodded down the narrow spiral staircase. Aranok wondered if it had been designed this tight to make it harder for prisoners to escape—they'd only be able to come up the stairs in single file. Easier for one well-armed guard to keep them contained.

"Mind your head." Bak ducked under the low wooden lintel at the bottom. The room opened out into a wide central corridor, with a number of heavy wooden doors squeezed into the side walls. The cells couldn't be large—but then, they hadn't been built for long-term use. Even under the circumstances, more than half of the doors stood open. Bak walked past the few closed doors nearest the entrance, right to the opposite end, where a solitary door was closed.

"In there?" Aranok asked.

Bak nodded. "He's noisy at night. Says he has nightmares."

"Hmm." Aranok wondered if that suggested he really was just an unhinged, cuckolded husband. Or if it meant anything at all. "All right. Open it."

Bak turned the key in the lock and drew his sword with his left hand, opening the door with his right. A fetid smell of sweat and piss hit Aranok in the face. He squinted into the dark cell, struggling to see anything, despite the strip of moonlight across the corner next to him. He could hear breathing. Was the man asleep?

"You! You bastard!" Aranok stumbled backwards as the slight man threw himself up from the bed, reaching for his throat. Bak stepped in front of him, putting his forearm across the man's chest, and his sword point at his belly.

"Step back!" the captain shouted. "Step! Back!"

Aranok regained his composure and his footing. What the Hell had just happened? Tilbark pointed accusatorily at him, his eyes nearly bulging from his florid face.

"He's the reason I'm in here!" he screamed at Bak. "That's the bastard who was fucking my wife!"

Aranok let out an involuntary guffaw. "What?"

"Back in the cell and sit, or you're never getting out of it!" Bak prodded the man with the end of his sword, just to emphasise the threat. He closed the door and turned to Aranok. "I take it that's as surprising to you as it is to me?"

Aranok realised his mouth was open and closed it. "I'd never seen the woman before. I honestly didn't even know her name until tonight."

Bak shook his head in confusion. "All right. Perhaps I should speak to him. You can listen from out here." Bak tapped the small hatch in the door. "What do you want to know?"

Aranok thought. What did he want to know? "Get some details from him. See if his story holds up."

Bak nodded. He was a sharp man. Aranok trusted he would ask the right questions. The guard flipped open the hatch. Aranok stepped away, avoiding the possibility of being seen from inside, but close enough to hear everything.

"Right!" Bak shouted, his hand on the key again. "I'm coming in. Alone. If you get up off that bed I'll stick you, no questions. Understood?"

There was a muffled grunt in reply. Bak pursed his lips, unlocked the door and stepped in, closing it behind him. Aranok leaned against the wall next to the door. This murder only got stranger the more he learned about it. He'd thought he was involved somehow, but not like this.

"Tilbark," he heard Bak say, "you were Evenna's husband?"

"You know I was." Anger and resentment were still clear in the prisoner's voice.

"How long were you married?" Bak asked.

"I dunno. Ten years at least." Tilbark's voice was fractured. It took sudden changes in pitch, as if he were in turns excited and miserable.

"Ten years?" Bak sounded impressed. "That's a long time. Where did you meet?"

There was a pause.

"In the tavern, I think. Auldun."

"Which tavern?"

"Don't remember," Tilbark answered. "What does it matter?" Defensive. Aggressive.

"It matters," said Bak. "How old are you?"

"Forty-five last summer."

"And Evenna? How old was she?"

Another pause. Good. Bak was asking the right questions.

"Thirty-eight. Thirty-nine," said Tilbark.

"Which one?" Bak asked calmly.

"She's not getting any older," Tilbark sneered.

Aranok felt a wave of repulsion toward the slimy little man and pity for any woman who had been his wife.

"No, she's not," said Bak. "Why did you kill her?"

"Because she was shagging that bastard out there!" Tilbark growled, raising his voice, presumably to be sure Aranok heard.

"How do you know?" Bak asked.

"I just do."

"How?" he asked again, still calmly.

"She was always wittering about him. 'Met the envoy,' she said. 'Very handsome. Real hero. Kind eyes. Nice hair.' I knew."

Aranok had met her? He had absolutely no memory of it. He'd met a lot of people since they took the kingdom, but... God, how could he not have any recollection of her? What did that say about him?

*Wait. He's probably lying.* Aranok hoped so.

"That's all? That's why you thought...?" asked Bak.

"I knew," Tilbark interrupted. "I could smell it on her. The stink of another man."

Bak cleared his throat.

Aranok realised he was digging his fingers into the stone behind him. He stretched them out, feeling the tips tingle as blood returned. He imagined Bak was having similar difficulty restraining his own anger now. Maybe not. Maybe dealing with criminals made him hard.

When he spoke again, his voice was still even and measured. "Where do you live?"

"We have a place. Havenport."

That seemed unlikely. The docks were one of the poorest areas in Haven. King's messengers were well paid. It was a difficult job to get. You needed people to vouch for you. Reputable people. She could have afforded better.

"Haven?" Bak asked. "But you met in Auldun?"

"Aye," said Tilbark. "So?"

"Where are you from?" Bak asked.

"Why?"

"Answer the question."

"Near Leet," said Tilbark.

"You work the docks?" Bak asked.

Tilbark didn't answer, but Aranok assumed he'd somehow indicated yes, because of Bak's next question.

"Started in Leet? Moved to Haven?"

"Aye." Tilbark's voice was more even now. Relaxed.

"What was Evenna's favourite meal?" Bak asked.

"What?" said Tilbark, as if the captain had poked him.

"Her favourite meal."

No answer.

"You were married ten years," said Bak. "What was her favourite meal?"

"I don't... I don't..." Tilbark stuttered.

"Favourite colour?" Bak asked. "Drink?"

"I... It's..."

"You must know something about your wife, surely?" Bak pressed.

"I don't... Stew!" he said, as if he'd found something lost.

"Beef or lamb?" Bak asked.

"Lamb. Beef." Tilbark was flailing.

"Interesting," said Bak. "Because Calador told me that every time Evenna stayed, she had the pork. Loved it, he said. That seems like something her husband should know."

Yes. He had him.

"Want to have a guess at the drink?" Bak asked.

"I...I don't...know," Tilbark sounded agitated now. His voice was almost a whine. A piteous, dying noise. Aranok could hear him moving, rustling, as if he was scratching at something.

"Steady," said Bak. "Come on. What did she drink?"

"I knew. I knew when he showed up. I knew. I knew. That was it," Tilbark rambled.

"Come on," said Bak. "What drink?"

"I don't know!" Tilbark screamed.

"Wait, don't..." Sudden panic in Bak's voice. Aranok turned and grabbed the door handle, throwing it open to see Tilbark lunge at the rear wall and smash his head against it with a sickening crack. He hit the floor with a dull crunch. Blood pooled on the floor. Bak had barely managed to get to his feet.

"Fuck!" The captain rolled the limp body over. Blood poured from a crack in the front of his skull, running down over his face, pooling in his right eye socket. Aranok had seen enough head wounds to know a bad one. Part of the bone was collapsed. Hells, how hard had he hit himself? Aranok looked up at the wall. The stone he'd smashed himself against had a crest, like a little wave of stone up the middle. Like an axe edge.

"Do we get a medic?" Bak's left hand was sticky with blood.

"If there's one close," said Aranok.

But it would only be to watch him die.

---

Half an hour later, they sat in Bak's office again. The guard still looked pale. They'd said very little to each other since the medic arrived and confirmed Aranok's belief. Tilbark's injury was catastrophic. It was difficult for Aranok to even imagine a man being able to hit his head that hard. What sickness in his mind would drive him to that level of self-harm? Presumably, the same sickness that convinced him Aranok was sleeping with his wife, who may or may not have actually been his wife, and whom Aranok had never met, as far as he knew.

He'd considered going to the Canny Man to bring Samily back, but it was at least half an hour, even if he ran. The medic was only three streets away, and even she had arrived too late. Samily had been very clear about her inability to "heal" the dead.

"What do we make of that?" Aranok asked.

Bak clenched a trembling fist. For all his experience, watching a man kill himself was disquieting. Especially like that. He stood looking out the window at the quiet night.

"I've no idea. Ramblings of a madman."

*Maybe.*

"He was obsessed with her? Followed her around, convinced himself he was in love with her, and she with him? Then got jealous when he imagined her cheating on him?" Bak suggested.

"Why me, though?" Aranok asked. "Why did I make him kill her?"

"What do you mean?"

"The last thing he said before he killed himself. 'I knew when he showed up.'"

Bak turned to face him. "You think he killed her because you were there?" The guard was still clenching and unclenching his left fist, as if it was painful.

"I do. I thought someone wanted her dead to prevent me from speaking to her. Maybe I still do."

"That doesn't seem right, does it?"

"Say someone did want to prevent me talking to her, and they knew about Tilbark—assuming you're right about him. Convincing him he needed to keep the two of us apart would be one way to do it. And keep their hands clean."

"I suppose," said Bak. "But that's awfully convoluted. Isn't him being deranged a more... straightforward solution?"

"It would be, if Evenna hadn't been spreading misinformation in the name of the king," said Aranok. "And tell me this—if Tilbark was obsessed with her, wouldn't he have known what she eats?"

"Oh, he might have been right about that," said Bak. "I didn't ask Calador what she ate."

"Ah." He'd made it up. And the fact that Tilbark hadn't been able to repudiate Bak's claim proved him a liar just as well as if Bak had been telling the truth. Clever. "But that still casts doubt on your theory, doesn't it?"

"God, I don't know." Bak ran his right hand through his hair. "Maybe. We'll never know either way now. The only people who could have told us anything are both dead."

"Exactly," said Aranok. "And isn't that convenient?"

Bak looked at him and then away, opening his hands as if in surrender.

"Do you know anyone in Haven? That you trust?" Aranok asked.

"A few. Why?"

"Ask them to poke around the docks. Find somebody who knew Tilbark. See what they have to say about him."

Bak frowned and nodded. "Good idea. I'll send a man tomorrow."

"Send three." Aranok moved to the door. "Tell them to travel by day and stay away from the Auld Road. Take shelter to sleep—even if it's mild. There are...things in the night."

"As you say, Laird," said Bak.

"And for God's sake, call me Aranok," he said. "I've never been a laird."

Bak moved to follow him to the main door. Aranok paused on the step.

"Thank you, Bak. I appreciate your help. So does the king."

"My pleasure, Aranok," he said, shaking his hand. "You know, it is possible this was just a madman convinced a woman belonged to him, and that nobody else could have her. I've seen it before."

"I know. But this smells funny, don't you think? If nothing else, Evenna deserves the truth." He'd have liked to believe that was his main drive, but he knew it wasn't. Her death was a tragedy, but if it was covering up a greater crime—Aranok needed to know.

"She does," the captain said. "Let's get it for her."

Aranok could have simply ordered him to investigate, but in his experience a person who believed in their cause was a greater ally than one following orders. Bak was a good man, and getting to the truth of the murder would be drive enough.

For Aranok, the whole kingdom was at stake. Still, he could hear Allandria chastising him for not caring enough about the messenger's death. And she was right.

At least he knew her name now.

# CHAPTER 31

The slope of Barrock Hill was just too steep to ride the horses up. Of course, that's why they had built it there. Attacking forces had to come on foot. The narrow road was edged by a stone wall on one side and a steep drop-off down toward Gaulton on the other. Nirea was picking her way up the path, horse in tow, choosing her steps carefully. Even with this need to concentrate, something was still niggling her. It was too quiet. "Where is everybody?"

"What?" Glorbad shouted from behind.

"I'm just saying, where is everybody?"

It was odd. Even if they were trying to keep Taneitheia's presence here a secret, there should have been some guards on post. Lookouts of some sort at least. But they hadn't seen another living soul since the half dozen Reivers they'd scrapped with after breakfast. They'd been scrawny, looked like they'd been on the road too long. By the time she and Glorbad had taken down one each, the rest had turned and run. Meristan had even drawn his axe. The Reivers had stayed well back from the big bear. It had barely been practice. Got her heart going, though.

But here they were, only a few hundred yards from the Barrock gates, and there wasn't a single sign of life. Barely a sound beyond the buzzing clouds of midges and the breeze in the trees.

"Aye," Glorbad called back. "Right enough. What do you reckon?"

What did she reckon? Maybe they were relying on the assumption the castle was abandoned. Maybe they were shorthanded. Maybe they had decided that keeping the defences inside the castle grounds was a more effective way of keeping their presence quiet.

Maybe not.

"I don't know. But let's keep our wits about us. I don't want an arrow in the head because some Gaul mistakes me for a Reiver!"

It wasn't long before the better options were ruled out.

The huge wooden gates to the Barrock courtyard hung open. Well, one hung; the other was mutilated—mashed almost beyond recognition. What was left of the lower half hung from the iron bar that had run across the middle.

Meristan frowned. "That's not good."

Something had battered its way in.

"God damn it." Glorbad drew his sword. "If we got here too late…"

It looked very much like they had. Had they spent so long on the Blackened that they'd lost the queen? Had Glorbad been right?

"Stay calm, my friend." Meristan crouched amongst the fragments of gate. "Look."

He pried up a large piece of wood, which came away with a wet, sucking noise. It was dark brown and stank of mould. The great muddy hole in the grass crawled with insects, scurrying away from the sudden invasion of light. "This did not happen yesterday. It has been this way for some time."

"Arse." Glorbad sheathed his weapon. "That's probably worse, isn't it?"

For Taneitheia, and maybe the kingdom, it was. For Glorbad's relationship with the envoy, it was probably better. If something had attacked the castle recently, there might be survivors. If it had happened a while ago, and nobody had repaired the gates, either they'd retreated or there was nobody left.

"More bad information?" Meristan wiped the dirt from his hands.

Nirea scanned the bailey. The stables stood empty. The grass grew high. People had not walked through here in some time. There was no sign of struggle. No bodies. Nothing. "Aye. Maybe."

"What does that mean?" Glorbad folded his arms across his chest.

Indeed. What did it mean? "Let's tether the horses, then have a look around."

Empty room after empty room greeted them. No clothing, no weapons, no discarded plates or half-drunk bottles of wine. Nothing to suggest the daily life of the castle had been interrupted. No bodies, no bloodstains, no sign of conflict. By the time they reached the castle's main kitchen, Nirea was struggling to come up with an explanation more complicated than that the inhabitants had packed up and left.

"Dust." Meristan swiped his hand across the huge iron oven. It left a dark swathe through the grey haze.

"Same as the rest," mumbled Glorbad. "What the fuck happened?"

The kitchen was one big stone arch, with an alcove taking up almost all of one wall, in which sat two large ovens. The workbenches around the room lay empty, the shelves bare. Nirea opened the pantry door and was met with a wave of dank air. She held up her torch. Aside from a few remnants of rotten vegetables, there was nothing to see.

"Well?" Glorbad leaned against a workbench.

"Nothing," she said. "There's just…nothing."

Damage to the gate aside, it looked like a castle that had been abandoned in a fairly orderly fashion. And not recently.

"What does this mean?" Meristan rubbed his hands together. The building was cold and damp. There'd been no heat here in a while.

"It means the queen isn't bloody here!" said Glorbad.

"And probably hasn't been for a long time," said Nirea.

"Aye," said Glorbad. "That too."

Meristan poked at a pot on the shelf. It rattled for a moment, and the noise echoed off the stone walls. "So are we all thinking the same thing?"

Glorbad nodded. "We're hunting a dead deer."

"Indeed." Meristan stretched his great arms above his head. "Which begs the question: Why?"

"Or how?" Glorbad thumped his hand down on a workbench. "How can Janaeus have thought Taneitheia was here when the place is like a damned tomb?"

But that wasn't the most worrying question. Not to Nirea's mind. More worrying was what if Janaeus did know? She suspected Meristan was thinking the same, based on the eyebrow he raised when she caught his eye.

Something scraped across stone above them.

Nirea looked up, then to the door. She raised a finger to her lips, creeping across the room. Nothing to see in the corridor in either direction. But the sound came again. Heavy, dull, like dragged meat. About thirty yards to the right, a staircase curled upwards. Glorbad appeared behind her, sword in hand. She pointed to the stairs, then carefully reached for her own swords, doing her best to quieten the draw. Slowly, they moved toward the staircase, Meristan following a few paces behind. He held the axe ready—more as a comfort to himself, she imagined, than anything else.

She paused as they reached the bottom of the stairs. The sound again. Closer. Louder. Nirea found herself thinking about that gate—and whatever had taken it down. As she moved to put a foot on the first step, she felt a hand on her shoulder. Glorbad pointed forcefully at himself. Nirea shrugged, brandishing her swords. She was perfectly capable of defending herself.

"Bollocks," he muttered, holding up his shield—Vastin's shield—even more forcefully.

All right. He had a point.

She stepped aside and gave him room to get ahead. He climbed slowly, minimising the noise from his armour. She turned to Meristan and gestured for him to stay there. He took a deep breath and nodded. She handed him the torch. It would only give them away to whoever—whatever—was upstairs. The monk moved to take up a guard position at the bottom of the steps as Nirea followed the soldier up.

The tight staircase curled past a small window. Outside she briefly noticed the view. From this high up, she could see all the way back to Archer's Hill, rising above the trees. It looked peaceful and majestic in the afternoon light. Her attention snapped back to the moment as she heard a new noise—a snick of metal on stone. From what she could see past Glorbad, the staircase ahead looked darker. There should be plenty of light from windows dotted all the way up, but they were leaving the light behind with every step. It was as if there were no more windows.

Or something was blocking them.

She reached to put a hand on Glorbad's shoulder and pain burst across her left cheek. Her eyes went black as her head smacked against stone. She lifted her hand to her face—it came away warm and red. There was a metallic clatter: Glorbad fighting whatever had hit her. Her head spun as her sight returned. She staggered back a few steps to give herself some space, see what was happening. She held her swords up defensively, begging her eyes to work.

"Glorbad!" She could see the soldier before her, but something was wrong—the image wouldn't solidify in her head.

Then it did.

Glorbad's wide frame hung before her, arms limp, weapons dropped. A glistening black metallic spike with razor edges jutted from his back.

*My God. It came right through him.*

Blood poured from the man like a burst wine barrel. The spike withdrew with a nauseating, wet slurp and what was left of Glorbad dropped to the steps.

Something screamed.

"Nirea?"

She stumbled downwards, trying to make space, before... Her head was still spinning, arms shaking. She battered off the walls, struggling to keep her feet. She was losing blood. She dropped the left blade and tried to stem the flow from her face. The darkness was coming, following her down. God, she hadn't even seen it yet.

She rounded the final corner and stumbled the last few steps into Meristan's arms. He dropped the axe to catch her.

"What happened? What is it?"

She spat out a mouthful of blood and did her best to say the word clearly. "Demon."

———

Nirea's head jerked to the side as her eyes opened.

"Wake up!" Glorbad bellowed at her.

*Wait. No. Not Glorbad. Meristan.*

She must have blacked out. Her eyes cleared. She was walking. Metal scraped on stone behind her.

*Hell, the demon! Oh God, Glorbad.* They had to run. They had to…

She stumbled. Meristan caught her again. He was supporting her on one arm, dragging the axe with his other. She slapped her right cheek. "Come on!" she shouted at herself, spitting blood. She could barely feel the left side of her face. It was hot, throbbing.

She glanced back over her shoulder. Slick black limbs dotted with spikes slipped around the bottom of the stairs. The skin glistened and moved with a wet scraping noise that made her skin crawl.

Her swords. She had no weapons. She'd left one on the steps, but the other—she looked back. Maybe ten yards. She could get it.

*Move.*

She pushed herself free of Meristan's arm, forcing herself to run. Her legs were like lead and the floor lurched beneath her. She focused on the sword. She had to get it, or they were all going to die here.

"Wait!" Meristan screamed. She fell forward onto her knees as she reached the sword. Pain seared her knuckles as she landed on them, grasping the hilt. She instinctively swung her blade up, parrying away a leg. No, not leg. Tail. She forced herself to her feet and backed away. Finally, she got a look at the thing.

It filled the corridor, its spindly, spiked legs running along ceiling, floor and walls. Its wide, globulous body blocked the passage, and its tail, that long black spike with razor edges, dripped with Glorbad's blood. And some of her own. My God, it must be strong, to have pierced Glorbad's shield and armour like it was nothing, and hit her too. Its head, though—its head was long and thin, with broken arrowheads for teeth, and soulless grey eyes.

The tail thrust again, and again she parried it. The force knocked her sideways. She caught herself against the wall. She could hardly see on her left. Her eye was swelling shut. Damn it! She'd have to do this quick. She steadied herself on the balls of her feet. Blood ran along the edge of her jaw, dripping off her chin.

"What are you doing?" Meristan called. "Run!"

She wasn't running. The moment she turned her back, this thing would spear her like Glorbad. She had to face it. A leg came at her from the right and she parried it away, darting toward the beast. The tail flicked at her legs, but she jumped and it passed under her. As she landed, she rolled forward and sprang up, thrusting her sword upwards toward its ugly head.

The weapon bounced off with a clang. Its hide was like stone. Just like the one at Mutton Hole.

She heard her sword clatter to the ground before she felt the pain, and her arm went limp. She looked down. The tip of the tail stuck through her shoulder. It had wrapped round—hit her from behind. It whipped away with a jerk. She crumpled to her knees, spitting blood.

*Fuck.*

That was it. She had no strength left. Her head was swimming in a haze of blood and pain. She was going to die. She slumped back onto the floor, grateful that she'd at least given the monk time to escape. At least he'd survive, as long as he had the good sense to run.

Black was closing in around the edges of her vision. She saw the long, dark mouth open above her, and hoped she'd pass out before it bit.

It screamed.

No, wait. It wasn't the demon. It looked up, away from her. A flash of metal. A wet rip and a spray of blood splattered her face.

*For fuck's sake.* It had all been for nothing. The idiot had got himself killed too.

*Why are men so fucking stupid?*

# CHAPTER 32

Wrychtishousis was an odd building. It seemed to Allandria to have started out as a somewhat modest, if impressive, home. But it had been built on and extended at various times in its history to become the sprawling, ramshackle collection of architectural styles that stood before them. Here a round spire stretching into the sky; there a squat, square building with huge windows. The outer stonework was spattered with various crests, probably each representing the family that had owned the house at the time of that particular building's construction. It was even a mix of different materials: sandstone, granite and a reddish-orange stone she didn't recognise. It looked like a child's drawing of a castle.

"Where's the door?" She couldn't see any obvious entrance.

"I'm not sure," said Samily. "I've not been here before."

"But you've met him?" Aranok asked. "Anhel Weyr?"

Meristan had recommended they stop here. Anhel Weyr, he said, was the most devout man in the kingdom—a great supporter of the brotherhood. It was his money that was buying the materials to rebuild Baile Airneach.

"I haven't had the honour," said Samily. "But he is known to all White Thorns as our benefactor."

"Hmph." Aranok crossed his arms. "Great. But if we can't get in…"

"We're not changing the plan now." Allandria knew where this was going.

"We could have made Gorgyn," said Aranok. He really was infuriating.

"Yes, we could have," Allandria answered. "And then what? The ride to Caer Amon is too long from Gorgyn. We'd have had to camp overnight in the Wilds. This way, we ride to Dail Ruigh tomorrow, and then we can make for Crostorfyn at daybreak."

"I know," he answered grumpily.

Crostorfyn—another of Meristan's ideas. Riding straight for Caer Amon would have them arrive at night. So he'd suggested they seek refuge in the nearby kirk and reach Caer Amon the following morning.

Aranok, however, was impatient—and not overly inclined to spend two nights in righteous company. It had taken Allandria some coaxing to convince him there was little point in getting to Caer Amon a day earlier if they were all dead.

It had been a convincing argument, though.

"Let's try around here." Samily nudged Bear forward around the southeastern edge of the buildings.

Aranok did not move. Allandria raised an eyebrow.

"Fine." He kicked Dancer into life.

They didn't go far before finding a great stone arch between two buildings, engraved with yet another coat of arms. The path there led into a small courtyard with a carved marble fountain depicting a naked man blowing a horn. The water in the fountain was a murky green and the grass edging the paths overgrown.

"Interesting," said Aranok.

On the other side of the courtyard, three large steps led up to a dark oak door lined with wrought iron. Finally—a way in.

"This'll be us, then." Allandria swung down off Midnight. They tethered the horses and gathered at the front door.

"Envoy?" Samily gestured toward the great iron knocker.

"No, no." Aranok waved his hands in abdication. "You're the envoy here."

Samily looked to Allandria. She shrugged. If he was going to be an awkward arse, they might as well take charge.

"All right." The knocker creaked in protest as Samily lifted it, then thunked satisfyingly back against the door. It resonated inside, echoing off the mixed stone.

"How long do we wait?" Aranok asked. Allandria scowled at him.

A latch slid open, and one of the heavy doors crawled inward. A round-faced bald man with an impressive belly appeared in the gap, wearing a plain cream robe with blue-and-gold trim, and weathered brown sandals. There was an odd flicker in his eyes as he looked at each of them. He lifted one heel slightly, as if to step back, but lowered it.

"Yes?" he asked.

"Is your master at home?" Samily asked, taking Aranok at his word.

The man laughed. "In a manner of speaking, I suppose."

"I'm sorry?" said Samily.

"Well, child, my only master is God"—he spread his arms wide— "so my master is always here."

Samily blushed. "Oh, I am sorry, sire, I mistook you for..."

"Nonsense. A White Thorn has no need to apologise to me, or anyone else. Anhel Weyr," he said, offering his hand.

The knight hesitantly shook it. "Samily."

"A pleasure to meet you, child," he said. "Please, have your servants take the horses to the stable, and let me arrange some drinks."

Allandria giggled.

"Oh! Oh, no," Samily spluttered. "These aren't my servants; this is..."

"Palomin." Aranok offered his hand. What was he doing?

Weyr looked sceptically at him for a moment, then took it. "Ah, now I'm sorry. I've embarrassed myself. Anhel Weyr."

"Not at all." Aranok gestured to Allandria. "My wife, Elana." Whatever it was, she had no real choice now but to go along with it, unless she was to cause an embarrassing scene.

"Lady Elana. It is my absolute pleasure." Weyr leaned down extravagantly to place a kiss on the back of her hand.

"My laird." She offered a slight curtsey, which felt ridiculous in her leathers. It felt ridiculous anyway. But still. Even worse.

"What brings you all to my home?" asked Weyr.

"We are accompanying Samily on a mission from the brotherhood," said Aranok. "The details, I'm afraid, are confidential. You understand."

Samily looked at Allandria, her eyes asking what on earth was happening. Allandria smiled and nodded, hoping it was enough to tell her just to play along. Whatever Aranok was doing, he could—and should—have given them warning. She was used to his theatrics, but Samily could easily have ruined this. He'd been lucky.

Weyr looked at Aranok questioningly. Finally, he broke into a grin. "Of course, of course. None of my business." He turned to Samily. "How can I be of service?"

"Brother Meristan suggested you might be able to give us lodging for the night," she said. "If it is not an inconvenience. We will be leaving at first light and would be in your debt."

Weyr smiled. "Brother Meristan? Did he now? Fine man. How is he these days?"

"He is well, thank you, sire. He speaks highly of you."

"Does he?" said Weyr. "I'm sure I don't deserve it. But, of course, my house is your house, as it is for any White Thorn. Allow my servants to stable your horses, and I will have rooms made up for you."

Weyr turned and walked into the house.

Allandria turned to see a pair of young men in plain brown clothing by the horses. She hadn't heard them approach. Weyr reappeared at the door.

"Don't mind the boys, by the way. They're penitents. They have taken a vow of silence and only speak when necessary to ascertain my needs."

Both men lowered their heads as Weyr spoke, only lifting them again when he had disappeared. It was creepy. *Penitents.* Did that make them criminals? Allandria wasn't sure, but the thought was discomfiting.

They followed Weyr into the house. The entry chamber was made up of the red stone. There were arches to each side leading into large rooms, and a staircase that began on the left wall and carried on up the back, ending at a balcony that ran around three of the walls. There was a large, dark statue of a king at the back wall, under the balcony. She couldn't make out which king it was intended to be.

Weyr was halfway up the stairs. "I'll send men to attend you," he called back. "And I shall see you all for dinner in a few hours!" He disappeared onto the balcony and was gone.

"What are we doing?" Samily whispered. "Why did you lie?"

"I didn't want to embarrass him," said Aranok. "He was already blushing when he thought we were just some laird and lady. Imagine how mortified he'd have been if he'd insulted the king's envoy. Besides..."

"You don't like people knowing where you are," Allandria finished for him.

He nodded and winked. But that definitely wasn't the full story.

"I suppose," said Samily. "But it doesn't feel right, lying to such a man."

"You didn't." Aranok smiled. "I did. And as the king's envoy, I order you to keep the secret. There, now it's not your choice. You are absolved." He made a sweeping gesture with his arm, as if he'd done her a great favour. Samily frowned. Allandria slapped his arm. He was being a cock—mocking her faith. She wished he'd stop doing that.

Another man arrived. He bowed to Samily, took her pack and gestured for her to follow him up the stairs. She looked at Aranok, who nodded, and she followed.

"What are you really doing?" Allandria whispered when the girl was out of sight.

"After Mournside, we need to be wary," he said. "I'm covering our tracks."

"You think the most righteous man in Eidyn is someone we need to worry about?" She heard the incredulity in her own voice.

"Of course not," said Aranok. "But his servants? The penitents? Maybe. And if someone comes looking for us..."

"He can't tell them we were here if he doesn't know." It wasn't unfair. The mess of that poor woman's murder in Mournside, and her "husband's" bizarre suicide, made no sense. Keeping their heads down until they understood it was probably wise.

Another two men plodded quietly down the steps toward them. Aranok leaned in and turned his head away from them.

"These guys are creepy, right?" he whispered.

"God, yes."

<hr />

At Allandria's insistence, Samily had changed into her doublet and trousers for dinner. Apparently it was appropriate etiquette. She would have happily stayed in her room, eaten rations and enjoyed some peace and quiet, but she didn't want to insult their host. There had been a basin of clean water and soap waiting for her, so she'd scrubbed off some of the dust. Aranok and Allandria had obviously done the same. The envoy now wore a black doublet and trousers, similar to her own; Allandria wore her cream dress with her hair braided.

"I hope you're all hungry!" Weyr welcomed them into the dining room.

The huge, dark wood table had decorative carved edges with leaves and acorns gilded in gold leaf. The design was reflected in the chairs too, which had high backs and cushioned seats. It was oddly opulent for a devout man like Weyr, she thought. Pretty, but opulent. He gave a great deal to support God's work, though. It was probably a small expense for him.

On the table was an impressive feast—too much food by far for four people. A platter of roast pork, a large pie, a steaming haggis, a mountain of roast potatoes, carrots and other vegetables. Samily had never seen a feast like it. Her astonishment must have shown on her face, because Weyr touched her arm and said, "Don't worry, child. The servants will eat what's left. Nothing is wasted."

"Still, this is too generous," said Aranok.

"Not at all," said Weyr. "Please, take a seat, take a seat!"

They did so, with Samily and Weyr facing each other at ends of the table, and Aranok facing Allandria across the middle. They seemed ridiculously far away from each other, to Samily's mind. She wondered if all formal dinners were like this amongst wealthy nobles—distancing themselves from one another with their opulence.

A penitent came in with a bottle of wine and filled each of their goblets. Samily had noticed they were all male, roughly her age or a little older. She wondered if that was by design, or whether young men were simply more inclined to penitence.

Weyr raised his goblet. "To unexpected guests, and the surprising pleasures they bring! *Slàinte.*"

"*Slàinte,*" they echoed, drinking with him.

Weyr smiled broadly. "Please help yourselves to whatever you desire."

Samily took a large spoonful of haggis, with some roast potatoes and carrots, and covered it all in gravy. It smelled divine, and she lost all thoughts of eating rations in her room.

"So tell me, Palomin," said Weyr, "what manner of *draoidh* are you?"

Aranok cocked his head. "None, I'm afraid."

"Oh? But surely that armour you arrived in is *draoidh*. No?"

"You have a fine eye, Laird Weyr," he answered. "It was a gift from an old friend. To keep me safe on the road."

"Well, that is a friend I'd like to have." Weyr turned to Allandria. "Would you be so kind as to pass the potatoes?"

"Of course." She handed them along.

"And you, Lady Elana, do you also have special armour?" he asked.

"Oh, not me. Just plain hunting armour."

Weyr nodded, dishing potatoes onto his plate.

Samily reached her hand behind her neck and stretched her shoulder. She was more tired than she realised. After this feast, she'd sleep well.

"None of it quite like the White, though, eh?" Weyr asked.

"Indeed not." Aranok looked at Samily. "Nothing matches the White."

"I hear it's very light too. Is that right, Lady Samily?"

Samily quickly swallowed her mouthful. "Mmm, yes." She used a hand to hide her mouth. "No heavier than leathers."

"Hmm. And have you fought many demons in it?" Weyr asked, tucking into his meal.

"A few," she answered demurely. Meristan had taught her it was always better to be humble about one's achievements. Better to be underestimated than overvalued.

"Oh, she's being modest. Only last week, we..." Allandria stopped mid-sentence and flinched. She looked questioningly at Aranok.

"Only last week Brother Meristan was telling us what a fierce warrior Samily is," he said.

Allandria pursed her lips but said nothing.

"Is that right?" Weyr raised his cup again. "Well then, I am even more honoured to have you at my table." He gave a deferential nod to Samily and drank again.

"May I ask, Laird Weyr, how you came into your money?" Aranok

asked. It was a question Samily would never have dared consider. Even
from the envoy, it seemed rude.

Weyr smiled and sat back in his chair. "Well, that is an interesting
question. Why do you ask?"

"Just curiosity," the envoy replied. "I simply wondered to what we
owe this fabulous meal."

"Well, I'm afraid I can't tell you," said Weyr. An odd answer. It also
seemed rude. Samily worried that a split was forming between their
host and the envoy. The two men smiled at each other, but there was
something unpleasant underneath. Something she didn't like.

"I'm sorry," said Aranok, "I shouldn't have asked."

"Not at all." Weyr raised a placating hand. "I wasn't being difficult. I
can't tell you because I don't know!"

*What?*

Aranok and Allandria looked as puzzled as Samily felt.

"No idea." Weyr beamed. "I inherited the lot. Didn't earn a penny
of it. It just"—he raised his hands toward the ceiling—"fell into my
hands, so to speak."

"That's fortunate." Allandria exchanged a look with Aranok.

"It really is," the envoy said. "No wonder you are so devout, when
God has smiled on you so warmly."

Weyr smiled himself. "Indeed. When a man inherits lands, title and
great riches out of the blue, what else can he do but put it to good use?"
He nodded to Samily. She smiled awkwardly and nodded back with a
mouthful of potato.

The difficult mood lifted, for which Samily was grateful. She felt an
odd responsibility to keep good relations here. Weyr was a good man
and a man of faith—a man who had all but put a roof over her head.
She owed him a great deal. All the Thorns did.

She had brought the envoy and his bodyguard here. She had effectively vouched for them, despite Aranok being faithless. She'd already
found him difficult, but not beyond handling. She'd assumed he
wouldn't be so uncivil as to press Anhel Weyr's beliefs in the way he
challenged hers. That certainty had been a little shaken.

Thankfully, the meal largely passed with Aranok telling stories of
his "tailoring trade," while Allandria and Samily avoided saying much

unless asked a question. Better to avoid accidentally exposing the envoy's strange lies. Weyr seemed very interested in Samily, though, and asked several questions about her encounters with demons. She attempted to answer them with as much grace and as little detail as possible. She didn't understand why it was necessary to disguise who they were, but Aranok seemed to have reason, and it was not her place to question him. Not in public, certainly. Besides, she was feeling incredibly tired and slightly nauseated. She had eaten too much. But it had been wonderful.

"Can I interest anyone in a small after-dinner drink?" Weyr asked when they'd all eaten their fill. "Some whisky, perhaps?"

"No, thank you," said Allandria. "I'm afraid I'm going to have to leave the rest of you to it. It's been a very long day."

"Of course, Lady Elana." Weyr stood and offered her a small bow.

Allandria made to stand, but as she did, the colour drained from her face. She collapsed back into her chair. "Oooh," she moaned. "I feel odd."

Samily looked at Aranok. He was blinking and shaking his head, as if shooing away a fly. Samily stood and moved to Allandria. Her head lolled back against the chair. Samily put her hands underneath to support it.

"What's happening?" she demanded. Weyr smiled serenely back at her. Three servants stood silent and unmoving.

"I thought about killing you when you arrived, you know." Weyr stood and moved to Aranok.

"What?" shrieked Samily. White foam was bubbling from Allandria's lips. "What have you done? Why?"

Weyr took Aranok's face between his hands. "But I had to be sure. You might have been acting. Testing me. But it's true, isn't it? You really don't know who I am, do you, Aranok?"

"What's happening?" Samily demanded again, as her legs weakened. She leaned heavily on the table, her vision blurring.

Weyr ignored her, still focused on Aranok. The envoy's eyes rolled in his head. "You sat here at my table and told me the most elaborate lies. Eating my food and drinking my wine as if we were complete strangers. I didn't believe he could do it. I had to see it for myself. And here you are. It worked."

"What worked?" Samily staggered back to her end of the table. She barely made it to her seat. "What have you done?"

"Oh, child, haven't you worked it out?" Weyr held up Aranok's goblet. "I poisoned the cups. Slow acting, so I'd have time. In truth, you were all dead from the first sip. Dinner was solely for my edification and entertainment. I'm sorry."

Aranok shook as foam poured from his mouth. Samily looked back at Allandria. She was still. Still and pale. Foam hung from her chin. Samily felt a wave of anger rising in her. She'd brought them here, to this man, and he'd betrayed them. Murdered them! How could this happen? How could this great man be…?

She felt it building, like a ball within her. A ball of fire and light.

"You've a stronger constitution than these two, girl." Weyr stepped toward her. "Impressive, for your size. You'll be a great loss to the Thorns. All the better."

The room was spinning. She could barely keep her head up now. Aranok was still. The fire built within her. Bigger, stronger, hotter. She leaned forward on the table, trying desperately to clear her head, just for a moment, just long enough…

"Don't fight it, child." Weyr placed a hand on her cheek. "You'll only suffer. And you're such a pretty thing."

She looked up at him, smiling beatifically down at her, and felt more rage, more anger than she'd ever known. Every injury, every unfairness, every moment of indignation rose up in her. Her skin burned with life—life desperate to be free, to be released.

She swallowed hard, choking back the foam she could feel rising in the back of her throat, took a breath, and screamed her final words:

*"Air ais!"*

# CHAPTER 33

Weyr raised his goblet. "To unexpected guests, and the surprising pleasures they bring! *Slàinte.*"

Aranok raised his goblet in return.

"No!" Samily threw her goblet across the table, splattering wine across the food. "It's poison!" She collapsed forward onto the table.

Aranok froze. He turned to Weyr. Their host's wide eyes darted between Aranok and Allandria. She looked at him over the mountain of food, dripping with dark red liquid. He nodded.

"Kill them!" Weyr shouted, standing.

"*Gluais.*" Aranok threw Weyr back against the wall. The servant who had been at Weyr's right leapt onto the table, perched like an animal. His skin had turned grey and thin, almost transparent. He had no mouth, and his fingers now ended in needlelike claws.

"Shapeshifters!" he called to Allandria. She was already on her feet, stalking toward the servant between her and Samily. Knives glinted in her hands.

The shifter on the table leapt high toward Aranok. He ducked and rolled away, throwing up an arm and pushing the creature at the ceiling. It hit hard and dropped back to the table with a crack, splattering food across the floor. Aranok scrambled to his feet, his heart pounding. He wasn't wearing armour. A hit from this thing would rip right through these flimsy clothes.

The last shifter, by the door to the kitchen, didn't advance. It stood like a sentry. Fine, Aranok would deal with the one in front of him. Its claws raked on the wooden table as it regained its feet. He needed to end this quickly.

"*Teine.*" Fire burst from his hand, engulfing the shifter and the food. It would have screamed if it had a mouth. Instead, it thrashed and hammered its hands against the table. It leapt at Aranok. Again, the *draoidh* moved too quickly, and it tangled itself in a curtain. The fabric quickly took the flames. That could become a problem.

"*Gluais.*" He punched the thing through the window into the garden. Let it burn outside. He turned back to face the room. The table burned with low flames, but it was spreading quickly.

*Samily!*

He rushed to the end of the table and carefully lifted the knight away. He rested her in a chair, watching the shifter at the other end of the room. It barely moved, except to follow him with its head.

Where was Weyr? He couldn't see him.

There was a clatter as Allandria's shifter landed on the table. It didn't move—probably dead before she dumped it. He quickly scanned her for injuries—a few rips on her dress, no sign of blood. She caught his eye and nodded. He moved back around the left side of the table; she moved slowly up the right. When he got halfway, he could see Weyr was gone. Must have gone through the kitchen door. That's why the shifter wasn't moving. It was the rear guard. As they drew closer, it raised its arms wide, spreading its claws. Had Aranok not seen them before, he might have hesitated. As it was, he knew exactly what to do.

"*Gluais.*" He pinned the thing's arms against its sides. Allandria stepped across, drawing a knife along its throat, jamming another in its heart. It jerked and slumped to the ground.

"Come on." He lurched for the door.

"No." Allandria pointed to Samily. "We can't leave her."

"But..." he began. She was right, of course. He nodded.

"We need to get to our rooms," she said. "Weapons, armour."

"Yes," he agreed.

"Can you carry her?" Allandria nodded to Samily.

"*Gluais.*" He lifted the knight onto his shoulder. With the magic assistance, she wasn't heavy, but maintaining the spell would drain him. They needed to move quickly. The corridor outside the dining room led back to the balcony overlooking the entrance hall. There was no sign of movement. Allandria took the lead, knives still in hand. It seemed ridiculous that they'd intended to eat with them just minutes ago. Both were black with demon blood. Shifters were minor demons. That almost certainly made Anhel Weyr Mynygogg's mysterious ally. Was he behind Evenna's murder? Mournside was only a day's ride away.

They passed the top of the stairs unchallenged and moved into the main upper corridor, where their rooms were. Still nothing. Allandria, of course, remained alert. Every door was closed. Under other circumstances, he would have suggested searching them. But he could feel himself lagging badly now. He needed to catch his breath, and Samily was already down. Allandria could defend them both, but not with a pair of dinner knives.

They reached Samily's room first. Allandria put a finger to her lips and leaned her head against the door. After a moment, she nodded, stepped back and threw it open.

Nothing. It looked just as Samily had probably left it. He heaved her onto the bed and sat down next to her.

"Looks like he just retreated." Allandria closed the door behind them.

"It does," said Aranok. "Where to?"

"More to the point, why the Hell did he try to kill us? And how did Samily know?"

"I have no idea why, but I have a suspicion how. And if I'm right, this girl is a lot more powerful than I thought." If he was right, Hells, the whole world was different all over again.

"You think you can guard her here, for a minute?" Allandria picked up Samily's Green blade.

Now that he'd put her down, he could feel the fatigue. But he'd be fine. "Yes. Go."

She returned with their gear in minutes. Aranok quickly dug for his mother's oil bottle and breathed it in before putting it under Samily's nose.

The knight jerked upright, her eyes wildly searching the room. "Poison!"

"It's all right, honey, we know." Allandria rubbed her arm. "We know. You saved us."

"Oh, thank God." She slumped back on the bed. "What…what happened?"

"I hoped you'd tell us," said Aranok. "How did you know?"

Samily took a deep breath. "He sat with us. All through dinner. We ate. We talked. We drank."

"What?" Allandria asked, but Aranok put up a hand to quiet her. This was what he'd guessed. And if it ended how he thought, it was momentous.

Samily reached out to Allandria and grabbed her hand. "You died. You both died." She turned to Aranok. "He knew who you were. The whole time, he knew. And I was dying, and he was smiling. Laughing. And I could feel it, burning inside me. So I used it. All of it."

"I know." Aranok felt a tingle of excitement run up his arms as she confirmed his suspicion. "And you are bloody brilliant."

"What's she talking about?" Allandria asked.

Aranok smiled. "She turned back time. For all of us."

Allandria's mouth fell open. "My God. How does that even work?"

"My guess is like a bubble. How big, I don't know. But it was enough to take us all back to before we were poisoned. I don't imagine the rest of the world was affected at all," he said. But that wasn't even the most exciting bit.

"Wait, we were dead?" Allandria asked. "Like, dead?"

Samily nodded sadly. "It was awful."

"But we're not, Samily. We're not dead. We're alive. Because of you."

"But why?" the knight asked. "I have tried before. The dead are dead. They are with God. I have never brought anyone back before. That's"— she paused, as if afraid to say the next word—"necromancy."

"No, no it's not," said Aranok. "You didn't bring us back, you stopped us from dying at all." There was a significant difference. He understood why a faithful knight would be worried about practising such magic— even by accident. Even if it saved her life. Regardless of how *draoidhs* in general were seen by the church, which varied, necromancers were universally considered to be working against God, against nature. Perhaps that's exactly why it had never worked before—because at Samily's core, she didn't want it to. But tonight, when she herself was dying—desperate and angry...

Or maybe it was something else. Maybe what she'd done tonight was a different use of her power—turning back time entirely, as opposed to focusing on a specific thing. Perhaps that explained the difference. They could dig into that when they got back to Traverlyn. Master Ipharia had a special interest in niche skills. She might know more about Samily's ability. Aranok didn't know her well, but she would surely be interested in the first time *draoidh* in living memory. Assuming, of course, she could be trusted—a worry with all of the senior masters. Maybe this discovery about Weyr could lead them to the traitor in the university—if they could get word back before he did. Aranok made a mental note to talk it through with Rasa if she arrived.

"So, wait, it's later than we think it is?" asked Allandria. "If time went back."

"Almost certainly." Aranok turned to Samily. She was a terrible colour. She'd likely used every ounce of her energy to save them and he couldn't even let her rest.

"Samily, I'm so sorry, but we need to move. We set fire to the house. It'll take a while to spread with all the stone and marble, but we still need to move. Do you think you can stand? And ride?"

She nodded.

"Good. Then get that armour on. We might need it."

"Where are we going?" Allandria asked.

"Where we should have gone in the first place. Gorgyn."

"That's a day's ride," she protested.

"Not cross-country," said Aranok. "And not on Calladells."

"It's already dark!" She gestured to the window. "What about a local cottage? There are tenants all over Weyr's land."

"Weyr's land," Aranok repeated. She took his meaning. "Honestly, we're probably safer out there than in here. And we've got this"—he held up the metal cage holding his sunstone, then pointed to Samily—"and her."

"All right." Allandria looked at him expectantly.

"What?" Why was she wasting time?

"Turn around, you dolt. Women are dressing for battle."

———

Within half an hour they were riding. They'd seen no sign of Weyr or his shapeshifters again, though wheel tracks outside the main entrance suggested he'd already run. As if he'd had it planned—probably what he'd been doing while they were dressing for dinner.

They had been relieved to find the horses unharmed. Aranok presumed Weyr had intended to keep the animals once he'd killed the three of them. Everybody knew the value of Calladells—even the wealthy.

Despite the danger of attracting unwanted attention, Aranok used *solas* to create a few balls of light—just enough to see where they were going. The light drizzle in the air was a relief. It was helping to keep him awake, along with his oil, which he and Samily passed back and forth. They couldn't really push the horses until they reached clear land. It was slow going, picking their way amongst the trees over the spongy, peaty earth. When they reached a small clearing, Aranok looked back. The orange glow in the sky told him the fire had fully caught. There would be little left of Wrychtishousis by morning.

That was surprisingly saddening. It was such an unusual building— buildings. It was a shame to see something so unique destroyed. Maybe more of a shame Weyr wasn't still inside. No, he wanted the man alive. He wanted to see him again. He wanted answers.

"Samily?" The Thorn turned to him. She looked like he felt. It would be better if they managed to avoid Thakhati tonight. Allandria was the only one at full strength. Still, that meant something.

"Yes?" she asked.

"You said Weyr knew who I was. What else did he say?"

"He was surprised you didn't know him. He said he wanted to have dinner to be certain you weren't 'acting.'"

That made no sense. He'd heard of Anhel Weyr, of course, but they'd never met. Aranok would have remembered. Weyr was a memorable man.

"Did he say why I would know him?"

"I don't think so," said Samily. "But he said something else. It was odd. He kept saying: 'He did it. He really did it.'"

"Who did what?" asked Allandria.

"I don't know," said Samily. "But he seemed impressed."

"Fuck," said Aranok.

"What?" asked Allandria.

"Mynygogg. It has to be."

"But what did he do?" she asked. "He can summon demons and control the dead, but how do either of those explain...anything?"

She was right. It didn't explain Weyr knowing him, or Aranok not "recognising" Weyr. Had he changed his appearance? Maybe Weyr was an illusionist—or a metamorph. No, he must have been a demon summoner to control those shifters. There had never been a dual-powered *draoidh* before Mynygogg. The chances of another one were—there was no chance.

None of it explained the messenger delivering misinformation. Evenna's murder. The Blackened...maybe. And then there were the Reivers and their bizarre crests. He was sure it all fit together somehow, but he just couldn't see where. Maybe the Weyr they met wasn't Weyr at all. Maybe the real Weyr was dead. But that didn't explain who "he" was, and what he'd done. There must be another Mynygogg acolyte. Worryingly, it did seem likely to be a master. He wished he had Meristan here to talk it through. The monk had a talent for clear thinking.

"I don't know," he finally answered.

"So what do we do?" Allandria asked.

"We do what we came to do. We get to Caer Amon. We find the heart of devastation and get it back to Traverlyn, so Conifax can cure the Blackening. That's still the most urgent threat.

"After that, maybe we can figure out what the Hell is going on."

———

Quarters were all but deserted at that time of night. Only during exams would students be found here in the evening. The oil lamps gave it a warm glow, but every step echoed off the cold walls. Conifax's back twinged with each stair, and he silently cursed the idiot who'd put the *caibineat puinnsean* on the top floor. He understood the reasoning: keep temptation away from the students. They'd even put the least popular

subjects, like herbology and ancient history, on the top floor to mini-
mise the number of students who might find themselves up there,
drawn to the alluring golden locks on the *caibineat's* door.

When he finally reached the third floor, Conifax stopped and rolled
his shoulders. His back gave a few pops and he sighed with the release.
He was too old to be working this late. It had been a long day of teaching, followed by dinner and drinks with a group of nobles. He hated the
fawning charade he had to perform for them, but their gifts would keep
the university going. It also meant accepting some of their idiot children as students, giving them an air of respectability and achievement
their talents were unlikely to merit. Perhaps, at least, they could be
educated to use their unearned power and wealth wisely. Benevolently.

Thankfully, other masters were better at the game than he. Rotan
and Dialla were both at home amongst the aristocracy thanks to their
own backgrounds. They were amongst the minority of genuinely talented highborn students who had come to the university and had stayed
to become full-fledged masters. Dialla's control of energy made her an
invaluable ally to a tired *draoidh*. Rotan's unfailing capacity to generate
conversation with even the wettest of dullards was equally valuable to
Conifax. Perhaps the day would soon arrive when he could unburden
himself of these tedious affairs altogether and leave it to the pair of them.

Despite the company, the dinner had been pleasant. His belly was
full of meat, his head full of wine. When he'd finally managed to
excuse himself, he'd been unable to wait for morning to get back and
look again at the book. It was such an oddity. Why did it exist? Why
would someone write it? And given that it was a work of fiction, why on
earth had it been placed in the *caibineat puinnsean*? He needed to read
more and find out what terrible secrets, what scandalous ideas had seen
it deemed too dangerous for general consumption.

He was halfway along the floor when he saw that the door to the
*caibineat* was not completely closed. Light shone from a narrow crack
along its edge.

*How odd.*

Other than his own current obsession, which he'd shared with no
one, there was little in there to prove so compelling as to have a master
doing research at this time of night, as far as he knew.

However, since he was here himself, clearly it was not unheard-of. He approached the door quietly, listening for any clue as to who was inside, but there was no sound beyond the turning of a page. Deciding not to startle whoever was inside, he loudly cleared his throat before pushing the door open.

When he saw the man reading, Conifax smiled. "Ah, good evening. What brings you here at this time?"

"Oh, Conifax." The man seemed a little startled at first but quickly regained his composure. "Actually, you're exactly the person I need to see."

# CHAPTER 34

They arrived in Gorgyn in the middle of the night. Despite Allandria spending most of their time in the forest convinced she was seeing movement in the trees, a campfire had been the only real sign of danger. It might not have been Reivers, but with both Aranok and Samily fatigued, she decided to avoid it.

The innkeeper, a middle-aged woman named Charia, was grumpy and extremely unwelcoming until she saw Samily. Respect for the White Thorns amongst the lower classes verged on reverence. It required something of a debate to convince her to take pay for the beds. She was adamant it should come under the Thorns' charity, and that the beds were empty anyway. Allandria tried to gently persuade her that they would pay. When that failed, Aranok flatly insisted. Sometimes his authority was useful.

They slept to midmorning, despite which Aranok wanted to set off immediately. A lot of persuading and some shouting convinced him not only that leaving from Dail Ruigh tomorrow morning made more sense, but also that Samily, at least, needed more rest. Allandria didn't press the notion that he did too, but it was patently obvious to anyone with eyes. He had a permanent scowl, and the dark circles under his eyes were the only part of his face that wasn't grey. He looked ten years older.

It didn't take long that afternoon to ride the horses around the edge of the Crags and up the hill slope to Dail Ruigh. If not for the horses, they could have taken the platform that was winched up and down the sheer cliff face throughout the day to allow for trade and travel between the twin towns, but it was only built for people and produce. They'd apparently tried, in the past, to set up a heavy-duty platform for horses, but too many animals had taken fright at the height. Local legend had it that one had burst out of its protective cage and fallen to its death, right on top of the winch operator.

That left them riding into Dail Ruigh midafternoon, with nothing to do for the rest of the day but find a bed and rest. Dail Ruigh and Gorgyn were both market towns, but the similarities ended there. Where Gorgyn dealt in meat, vegetables and fruit, Dail Ruigh dealt in clothes, exotic trinkets and jewellery. There was food, but it was bread, pastries and pies, with wines by the case. This was where the nobility came to shop while their servants gathered essentials down in Gorgyn.

The market lacked the particular stench that permeated Gorgyn, with a pleasant aroma of fresh bread mixed with the perfume of its female customers instead. It also generally lacked the flies.

They'd taken a gentle pace, coming in on the main southern road and heading out of town again until they reached the northernmost inn. The Wheatsheaf was named for the mill just outside of town, where wheat from Mutton Hole was ground into flour for local bakers. It was a large, two-storey white building with a dark, thatched roof. The front was half-covered in ivy, and a small burn ran behind it. It was most likely commonly used by farmers and merchants, with the nobility who visited the town preferring to stay in the centre, where they could be more easily seen.

Aranok approached the bar, while Samily and Allandria waited by the door.

"How are you feeling?" Allandria asked. The girl was as pale as her armour.

"Tired still," she answered. "It's like having a mist around me. Nothing feels quite real. It's difficult to concentrate."

"You'll feel better tomorrow, after a bath and a good night's sleep."

Samily gave a watery smile.

"Fine," she heard Aranok say, and turned to see him stomping back

toward them. He walked straight out the door. They followed him out
to find him digging in Dancer's pack with a look that would melt iron.

"What happened?" she asked.

"They don't serve *draoidhs*." His voice was cold.

"No! Did you tell them who you are?"

"I shouldn't fucking have to," he spat.

Allandria put up her hands. "All right, don't bark at me. I'm on your
side."

"Fine." Aranok swung back up on his horse. "Let's go."

"No," said Samily.

They both turned to her.

"We can't stay here, Samily," said Aranok.

"No. This will not stand." She turned and walked back into the inn.

"Shit. I'd better…" Allandria pointed after her. Aranok rolled his
eyes and nodded. She hurried back in to find Samily facing the innkeeper across the bar. He was a portly, ham-faced man with a blue
apron. Twice if not three times her size. And yet, somehow, she tow-
ered over him. "Innkeeper, I require two rooms for the night."

The man looked at her, wide-eyed. He looked Allandria up and
down.

"M'lady, we'd be delighted to put up you and your friend here. But
that other one," he shook his head, frowning, "I'm afraid not."

"Why not?" the knight asked in an even voice.

"We don't serve his type."

"What type?" Samily asked.

The innkeeper shifted uncomfortably. "*Draoidh*. I wish you no disrespect, of course, m'lady. I'd be happy to offer your own room on
charity."

"What do you have against my companion? Have you met?" Samily
ignored most of the innkeeper's answer.

"Well…no. But they're dangerous."

Samily cocked her head. "I'm dangerous." The innkeeper swallowed
hard.

Allandria glanced behind her. There were maybe eight people in the
bar—all men. The nearest three were clearly listening to the exchange,
pretending to be absorbed in their drinks.

"With respect, that's not the same. You're doing God's work," said the man.

"How do you know he's not?" asked Samily. "What if I was also a *draoidh*?"

"Look, the last *draoidh* we had through here, she befuddled my wife and stole a day's coin. Took us an age to recover," he said. "Heard of another one, killed half a flock of sheep. Set 'em on fire. Trouble follows 'em around. You can't trust him, lady, whoever you think he is…"

Samily leaned across the bar. "I think he's the king's envoy," she whispered, "and there's a good chance you owe him your life."

The man's pink face turned white, which Allandria found deeply satisfying. He looked from Samily to her, then the door. "That's…"

Samily nodded.

He looked to Allandria; to her bow. "Are you…?" She nodded.

"So we'll need two rooms for the night and stabling for three horses." Samily spoke as if it were a routine transaction. "We'll take them all on charity, thank you."

"I…What?" the man stumbled.

"Will that be a problem?" she asked, as if it was the most innocent question in the world. "If you're only happy to offer me the charity, I can let the brotherhood know we have a preferred inn in Dail Ruigh that all Thorns should stay in when nearby."

Allandria wouldn't have thought it possible, but the man's eyes opened even wider at the thought of having to give away all those rooms.

"I…I can do two rooms." He swallowed again, smacking his tongue. "Of course."

One of the drinkers snickered into his beer. Allandria was grinning openly. She'd had no idea Samily had this devilment in her. Not a girl to cross.

"Excellent. Follow me." Samily turned and walked for the door. Allandria followed her back out, feeling an odd sense of pride she wasn't entirely sure was appropriate.

Aranok sat impatiently on Dancer. "Can we go now?"

"Turns out we've got two free rooms for the night. All welcome," said Allandria.

Aranok's forehead crinkled. "How?"

"Our lady knight had some words for the innkeeper."

Aranok looked down at Samily. She looked back with a straight face, but a smile lit her eyes.

It spread to Aranok's face. "Thank you, Samily. But I can't stay here." He looked up at the building. "Not now."

"I understand." She moved to remount Bear. The inn doors swung open. When the innkeeper saw Aranok's dark look, he blanched. He approached slowly, chastened.

"I'm sorry, Laird Envoy. I didn't know who you were." The man fumbled with his hands. He would be calculating the cost of his bigotry by now. Having the king's envoy and a White Thorn to stay would have made his inn the talk of the town for a while, likely brought custom with it.

"No, you didn't." Aranok glowered down at him. "And yet you turned me away."

The innkeeper dropped his head.

"But we have something in common," said Aranok.

"Do we?" The man looked up from under his brow, a twinkle of hope around his eyes.

"I didn't know who you were either." The *draoidh* nudged Dancer to walk. "I do now."

---

She opened her eye, slowly, painfully. Everything hurt. Especially her face. She moved to sit up, but the shuddering pain in her shoulder forced her back down with a grunt. Something moved next to her in the dark. A rustling, like cloth. Where the Hell was she?

A light flared to her right. She flinched away from it, jerking again as pain bit her shoulder.

"Nirea?"

She opened her mouth to answer, and groaned as a burning pain stabbed the left side of her face. She held her hand up to it instinctively and felt... stitches. Her left eye was swollen shut, but she could see the huge form looming over her with her right.

"Me-stan?" she slurred. "Wha' happa?"

The monk took her hand gently.

"It's all right. You're safe. We're in the hospital. Traverlyn."

"Glohbah?" she asked.

Meristan's face fell. "I'm so sorry. There was nothing I could do."

Her vision blurred as tears welled. Tears of relief for her; tears of grief for her friend. She freed her hand from Meristan's and wiped her good eye.

"How?" How had they survived? Who had saved them?

"Well," Meristan said, "that's a rather unlikely story. When I... When you were...Well, I noticed something. When you struck the demon's skin, your sword glanced off. But when it reared to bite you, I noticed that inside its mouth was pink. Pink and fleshy. So I thought that must be a weakness, and...I hit it. In the mouth. With the axe."

If her face hadn't been so swollen, it would probably have been more apparent that Nirea's mouth hung open. The monk had saved them. The monk.

"An...?" she asked.

He looked confused for a moment. "Oh, 'and'? Took the jaw right off. That boy knows how to make an axe. Then it was screaming and thrashing, and I just swung it up, and..."

He opened his jaw and moved his flat hand as if it were an axe, lodging in the roof of his mouth. He shrugged and smiled.

*The monk.*

The monk had slain a demon. Single-handed. With an axe. God was working hard to make her believe.

"Heah?" she asked. "How we heah?"

"I picked you up and ran. I did what I could for your wounds, strapped you to your horse and rode. We arrived this afternoon. Egretta stitched you. It's night. You should rest."

Incredible.

"Glohbah?" she asked again.

"There wasn't time. You were dying." The monk sat down on what Nirea could see was another bed. He placed the lamp on a table. "I had to get you here. Once you're healed, perhaps we can go back for him."

Nirea nodded. It was the right choice. Prioritise the living. But there was something else. Something he was not saying.

"Wha ess?"

He sighed. "Nirea, I'm not sure how much you remember, but…that was a trap. We walked into a trap. Taneitheia hasn't been in Barrock in at least weeks, more likely months. I don't know where she is—if she's even alive. But that demon—it was waiting. Waiting for someone to go looking for the queen." He looked intently at her. "How did that happen?"

Indeed. How did their king send them on a mission that was likely to end in their death? How could he have got it so wrong? Who could have convinced him Taneitheia was still there?

*Wait.*

*Aranok.*

He had the king's ear. He was more than capable of usurping information like that, and he had been constantly delaying their trip. And then he didn't come. And he'd taken their bloody healer with him—the one person who could have saved Glorbad if she'd been there. In fact, if the monk he'd sent with them instead hadn't somehow enacted a miracle, they'd all be dead. The whole council. The council Aranok clearly wasn't enamoured with from the beginning. It was all a bit convenient, even if he had objected to the mission in that first meeting. Was that an elaborate act to avoid suspicion? Had she completely misjudged the man from the start?

But then, what purpose did it serve? If he wanted them dead, there were easier ways than an elaborate demon trap. He could have murdered them in their sleep several times over. No, there was no easy answer there.

"And, I'm afraid there's something else. I don't know what it means, but…" Meristan crossed his arms and stroked his beard with one hand. "They found him last night. In the library.

"Conifax is dead."

———

Aranok lay awake, staring at the ceiling, his arm under Allandria's neck as she slept with her back against him. They'd found another inn. Not as near the edge of Dail Ruigh, but not far away enough to matter.

That fucking innkeeper. He was annoyed at himself for even being angry. But every time he experienced the prejudice of ignorant bastards, it reminded him of Korvin. He felt their hate, not for himself, but for his dead friend, for his niece, for every *draoidh* child.

He could see him as if it were yesterday. Lying in the dirt, his stage as broken as his neck. He remembered the light shows. Not the ones he did onstage; the ones when they were children—when they'd sneak into his father's warehouse, and Korvin would make the lights dance for them. It was magic as pure joy, the happiest he ever remembered being. Korvin and he got each other through childhood—all but raised each other. They sat together in school, ate together. Fought together.

As young men, they drank, studied, chased girls and still, sometimes, fought together.

When Korvin and Ikara had fallen in love, at first he'd been uncomfortable with it. She was a lot younger. But they were so happy, and the man he thought of as his brother actually being his brother was a nice idea. Which made Pol all the worse—knowing how it should have been. His father would have been unhappy, of course, but Ikara would have cared about that as little as Aranok did.

He'd been supposed to meet Korvin after his show, to go to the Canny Man. When he'd arrived in the square, it was immediately obvious something was wrong. He still remembered the sickness, the feeling of his legs turning to water beneath him. The crowd standing, staring.

Staring at the illusionist dead on his own stage.

It took him eight months. Eight months of living amongst them, pretending to be one of them. Listening to their bile and ignorance, repeating it back at them. Drinking in their scummy inns. Eight months until three of them drunkenly boasted about killing Korvin. Altric, Hammon and Kulan. Another two weeks to get them all together, out of sight of the guard.

A moment to kill them. A gesture. A word.

He remembered the screams. The pleading. He remembered the smell as they burned. It made him smile. A painful, bittersweet smile.

Then he drank. A lot. More months. He wasn't sure how many. He was almost barred from the Canny Man. Probably would have been if Calador hadn't known him, hadn't taken pity on him. By the time Janaeus dragged him out of the bottom of a bottle, Emelina had been born and Ikara married to Pol.

A year later, a year of listening to Janaeus talk about a better world—a better kingdom, where taxes were spent for the people, not the king, where everyone was equal, including *draoidhs*, where children didn't starve to death on the streets of Auldun—a year later, they took the throne. They built the better Eidyn. And the country loved them for it.

A *draoidh* became the second-most powerful man in the land. And everything was better. The best it had been in his lifetime. And he felt like he'd done Korvin some justice. More than when he killed the bastards who murdered him. He'd made a better world for Korvin's daughter. That was justice.

Until Mynygogg. Until the Reivers. Until the war. He barely recognised the country he and Janaeus had built. People starved in the streets again. Scum who belonged in gaol worked the towns, because the good people, the men and women who should have been doing their jobs, had given their lives fighting Mynygogg's monsters. Some of them had become his monsters.

But maybe, maybe they could start to build again. Maybe, if they could find the relic, they could cure the Blackening. That would be a huge step forward. Then they could go back to Haven and regroup properly. He and Janaeus could root out the traitors. Anhel Weyr and whoever "he" was.

They'd build the better world again. For Korvin. For Emelina. For Vastin.

For all of them.

# CHAPTER 35

Crostorfyn lay only a few miles from Caer Amon. It had been built to be the heart of a new settlement as Caer Amon expanded—until it didn't. Thus, the kirk only served a relatively sparse rural community, despite being an impressive feat of ancient architecture, built to house many more. As they approached in the fading light, Samily was struck by its beauty. It was an impressive monument to God's work.

The kirk sat atop a slope that rolled down toward the ruins of Caer Amon and the sea. The main spire rose majestically against the setting sun, the Light emblem carved into its stone mirroring the ones on her pauldrons. It was times like this when she truly felt the presence of God: a warm, gentle sensation of love and beauty.

"Some building," said Aranok, dismounting. Another day of cross-country riding had been hard on the horses. It had been worth it, though. They'd made it to Crostorfyn in daylight. Tomorrow morning they would make for Caer Amon.

"Are you sure this one isn't going to try to kill us?" Aranok smiled, but it wasn't funny. Anhel Weyr was supposed to be a brilliant man and a devout servant. Either he wasn't or, perhaps worse, he was dead. Either way, it was not a joking matter. Aranok's smile faded when he saw Samily's reaction. Good.

She climbed down off Bear and stroked his huge neck. "We should walk to Caer Amon. The horses need rest."

"That's not a bad idea," said Allandria, tending her pack. "It won't take long to walk, and there's no road to speak of. We should travel light."

"Fine," said Aranok.

The arched wooden doors of the kirk creaked open and a small man in a black robe, similar to Meristan's, stepped out. His silver hair was almost at odds with his clean-shaven, youthful face. It was difficult to age him at all. Not that it mattered.

"Good evening, friends," said the priest. "Welcome to Crostorfyn."

Samily shook his hand. "Thank you, Faither. My name is Samily. My friends and I seek solace for the night."

"And you shall have it." The priest folded his hands on his chest. "I am Dalim. All are welcome here, of course, but especially those who wear the White."

"Is there somewhere we can stable the horses?" the envoy asked.

"I'm afraid we have no stable." Dalim pointed to his left. "But a pole runs around the side of the kirk, where they can be tethered for the night..."

"We need them inside overnight." Aranok looked around at the trees. "We all need to be inside."

Dalim frowned. "Hmm. Well, I suppose we could bring them into the aisle. Or perhaps the transept. May I ask why they need to be inside?"

Samily placed a hand on his arm. "We will explain, but first, may we go inside?" The sun was almost completely gone now, and while she hadn't seen any cocoons in the trees, it wasn't worth risking a fight they didn't need to have.

"Certainly," said Dalim. "And, by an interesting coincidence, there is someone else you should meet."

———⋄———

"Tull!"

Samily ran to the man and threw her arms around him. He looked not much older than her, but substantially larger, and while his dark skin and hair contrasted with the girl's pale complexion, he wore the same glistening white armour. Another Thorn. Aranok had not met many, and here were two at once. It was comforting knowing they were scattered around the kingdom, but actually seeing another made it more real.

"Samily!" He held her at arm's length, beaming back at her. "What are you doing here?"

She glanced quickly at Aranok. He shook his head. He didn't need to know.

"What are *you* doing here?" Samily asked instead.

Clever deflection.

"Reivers," he answered. "There's a breach in the Malcanmore Wall just west of here. It's a straight run to Haven, so we were asked to patrol."

"We?" asked Samily.

"Asha and I were assigned here."

"Asha's here too?" Samily looked around excitedly. This was maybe the first time Aranok had really seen her youth. She was usually so sensible.

"No," said Tull. "She rode back to Baile Airneach a few days ago. Reporting for new orders. She may come back."

"Oh." Samily's shoulders dropped.

Tull nudged her playfully. "Hey. We took a demon. Winged. Six legs. Just the two of us."

Samily brightened again. "Where?"

"Down at the coast. Took some doing, even with two of us. Burned it on the beach. It was...kind of pretty. Stunk like Caparth's feet, though." Tull grinned widely and Samily laughed. "What about you?"

Samily cast a surreptitious glance at them and looked down. "Oh, um..."

She clearly wasn't sure what to say, through either modesty or fear of saying too much. It took Aranok only a moment to recognise it would be cruel to leave her dangling. "Samily saved us from a demon. It's how we met, on the road."

The Thorn jerked her head around, eyes mixed with surprise and gratitude.

"Very nice. A big one?" Tull asked.

Samily turned back to him. "Yes. Maybe ten feet. Fire breather. I had help."

"Oh, who was with you?"

Samily waved a hand. "Oh, nobody. I mean, well, Brother Meristan, and...some fighters."

Tull stopped smiling and stood tall. "You took it on your own?"

Interesting. It seemed that, in a demon battle, only Thorns counted. Was this a competitive thing? Or did they just see anyone else as effectively useless against demons? To be fair, they wouldn't be far wrong.

Samily scrunched up her mouth awkwardly. "Well..."

"Entirely alone," said Allandria. "She split its head with one strike."

Tull's eyes opened wide. "S'grace, girl. Very nice."

Samily smiled appreciatively but still looked uncomfortable. "Anyway, it's wonderful to see you. How long have you been here?"

"Uh, Dalim's been putting us up for, what, a month now?"

The priest nodded in agreement.

"That's a good sign," Allandria whispered. She was right. Hopefully this "righteous" man actually was. Aranok hadn't really suspected him. What were the chances of both of the holy men they went to for shelter being frauds? Then again, he'd have said the chances of one were low.

Samily looked delighted to see Tull—almost as happy as she'd looked when they brought Meristan back from the dead. Actually, she'd mostly cried at that point, so she probably looked happier now.

"I am afraid we'll be a little short on space," Dalim said. "There are only three bedrooms in the building. It is not really designed for visitors."

"That's fine," said Samily. "Palomin and Elana are married, and Tull and I have shared a room before." She gave Aranok and Allandria a subtle smile, which suggested to him that the secret of their relationship was not as secret as he'd have liked. He wondered how close these two were. Did White Thorns have partners? Did they marry? He didn't really know. He turned to Allandria and raised his eyebrows, nodding toward them. She closed her eyes and shook her head. She seemed confident. She knew something he didn't. He'd get it out of her later.

"Ah well, that's all fine," said the priest. "In that case, I suppose you should bring the horses inside, and I'll see what we can do about dinner."

"You're bringing the horses inside?" asked Tull.

"Yes," said Samily.

"Why?"

"Have you seen any odd creatures at night? Like..."

"Giant insect people?" Tull interrupted her.

"Yes! You've seen them?" Samily's enthusiasm was a little unsettling. Aranok could easily have assumed the two were talking about some training competition rather than murderous beasts. In fact, they both seemed a little too excited for the conversation.

"I have." Tull shrugged. "But they're not that difficult to kill."

Easy for him to say with that Green blade on his back.

Allandria snorted.

Samily glanced awkwardly at them before answering. "For us, no, but...how many have you encountered? At once?"

"A few."

"We've seen a swarm," said Samily. "We were lucky."

"I want to hear that story," said Tull.

Samily glanced surreptitiously at Aranok. "You only see them at night, right?"

Tull looked thoughtful. "I suppose. Hadn't thought about it."

"They die in sunlight. We...had a *draoidh* with us. He used a spell to store sunlight in a rock, and..."

*Good girl.*

"Wow," said Tull. "That sounds miraculous! I'd like to meet that *draoidh*."

Samily smiled. "I'm sure you will."

---

Samily felt completely at peace for the first time in a long time. She and Tull had prayed together, then settled into bed for the night. He'd tried to insist she take the bed, but once she explained she'd been sleeping in inns for weeks, he relented. She'd set up her bedroll on the floor but did take the offer of a pillow. She lay on her side, in the dark, just listening to her friend breathe. It was like being back in Baile Airneach. Even the smell of him reminded her of their bunks. She found herself smiling.

She hadn't felt like this with Meristan, she realised. Which was unusual. If anything, he was her closest family, and yet, she'd been uncomfortable with him. Ever since that night in Baile Airneach. He seemed so sad. Full of doubt. He showed a braver face to the others, but she could still see it in his eyes—the darkness that was eating him. She prayed he was safe.

"Tull?" She spoke quietly, testing whether he was awake.

"Mm-hmm?" he answered sleepily.

"Can I ask you something?"

He rolled onto his side and looked over the edge at her, rubbing his hand over his face. "You can ask me anything, Sam."

He was right; she could. And that felt good too.

"Have you seen Meristan recently?"

"When I was back at Baile Airneach, I suppose. That was a while ago."

"Did he seem...odd?"

He was silent for a while. "I don't think so. I can't remember anything specific. I mean, I know I must have seen him, but nothing sticks in my head, you know? So I guess I mustn't have noticed anything odd. Why?"

"Something's bothering him," she answered. "He's always been happy, loud, just, you know...?"

Tull laughed. He knew.

"He seems small. As if something has squashed him. Disappointed. I don't know why."

"Huh," said Tull. "That doesn't sound like him at all."

"I know. That's why I'm worried. And on top of that..." She stopped. Could she tell him about the Blackening?

"What?" Tull's brow furrowed.

She sucked air through her teeth. Tull was one of her best friends. She trusted him with her life. Aranok didn't. But in this case he was just going to have to take her word for it, because she needed to talk. She sat up in the dark, cross-legged on the floor. Just like they used to, as children, talking through the night when they were supposed to be asleep.

"All right. I have a lot to tell you."

Aranok woke to banging on the door. He brushed Allandria's hair out of his face and looked around. He did not want to be awake. His eyes stung, pleading to be closed again.

"What's wrong?" Allandria asked.

"I don't know." He clambered over her and fumbled for clothes in the dark. Who would be knocking at this time? Why?

"Was that the door?" she asked, disgruntled, pulling the blanket over her head.

"I think so." Aranok struggled into his trousers. His left foot stuck and he tumbled backwards onto the end of the bed.

"Ow!" Allandria drew her feet from under him.

"Sorry."

More banging.

"It *was* the door." Aranok felt his way across the small room, stubbing his toe on something as he went. Felt like a boot. He opened the door a crack to find Samily and her friend standing in the hallway, half-dressed and looking at him eagerly.

"Yes?" He covered a yawn.

"We need to talk," said Samily.

"Now?" he asked incredulously.

"Now."

Aranok sighed. He was not destined to get a decent night's sleep. "All right, give us a minute." He closed the door again. "Allandria?" he whispered loudly. No answer. "Allandria?"

"What?" she mumbled from under the blanket.

He sat on the end of the bed. "Samily wants to talk to us."

"About what?"

"I don't know."

"But I'm asleep," she said with a hint of ire.

"No, you're not."

"I bet she doesn't need to talk to *us*. I bet she could talk to *you* and you could tell me about it tomorrow."

He nudged her leg and she gently kicked him with it.

"If I have to be up, you have to be up," he said.

"I am absolutely certain that's not true."

"How are you going to guard my body while you're asleep?" He pulled his shirt over his head.

"Not fair," she said huffily. "You're not allowed to pull rank when I'm naked."

"Either way, I'm letting them in when I'm dressed, so..."

"Don't you dare!" She shot upright, the blanket dropping to her waist. He smiled at her in the moonlight.

"You are definitely not asleep."

"I'm not getting out of bed." Her face was dead serious.

"You should probably put this on, then." He threw her a shirt.

Allandria pulled it over her head like a petulant child, wrapped the blanket tight around her waist, curled her legs up and leaned back against the wall. She raised her eyebrows, daring him to argue any further. It was surprisingly alluring. Which was not helpful. He lit the lamp and kicked the clothes they'd shed onto the floor under the bed. It was as tidy as it was getting.

He opened the door. "All right. What's so important?"

Samily and Tull entered. She opened her mouth but stopped as she looked at the floor, then recovered and carried on.

Oops. No bedroll. Oh well. It would only have been confusing for Tull, who thought them married.

Tull closed the door behind him.

"I told Tull everything," Samily said quickly. "I understand you didn't want me to, but I trust him, and you have to trust me."

"Laird Envoy." Tull nodded slightly. "It's an honour."

Aranok took a breath before responding. It was irritating, but there was little point arguing about it now. "All right." He gestured to Tull's head. "But please don't do that."

Samily visibly relaxed. "Good. Well, he has information. He's been to Caer Amon. Tell them." She turned to him.

"She's right," Tull said. "You don't want to go down there."

"Why not?" Aranok sat on the bed.

"Well, firstly, there's nothing there," said Tull. "I mean nothing. There's barely even a trace of the buildings that used to be there. Just some foundation stones, and sometimes not even that. It's just...remnants."

"But..." Aranok began, halting as Tull put up a finger.

"Most of the time."

"What do you mean?" Allandria sat up a little straighter.

"I've heard the ghost stories," said Aranok.

"They're true," said Tull. "And more."

"Tell me." Aranok had never heard a firsthand tale from Caer Amon. Few living had.

"We haven't seen that many Reivers, despite the damage to the wall. To be honest, those we've seen have been leaving, not invading. It's been quiet. So I went looking down toward the coast—in case they were slipping in down there. Being that close to Caer Amon...if I'm honest, my curiosity pulled me.

"It was early afternoon when I reached the edge of the old settlement. There were a few foundation stones here and there. Overgrown. Nature has reclaimed almost everything. It's actually very peaceful. I walked for a mile or so—there were a few other remnants. When I found a stone slab, I stopped for a seat and some rations. I'd not been there a few minutes when I heard something completely wrong. Amongst the birds and the insects, I suddenly heard laughter, clear as day. The laughter of a small girl."

The tale was starting to sound like the stories he and his friends told one another as children, in the dark, to make them feel scared and alive.

"I jumped up and drew my sword—I assumed it was a party of Reivers, though why they had a young girl with them...I suppose it didn't really make sense, but I hadn't seen another person all day. I couldn't see her, at first. Then she giggled again, and I turned. She was maybe twenty feet away. She was playing. She looked at me and smiled. She waved. She saw me."

"So you saw a little girl? I mean, that's a bit odd in Caer Amon, but..."

Tull carried on as if Aranok hadn't spoken. "I heard another voice. A woman's. Calling a name. Shashak, I think. The girl turned and ran across the clearing..."

That was odd. Shashak wasn't a name Aranok had ever heard, but more than that, it broke with the entire form of male and female names in Eidyn. Traditionally, boys' names ended in consonants, girls' in vowels. It had been that way for centuries. Nobody had ever been able to explain to Aranok why, but a boy with a girl's name, or a girl with a boy's would have been ridiculed. It would be almost cruel for a parent to break that particular tradition. And yet, it served no discernible purpose.

Aranok realised Tull's face had lost some of its colour.

"She ran to a cottage," he continued. "A cottage that wasn't there when I sat down. A cottage that looked primitive. A woman stood at the door, watching me. She looked...she looked like she thought I might be a threat to her child. She didn't recognise me—or the armour. She didn't recognize the White. She ushered the girl in, looked hard at me and closed the door. I heard the bolt latch.

"And then it was gone. Vanished right before my eyes. I swear by God's grace I watched that cottage disappear as if it were never there."

There was a long silence.

"So the ghosts are real?" Allandria finally asked.

"No," said Aranok. "That doesn't make sense. In any ghost story I've ever heard, the ghosts are unaware of people. They don't know they're dead—they're reliving moments of their lives. They don't interact."

"It seems the ghost stories were wrong," said Samily.

"Maybe." Or maybe there was something else entirely happening.

"There's more," said Tull. "I was coming back up the hill. I heard voices. Lots of them, carried on the wind. Shouting. Angry. Then a scream. A scream like nothing I've heard before. A howl of pain. I can't swear it was human. Then it stopped, and there was nothing. Nothing but gulls on the breeze."

"That's given me gooseflesh." Allandria rubbed her forearm.

"What do you think it was?" asked Aranok.

"I don't know, Laird. But I believe something awful happened there. Something evil. Something so terrible it cursed the soil, and the land still echoes with it."

"That'd be new," said Aranok. "I've never heard of a place being *damainte* before—though I suppose it could be possible. Theoretically." He found himself wishing he could confer with his old teacher, who would have a much better idea than he what was happening in Caer Amon. He'd be able to discuss it with him when they got back to Traverlyn, hopefully with the heart of devastation.

"What do you think, Envoy?" Samily asked.

"I think I need more sleep," said Aranok. "But thank you, both, for coming to me. Tull, I appreciate your help. I'd also appreciate it if you'd keep this between us. Especially..." He gestured to himself and Allandria.

"Of course, Laird." Tull began to bow, then stopped himself. "I consider your confidence a sacred trust."

The Thorns withdrew, leaving Aranok to climb back into bed.

Allandria snuggled up against him. "What do you think?"

"Could be several things. Ghosts. Curse. Maybe Tull ate something poisoned. Maybe there are plants down there that give folk visions. I don't know."

"But we're still going?" she asked.

"God, yes. The entire kingdom's at risk from the Blackening. We can't let a creepy story keep us away. Can you imagine explaining that to Janaeus?"

"Just checking," she said sleepily. Moments later, her breathing changed and she was asleep. He envied her that—the ability to drop off so quickly. It would take him an age. Ah well, he was slowly becoming used to a lack of sleep. Perhaps that would have him seeing visions tomorrow too.

# CHAPTER 36

Allandria closed her eyes and breathed in the crisp morning air. For a moment, she was back home, picking mushrooms in the forest outside Lochen.

They'd come down to Caer Amon early, as Aranok wanted. A light mist was just dissipating, leaving a chill dew over the grass. They'd been on guard against Reivers, but Tull was right about their absence. In the silent solitude of nature, Allandria felt a long way from civilisation. It was nice. The Thorn had been right about the remains too: little but rocks. You'd barely know there had been a settlement there. And yet, nobody had built there since. In hundreds of years, every generation had avoided the place. Allandria thought there must be something to that beyond folklore. There was a certain presence about it—an indescribable tension in the air, a tingling on her skin. As if something were humming on the edge of her hearing.

They found Tull's clearing midmorning. The stone slab was as he'd described, but there was no cottage, no girl. They made their way to what seemed to have been the centre of the old settlement. Allandria suggested there was little point searching, because there was nothing to search. No buildings. No entrances to underground passages. Just dirt and grass and rocks.

Still, Aranok insisted they try. With what was at stake, she agreed. They each chose an area and combed over it carefully. Picking through rocks, pushing aside grass—an anthill was the most notable thing she discovered. Down toward the water, she expected to see the remains of a port, a pier, even some kind of dock, but again there was nothing. Just sand, stones and water. She stood for a while, looking out over the sea, breathing in the salty air. There was something about the coast— like being at the edge of the world. In some ways, she felt more alive here, more energised. It was, she imagined, a small taste of what Nirea missed. Would it be nice to just sail away from everything? To leave the world—the Blackened, Mynygogg, everything. Just pick up and go?

It was tempting.

She turned away and trudged back up the slope. There was nothing here. She wanted to hope Aranok and Samily had had better luck, but a resignation within her knew they hadn't. This place was dead.

"Anything?" called Aranok as she approached.

She shook her head. "Not even a ghost." She realised as she said it that she was almost disappointed. The idea of seeing a ghost was exciting. She'd seen amazing things, but an actual ghost would be something new.

"Damn it." Aranok threw down the rock in his hand.

"Nothing here either?" She already knew the answer. He shook his head.

"Now what?" Aranok sat on a stone platform.

She sat next to him. "What do you think this was?"

He tapped the stone. "This? I don't know. It's survived better than everything else. From the space around here"—he spread his arms, indicating the ground around the stone—"and the buildings I can make out over there, I think we're probably right in the middle of the settlement. Could have been the market, I suppose. Maybe this was for announcements? Or maybe something religious? Samily might know…"

"Any sign of her?" Allandria asked.

"Not yet."

She put her hand on his. "I'm sorry. I'm sorry this didn't work. I know how much you wanted it."

He looked up at her, his eyes tired and dull. "We all did."

"Of course, but I think it meant more to you." She didn't say that he expected too much of himself, or that he wrapped his own value too much in the things he could achieve—in the people he could save. She didn't say that she worried he'd never be happy, no matter how much he did. It wouldn't help.

"Shall we look for Samily?" she asked instead.

He nodded, and they started back toward the southern end of the settlement.

"We can still cure the Blackening," she said after they'd walked in silence for a while. "It'll just take longer."

"Maybe. But I'm not sure we can…" He stopped, staring ahead. Allandria followed his gaze to the girl running toward them. She wore a plain cream dress with a brown apron and no shoes. She was crying. And she ran like the Devil itself was chasing her. She barrelled past them, not quite avoiding them, nudging Allandria against Aranok. She grabbed his shoulder to catch her balance and turned to see where the girl had gone. She half expected her to have disappeared, like Tull's cottage, but what she saw instead flushed a tingle through her.

A muddy road, lined with houses. The girl, running down it, past others. An older woman, feeding chickens beside her house. A boy leading a goat on a rope. A man carrying a great axe over his shoulder, a sling full of wood in his other hand. There was an entire village behind them and, as she looked, it was all around them, as if it had always been there, waiting. Only the slight green haze prevented it from looking exactly as if they'd been transported to a primitive village.

"What the fuck?" Aranok breathed out.

But Allandria was focused on one thing: the girl. Tull said something evil had happened here. She had a feeling that girl was running from it.

"Come on!" She pulled Aranok's arm. "Follow her!"

---

Tempit stumbled in the mud and slipped to her knees. She landed hard on her hands, jarring both wrists—but she barely noticed the shooting pain, pushing herself back to her feet. She had to get to the square. Up and running again, she battered into the back of old man Gorshin.

"Hey!" he shouted after her.

Tempit barely noticed him. All she could hear was the pounding of blood in her ears; she felt the earth beneath her bare feet, the burning need to run.

She rounded a corner, knocking Hardia off her feet and sending her sprawling with her basketful of chickens.

But she could see the square now—could see the throng of bodies, crammed in, fighting to see the show. *Ghouls.* She barged her way past another few people—didn't stop to see their faces, just heard their grunts of derision and disapproval. She didn't care. She had to get there. Had to stop this. She reached the edge of the square. The bodies were packed tight. She tried to squeeze in, but a large man in grey robes stubbornly refused to move, to give her any leeway. She was stuck here, too far from the platform.

"Stop!" she called out. "Stop, you don't..." A hand over her mouth, and an arm around her waist, dragging her backwards. She thrashed frantically, trying to get free.

"Shh," a familiar voice said in her ear. "You'll get yourself killed."

"Father?" She turned her head to him.

"You can't stop this," he said. "You can only get yourself killed too."

"No." Her voice broke. "No. It's not fair. I won't let him die!"

"You'll shut up and do as I tell you," he said.

"As we all know..." a voice began from the platform. "This year's crops flourished very late. It should have been a hard winter. A winter spent eking out our rations."

It was the pastor, Harden. The sanctimonious old bastard. The self-appointed guardian of their souls. He'd have had half of them die rather than save the crops. The damned idiot.

"And as you all know, we've been able to harvest on time, because the crops grew at an unusual rate. An unnatural rate. While that might seem like a blessing from God, I am here to tell you it is not. It is the opposite. It is the work of the Devil. The Devil working through this witch!"

He gestured down at the platform he stood on. Tempit couldn't see what was there, but she knew. She knew it was Goardem. She knew, like she knew the sun would come up tomorrow—for most of them.

"Now, you may think what he did for us is a blessing! A good thing! But anything that usurps God's will is evil, my friends. God is not working through this man—this is the perverted work of Hell!"

Tempit bit her father's hand. He yelped and pulled it away. "No, it wasn't!" she screamed. "I can prove it!"

"What? Who spoke? Come forward!" Harden beckoned benevolently.

Tempit looked back at her father, who scowled angrily at her. She'd have to fix that later. For now, she strode toward the platform, gawkers and murder fetishists parting like leaves in a breeze.

"It wasn't him." As Tempit got close to the plinth, she saw Goardem, hands chained to the ground, his head strapped against the block. His pale blue eyes pleaded with her to save him.

"We have a witness that says otherwise, Tempit," Harden said. "Are you saying she's lying?"

"I'm saying she's wrong! But even if she wasn't, why does it matter? The crops grew. We have enough food. We'll have enough for the winter!"

"It matters because we are godly people, Tempit," said Harden. "It matters because God does not tolerate witches."

There was a grumbling agreement from the crowd around her. Someone nudged her shoulder from behind.

"It wasn't him!" Tempit was all but begging. "Please, you have to believe me!"

Harden looked hard at her for a moment, then took a step back and put out an arm. "Come forward, child." The little brown-haired girl in a plain heather dress stepped timidly to the front of the plinth. Tempit's breath caught in her chest. Not her. Not Delfia. Not Goardem's own little sister.

"Tell the people what you saw," said Harden.

"Don't want to." Her voice was tiny, watery. She was terrified.

Harden crouched down beside her. "Come on, now, child. We talked about this, remember? God knows the truth, and only the truth will save us. Did you see Goardem use magic to make the crops grow?"

Tears streamed down the girl's face. She was literally feet from her own brother, strapped down and trembling.

"Tell the truth, Delfia!" Harden pointed to the sky. "God is watching!"

With a quivering lip, the girl nodded. She looked at Tempit and opened her mouth as if to try to speak, but no words came out.

"It's all right," Tempit mouthed to her. "It's all right." She was going to have to do this herself.

She breathed in deep and pushed toward the plinth. "Goardem did not make the crops grow."

"How do you know this, Tempit?" asked Harden.

"Because I did."

There were gasps from the crowd. People stepped a little farther back. She saw Maren, her friend since before they could walk. She looked her dead in the eye, hoping for some comfort, but the girl dropped her head and looked away.

*Fine.*

"Witch!" someone shouted. "She admits it!"

"Get her!" another voice cried.

"No!" Tempit put up a hand. "The first person to touch me will regret it!" That was enough to give them pause.

"Listen to me, please!" Now standing directly in front of the platform, she reached up and stroked Goardem's face. It was clammy and pale. He was trembling.

"We were going to starve!" she said. "And I have a gift. A gift I believe came from God. You all know me! Have I ever harmed you? Any of you?"

Every face she looked at turned away—looked at their feet, or the sky. Damn them and their cowardice. Harden had them afraid of their own shadows in the name of God.

"Then why would Delfia tell me it was her own brother?" Harden asked.

*Damn it.*

"Goardem just helped me. He helped me focus. But it is my ability. It is my gift, not his."

She was just going to have to do it. Bilbry's axe was looking twitchy. She needed to get Goardem free before Harden took matters into his own hands.

She knelt at the base of the plinth and gently caressed a small weed that grew there. *"Air adhart,"* she whispered, and stepped back as the weed grew up the side of the platform. It kept growing until it was taller than her, until everyone in the square could see it.

More gasps. More people stepped back. She was in a little circle, completely alone. There was a shuffling, a murmuring in the crowd, and suddenly Jakobil was pushed aside as Tempit's father strode toward her. His face was a confusing mix of anger and fear. When he reached her, he put a hand to her cheek and shook his head. His eyes were pale, with tears just forming at the edges. He turned to face the crowd.

"You all know me," he said loudly. "You know I'm a God-fearing man. And you all know what I've done for you. For each of you."

As the town's medic, many of them owed her father their lives. And they knew it.

"Now I ask something in return. Let the children go."

Tempit felt the words like a hammer in her chest. Go? Go where? Were they to be banished? Banished for saving the village from starvation? "No!"

But her father raised a finger, the way he had since she was a young girl. The one gesture that always quieted her.

"You'll let them go—both of them. And I'll stay," he said, his voice shaking. Of course. Because the town would never agree to their medic leaving. But if he stayed...

There were murmurs of agreement. After all, what was being asked of them? Eat the crops she'd grown for them? Keep their medic and let a couple of fourteen-year-olds leave? Did they really want to see them executed instead?

"No."

It was Harden. Of course.

"No. The girl must not be permitted to live. Our tradition is clear. God will not suffer a witch to live, and neither must we. I'm sorry, Vind, but you know it's true."

Her father stepped between her and the foot of the platform. "You can't have her, Harden." Tempit felt her legs weakening beneath her. She glanced again at Goardem, horribly aware of how vulnerable he still was. He looked terrified.

Harden stared at her father. The crowd was ominously silent, as if speaking would unleash chaos.

"I'm sorry," Harden finally said. "Take her." He nodded to two men in black shirts. The crowd burst into life. Some voices rose in panic, others in anger. The two men came toward them. Jeral, the farmer, and Mink, the butcher. Men who attended service every week. Men who would do whatever Harden asked of them.

Vind pushed her back toward the crowd, keeping himself between her and the advancing men. Someone behind her prodded her in the back. But she was bumping into people now and couldn't tell who. Minever, a woman whose clothes she'd helped wash, screamed "Witch!" in her face. Someone spat on her dress. She fleetingly worried about having to wash it later.

"Please?" she said in a tiny voice. "Please."

Her father collapsed before her, a red wound blossoming on the top of his balding head. Tempit looked up to see Jeral lowering his club.

"Father!" She dropped to her knees in the mud, cradling his head. The dirt mixed with the blood from his wound, smearing the front of her dress. Her beautiful dress.

"Move, witch." Jeral grabbed her arm and lifted her off the ground.

"No, no!" she screamed, desperately trying to hold on to her father. But Jeral's thick arms were too much for her, and he yanked her to her feet. "No!"

As he pulled her away toward the platform, she looked back and saw Maren take her place, lifting her father's face and wiping it clean. At least it meant something, their history.

Jeral yanked her toward the platform. She was going to die. She was going to be executed here in front of her friends. Her family. Because she had tried to save them. And they were all going to stand by and let it happen.

They were going to watch.

Tempit felt a stone building within her. She closed her eyes. Fear melted away and, as she breathed in, a deep, soulful calm came with it.

"Let me go," she said. "Let me go or die."

She opened her eyes. Jeral had paused, looking to Harden for support.

"Bring her to me," said the pastor. "She can't harm you with a weed, man."

Hesitantly, slower than before, Jeral pulled again.

"Last warning," said Tempit.

He ignored her this time, confidence boosted by his master's assurance. His master was wrong.

Tempit reached her free arm up and touched the farmer's ruddy cheek. *"Air adhart."*

Jeral took a deep, rasping breath, and his strength faded as he instantly aged ten years. Twenty. Thirty. He stumbled back from her, releasing her arm. The hardy man was now elderly, bent, and frail.

"You should have listened," Tempit said.

"Witchcraft!" screamed Harden, and the crowd erupted.

She ran for the steps to the platform. Nobody moved toward her, but a stone hit her in the side, winding her. She caught her breath, but then another, and another. God, what did these people want from her?

She reached out to Delfia, but the girl shrank away, her eyes the size of cartwheels.

*Damn it!*

It didn't matter. She just had to get to Goardem. She'd free him and they'd leave, just like her father said. They could grow their own crops, have their own farm, away from these vile, fearful people. She lurched toward Harden, who flinched away from her.

"Do it!" he cried. "Do it!"

A hiss of wood through air. The sickening crunch of metal on rock. The thud of meat hitting stone. Tempit felt her soul splinter. The crowd was silenced.

She staggered to him. To her love. To the one boy who'd understood her completely. Who'd known her entirely and loved her. The boy who meant everything. She knelt next to his lifeless body. Blood spurted from his neck. His head rolled a few feet and stopped—his blank eyes staring back at her, still scared. Still pleading for her to save him.

"Again!" Harden barked. She heard Bilbry raise his axe again— knew it was coming for her next. She held up an arm in defence, never taking her eyes from Goardem's.

*"Air adhart,"* she whispered. The axe head crumbled to flakes of rust as it reached her, the wooden handle snapping like sun-bleached drift-wood. More gasps from the crowd.

"Get off," she said flatly. Nobody moved.

"Get off!" she bellowed. Delfia was crying. Hardly a surprise. Goardem's blood was pooling in front of Tempit, leaching into the edges of her dress. Her dress. Her ridiculous dress. As if that mattered. As if it had ever really mattered. She heard Harden and Bilbry retreat down the steps, leaving just her and Goardem on the platform, raised above the whole village.

"We did it to save you," she said quietly. "We did it to save all of you."

She reached forward and lifted Goardem's head, cradling it in front of her face. Blood and gristle poured down her arms. But still, she felt the power. She felt the additional strength he'd always given her. She felt it rise within her. She pulled him close and pressed her lips against his.

"Wait for me," she whispered. "I'm coming."

She stood, surveying the crowd, holding Goardem's head like a precious jewel.

"We tried to save you. But if you're all in such a hurry to die, we might as well get on with it."

The power rose in her, burning like the sun. She closed her eyes and pictured his face. Smiling. Laughing in the fields. Dancing in the rain. They would dance again. She held his head high above her.

*"Air adhart!"*

And then there was nothing.

# CHAPTER 37

The girl knelt on the stone block, cradling the boy's head. It was a scene from Hell itself. Allandria felt her hands shaking. "We have to do something."

"We can't," said Aranok. "This happened. We can't change it."

"They're going to kill her for being a *draoidh*," she said. "You of all people..."

But when she turned to look at him, his face was streaked with tears, his jaw clenched. The girl kissed the boy's head, and Allandria felt a stab of despair in her chest. That poor child. Was the past really this bad? Then again, Korvin had been killed for the same reason. For nothing. But not in the name of God.

"We must leave. Now." Samily came up behind them.

"Why?" asked Aranok.

"This is real," said the knight. "I can feel it. Time is broken. These are not ghosts. We are here. In the past. I've seen others. Others who don't belong here."

"You think they're the people who went missing?" asked Aranok.

"I do. We need to leave. Quickly."

"The relic!" Aranok pleaded. "We might find out what it is!"

"What good will it do you if you are dead, Envoy?"

Out of the corner of her eye, Allandria saw the girl stand. A hush fell over the crowd as she raised the severed head high above her. The pretty young girl, covered in mud and gore, like a demon herself.

"We tried to save you," she shouted. "But if you're all in such a hurry to die, we might as well get on with it."

"Heaven, no," said Samily. "We're too late."

"*Air adhart!*" the girl screamed.

Samily lunged at them, throwing them to the ground beneath her. Allandria grunted as she hit the ground hard.

"*Air aaiiiiiissssss!*" the knight bellowed, her voice straining with the effort. A wave blew over them, like a blizzard of broken glass. Allandria raised a hand to cover her face—to protect her mouth. Over the rushing air, she couldn't hear Samily screaming, but she could see the knight's face, stretched and distorted. She felt the grass beneath her grow up past her head, die, and grow again—it tickled, in a nauseating way. Her stomach flipped and she leaned to the side, vomiting into the dirt, watching as it was absorbed by the soil, as if it had never been.

As quickly as it began, it was done. The earth shuddered and there was silence. She could breathe.

Samily slumped on top of them. Allandria sat up carefully, turning the knight, who made no resistance. She was unconscious.

Aranok rolled toward her. "You all right?" His eyes were like saucers.

Allandria looked down at herself. Except for being a lot dirtier, she seemed fine. Physically. But her head spun and her heart raced. She nodded.

The people were gone. The buildings were gone, almost as if they'd never been. All that remained were ruins, reclaimed by nature. But not quite as they had found them this morning. There was more. More structure, more stone left unweathered. And the faint green haze remained.

Aranok rested Samily's head on his knee and gently poured from his waterskin into her mouth.

"What happened?" Allandria asked.

"I think Samily just prevented us from being turned to ash."

"How?"

"That girl was a time *draoidh*. She sent the whole village forward in time—hundreds of years by the look of it. Samily balanced it by sending us back at the same time—the two cancelled each other out. But it must have been exhausting. That girl must have been incredibly powerful, to do this to an entire settlement. You saw how hard it was for Samily just to take us back a few hours."

"But that doesn't make sense," said Allandria. "If she was a time *draoidh*, why kill everyone? Why not save the boy instead?"

"Until a few days ago, Samily thought her power was healing," he said. "Maybe the girl thought all she could do was speed things up. Everything she did—making the plant grow, destroying the axe—it was always forward, not back."

"Oh God." That was so much worse. If she'd known everything she could do… Allandria's heart broke for her again.

Aranok nodded. "I know. It's horrendous. But listen, quickly, I don't know how long this will last. I'll see to her—can you search the square? Look for anything left behind. Anything that could be the heart of devastation."

He paused as he said it. The name made sense now.

Allandria made her way carefully toward the stone altar that, moments ago, had been surrounded by life. She was extremely aware that every crunch beneath her feet was likely tiny fragments of human bone. All those people. For what? Nausea rose in her gullet and she stepped as lightly as possible. It was horrible. There was just nothing left.

Except… on the platform. There was something there.

*Is that…?*

"Allandria, hurry!" Aranok called. The green haze was lightening. Time was returning. She stopped walking gingerly and ran to the stone.

*My God. It is.*

She reached the platform as the last hint of green faded. The stone weathered before her eyes. The grass grew. The ruins fell apart. And the one thing left behind faded away. But it had been there. It had been there after everything. For some reason, it hadn't been affected.

"Did you find it?" Aranok called. Samily was sitting up now, inhaling from Aranok's oil bottle. Allandria walked back across the square.

"Well?" Aranok asked, an urgent edge in his voice.

"I found it." She wished she hadn't. She wished she'd never seen it.

"Where is it?" He scrambled to his feet. "What is it?"

"Wait." She waved him down. "I don't have it. It faded with the light. But it was there. It survived the magic. It was the only thing left."

"What was it?" Samily's voice was still weak.

Allandria took a moment to get control of the emotions that were threatening to overrun her. The anger, and the awful, awful sadness that clawed at her. She took a deep breath, clenched her fists and spoke.

"The boy's head."

---

"Fuck," said Aranok. "His head? That's what we're looking for?" No wonder Allandria looked ill. Hells, after what the bastards had done to those kids, and now the very thing they had to find...It was hideous.

"That makes sense," Samily said drowsily. "In the kirk's terminology, a relic is usually the remains of an especially devout person—often someone with an unusual ability. And must you be so profane, Envoy?"

Aranok tried not to roll his eyes. Allandria grinned at him. "A special skill like yours?" he asked.

"I suppose so," the knight answered thoughtfully.

So chances were the kirk's holy relics came from *draoidhs*. Interesting.

"You think the boy was *draoidh*?" Allandria asked. "It seemed like she had the power."

"She did, but she said he helped her focus. What if she meant it literally? We're looking for a relic that expands the range of a spell—what if it does that by focusing the *draoidh*'s energy—making them more powerful? Maybe that was the boy's skill."

"Is that possible?" asked Allandria.

"I've never heard of it. But nobody's pretending we know every *draoidh* ability. And something passive like that could go unnoticed a person's whole life. Imagine they never encounter another *draoidh*..."

"Well, we know what we're looking for." Samily tried to stand, but her legs gave way, dropping her back on her arse in the grass.

"Wait," said Allandria. "Before anything else, aren't we going to talk about what just happened? We went back in time. We saw something horrific." She looked directly at Aranok as she said it. He knew why. "Are we all right?"

Aranok wasn't. He'd been distracting himself since it happened, but seeing those kids had brought everything back. The bullying. The abuse. Korvin. All of it. There was a black pit screaming inside him, waiting to suck him in. He needed to bury it. Again.

"I'm fine," he lied, "but Samily isn't. Take her back to the kirk, please? She needs to rest."

"I'll be all right." But Samily made no move to stand again. "Just give me a few moments."

"No. That's an order. Go back and rest. You saved our lives. Again. You need to sleep." Aranok raised his eyebrows at Allandria. She looked at him for a moment, her brow furrowed. She saw right through him—which was part of why he needed her away from him right now. He couldn't bury these feelings if he saw them reflected every time he looked at her. And he couldn't afford for them to overwhelm him. They didn't have time.

"Fine," she said flatly. "Don't do anything stupid. There could be Reivers out here. Or worse." She helped Samily to her feet and supported the girl until she found her balance.

"I'll be back before dark," Aranok said. "I promise."

Allandria's mouth contorted into her "I don't believe you" frown, but she didn't argue. "Be careful" was all she said, turning up the hill with Samily all but hanging from her side.

He went straight to the platform. The eerie green light had gone, and all was as it had been. Except him. He leaned on the edge of the stone, feeling chills run up his arms. The stone block the boy had been strapped to was all but dust, though now he knew to look for it, he could see discolouration where it had been. He ran his hand over the space, feeling a chaos of fury and almost unbearable sorrow. Sorrow for these poor children who'd died so many years ago; fury at the ignorant bigots who'd killed them. He understood the girl. Why she'd done it. It could have been him. If Korvin had died at the same age...or Allandria. He felt himself shaking, so balled and opened his fists to get it under control. He needed to focus. All of his feelings aside, he needed to find that...head. God almighty. Lives depended on it.

A lot of them.

Would the boy want him to save them, though? He hoped so. There was less ignorance these days. A lot of the people cursed with the Blackening were innocent, decent human beings who had no problem with *draoidhs*. Some were not. But better to save ten arseholes than sacrifice one innocent, Janaeus said. That hadn't been a common sentiment in Eidyn under Hofnag. To be fair, Hofnag was an arsehole.

Aranok slowly walked around the huge stone, carefully moving the long grass with his feet. Slowly, studiously, he walked around and around the stone in circles, moving a little farther away each time.

After maybe an hour, he'd covered the whole town square. All he'd found was dust. It would take forever to search the whole settlement at this speed.

*Damn it!* Where the Hell could it be? He ran his hands through his hair. If not for the grass, he could look more quickly.

*Wait.*

He could get rid of the grass.

---

It had been slow going back up the hill. Much slower than coming down this morning. All but carrying Samily wasn't helping either. In fact, if Aranok didn't hang around too long, he might well catch them before they reached the kirk. Especially if they had to keep stopping for them both to rest.

Samily pulled a wildflower from the grass. "It's beautiful from up here, isn't it?"

It was. The sweep of wild green back down the hill toward Caer Amon was idyllic. Beyond it, the swathe of blue sea gave way to the white and grey of the clouds that covered Eidyn.

"Some sun would be nice," Allandria said.

"Ah, but then we'd be too hot." Samily tapped her armour. "God watches over us."

"You really believe that? That God is so active in our lives?"

"Why not?" said Samily. "Think about what's happened to us. Today, I was able to save us because I learned that my power is not healing, but time. Had I not known that, we would be dead, like everyone else in Caer Amon."

"I suppose."

"I would not have learned about my ability if I had not tried to heal Vastin. And I would not have needed to heal him if he and Meristan had not been Blackened.

"And then, there's the question of whether I should even be here at all. I was not assigned to the envoy's team. Had Meristan left Baile Airneach when he was called to Haven, I would not have been with him. I would not have been here, today, with you. You'd both be dead."

"Dead hundreds of years in the past," Allandria mused.

"With all that had to happen for me to be here, and to know how to save us, how can you question that God is working for us?"

"Aranok would call that a lot of fortunate coincidences," said Allandria.

"I do not believe the envoy would see God if God stood before him. He is too closed."

It was true. She couldn't imagine a scenario where Aranok found faith—short of divine intervention. "He's not closed. He's angry. He's bitter."

"At God?"

"Not so much at God. At the world. And the idea that a god has been directing his life, that God caused his unhappiness—he would choose not to believe in that God."

"And look what he has become, for all God's influence on his life," said Samily. "A man who would risk his life for others. Who, despite his own unhappiness, seeks happiness for others. There are few more righteous callings. I believe God works through him, even if he does not."

Allandria smiled. "Don't expect him to see it that way."

Samily lay back on the grass and closed her eyes. "He doesn't have to believe in God. God believes in him."

Allandria batted the girl's hip. "Hey, don't go falling asleep on me. We've still got a lot of walking to do before dark."

Samily smiled and raised her head. "I know, but... what's that?"

Allandria followed Samily's gaze down the hill. An orange glow was growing from Caer Amon. Smoke rose above it.

Samily clambered to her feet. "Should we go?"

"No." Allandria sighed. "He most likely set it himself, and he's more than capable of putting it out."

"Why would he do that?"

Allandria clambered to her feet. "Well, he either thinks it will help him find the relic or he's having a tantrum because he can't. Either way, he can look after himself and you can't."

"I am fine," said Samily.

"You can barely keep your eyes open. He'd kill me if I left you to go back for him." She reached out a hand. "Come on. Best we can do is get you back."

"I think I can walk on my own."

Allandria reached out for her. "Well, why not take my hand anyway—just to keep you steady."

The knight smiled and took the hand, and they started back up the hill again. Allandria couldn't help but look back over her shoulder, though, at the increasingly dark smoke billowing up from the ruins. The fire burned like a beacon. A beacon that might attract anyone. Or anything.

*You better be alive, you fucking idiot.*

<hr />

Aranok sat amongst the charred ruins of Caer Amon. He'd burned as much of it as he could without risking the fire spreading beyond his control.

Still nothing. Of course, if the skull had never moved from this spot, nobody would have ever discovered its power. There would be no rumours—no vague mentions in banned tomes. It would just be a dead boy's skull, bleaching in the sun. But he'd hoped to find something—anything to give them a clue as to where the relic might be now. A tomb. A passage. Something.

At least now they knew what they were looking for. And exactly what it could do, assuming it retained the boy's ability—though why it would was a mystery. Maybe the girl's time power had affected it? Samily had said time was "broken" here...Could the skull be trapped in its own time bubble? In that case, Hells, was he looking for an intact severed head? A chill ran down his arms.

He'd spent hours covering the settlement—probably too many—and the sun was already low in the sky. Allandria would be hurrying him to leave if she were here. And he was tired. Tired to his bones. It had only been a few weeks, maybe a little more, since they left Haven—but it felt like a lifetime. They'd covered half the country and almost died several times just to get here. For nothing. He couldn't save the Blackened. He couldn't save the country. And he'd used all but his last energy burning out a ruin.

For nothing.

It had been cathartic, but otherwise useless.

*God damn it.*

What was he going to do now? He lay back on the stone plinth and stared up at the sky.

"Anybody up there?" he muttered to himself. "If so, you're making a shitty job of the place."

The clouds hung lazy and unmoved.

He stayed there for a while, quiet. Listening. There wasn't much to hear. Wildlife and insects had no reason to come near now he'd charred the place like a suckling boar. The wind, brushing over the remains of the town, was all that disturbed the quiet. It was peaceful.

Perhaps he'd just stay here. Away from other people. Away from responsibilities. Away from the chaos.

He breathed deep. The burnt aroma was acrid in his nostrils. Sitting up, he placed a hand where the stone had been—where the boy was murdered. Maybe he should have saved him. Changed history. But then what? If Caer Amon had survived, the entire history of Eidyn would be rewritten. Hundreds, thousands of people would be born who weren't. People who were alive today would never be born. How many lives would he have been erasing to save the boy? How different might the world have been? Did he have the right to make that choice? Did anyone?

He rubbed his hand across the surface, feeling the rubble that barely served as the boy's headstone.

"I'm sorry," he said quietly. "You deserved to live."

# CHAPTER 38

He was definitely going to die.

Two hours of trudging up the damned slope and Aranok felt every ounce of energy he'd used to burn Caer Amon. His legs felt like stone and every step was like dragging an anchor. His knees ached, the joints burning. His lower back was seized tight and daggers stabbed him with each footfall. The headwind that had blown up just after he started the ascent was the biggest problem. He could barely keep his head up. All he was seeing was his feet—his throbbing, tired feet, as they slowly dragged him farther up the never-ending hill.

The sun was dipping below the horizon to his right. There was nothing out here. No farms, no cottages, no ruins where he could hole up for the night. He was maybe another hour from Crostorfyn, but he wasn't going to make it. Not before dark. And at that point, he was vulnerable. The open landscape meant he could see a long way in every direction, and there was nothing out here but grass, gorse and heather. Once it got dark, he'd be lucky to see his own feet, and he didn't even have enough energy left for a light spell.

Hells, he was such an idiot! How had he done this to himself? He'd underestimated the walk, overestimated his reserves. He'd done exactly what Allandria was worried he'd do.

He focused on walking. One foot at a time. Tried not to think about the pain—though it may have been the only thing keeping him awake.

That thought made him think about sleep, which was a mistake. His eyes closed involuntarily, and he pictured himself in a soft, warm bed. The aches melted away and...

He woke as his knee hit the ground hard. Falling forward onto his hands, he realised how heavily he was breathing. All right. A little rest. Just a little break here to catch his breath and get off his feet. He rolled onto his back. Every bone seemed to click into place. His feet throbbed with a tingling heat, grateful to be relieved of his weight at last.

He stared up at the darkening sky, full of pinks and oranges as the sun dropped from view.

*This is pretty*, he thought. Then it was dark.

*Horses.*

He shook himself awake at the sound. How long had he been asleep? It was pitch-black. Damn it! If he couldn't see the horsemen, they shouldn't be able to see him. If he kept low, they should ride right past. He lay back down and turned his head toward the sound. They were coming down the hill. Reivers? Who else went out riding at night in the middle of nowhere?

He primed himself to use magic. He felt very little. A tiny spark at best. Maybe enough for a small plume of flames. The hooves came closer. They were not in a hurry—sensible enough, coming downhill on uneven terrain in the dark. But they were getting closer. Almost as if they were coming right toward him. The clouds above parted and allowed the moon to shine through, and Aranok could see them. Two horses, maybe two hundred yards away, up the hill. And if he could see them...

*All right, Aranok, get the fuck up.*

He rolled onto his knees and, placing his left hand on the ground for balance, raised the right beside him.

"*Teine.*" His fist flickered into a ball of flames. As it lit, the horses sped up, moving toward him at a trot now. If he was going to escape this, they needed to believe he was at full strength. He used everything he had to force himself up to standing, leaning into the wind at the horses' backs.

When they were maybe fifty yards away, he held his fist high.

"Stop there!"

Both horses drew up. Good. They were clever enough to be afraid of a *draoidh*. If he could just keep his hand burning for long enough to get rid of them...

"Turn around and ride away!" He did his best to sound confident, but there was barely any breath left in his lungs, and he was shouting into the damned wind.

"Envoy?"

He recognised the voice but couldn't place it.

"Envoy, it's Tull! Allandria sent me!"

*Oh, thank fuck.*

He collapsed back to his knees, letting the fire burn out. He heard the horses come closer, heard Tull's armoured feet hit the ground.

"Envoy, can you stand?"

The first spits of rain stung Aranok's face. He nodded but used Tull's proffered hand to help him upright.

"She was worried about you, when you didn't return by dark. And with the storm coming in..."

"I misjudged the slope."

Tull nodded. "Let me help you, Envoy." All dignity abandoned, Aranok allowed the young Thorn to all but lift him onto Dancer's saddle. The horse shook its head in a gesture of frustration—probably similar to the one he'd see from Allandria. Tull practically vaulted back onto his own mount and brought it alongside Dancer. "Can you ride?"

Aranok tried to focus on the reins, but the best he could manage was to grip the edge of the saddle.

"All right." Tull took up the lead he'd used to bring Dancer down. "You rest."

Aranok slumped forward against the horse's neck. It was warm, if a little dampened by the rain. He reminded himself not to fall asleep. He could stay awake at least to the kirk...

His eyes opened to candlelight. He had no memory of getting there, but judging by the feel, he was in the soft bed he'd been imagining earlier. He was warm. And dry. That was nice.

He lifted his head to see the room at Crostorfyn.

"You're alive, then." Allandria's voice. He turned to see her on the floor, lying on the made-up bedroll.

"Apparently so." He dropped his head back onto the pillow.

"You're an idiot," she said.

"I know. Any chance you could shout at me tomorrow?"

"There's a very good chance I will shout at you tomorrow."

They lay in silence for a while.

"You didn't find it?" she asked quietly.

He sighed. "No."

"I'm sorry."

"So am I."

"Aranok?"

"What?"

"It's not your fault."

"I know," he answered quietly.

"Do you?"

This time he couldn't answer.

"Get some sleep," she said. "We'll make decisions tomorrow."

Aranok wasn't going to argue. It felt too good to close his eyes. He heard Allandria blow out the candle, and everything was peaceful, cool dark.

———⊙———

Nirea carefully put the spoon to her lips and tilted her head to the right as she supped at the warm soup. The opium was helping with the pain and the stitches would hold her left cheek together, but she'd rather not test the wound's resolve against the broth.

It was the middle of the night. She'd only awoken a few hours ago after sleeping for almost two days. Meristan still occupied the bed next to hers—apparently he refused to leave her.

She tried hard to switch off her mind, concentrate on eating and resting, but it stubbornly refused to be quiet. The image of Glorbad, hanging limp, blood pouring down his armour, would not go. And then Conifax's murder. They had to be connected. They'd walked into a trap and Conifax had been murdered as soon as they left. Too much of a coincidence. But who gained?

She didn't want to suspect the envoy. But she did. Though now she'd calmed down, she could see that a lot of her initial reaction was anger. And grief. There was also maybe a little underlying prejudice against him for what he was, which made her itch. She didn't like it, but it was there. And the case against him still existed, in theory. He'd sent them. He'd walked away. Conifax was killed just after he left—but that would go against everything she'd experienced. She'd seen nothing between the two except an old friendship—it would be shocking if she'd read that so wrongly.

But where did that leave them? With everything he'd told them before... Could it really be Mynygogg's allies behind this?

Nirea put down the spoon. "Mehsan?" She had to keep her lips tight, moving her jaw as little as possible. The words were barely understandable, but he'd know what she was saying. Still, she'd have to keep the conversation as simple as possible.

"Hmm?" The monk sat up in bed, as he had done when she woke him asking for food, but he must have dozed off.

"What we know bout muhduh?" She sucked back in the saliva that escaped as she spoke.

Meristan shook the sleep from his head and swung his legs round to face her. "He was found in the library—in a room called the *caibineat puinnsean*. He'd been stabbed in the back. One strike, through the heart."

"Whass in it?"

"The room? Books, I'm told. Books restricted to the masters."

"Massuh kill him?"

"Well, maybe. The door was found open. It was late. If he'd gone in and left the door open behind him..."

"Cayless." That was not her impression of Conifax. "You thing he cayless?"

"In the time I knew him, he did not strike me as careless. Quite the opposite," said Meristan.

"Someone he knew."

"Why do you say that?" Meristan scratched at his beard.

"Gaw close, behine. If came ah fronn..." She pushed her hands out the way she'd seen Aranok do to push or grab an enemy.

Meristan nodded.

"Poins to Massuh," said Nirea.

Meristan smiled. "I'm glad you agree, because that's exactly the line I've been following."

Nirea cocked her head. He'd been following? What had she missed while she slept? Her question must have been clear to the monk, because he wasted no time in explaining.

"I've been looking into his murder. I mean, the local guard have too, obviously, but I'm not convinced of the competence of their commander. He seems intent on the idea that it could not have been a master, and that Conifax must have left the door open. Either that or he let in a student who shouldn't have been there. Neither seems likely to me. So I've been investigating the other masters.

"Many can account for their locations when the murder occurred. Some cannot. Some, I'm told, did not entirely like Master Conifax—though their grievances are mostly academic, or administrative. I have yet to find one with a motive that would explain murder."

"Connec do Mynyaw?" Hells, *Mynygogg* was particularly difficult to say. It seemed almost appropriate.

Meristan's face darkened. "As yet, no. But there are a few who have studied darker magic. They are not skilled with it, but they have taught its capabilities."

That didn't necessarily mean anything. Even if they had been given the dark *draoidh* abilities, having the capacity to do something and doing it were different things. Though she recognised again her predilection for believing they were more likely to be guilty because of the association. It bothered her a little less this time.

"Who you suspec?"

"I'm not sure yet. The two most obvious have no one to verify their whereabouts and were at least on unfriendly terms with Conifax."

"Who?" She winced as a stabbing pain in her left cheek reminded her to be gentle with herself. She nearly spilled soup on her lap. Meristan instinctively stood and placed a hand on her arm.

"All righ." She waved him away.

"Are you sure? Can I get you anything?" The monk's tone was earnest, but Nirea had to fight an instinctive irritation at being coddled. It wasn't him she was angry at. She shook her head but gave him as much of a smile as she could. It was a crooked, broken thing.

"Who?" she asked again.

"The first is Opiassa. She is a physic *draoidh*—has the ability to increase her own strength and speed. She and Conifax disagreed over the punishment of some unruly students last year. Apparently they've been cold since."

Physic. Her speed could have got her behind him. Her strength certainly enough to kill him. That was plausible.

"And?"

"The other is Macwin. He is a nature *draoidh*. Controls plants and animals, I believe. Or can communicate with them. I'm unclear on that point. Anyway, apparently he and Conifax have an old grudge over seniority. There was rivalry for a promotion to a higher rank."

"Conifax won?"

"No. Macwin did. But as I understand it, Conifax believed the process unjust and demanded they change their decision. They did not. But this was many years ago."

That made less sense. If Macwin had been passed over and held a grudge—maybe. But the other way around—what would it benefit him to kill Conifax? Why would he? It was a weak motive at best. Again, her face must have given away her thoughts.

"I know, neither seems very likely, does it? And then there's the question of our own entrapment. It seems unlikely to me that the two are unconnected. Which leads me to think there is something bigger here."

The monk was sharp. Fit, clever and braver than he first appeared. Shame about his vows.

"Wha Conifas doin?"

"We believe he was researching a cure for Morienne. But we can't be sure. He had no books open or near him when he was found."

"Nec queshion." She pointed at him.

Meristan smiled. "I agree. And it will be a pleasure to be able to discuss my findings with you. For now, finish your soup. You need to keep up your strength, to heal."

Nirea nodded. She picked up the spoon again but used the wrong arm and felt her injured shoulder complain. She grabbed it with her good hand.

"It's all right." Meristan gently took the spoon from her. "Here, let me." She leaned back against her pillows and let him feed her the rest of the soup. It was barely warm and tasted pretty terrible.

But it was sweet.

# CHAPTER 39

The downside of keeping the horses inside was all the shit on the floor. They'd moved them back outside once it was light. The smell was not helping Aranok's tired brain clear.

Thus he was using *gluais* to clean up horse dung for the first time. Tull held the door open as he shifted and deposited several heaps onto the kirk's rosebeds. Tull and Allandria had volunteered to mop the floors, since both he and Samily needed to recuperate. The girl was a lot worse than him. She was still sleeping, and it was near lunchtime. It must have taken a Hell of a lot out of her to do what she did, and then walk back up that rise. She'd only made it because of Allandria. As had he.

"May I offer you a cup of tea? I find it extremely rejuvenating myself." Aranok jumped, turning to see the priest smiling at him. Had he seen the magic? Would it really matter if he had? Dalim held a steaming cup toward Aranok. It was warm, and a tingle of heat ran up his arms as he took it, making him shiver.

"Sounds good." He raised the cup as a gesture of thanks.

The priest sat on a pew and gestured for Aranok to join him. "How are you feeling?"

Aranok sat and sipped from the cup. It tasted of winter. Cloves and cinnamon maybe? It was very different from any tea he'd ever had. But it warmed him, and he felt himself shiver against a bone-cold exhaustion.

"I'm fine."

Dalim nodded and gave a sympathetic smile. "I'm pleased to see you looking better. You gave us a fright last night."

Aranok still had no memory of getting back. What with Allandria bringing Samily home in a similar state, and Tull having to rescue him, the priest must have been wondering what he'd got himself into.

"Sorry about that. Things got out of hand."

There was a clatter as Tull banged his bucket of water against a pillar. Aranok jumped again, more than he should have. Seemed his nerves were a little on edge. Dalim put a gentle hand on his shoulder.

"Is there anything I could do to be of help? You look like a man carrying an awful weight."

Aranok laughed gently. He'd been avoiding thinking about yesterday's failure, and the sting of it came back like a punch to the head. Allandria's mop slapped against the stone floor behind him. He turned and smiled at her. He owed her his life again. It was a lengthy tally. She puckered her mouth back at him—only half seriously objecting to the job she was stuck with.

"It seems to me your mission must have been awfully important to the brotherhood, for you to risk your lives in Caer Amon," said Dalim.

"It was. Very important."

"Life and death?"

"A lot of lives."

"I thought it might be." Dalim looked at Tull, wringing his mop into the bucket, and back to Aranok. "Your friends speak highly of you. When a White Thorn speaks so well of a faithless man, it behooves a man of faith to take notice.

"Last night, before you got back," the priest explained, presumably seeing the confusion on Aranok's face, "I made some dinner. We talked a little. Both of the women seem to think well of you, despite finding you a little difficult."

Aranok laughed. That sounded about right.

"As I understand it," said Dalim, "you risked your life last night, and sent the two of them away to protect theirs. I don't know what happened down there, or why you were there, but, well, this kirk has more information on Caer Amon than anywhere else in creation, and it seems to me that if I knew what you were after, I could perhaps be of some use?"

Could he? What harm could it do now? Tull seemed to trust him. Though Samily had expected Anhel Weyr to be…

*Oh fuck it.*

They were nowhere, as it stood. If there was any remote chance the relic existed and Dalim could help them find it, it was worth the risk. Aranok turned to face him.

"We were looking for a relic. It might not even exist. The 'heart of devastation.' It's a legend. But we think we know what it is."

Dalim's face was hard to read. "May I ask why you're looking for it?"

That wasn't the question he'd expected. "It's a long story, but we think we can cure the Blackening."

Dalim sat upright. That clearly wasn't the answer he was expecting either. "The Blackening? How?"

In his side vision, Aranok noticed Allandria had stopped mopping and was leaning on a pillar, listening.

"We discovered that it's a curse, not an illness. And it can be lifted by a *draoidh* who knows how."

"A curse?" the priest said. "Well, that is interesting. Do you know who made it?"

"We don't. But we think, if it wasn't Mynygogg, it was someone helping him."

"Someone helping him?" Dalim's voice went up a few notes. "That is worrying."

Aranok nodded. Mynygogg had Anhel Weyr on his side at least. In fact, they should really warn Dalim, in case Weyr came here. They assumed he'd made for Auldun, but it was a guess at best.

"How would the relic help?" asked the priest.

Still, he hadn't asked the question Aranok was waiting for. And now he needed to know why not. "Faither, I'm sorry, but do you know what the relic is?"

Dalim smiled. "I do."

Allandria moved over to lean on the back of their pew. "You do?"

He nodded. "It is commonly believed that when Pilar, the first priest of Crostorfyn, visited Caer Amon after the devastation, there was nothing left of the settlement. That is not entirely true. What he did find was disturbing."

"A boy's head," said Aranok.

Dalim's expression turned from conspiratorial to shocked. "How did you know?"

Aranok waved his hands dismissively. "Another long story. Please, go on."

Dalim recovered his composure. "Well, that being all that was left of the whole settlement, he felt it best to bring it here, for safekeeping. It's not entirely clear why. But the kirk does have a history of maintaining relics of 'special' people."

"We know," said Allandria. "Samily told us. What happened to it?"

Dalim opened his hands as if offering something. "It's been here since."

"It's here?!" Aranok jumped to his feet. "You have it?"

Dalim smiled. "Understandably, it is just a skull now. But yes, we have it."

Aranok's head spun. They'd gone from nowhere to having the answer in their grasp! And it had been right under them—they might have walked away without it! He looked at Allandria—her surprise and excitement mirrored his own.

"My God, can we have it? Please?" he asked.

"Try not to take God's name in vain, my friend. At least not here." He raised his arms to indicate the kirk. "But yes, if it will help save lives, of course you can have it. Besides, who am I to say no to the king's envoy?"

Aranok looked at Allandria, confused. "Did you...?"

"No." She looked at Dalim suspiciously.

He smiled beatifically. "Don't worry. Nobody betrayed you. We've met. There were a number of us—priests—petitioning the king to expand payments for the poor. You argued in our favour."

"I remember." Janaeus had been unsure they could afford it, not long after they overthrew Hofnag. Aranok had said they had to look to the weakest first—an argument Janaeus had made himself before the revolution. "Why didn't you say something?"

"Laird Aranok, from that day I have known you to be a good man. A man of your word; we received the payments. That has not always been the case. If you had reason to keep your identity concealed, it was not for me to pierce that veil."

"Then why now?" Allandria asked.

"I flatter myself that I am an observant man. I gathered from the hushed conversations that stopped as I arrived that you had brought Tull into your circle. Since I was the only one on the 'outside,' I thought maybe it best for you to understand you are amongst friends. If there is anything I can do to assist, Envoy, you need only ask."

Aranok smiled. "Thank you, Faither." He offered his hand, which the priest took, and rather than shake it, held it between his own. It was surprisingly comforting.

"Hey. What's happening?" Tull had finished mopping and clearly been attracted by the commotion.

"Dalim has the relic," said Allandria excitedly.

The Thorn grabbed the back of a pew. "No! You never mentioned a relic, Faither."

"It is not something we shout about, sir knight. But the keepers of this kirk have looked to the relic for centuries, in the hope that it would prove useful. So that those who died at Caer Amon might not have died in vain—whatever evil wiped them from the earth."

"Ah well," said Aranok. "That's a story we can tell you."

———◇———

Allandria brushed her arm against the cold stone wall, stirring up a cloud of dust that made her sneeze. She wasn't keen on being underground. It had always felt too close—too tight, like a weight. It put her in mind of crypts, and she felt a compelling urge to run, to escape back to the light and the sky—to be able to breathe. Despite the stone and the flickering torch, she was extremely aware of being under the earth, and that made her feel terrifyingly mortal.

"Not been down here in a while?" she asked Dalim, trying to distract herself.

The priest turned at the bottom of the steps, the torch in his hand providing the only light. "No, I do not visit the crypt often. The company does not agree with me."

*An actual crypt.*

They followed Dalim through a doorway into a larger, equally dark chamber. The priest put up a hand to stay them. He stopped fifty yards ahead and lowered his torch. After a moment, a second fire crackled into life. As the brazier lit up what she could now see was only the nearside of the room, Allandria realised just how large a space they'd come into. It explained the long descent. The room was like an underground mirror of the kirk, with a high, vaulted ceiling. But instead of stained-glass windows, there were rows of shelves up the walls—most of the lower ones occupied by dusty human remains. Instead of pews, there were granite sarcophagi lined up in two rows, creating a morbid aisle down the centre of the room. The size of the place alleviated her discomfort a little; the corpses did not.

Dalim lit another burner farther down the room; he waited for it to rise and gestured for them to join him. The smell of burning dust overcame the damp odour of mould and rot.

"You realise, if he's another Weyr, we're in trouble?" said Allandria quietly.

"How so?" Aranok asked.

"If all these skeletons decide to get up, we're a long way from safety. And arrows are pretty useless against bones."

"Thank you. That's a comforting thought."

"Spooked?" she teased.

He glanced sideways at her but didn't answer. Regardless, she was certain he'd have a spell ready now—if he hadn't before.

"Come, come!" Dalim ushered them toward what Allandria assumed was the end wall. She certainly couldn't see anything past it, and it seemed to be in about the same position as the upstairs wall—allowing for how difficult it was to judge distance down here.

Their footsteps echoed around the chamber, slightly cushioned by the dust. She'd want another bath when they got out of here. It was already making her itch. She rubbed at her face but felt another layer of decay settle on her even as she wiped it clear.

When they reached the far wall, she could see Faither Dalim was standing next to a small, ornate metal door. It was hard to tell in the light if it was gold. It could have been copper or bronze glinting in the firelight. Either way, it stood out from its dark stone surrounds.

"Bit of an obvious place to store something valuable, isn't it?" Aranok asked.

"Only if somebody knows to look for it." Dalim tapped the side of his nose. "And there's only one key." He reached inside his black tunic and lifted out a large metal key that hung on a chain around his neck. He lifted the chain over his head and slid the key into the lock with a slight jiggle. It clicked as it found the right position.

Dalim cocked his head.

"What?" asked Aranok.

"Nothing, really," said Dalim. "Just an odd sense of...something."

"Something like what?" Allandria was well used to dealing with tricks and traps, and in her experience, an instinct that something was wrong should always be investigated.

"I don't know," said the priest. "Just something nagging at me. I can't place it."

Aranok nodded to her.

Allandria stepped forward. "Take your hand off the key, Faither. Gently."

Dalim did as he was told and stepped away from the door. "It's probably nothing, you know." But there was a tinge of nerves in his voice that Allandria didn't like. She moved to the door and carefully ran her fingers around the edges. No sign of anything unusual. She felt the key, jiggling it slightly and listening for any telltale clicks. Nothing. It would have been easier to check it without the key in place, but this would have to do. A few minutes later, after thoroughly searching for every kind of trap she could imagine, she nodded at Aranok.

"Nothing?" he asked.

"Nothing that I can see."

"All right." Aranok turned to Dalim. "Faither, please step to the side."

The priest looked almost embarrassed. "Are you sure this is necessary?" But he stepped back all the same.

Allandria drew her sword. She had no idea what would happen when Aranok turned that key, but better to have her weapon in her hand than waste time floundering to draw it. She also stepped back and away from the direct line of the little keepsafe.

Aranok, having moved to the other side, gave them both a tiny nod, raised his hand and said, "*Gluais.*" The key turned in the lock with two loud thunks. Allandria breathed out. Nothing happened. But they still had to open it.

Aranok turned his hand and the handle rose with a creak of protest. Finally, he pulled and the door creaked open.

The three of them stood in silence for a long moment, waiting.

"You see?" Dalim walked forward. "Nothing to worry about. Just a silly man's nerves getting the better of him." He reached the open door and stopped. "Dear God."

Allandria and Aranok both rushed forward. "What, what is it?" she asked.

Aranok grabbed him by the shoulders to pull him away, but the priest just shrugged him off.

"No, no—you don't understand," he said. "There's nothing."

"Oh," said Aranok. "Then what were you...?"

Dalim gestured urgently at the hole in the wall. "No, look." Allandria did, and only then realised she could see... "Nothing! There's nothing there!

"The relic is gone!"

# CHAPTER 40

Aranok burst through the door into the back of the sanctuary. "How can it be gone?" He was trying not to sound aggressive, but by the depths of all bloody Hells he was frustrated.

"Calm down," said Allandria.

He took a deep breath and turned to face Dalim as the priest exited behind them.

"I do not know, Envoy. There is no explanation. I have the only key. I have seen the relic only once, when I took possession of the kirk from my predecessor. Since he died eight years ago, I am the only one alive who knows where it is, as far as I know. Or that it even exists."

Well, that clearly wasn't true. "Then how can it be gone?"

"Honestly, Envoy, I have no explanation." Dalim sat on the front pew. "The relic has been a sacred trust of this kirk for centuries. I cannot...I don't..."

"It's all right, Faither." Allandria put a hand on his shoulder. "It's not your fault."

He put his hand over hers. "Thank you, my lady. But I feel it must be, somehow. It was my sacred trust, and I have failed."

It was hard to be angry at a priest who already blamed himself. And Allandria was probably right. If he was against them, why even tell them about the relic in the first place? He could have let them go on their way, never knowing the relic was right beneath them. Except now it wasn't.

"Damn it!" Aranok shouted at nobody. Every time he thought they were onto something, that things were going their way, it all came crashing down on his head.

And Samily thought he was an agent of God. If so, God was playing a cruel game.

"Laird Envoy! You're back," Tull called from the other end of the kirk. "There's someone to see you."

*What?* Who would be here for them now? And why?

Aranok stalked up the aisle, his black mood clearly showing on his face, as Tull literally paused mid-stride. "Oh. It didn't go well?"

"It did not," said Aranok flatly. "Who's here?"

Tull stepped to the side to reveal a beautiful young woman standing behind him, wrapped in a cloak.

"Rasa. Is everything all right?" Before she could answer, Aranok turned back and called over his shoulder. "Allandria! Can you get Rasa some clothes?"

His lover looked a little confused but raised a hand in acknowledgement. She spoke to the priest and both moved off toward his office.

"Laird Envoy," said Rasa as he turned back to her. "I've been looking for you. I saw the horses and... I thought he was the Thorn you travel with." She gestured to Tull, who looked a little off-balance and glanced away. Then he realised—Rasa would have arrived without the cloak.

Aranok gestured to the pews. "Sit, please."

"Thank you, Laird, but I have important news. Everyone should hear. Is the Lady Samily here?"

"Ah, yes. I'll wake her." Tull quickly headed for the chambers, seemingly happy to escape his own awkwardness.

"Rasa, what's happened?" Aranok asked, seeing that the woman's face was paler than usual; her eyes were bloodshot and haunted.

"I'm sorry, Laird." She placed a hand on his arm. "I can only tell this once, and then I must return to Traverlyn."

Aranok felt his heart sink. It was bad. "All right. We'll wait."

They sat in awkward silence until Allandria returned with some basic clothes. The kirk kept a small store for the needy, donated by locals. Probably from dead relatives, Aranok assumed. What with his father's business and his mother's skill as a seamstress, he'd never wanted for clothes in his life. It hadn't really occurred to him to be grateful for that before. It did now, as his mind looked for anything to distract him from thinking about why Rasa was here.

The metamorph retired to a private room to dress, and Aranok briefly explained to Allandria who she was and how she had found them. Samily joined them shortly, looking better than she had the day before.

"I am told you got yourself into trouble after all," the knight said with an uncharacteristic glint in her eye. "I may stop saving your life if you're so determined to throw it away, Envoy."

Aranok might have bantered with her in other circumstances, but at the moment he could think of no witty replies. He stood a condemned man with the noose around his neck—the waiting felt worse than whatever was coming, but at least every moment of waiting was one where the worst had not yet happened. He dared not think on what her news might be. Aranok, Samily and Allandria sat in a row on the front pew, like an audience awaiting a show from the pulpit. Eventually, Rasa returned and stood before them, eyes on the ground, her hands fidgeting at the front of the plain brown dress she now wore.

"All right, Rasa, we're all here," said Aranok.

She looked at the two women with a slight nod of acknowledgement and took a sharp breath. "Master Conifax is dead."

Aranok's world crumbled beneath him. It was worse than he'd feared. "What? No…" There had been some ridiculous mistake. Allandria put a hand on his thigh. Samily one on his shoulder. No, no, he'd misunderstood. "What do you mean? How can he be dead?"

Rasa raised her eyes; they were heavy with tears and her bottom lip trembled. She nodded as the tears streamed down her cheeks. "I'm sorry."

"But…how?" Aranok was completely numb. This obviously wasn't happening.

"Murdered," said Rasa.

"What?" Allandria asked. "By who?"

"Don't know," said Rasa. "The guard are investigating, but…Oh God, I'm sorry. There's more."

"More?" asked Samily.

"Meristan and Nirea…Barrock was a trap. There was a demon."

"No!" Samily stood. "No!"

Rasa raised a shaking hand to the girl. "Meristan and Nirea are fine—well, Nirea will be all right."

There was an awful, hollow silence, until Allandria finally spoke. "Glorbad?"

Rasa chewed her lip and shook her head.

Allandria raised a hand to her mouth as Samily collapsed back into her seat.

"Meristan sent me," said Rasa. "He said to tell you it was definitely a trap. The demon was waiting. Nobody had been there in months."

*God damn it.*

Aranok's head was swimming. Rasa said something else, but he didn't hear it. He felt Allandria wrap her arms around him, place her head on his shoulder, but he was watching it happen from a distance. It was a dream. Surely, a fever dream. He was still in bed, sick from the walk back. They couldn't have been so close to having everything, to curing the Blackening, then lost the relic, as well as Conifax and Glorbad.

The day he met Conifax, the old man was so condescending that Aranok had nearly walked out of the office and left the university before he started. Korvin had convinced him to stay. He later learned that his arrogance was just confidence. Justified, in a man who had such exquisite control of his abilities—both as a *draoidh* and as a teacher. He'd taken a raw, angry, confused boy and turned him into a *draoidh*. Conifax had been far more of a father than his own was. And Aranok had loved him for it.

And Glorbad. Barely even a friend, but a man he'd fought beside. A man who'd risked his life for him. A man who died because he wasn't there. Because he brought Samily with him. Because she wasn't there to save him. Because he was selfish. He hadn't listened. And Glorbad died for it.

Aranok's vision blurred and his stomach flipped. How would it look for the king's envoy to vomit on himself? He'd have to have his outfit cleaned. He breathed deeply, focusing on the flagstone beneath him. People were still talking—hushed, grave tones and sympathy. Noise.

Then it snapped into place. He knew where the relic was. He knew who'd killed Conifax. He knew who'd laid a trap for him and killed his friend instead. He knew who was behind everything.

It was all so ridiculously simple. How had he not seen it until now?

"Mynygogg."

"What?" Allandria lifted her head from his shoulder.

"Mynygogg has the relic," he said, as if explaining it to a three-year-old. "That's how he's doing it. That's how he's doing all of it. We think he's trapped in Dun Eidyn, but he's controlling the whole country from there. Because he has the relic."

"How could Mynygogg have the relic?" asked Allandria.

"I don't know. But he does."

Aranok felt a cold calm fall over him. He stood and walked toward the bedchambers. Allandria said something he didn't hear. Rasa too, maybe. None of it mattered. Just noise. He knew what he had to do now. Everything had been directing him here since they began. There was only one solution. Only one destination. Only one way this was ever going to end.

He had to kill Mynygogg.

---

"Is he going to be all right?" asked Samily.

"I don't know." Allandria did know he would blame himself for both deaths. For causing them—for not stopping them. It didn't matter. It would be his fault. For now, she thought it best to give him space. Let him breathe. Let him grieve.

"How are you?" she asked the knight.

"I'm saddened about Glorbad, but...is it wrong that I'm relieved it wasn't Meristan?"

It was odd to hear such uncertainty in her voice. But Allandria understood it.

"No. It just makes you human."

"I pray he will be with God," said the knight. "He was a good man. Damaged, but good."

He was. She had not long begun to consider him a friend, only to see him die needlessly. Pointlessly. Just like the war.

"I must go," said Rasa. The poor woman was a mess.

"Please, wait. Here. Sit." Allandria indicated the seat where Aranok had been.

The woman paused for a moment, then slumped down as if releasing a huge weight, and sobbed. Allandria put her arms around her shoulders. She barely knew her, but clearly the loss was hers as much as Aranok's. Their master must also have been important to her, and sometimes speaking a thing out loud made it impossible to bear.

"You were close to Conifax?"

Rasa nodded. All Aranok had said was that she was one of his students, and he'd hired her as a tutor for Emelina. And that she was a metamorph.

"I'm so sorry for your loss." Samily placed a hand on her leg. "May I pray with you?"

Rasa looked up at her. "Thank you, but I don't...I don't pray."

"Then may I pray for you?" the knight asked, unfazed. Rasa shrugged and nodded. Samily sat cross-legged on the floor and closed her eyes. For her, Allandria supposed, there was no greater kindness than praying for someone. She didn't know if Rasa would understand that, but she hoped so. She hoped it was a small comfort.

They sat in silence for a while. Allandria knew nothing she said would help, and holding the woman was the best she could do. It hadn't even occurred to her yet to grieve, herself. She hadn't known Glorbad long, but his loss felt like a wound. Both to her and to them all. They'd somehow become a group, a company, in the last few weeks, and now they'd lost one. The company was wounded. Conifax had done a huge amount to help them—to help cure the Blackening. And he meant so much to Aranok. She didn't know how he'd cope with the loss. It could break him.

She couldn't tell how much time passed, but it felt like a lot. Tull and Dalim seemed to have sensed they needed privacy and stayed away. When Samily finished praying, she stood and placed a hand on Rasa's shoulder. As if it were some sort of sign, Dalim appeared from the door to the chambers. He looked agitated.

"Faither?" Allandria asked.

"Has something happened?" The priest still looked ashen and awkward.

"Two of our friends have died," Samily explained.

"I am so sorry." Dalim's face fell. "Is...is the envoy all right?"

"Why?" Allandria was beginning to worry about the priest's discomfort. "Have you seen him?"

"He just brushed past me. As if I weren't there. At first, I thought he was angry with me. I tried to speak to him, but..."

"But what?"

"He left. Out the back door." Dalim pointed behind himself.

"He probably just went for some air." Allandria released Rasa and stood. "I'll check on him."

"No," said Dalim. "He was carrying his pack."

*Shit.*

Allandria ran. As she burst through the outer door, she saw Aranok riding away in the distance.

"Aranok! Aranok, stop! Wait for us, at least!"

He didn't slow, or even turn his head.

"Is that...? Is he riding Bear?" Samily had followed her out. Allandria quickly glanced at the horses. Right enough, Dancer remained, tied up next to Midnight and Tull's horse. He'd taken the biggest, the strongest, the fastest—which only confirmed her worst fear.

"Yes."

"Where's he going?" asked Samily as Dalim and Rasa also arrived outside.

Allandria turned to the metamorph.

"Rasa, I'm so sorry. I really am. But I have to ask you something. Please. Can you follow him? Keep an eye on him? He's not in his right mind. He's going to do something really, really stupid. Please."

"Of course, my lady." The woman wiped her eyes. She slipped out of the dress she'd only just put on.

"Heavens!" Dalim raised his hands to give her some modicum of privacy. But what came next was miraculous. Allandria and Samily watched as her body stretched and shrank. Hairs retracted to be replaced by feathers, which sprouted all over her body, as it twisted and contorted itself, until she was completely re-formed as a large raven.

"Thank you," Allandria said as the bird took flight after Aranok, who was already all but out of sight.

"Did she just…turn into a bird?" Dalim's mouth hung open and his hands now dangled limp.

"That she did," said Allandria. "And it was magnificent."

"It was!" No small trace of excitement in Samily's voice. "I've never seen such a wonder! She's glorious!"

"She certainly is." Allandria watched the bird shrink into the distance.

"What will you do?" asked Dalim after a moment.

"We'll pack, and we'll follow him." Allandria walked back toward the building.

"You know where he's going?" asked Samily.

Of course she knew. He'd gone northeast. No consideration for roads. He had no intention of planning a route, of being safe. He was going to ride cross-country, and they were going to have to do the same to have any chance of catching him.

"Dun Eidyn. He's going to Dun Eidyn."

# CHAPTER 41

Four days later and it still hurt like Hell, even through the opium. Nirea gently ran her finger down the outside of the bandage, feeling the tiny ridges of the stitches that held her face together. She hadn't seen a mirror since it happened. God knew what she looked like. But the scar was hardly going to make her look out of place when she finally got back on a boat.

After all that had happened, she felt the pull of the ocean more strongly than ever. She felt out of place here. More so now Glorbad was gone. He'd made her more connected. Grounded. But now she couldn't shake the nagging feeling that this just wasn't where she was meant to be.

As soon as she was well enough to travel, she was going back to Haven to ask Janaeus to release her from the council. If Leet was under siege by pirates, that's where she should be: helping her brothers and sisters. Not here, pissing about on land in matters well above her rank.

She might try to find Glorbad's killer first, though. She should. He would have done it for her. He deserved that.

The door to her room creaked open. She opened her eyes, expecting to see Meristan back to check on her, as he did several times a day, but it was Egretta who greeted her instead.

"How is the patient?" The medic smiled kindly.

"Alive." Nirea touched her face. "How you?" Egretta had seemed close to Conifax. She must have been feeling his death more than most.

"I'm fine, dear." But her eyes were grey—they'd lost their blue shine. She'd been crying. "I've brought a visitor, if you're up to it?"

Nirea shrugged and nodded. Who would be visiting her, other than Meristan? Egretta moved out of the doorway and gestured to whoever was outside. A young woman stepped in. She had dark hair with a fleck of red at the front, and strong features—high cheekbones and a sharp chin. She smiled at Nirea like an old friend, but it took her a moment to recognise her—and then to realise why she hadn't.

"Moyenne? Wha happen?"

"Hello." The woman stepped toward the bed. Nirea felt no nausea. Her eyes didn't water. In fact, she could clearly see her for the first time. Morienne pulled a small stone amulet out from under her top and held it out for Nirea to see. It looked like a knot, or some form of intricate rune.

"Cuah?" Nirea asked.

"No, but the totem protects others from the effects of my curse." Morienne smiled.

"Wonnuhful!" Nirea instinctively held out her arms to the woman. She ignored the twinge from her shoulder. Morienne hesitated a moment, then stepped toward her and accepted the embrace. Nirea wondered briefly if her mangled face had given her pause, but then she realised—Morienne was not accustomed to being hugged. Whether it was joy for her, or sadness at that thought, tears welled in her eyes and she pulled the woman tighter.

Which was a mistake, as pain shot through her shoulder. She winced involuntarily and Morienne jumped back as if she'd been bitten.

"I'm sorry!"

"No." Nirea tapped her shoulder gently. "My faul." She pointed at the necklace. "How?"

Morienne grabbed it protectively and held it against her chest. "Master Balaban. He found it in a book. It works!" She looked about to burst.

"Wonnuhful. Haffy." She attempted a smile, but her swollen face didn't move much. She hoped it was evident in her eyes.

"Thank you." Morienne's face was a wide, joyful grin. It was really something to see the light in her eyes. She was like a young child. In fact, she might be younger than Nirea had originally thought. The joy of youth.

That reminded her. "How Vassin?"

Egretta's face darkened. "He's healing. But he fights the feeding. I'm not surprised, really. Awful thing to do to someone. Just awful."

"It's saving his life." Morienne put a hand on the old woman's arm. "He'd want you to do it if he understood. And he will. Once he's cured, he will. He'll thank you."

"Bless you, child." Egretta patted Morienne's hand. "You'd make..."

"Nirea!" Meristan burst into the room. He stopped when he saw the other women. "Ah, hello, Egretta. Morienne."

Both smiled and stepped aside to give him room to enter.

"You know?" Nirea gestured to Morienne. He looked confused for a moment, then realised what she meant.

"Ah, yes, we saw each other this morning. Wonderful, isn't it?" Nirea nodded.

"Well, allow us to get out of your way." Egretta backed toward the door. Morienne stood to follow her.

"No," said Nirea. "Say. Cose door." Everyone else in the room looked slightly confused, but Egretta did as she asked.

Once the door was shut, she pointed at Meristan. "News?"

"Ah, um, all right, I've, uh, I've been granted special dispensation to enter the *caibineat puinnsean*. I spoke to the masters' council and, well, as the head of the brotherhood, they felt it appropriate to allow me access. Master Balaban spoke on my behalf."

Nirea nodded.

"Why would you want to do that?" asked Egretta suspiciously.

"Well, we've, um, I've been looking into Conifax's death."

"Why?" asked Morienne.

"Because he doesn't think the guards are doing it right, do you?" Egretta answered for him.

"We have concerns," said the monk.

"Good. So do I." Egretta sat on the end of Meristan's bed. "Conifax was too wily to be snuck up on by a student, and too careful to leave the door open. Something doesn't smell right."

"Well, that's the thing," said Meristan. "That only leaves..."

"Another master," said Egretta. "That's what I think too. I just don't know why. Could it be connected to all this?" She gestured to Nirea and Meristan.

"Well, I'm hoping to figure out what he was doing in the *caibineat*," said Meristan.

"Not cuhse." Nirea pointed to Morienne. "Bahban."

"Ah, good point," said Meristan. "If Balaban was looking into Morienne's curse, why would Conifax also do it himself?"

"You don't think...someone killed him because..." Morienne struggled to get anything else out.

"No, no." Meristan grasped her arm. "No, that's the thing, we don't."

She seemed to settle, relieved. The thought that she had somehow instigated Conifax's murder must have been horrifying, even for a moment.

"He'd found something," said Egretta. "I spoke to him that day. He found something that shouldn't have been there."

"What?" Nirea asked.

"He didn't say. Mostly, he complained about not being able to get back to the *caibineat* until later. And, if I'm honest, I was only half listening. I was busy with something else. If I'd known it was the last time I'd see him..." She clenched her hands together and her face twitched as her mask slipped for the first time.

"Something that shouldn't be there?" asked Meristan. "Do you have any idea what he meant?"

"No. Best I can remember, he was asking why someone would write it, and then why they'd put it in the *caibineat*. Said it was odd, but not dangerous. I think he was going to try to figure out who had it put in there."

"Recohs?" Nirea asked. If that was what Conifax had been looking into, it might lead them to the killer.

"Yes, there's a record of each book and who proposed it be entered into the *caibineat*," Egretta said. "But you'd need to know which book."

Well, that was a starting point at least. Now they had some idea of what they were looking for. Somewhere to start.

"I'll go this evening," said Meristan. "When it's quieter."

"Tae guahd. Moyenne." Nirea pointed to the woman.

"Oh, I don't think that's..." Meristan began, but stopped when he saw Nirea's raised eyebrow.

"You want me to watch his back?" Morienne asked.

Nirea nodded. She had seen the woman move. She was formidable, and he needed someone he could trust. Which, considering what had already happened, was a very short list. It might be limited to this room.

"I wou, buh..." Nirea gestured to her shoulder and face.

Morienne laughed. "It would be my honour."

"Well, your company will be most welcome, Miss Morienne." It was good to know the monk meant it, and Nirea was sure that was not lost on the woman.

Egretta bustled to her feet. "Right, then. I have patients. Let me know?"

"Of course," said Meristan. "Morienne, may I meet you in the library after dinner?"

"Yes," she answered brightly. "But nobody calls it the library. It's 'quarters.'"

---

Allandria dipped her flask into the stream, watching it bubble as the cold, clear water rushed in. She was already tired—as were the horses drinking deeply beside her. She and Samily had taken off the saddles and packs to give them more of a rest and a chance to cool down.

They'd left Crostorfyn within half an hour of Aranok and ridden hard, yet they'd seen no sign of him. The sun was already starting to dip in the sky. She hoped he had the sense to stop at Dail Ruigh for the night, like they were going to. But she doubted it. He was careful with everyone but himself.

They were nowhere near a road, but just within sight of the edge of the Mutton Hole farmlands. The stream seemed to have once been a larger river, but its route had likely been diverted at some point to feed the farmlands instead.

"How do you think it works? Her power?" Samily sat in the shade with her back against a tree. She looked up at a large black bird, pecking at something on a high branch. Every now and again it stopped to look back at the knight, as if to be sure she had no intention of climbing the tree.

"Who, Rasa?"

"Yes. She must retain her mind, but otherwise...does she 'become' a bird? Is she a woman in the shape of a bird, or a bird with the soul of a woman? And how does a bird's tiny brain hold the memories of a person? What about her organs? What happens to food she has eaten? It would be too much for the stomach of a bird, so where does it go?"

Allandria found herself blinking. "I've no idea. I honestly haven't thought about it. But I think that, whatever her shape, she is always a woman at her core. You should ask her."

Samily perked up at the idea. "You think we'll see her again?"

"I hope so. When we catch up to Aranok."

*If we catch up with Aranok.*

"Do you think she can change into anything? Like a demon? Or a tree?" the knight asked.

Allandria smiled. "I really don't know." If she could, she'd be a Hell of an ally. Having your own tame demon would be quite an advantage in a fight. Especially one with the mind of a woman. She'd always thought of Aranok as the most powerful kind of *draoidh*, because his earth powers were so...direct. Well, aside from Mynygogg. But nobody had ever held two skills before. Being able to control the dead and demons was...She struggled for a word to encompass it. He was frightening. Monstrous.

Mynygogg aside, though, perhaps Rasa was the most powerful. If Samily's guesses about her were true, she could deceive as well as an illusionist, and fight alongside an earth *draoidh*. Could she turn herself into a Thakhati? And would she have their weakness to sunlight if she did?

Allandria laughed at herself. She was off into a labyrinth herself now, following Samily's thread. She took some bread from her pack and offered half to the knight. "We should eat. Build our reserves. We'll need to go again soon, to reach Dail Ruigh by nightfall."

Samily took the food. "Do you think we'll find the envoy there?"

"Honestly? No." Saying it out loud was harder than she expected. But she knew it was true. "He's only going to stop when the horse is exhausted. He'll sleep as little as possible, then start again at daybreak."

"Why?"

"Because he's angry, and grieving, and guilty. And the only thing he can do to make any of it better is kill the man responsible. He'll obsess over it until it's done. He's done it before."

*And it was bad.*

"Do you think Mynygogg is responsible?" Samily asked.

"I don't know. He could be. Especially if he has the relic, though I still don't think that explains everything."

"Weyr." The Thorn's voice turned cold.

"And the messenger," Allandria agreed. "Or why Janaeus sent us on a fool's errand to serve a queen who was long gone. How did Mynygogg manipulate him into doing that?"

"No." Samily stood and stretched. "None of that makes sense. May I ask, what did Aranok think?"

"Before today? He suspected someone within the king's messengers. Maybe the head messenger, Madu."

"Hmm." The knight lifted her saddle and moved toward Dancer. "I suppose. But wouldn't they need someone closer to the king? To convince him Taneitheia was still in Barrock?"

"We've been at war," said Allandria. "In war, communication is king. She who controls the truth controls the country. It could be the messengers."

Samily threw the saddle over Dancer's back. The horse recoiled slightly. She was probably unhappy to have the weight back so soon. She should really get Midnight ready too. Thank God for the Calladells. They would never have made Dail Ruigh by dark without them.

Then again, maybe Aranok wouldn't have run off without Bear.

*Maybe.*

# CHAPTER 42

The White Hart sign hung limp in the dead evening air. It seemed not long ago the place had been their haven, full of life. Fear too, but life. And hope. They'd run here from the Blackened. Sheltered together. It was a lifetime ago. Another country.

The building had deteriorated quickly. Or maybe it had always been this tatty, and it was the absence of light that rendered it clearly. A corpse of wood and stone standing sentry on the road to Auldun.

Bear breathed heavily beneath him, the huge animal's chest pressing against Aranok's legs. They'd ridden fifty miles that day on top of the same the day before, he reckoned. Even for Bear, that was a lot. He'd need to rest. That was fine. Aranok couldn't take him into Auldun anyway—not without getting him killed. He'd lock the horse up here and return for him once he was done. And if he didn't...Allandria would track him here eventually. She was likely already on the way.

Aranok briefly considered walking straight into Auldun tonight, but knowing what he'd face there, it would be suicide to go in so tired. Plus, in the dark, the added threat of Thakhati. He needed to rest. He jumped down from his mount and tied him to a post beside the door. It wasn't dark enough for Thakhati yet, and the Blackened were only drawn by human prey. Reivers...Actually, he'd seen very few Reivers, now he thought about it. None at all on his ride here, which he'd been expecting. In fact, only now it occurred to him how few they had really come across. Were they planning something? Gathering? Something to worry about later.

As he reached for the door handle, he stopped. It wasn't closed. He'd assumed when it was evacuated, they would have locked it up. Blackened didn't pick locks.

Perfect. Another fight he didn't have time for.

Aranok shoved the door open and waited.

Nothing.

With a deep breath, he pulled up his hood, raised his scarf and stepped inside. It was much as he remembered it. The double-sided bar split the ground floor in half. So he had two rooms to clear. And the upstairs. He should clear that too. Then he could sleep on a bed.

Aranok walked to the middle of the room, listening for any sound, any movement, a breath. Still nothing. He crossed to the end of the bar and peered through into the back room. Nothing there either. But it was too dark to see every corner, since the windows had been boarded up the last time he was here. He needed light.

He walked back in front of the bar and positioned himself where he'd be able to see the whole room when it lit.

"*Solas.*"

He threw the glowing ball out to the middle of the room. Nothing. Just empty tables. Where Meristan had spoken beautifully, raising the hairs on Aranok's arms. He'd drunk with the monk, and Vastin.

And Glorbad.

Before.

They'd laughed, despite the threat. There had been a fire in the hearth and food in their bellies. It was madness that he was nostalgic for that night now, but if he had Samily's power, he might well go back to that evening and prevent everything that had happened since.

"Come on!" His voice echoed off the stone without reply. Silence lay on the inn like fog.

He turned his back on the room, gesturing for the orb to follow. The back room was equally empty, as was the kitchen—though he found a small stash of salted beef that had been missed in the evacuation. It was tough, but welcome.

The stairs groaned as he walked up them. There were fifteen rooms in the White Hart. Eight on the first floor, seven more on the second. The first floor was empty. Just unmade beds and empty wardrobes. By the time he reached the last door on the top floor, he was thinking of little more than getting into the bed.

The last room was empty. He found himself laughing. Laughing at the absurdity, the irony. There was nothing here. Just a shell of what Eidyn had once been.

He trudged back down the stairs and brought the horse inside. The stables would have been easier to get him into, but he wanted the animal here, where he knew it was safe. He collected some straw from the barn, though. It occurred to him it was probably wise to stay in the same room. Twice the chance of one of them waking up if something else came in. He used *gluais* to carry a bed down from the first floor to sit near the fireplace and burned some peat he found in a store cupboard.

They might as well both be comfortable. The fire would prevent anything coming down the chimney. He needed to sleep.

But lying in bed, fully clothed in his leathers, he found himself staring at the ceiling instead, listening to the crack of the fire and the breathing of a soundly sleeping horse.

He must have passed out, though he had no memory of when. When he woke, the fireplace was cold. Bear was still asleep. Unsurprising, he supposed, considering the distance they'd travelled.

He got up and searched the kitchen for food. There was nothing more. Everyone who'd been there that night would have taken whatever they could carry. The salt beef was probably an oversight. But he needed a decent meal this morning. He needed everything.

It took him half an hour to catch a rabbit out the back, and another hour to dress and cook it. It was an unusual luxury to have a full kitchen to work in. Much easier than doing it in the wild with a hunting knife. In fact, a bed, a fire—they were still luxuries after the war. It was easy to forget. The nights huddled in the rain, trying to sleep through the shivering. It was all a blur really. Little things were clear, though. The sound of the dying. The smell of the dead. The taste of blood in his mouth.

He tore a strip from the rabbit. It was good to have hot, fresh food.

He found some salt, and that made it even better. It wasn't his mother's stew, but it was better than old salt beef. After breakfast, he brought another bundle of hay in for Bear. The horse seemed quite relaxed about his surroundings. He'd been in some odd "stables" of late.

Aranok dug through his pack. What should he take with him? Ideally, as little as possible. He was going to have to fight his way through Auldun. The bastard had made sure of that. And the irony, the salt in the wound, was that he'd be fighting his way through what was left of its citizens. After Mynyggog's demons had devastated the city and murdered half the inhabitants, the evil bastard raised the dead and marched them on Dun Eidyn. It was horrifying. Survivors watching their murdered family rise again, only to attack the living. It was inhuman.

Once Mynygogg was trapped in the castle, Aranok had assumed the dead would simply wander away, or perhaps even return to their natural state, but they hadn't. They lingered in Auldun. He'd wondered why and how before, not having studied necromancy. Now he knew: the heart of devastation. Its name had new meaning.

Trapping Mynygogg in Dun Eidyn had always been a temporary plan. They couldn't leave him in there forever. But it gave them time. A chance to breathe. To retreat. They'd called it the end of the war, but it was a gentle lie. The war wasn't over. And now that he knew about the relic, he realised it had never really stopped. They'd been at war the whole time, without realising. In fact, they'd almost lost.

This was the only way to end it. No more deaths. No more losses. One more fight. Him against Mynygogg.

To take back Eidyn. To end it all.

He picked out two days' rations and filled his water flask. In two days' time, either he'd have control of the castle and its resources, or he wouldn't need them anymore.

Either way, it would be over.

---

Nirea woke to the smell of porridge. It took a moment for the pain to kick in. How was it still so painful? She opened her eyes to find

Meristan sitting on the edge of his bed, looking at her like an excited puppy.

"Mohnin." She wiped saliva from the corner of her mouth. The swelling made it hard to sleep with her mouth closed, though it was slowly getting better.

"Morning," said the monk. "I brought you breakfast—and your opium."

"Thangs." She pulled herself up to a sitting position, lifted the glass first and drank the opium solution. She'd give it a minute to work before eating the porridge. Leaning back and breathing deep, she realised she smelled less than ideal. She could do with a bath, which meant kicking the monk out—unless he wanted to help, of course.

She turned to look at him, still perched on the bed, as if waiting for something.

"Yes?"

"Are you…I mean, I don't want to…Are you awake? Enough to talk?" he asked.

Was she? Probably. "Yes."

"Ah, good. I think we found it." Meristan produced a heavy dark-leather book from behind him. "This was in the *caibineat puinnsean*. It fits what Egretta said—it makes no sense. I can't see why someone would write it and I can't imagine who would put it in the *caibineat*."

Nirea gestured for him to hand it to her. It was as heavy on her lap as it looked. She ran her fingers over the golden letters engraved on the cover. *A History of Eidyn, Vol. 22.*

"Up to a point, it all seems accurate. But look here." Meristan opened the book where he'd left the ribbon—page 312. "From here, it's all wrong."

He sat back down on his bed, with his hands spread wide, inviting her to read it herself. They sat in silence as she did. When she'd finished scanning the pages and grasped the major fiction of the book, she closed it and sighed. "Why?"

"Exactly." Meristan folded his arms. "It didn't happen like that. Well, it did, but not…"

"Indeed." But there was a more important question. "Why khill Conifah?"

"Exactly!" The monk seemed pleased someone else saw something he'd been alone in noticing. "I thought the same. So Morienne and I went to the shelf where the real book is kept. It's not there."

"Wha? Where?"

"I don't know yet, but it looks very like someone is planning to rewrite history."

"Shih." Nirea realised where this was all pointing. "Time."

Meristan's face fell. "Yes, I thought that too. It seems a terrible coincidence, doesn't it? If Samily really is a time *draoidh*, then is it possible there is another? More powerful? An ally of Mynygogg?"

Yes, it was possible. Horribly possible. Regardless of her suspicions, they needed to tell Aranok. Assuming he wasn't a traitor. "Aranoh nees know."

"I agree," said Meristan. "But Rasa has not returned. She was going to come straight back, but perhaps she hasn't found them yet?"

"Mayee." But a knot in her stomach suggested otherwise. Something was wrong. "Wha neht?"

"Well, as Egretta said, there are records as to who checks books out of the library, and who puts books in the *caibineat*."

"Hmm. Danzhous." If that was what had got Conifax killed...

Meristan perked up. "Why?"

"How killah know?"

Meristan cocked his head. "I'm sorry, I don't understand. How will the killer know what?"

This wasn't a sentence she could shorten, apparently. Nirea took a deep breath, then spoke slowly and clearly.

"How. Did. The. Killer. Know. Conifax. Found. The. Book?"

Meristan turned pale. "You think he asked about the records?"

Nirea nodded. Meristan leapt to his feet and rushed to the door.

"What?" Nirea asked.

The monk threw open the door and burst into the hallway. She just made out his shouted response as he pounded away down the corridor.

"I sent Morienne to the records keeper!"

---

The great stone gatehouse of Auldun rose before Aranok. The naturally light brown sandstone was dark and grey, as if the walls too had been infected by the death inside. He approached the huge wooden gates and placed a hand against them. He'd been through these gates so many times before—and still, despite everything, he felt the tug of home. The great, imposing castle Dun Eidyn rose out of the Nor Loch, but it was Eidyn's sprawling capital, Auldun, where the life was. The people. The markets. The taverns. The joy. But the thriving city of his memory no longer existed. It was a cemetery, a monument to their failure, an open wound.

He couldn't allow himself to be overwhelmed. He had to focus, to shut himself off from his emotional attachment to the people. He couldn't be human here. Being human would get him killed. These were no longer the people of Auldun; they were Mynygogg's reanimated puppets. Attack dogs. Set, he now assumed, to prevent anyone from getting into Dun Eidyn.

The portcullis was raised, but he couldn't open the gates and allow the Dead to spill out into Eidyn. Thankfully, being the king's envoy had privileges, like a skeleton key that opened the guard tower. He pushed on the heavy iron door and it creaked open, scraping across the dirt.

*Shit.*

The Dead weren't like the Blackened. Sound would bring them. He had to hope there weren't many close enough to hear. Fetid air caught in his throat, making him cough. There was very little inside. A few barrels stocked with arrows in the corner and a motley collection of dusty weapons on the wall. A few swords, a few axes, some shields leaning against the bottom of the wall. One had fallen over and a spider had made a huge, intricate web within its rounded back. The gossamer strings were peppered with the carcasses of smaller insects.

Mostly, this was an entrance. The wooden stairs that wound their way around the walls to the upper floor of the guard tower were what was important. They also creaked as he walked up them, but not enough to be heard over the wind outside. Through the hatch at the top was the guard station. Here, a stove, table and chairs, even a small bed to allow a guard to take a break on long shifts. There were cards on the table, scattered where they'd been abandoned. Tankards thick with mould.

Auldun had been peaceful. Eidyn had been peaceful. It felt like another life.

As Aranok walked, little clouds of dust rose in his wake, dancing in the light that crept through the slatted windows. He crossed to the inner wall, where the window was wider, and looked out on his city.

The stone tenements of Auldun sprawled before him, split by the wide, cobblestone-paved High Street, which led all the way from the gates to Dun Eidyn itself. The street was made for royal processions, and locals referred to it as the Royal Mile, despite it being more like five miles long. Janaeus had never been one for processions. "Public masturbation" he called them. One of his first orders as king was to plant trees up the middle of the road and encourage market traders to gather there instead. It had soon become a home to artists and artisans, offering their wares or performing for coins. Aranok had always felt at home walking the High Street, as if part of Traverlyn's diverse soul had been transported to Auldun.

Janaeus had expressed the hope it might come to be known as the People's Mile, but tradition and habit had kept the old name. Aranok liked to imagine the people thought of it differently, though, and that the name itself had a different meaning now. Then.

The trees that remained were sickly, the market stalls and stages derelict and broken. Chimneys breathed no smoke and windows were dark mirrors, reflecting the misery below. For miles east and west, it was the same. Auldun had grown organically at the entrance to Dun Eidyn, centuries before. The stone tenements, designed to house many people in a small area, varied in size and position, like a ramshackle puzzle hastily put together. And yet the city had a character, a life of its own. The tight closes between buildings and the enclosed courtyards gave it a sense of wonder and discovery. It was a place to explore, to marvel at the skill and artistry of the men and women who carved it out of stone, wood and glass.

Despite everything, despite the rot and the death and the bleakness of it all, Aranok still saw life in Auldun. Maybe the old city wasn't done. But a closer look at the streets brought him back. A body strewn over a doorstep. Another slumped against a tree. Another, standing, as if staring at itself in the window of a bakery.

The Dead. Mynygogg's defences. He couldn't burn his way through them—he'd only end up bringing Auldun down with them. And the fire would surely alert Mynygogg to his approach. His best hope was that the *draoidh* wouldn't expect anyone to attack the castle—especially not alone. That meant not announcing his approach, which might be easier said than done.

But he had a plan. He pulled his riding cloak tight about him and raised his hood.

It was time.

—◦—

"Are you all right, miss?"

Nirea leaned against the doorframe. The world had gone a little sideways there for a moment. No, she shouldn't be out of bed, and no, she clearly wasn't all right, but it had taken only a few minutes for her to realise she couldn't just sit and wait for Meristan to come back. The opium that was keeping her from feeling the throbbing pain in her face was also making her light-headed. That, and the weight of the one sword she'd managed to strap on her good side had meant she needed a moment to regain her balance.

"Fine," she lied, pushing herself back upright. "You Calavah?"

The man adjusted his round spectacles and looked at her like a specimen in a museum, with a kind of interested detachment.

"I am Master Calavas. Can I help you?"

"You records keeper?" She carefully pronounced each word.

"I am. Would you like to sit down?" Calavas gestured to a chair in front of her. On principle, she wanted to stand. It was a better position if he attacked, or if she needed to leave quickly. But her legs had other ideas—so she sat.

"Friends came. Seen them?"

Calavas sat back in his red leather chair and stared at her across the dark wooden desk, half-covered in ledgers. He must have been around forty, which was somehow younger than Nirea expected a records keeper to be. His smooth bald head and narrow frame gave him an almost serpentine look.

"I'm sorry," he said. "You are...?"

"Nevah mind." Nirea attempted to add some authority to her voice. "Friends?"

Calavas cocked his head at her. "Are you sure you're all right, miss? Does the hospital know you're here?"

"Course," she lied. "Monk and girl. Red streak." She gestured to her own hair. "Seen them?"

Calavas leaned forward, his elbows on the desk and his hands at his mouth. "They're your friends, are they?" His tone was odd. Hard to read. Nirea couldn't tell if he was dangerous or not. She slipped the knife up her sleeve into the palm of her hand but kept it covered.

"Yes."

Calavas looked long and hard at her before speaking. "There's been no monk here. No girl with red hair either. Now, if there's nothing else?" He gestured to the door.

"Sure?" Nirea asked. "They came here."

"I am sure. I'm the only one here and I have been all morning. If your friends were coming here, I can only assume something distracted them. I trust no misfortune has befallen them. As I...suppose it did you."

Was that a threat?

"May I ask why they were coming?" he asked, a little too casually. Every instinct was telling her not to trust this man. He made her skin crawl.

"Book," she said. "Curses."

"A book on curses?" The man's eyebrows rose. "Well, I'm afraid those books are kept in the *caibineat puinnsean* and, as you may know, only masters are allowed in there. Particularly after what happened to Master Conifax. Why would they want a book on curses?"

*Shit.* She'd thought she was being clever, but had she given away more than she intended? She frowned and felt a stab of pain in her cheek, instinctively wincing and covering her wound with her hand. It took her a moment to realise that meant she'd left her knife on her lap, clearly visible to the man across the table. Their eyes met for a moment.

He looked down at the knife and back up again. "May I ask what that is for?"

"Nuhing." She quickly slipped the knife back in her sleeve. "Fell out."

Calavas stood with an impatient sigh. "I'm going to have to ask you to leave."

Did he know something? Had he done something to Meristan and Morienne? She couldn't have been that far behind them. It had taken her a little while to get dressed, and then to slip out of the hospital. She'd got directions here from a helpful student, who was also very concerned to know what had happened to her...Less than half an hour, no more. If they had come here, they couldn't be far. Nirea scanned the room for signs of a struggle. Both side walls were lined with huge bookcases, holding leather-bound ledgers of green, blue and red. Behind Calavas was one of those huge windows. If anything had happened in here, would it have been visible from the street?

No, out the window was a large tree, obscuring the view. The thick burgundy rug would have muffled the sound too. But he couldn't possibly have cleaned up in time, and the place was extremely tidy, if very full. Maybe they came and left. Maybe he was going to bide his time. Maybe he wasn't the killer at all, just a scout, who would pass on that someone else had found the odd book. But she needed to know. Her friends' lives might depend on it.

She stood and drew her sword with her good arm.

"Where. Are. They?"

Calavas, she'd been assured, was a mundane master—a non-*draoidh*—promoted for his academic skills. That meant she should be able to take him, even in this state. The man moved cautiously back toward his window.

"I don't know where you think you are, miss, but this is the university and I am a master here. You cannot simply come in here raving and pointing a sword at people! This is a place of learning!"

If he was innocent, he was doing a good job of bluffing. Nirea moved around the desk to his side. She gestured with the sword for him to move around and take the seat she'd just vacated.

*Damn it.* She'd left the door open. Well, there was nobody visible in the hall. She began searching through Calavas's drawers with her free hand, which wasn't easy, since her shoulder complained with each movement.

Papers, mostly. Signed documents. A letter with the royal seal. A bottle of whisky—Meristan would approve. She leaned over to look in the bottom drawer and immediately regretted it as the world spun beneath her.

"Shit." Nirea slumped back into the big leather armchair. She gripped the seat tightly, but the spinning only worsened. A wave of nausea rose. She tried to shake her head, to clear it, but that only made it worse. Only then did she notice the blossoming red stain on her bandaged shoulder. She must have torn her stitches.

"Well, that's no surprise, is it?" she heard Calavas say, just before everything went black.

---

She rose sluggishly from the darkness to the sound of raised voices.

"I'm sure that's not what Master Calavas is saying." *Male, calm, controlled.*

"Well, why not? Why shouldn't she be arrested? We can't have people wandering around the university swinging swords at people. They shouldn't even be allowed on campus." *Male, oily.*

"The woman is clearly not herself, Calavas. And there's no harm done." *Female, strong, irritated.*

Nirea could feel her head again. Slight nausea as it swayed gently to the side.

"Nirea?" *Female, close, familiar.*

"Mm-hmm?" she responded. The other voices stopped chattering.

"Is she awake?" *Meristan.*

"I'm not sure." *The second female. Morienne?*

Nirea's eyes fluttered open. Morienne leaned over her. Where was she? This wasn't her room. She wasn't lying down. She was sitting. Her feet were on the floor. Everything was...wobbly. "Where m'I?"

"You're in the university, Nirea. Do you remember?" asked Morienne. What did she remember? The university. The records. *Calavas.*

She leapt to her feet, reaching for her sword, but it wasn't there and her legs were water. She crumpled. Morienne and Meristan grabbed a side each before she slammed into the desk. Her shoulder flared with pain and she winced away from Morienne. They gently guided her back into the chair. Nausea rose in her gullet. She swallowed it down.

"Nirea, it's all right. You're safe. Just stay still. We've sent for medics." She looked up to see Meristan smiling at her. But there was something in his smile. Something desperate. Something nervous. Across the room, Calavas glowered at her like a pile of shite on his ornamental rug. Balaban stood to his right, between the records keeper and a woman she didn't know—a master, by her dress. She had dark hair streaked with grey, half of which had been pulled into a bun. Her face was hard to read, but she seemed to be regarding Nirea with a mix of curiosity and fatigue.

"Nirea, this is Master Opiassa," said Meristan. "She is in charge of the university's guard." That look again. She needed to be careful. Perhaps she just needed to keep her mouth shut. She blinked at Meristan, hoping it conveyed her understanding.

The woman smiled and nodded. "Captain Nirea."

Nirea half raised her left hand in a fairly pitiful wave. The name rang a faint bell in the back of her mind. Hells, her head was spinning. She looked down at her shoulder, where a bright red sun bloomed on her bandages. *Damn it.*

"For goodness' sake, is this the time for introductions?" Calavas whined. "I want her out of my office."

"Of course, of course." Agitated, Meristan leaned out of the door to look down the corridor. "As soon as we can, Master, I assure you. Please accept our apologies." It was odd seeing the huge man nervous before such a weedy little snake.

Calavas took a deep breath in and snorted it out. His face turned pink as he screwed up his mouth. "I have work to do."

"I understand, Master Calavas—but as you can obviously see, Captain Nirea is in need of medical attention, and moving her could be dangerous. Are you prepared to accept responsibility if she bleeds to death?" Opiassa seemed to grow a few inches with pure irritation. Nirea wondered if there was history between these two. It looked like it.

"Master Calavas, maybe it would be a good time to get yourself a cup of tea?" suggested Balaban. "Something soothing, perhaps. For the nerves. You must be rather rattled after your experience." He looked earnestly at the records keeper. Calavas stared back at him a moment and wordlessly slipped out of the door. Nirea could practically see steam coming off him.

"Thank you," said Meristan. Balaban nodded serenely.

"So, Lady Nirea, can I ask, do you know why you are here?" Master Opiassa perched on the other side of Calavas's desk. "To hear Calavas tell it, you are a raving lunatic."

What should she tell her? That she suspected Calavas was working for Mynygogg? That she had thought he might have murdered her friends? She looked to Meristan, standing behind Opiassa. Barely— just enough for her to notice—he shook his head. It could almost have been a twitch. But it was plain in his eyes.

Then she remembered the name: Opiassa. One of the masters Meristan suspected of Conifax's murder. The physic *draoidh*. Nirea leaned her head back against the chair, fighting the dizziness that threatened to overwhelm her.

"Don't know. Don't member."

"Oh! I'm sorry, I was looking for Master Calavas." A new face at the door. This one a redheaded, freckled young man with a thin beard— too young for the master's robes he wore, Nirea thought. Like a boy in his father's uniform. Like Vastin.

"Master Rotan." Balaban nodded politely. "Master Calavas has stepped away for some tea while we make use of his office. We'll be out of the way momentarily."

Rotan looked at Opiassa, glanced around the room at the others and nodded.

"There's been an incident," said Opiassa. "It's all in hand. No one was hurt." She smiled at the new arrival.

Rotan looked curiously at Nirea, who was obviously hurt and in no shape to be going anywhere. "Umm?"

"Oh, that happened elsewhere." Meristan waved away his concern. "Days ago. Nothing to worry about." Rotan looked unconvinced, tilting his head at Meristan. It took the monk a moment, but he stepped toward the man with an outstretched hand. "Sorry, Brother Meristan, of the Order."

Rotan's eyebrows rose as he took the hand. "*The* Meristan? Head of the Order?"

Meristan nodded demurely. "I have that honour."

"Well, it is my honour." Rotan shook the monk's hand vigorously, demonstrating his enthusiasm. "A pleasure to meet you in person, Brother."

"Rotan is one of the youngest masters ever inducted," said Opiassa. "Seems only a few years ago you were sitting in my history class."

Rotan crossed his hands on his chest and bowed slightly. "I was fortunate to have such excellent tuition." The boy had a silver tongue. Nirea wondered how much that had helped with his early promotion. It wouldn't have hurt. "Anyway, don't let me get in your way. I'll come back later. Nice to meet you, Brother. Ladies." Rotan smiled, nodded briefly at Nirea and Morienne and scurried away.

Nirea shut her eyes as a wave of exhaustion washed through her. She'd have given anything to be back in that hospital bed right then, with the soft pillow under her head.

"Perhaps she is fevered?" said Balaban. She felt a hand on her forehead. Morienne's.

"Is she warm?" asked Meristan.

"Quite. Could be fever, I suppose," said Morienne.

"There we have it," said Balaban. "A fevered patient consumed with delusions. Nothing in the world more simple."

Opiassa "hmphed" and stood. Just as well, because at that moment, Nirea was finally overcome by nausea and violently spewed porridge over Calavas's desk. She slumped back into the chair, feeling herself sinking again.

After what seemed like a long quiet, pierced only by dripping, she heard Opiassa say, "I think I'll leave you to it." Bootheels clicked on marble as she retreated.

"Well," said Balaban. "That could have gone worse."

Nirea fell again into the dizzying black.

# CHAPTER 43

Aranok pulled his cloak tight and kept his head down. He needed to move slowly—to get as far as possible before any of the Dead realised he wasn't one of them. He'd made it several miles without any of them taking an interest. But he must have upped his pace just a bit too much. A groan to his right. First, all he saw was a face—a ravaged, decaying mess, leaning at an odd angle. As she stepped out of the shadow, he saw it was because one side of her body was mangled—an arm missing, organs hanging out like fair-day bunting. Her head was slumped to the side too. She looked hard at him.

All right. Time to go. "*Solas*," he whispered. A glowing orb appeared in the air between them. The woman's head jerked as she followed the light like a cat. Noise from his left—another corpse lifted itself from the ground and groaned, hypnotised by the light. It barely had any flesh left on it; scavengers had been at it. But still it stood. From a building ahead of him, another woman, this one with her throat slit so deep it was a wonder her head was still on. And another, and another—they appeared like insects crawling from the dark, fascinated by the glowing orb hanging in the air. Aranok also turned to face it, careful to avoid looking out of place. Altogether, there were about twenty of the Dead milling around, watching the light. With a gesture, Aranok sent it back down the street, the way he'd come. The corpses burst into life, lurching after it in a frenzy.

He stood completely still, allowing them to run past him, holding his breath. One brushed against him as it passed and for a moment he thought it was going to stop, to turn and look right at him, but it stumbled, rolled, righted itself and carried on.

It looked like the Dead had a similar herd mentality to the Blackened. Set off a few of them, and they'd all go running.

But that would mean…

It began as a low rumble. Aranok closed his eyes, praying it wasn't what he thought. But in his soul, he knew. He turned to see the first of the Dead barrelling out of Cockburn Street. Moments later, they were swarming from everywhere—doorways, alleys—one threw itself from a window to shatter more bones on the cobbles. Still, it dragged itself to its feet and ran at him.

He already stood out too much now. No way were they all going to pass him by—and it only took one to latch onto him and attack before the rest followed suit. He was going to have to run.

*Damn it.*

"*Gaoth.*" A burst of air poured forth in front of him, blasting a path through the onrushing Dead. Their bodies crunched and squelched as they battered against one another and into walls and carts, thrown aside like broken puppets.

Aranok ran, pulled along in the wake of his own storm.

His feet pounded on the cobbles as the Dead parted before him. Windows shattered as twisted bodies hammered against them. Small branches ripped from trees.

His heart pounded in his ears. This had always been a backup plan. He'd hoped only to use it at the end, to get across the causeway, but he still had at least two miles to go, and he couldn't keep up a *gaoth* spell that long—he'd pass out first.

His breathing became laboured, his lungs stinging, begging him to stop. Running flat out like this was hard. Allandria was the runner. But he had to keep going, had to ignore the pain, the aches in his knees, the muscles screaming for respite.

*Run, run, run.*

He glanced over his shoulder to see that the Dead in his wake were chasing him. They were a long way back, but they wouldn't tire. When they got close enough, they'd have the same pull he was using to move faster.

*Run.*

*Run.*

The Dead seemed to be thinning. Ahead, he could see the entrance to the causeway. Most of them must be behind him. He ignored the morbid urge to look back again, knowing what he'd see. He had to keep going. Maybe a mile now.

Still the Dead scattered before him. One boy flew up and over his head, a sword jutting out of his chest.

*Not real. Not human.*

*Run!*

Aranok's mouth hung wide now, gasping air in and out in burning breaths. His shoulders ached; pain stabbed his knees with every impact.

Still he ran.

His foot caught the edge of a wet cobble. The ankle turned beneath him and he sprawled face-first onto the road, cracking his elbow hard on the stone. Pain shot up his arm as the air was pressed from his lungs.

His concentration broken, the *gaoth* spell abated. He was breathing so hard he could barely speak.

*Get up!*

A body landed on him. He heard its grating breath as it scrabbled at his back. Another impact. Another. The bodies piling up on him were making it hard for the ones immediately on top of him to move. His armour was preventing any real damage, but he couldn't escape either. The more that came, the worse it would get, but he needed to give them time to get close enough. Another body, another—they writhed on top of him, each desperately trying to reach him, to tear at him.

He was on the verge of running out of breath. It had to be now.

"*Clach,*" he wheezed.

With the next impact, his armour pulsed back, throwing the pile of dead off him like a cannonball hit.

Aranok breathed deep and forced himself back to his feet. His energy was all but spent, but he could see the causeway. He was right, it wasn't far. But there were too many of them. He was never going to make it.

With a scream of frustration and rage, he ran again. This time, without the wind to clear his path, he had to break his way through them. The first corpse to reach him came from the right; his raised forearm battered it out of his way, the armour providing enough resistance to protect his arm from the jolt. Another from the left grabbed his shoulder. He rolled his arm forward and swung a punch with his right, catching it square in the face. It fell away but left its hand behind, caught on the edge of his armour.

Another from the front—he ducked and caught it with his shoulder at chest height, lifting it off its feet and throwing it forward. It landed hard on its back and he stumbled over it. Its chest gave a wet crunch beneath his foot as he trampled it into the cobbles.

Not human. Not real.

Another from the left, this one with a blade, which it swung down toward him. He raised his left arm to deflect it and the blow bounced off, but he staggered, and a shooting pain in his ankle threw him off-balance again. He stumbled forward, arms flailing. He just had to reach the causeway. He had enough left for a wall across the entrance.

His weak ankle gave way on the slick cobbles again. He fell into a roll, pain cracking his kneecap as he landed hard. He yelped in pain as he rolled over his left shoulder, panting, to land on his back. A corpse was on him before he could even lift his head. Facing up, this way, his eyes were exposed. The dead thing scrambled desperately to get at them. He caught its hands, holding them up away from his face, and was briefly grateful for the rot that had wasted its muscles, giving him the strength advantage he desperately needed.

He had to get up. He lifted his left foot and pressed it against the ground.

*Fuck!*

Pain shot up his leg. Between the ankle and the knee, something was too damaged. He focused on keeping the Dead away from his face, as another landed on his legs, and another over the back of the first.

He'd walked himself straight into a trap.

Something roared above him. A demon? He couldn't see, but it was big and dark and falling toward them. A demon; he was finished. It was difficult to make out as he dodged the skeletal hands tearing at

Justin Lee Anderson

his face, but from what he could see, he would swear it looked like...a bear.

The beast hit the ground with a thud. It growled and, with a judder, the weight on Aranok lessened. A huge paw swiped the last few Dead away, battering them to the side. Now he could see it properly, but he struggled to believe his eyes.

A giant bear had fallen from the sky.

It roared and he scrambled back, managing to sit up. The animal stared back at him, and it took Aranok a moment to recognise there was more than just animal there. There was...recognition? Intelligence?

Then he realised.

"Rasa?"

The bear nodded its huge head and roared again. He didn't need to hear the words; she was telling him to run. He pushed himself up onto his good leg as more Dead arrived, but Rasa raised herself up to her full ten feet and swatted them away like insects.

He couldn't run. His left leg was useless. When he tried to put weight on it, it crumpled beneath him, and he fell back onto his good knee.

"I can't!" he yelled at the bear, hoping she could hear him over the noise. They were almost backed against a building. Aranok limped toward it, but two corpses cut him off. Rasa was behind him, on the verge of being overwhelmed by sheer numbers. He had to do something now, but what?

One spell, that was about all he had left. They needed a safe space. To rest. Aranok looked up. The building had three floors. The main door was closed. It looked solid. Solid enough.

He turned and shouted over his shoulder.

"Rasa! Window!"

The bear turned her head briefly—enough to see him point to the top floor. Did she nod? It didn't matter. He was out of time.

One last spell.

He held his palms flat toward the ground. *"Gaoth."*

The wind threw him upwards. It was a dangerous trick he rarely used, because it was easy to get it slightly wrong and find yourself falling from a great height. It required balance and strength to keep his arms at just the right angle. Past the first window, past the second. As he drew near level with the top window, he twisted and lifted one arm, pushing himself suddenly backwards and hammering against the glass. It shattered as he fell through, landing hard on his back.

He rolled over on the broken glass and pressed himself up to look around. Bedroom. Sparse. There was a bed against the far wall and a chest of drawers to his right with wooden toys on top. A child's room. The door was open.

He used the chest to haul himself to his good foot, just as the child itself came barrelling into the room, followed by one of its parents. There was so little left of the adult's flesh, it was hard to tell if it was mother or father.

The child reached him first. He grabbed it by the head as its small arms flailed toward him, trying to reach him. He lifted it and shook, then twisted. Its rotting neck crunched and smacked as the weight of its body pulled away, slumping to the floor. He threw the head out the window, just missing the crow as it flew in.

The remaining corpse lunged toward him but tripped over the child's body and stumbled into him. He punched up at it, connecting hard with its chin, and its head snapped back. As it landed on the floor at his feet, he leaned heavily on the chest of drawers and jumped on its neck with his good foot, feeling it crack beneath him. A second jump, a second crack, and it stopped trying to get up. Its head rolled off, coming to rest upside down a few feet away.

He turned his head, noticing another figure in the room. Oddly, the first thing that struck him about Rasa wasn't that she was naked, but that she was whole. It seemed incongruous that her body was flawless—complete. He noticed a few scratches, one in particular that looked painful, on her belly. Wordlessly, he turned his head away, untied his cloak and held it out for her.

"Thank you." She took it and wrapped herself.

"Thank *you*." He'd be dead without her. He might still be dead, truth be told. When he could hear she'd finished dressing, he turned back to her. "We need to check the rest of the house."

She nodded. "Your leg?"

"I don't know. My knee—my ankle—something's wrong." His blood was still up, so he knew he wasn't feeling the full effect of the pain, but when he put weight on it…

"I'll look." The woman moved to the door.

"Wait." Aranok reached out to stop her.

She smiled, pulling the cloak tight about her. It was splattered with rank blood and looked ridiculous, framing her angelic face.

"I can look after myself." True—she had proved that. Aranok let her go, realising he was glad to do so because he badly needed to sit down. He hopped carefully to the bed, avoiding the headless bodies on the floor. Slumping down on it, he lifted his left leg carefully. He pulled a pillow from behind him and placed it under his knee. Hells, it hurt!

He leaned back against the wall and closed his eyes.

*What a fucking mess.*

After a few minutes, Rasa returned. "It's empty. Just these two. I checked the front door. It's locked. Solid."

"All right. Good."

"How's your leg?"

"Not good. I can't bend it." If anything, it was getting worse for him sitting down.

"May I?" She sat at the foot of the bed.

Aranok nodded. "I don't suppose you studied medicine, did you?"

"I'm afraid not." She gently ran her hands up his calf, squeezing every inch or so. He flinched as she reached his knee.

"Hmm. I think we need to get these off." She nodded to his trousers.

Aranok hesitated. "All right."

"I've seen one before, Laird, if that's what you're worried about." She smiled.

Aranok laughed. "No, I just… I'm not sure how easy that will be. I think I'll need your help."

He was right. Not being able to bend one leg, he pretty much needed Rasa to undress him, which might have been embarrassing had the situation been less grave.

Once she had, it became apparent his knee was the size of a winter melon.

"Ouch," said Rasa. "I don't think there's much we can do with that. It might be dislocated. No wonder you can't bend it."

"What about the ankle? How does it look?" Now that his boot was off, it also ached.

Rasa poked around it, and he flinched again as she poked behind his ankle bone.

"Not as swollen, but you've damaged something back here."

"Fuck." As soon as he'd said it, he realised he didn't actually know the woman that well, despite them both being semi-dressed in a bedroom together. "Sorry."

Rasa smiled. "I've heard worse." She stood and left the room, returning with more pillows. One went under his ankle and the other behind him. "You should rest. Get under the blanket."

Aranok looked around. It didn't feel right. He'd just torn the head off the child who belonged in this bed. Their body was still on the floor. Rasa followed his gaze.

"Oh, of course."

She lifted the child's remains first and dumped them out the window with ease. Aranok heard the body land, and the resultant clamour from the dead gathered outside. She returned for the second body and sent that after, finally tossing the head with it. Aranok realised he still had a hand attached to his shoulder and tugged it free. The crunch as it came loose made him shiver. He shrugged and offered it to Rasa, who smiled flatly and dropped it out the window.

"You're stronger than you look," said Aranok.

She smiled. "I am as strong as I need to be. I choose this shape because I like it. It reflects who I am. But I'm not limited to it, any more than I am to the bear, or the bird."

Aranok hadn't considered the notion that this wasn't necessarily her natural form, but of course, she could take any shape she chose. It also explained her obvious comfort with her own nakedness—she was happy in her own body, not a luxury everyone had.

"Rasa. Why did you follow me?"

"Allandria asked me to."

Of course she did. "Did she know where I was going?"

"I'm not sure. It was all very rushed."

Aranok felt his eyes beginning to droop. "Thank you for saving me. I'm not sure I deserve it."

Rasa sat on the bed again and took his hand between hers. "Laird Aranok, since I met you a matter of days ago, you have hired me to help your niece, risked your life looking for a cure for the Blackening and—perhaps foolishly, I admit—attempted to take on Mynygogg single-handed. I need know nothing more about you to know what kind of man you are. But if I did, Conifax spoke well of you. There is no higher praise."

Her voice wavered on the last sentence and tears welled in her eyes. Aranok realised his hands were shaking. He lifted his arm and Rasa leaned into him, rested her head against his chest and cried. He wrapped his arms around her and was soon weeping like a child. Rasa might be the only other person who truly understood his loss. And, perhaps, he hers.

The two students sat for a long time holding each other in the tiny, dark room of a murdered child, mourning their lost mentor.

The Dead waited below.

# CHAPTER 44

W hat on earth did you think you were doing, you idiot child?"
It had been a long time since anyone had called Nirea a
child. But Egretta's scowl was doing a good job of making her feel like
one.

"Morienne? Merisan?" she asked, pushing herself up. Egretta put a
gentle hand on her shoulder.

"Don't bloody move. Your stitches are just redone and if you burst
them again, I might not replace them! Do you have any idea how dangerous that was? You could have bled to death!"

"Sorry," Nirea said quietly.

"Meristan and Morienne are fine." The medic lifted a bloody rag and
threw it in a cloth sack. "In fact"—she glanced over her shoulder at the
closed door and continued in a hushed voice—"they've gone to search
Calavas's accommodation. If you were right about Conifax asking for
the records, he's the most likely suspect. Which makes it even more
stupid that you went after him alone."

Nirea nodded and held her hands up placatingly. *It seemed like a good
idea at the time* was probably not an answer Egretta would appreciate
and, frankly, she'd struggle to say it.

"I don't know, though," she said. "About Calavas, I mean. He's an
odd fish, right enough, but to be working with Mynygogg? Doesn't
seem right."

Nirea shrugged. "Odd fish" was her impression too.

"Now," said the medic, "can I leave you here by yourself while I go and clean up, or are you going to go off wandering around the corridors trying to kill yourself again?"

Nirea smiled—as much as she could.

"There's more opium there." Egretta pointed to the glass on her bedside table. "Drink it and get some more sleep. You need it."

Nirea wasn't about to argue. She could barely keep her eyes open as it was.

---

"Wake up, you fucking idiot!"

Aranok jolted up and winced as a stab of pain reminded him about his leg. That also helpfully reminded him where he was. The room was mostly dark, but by the moonlight coming in the broken window, he could see the shape of a woman. But that wasn't Rasa's voice.

"Allandria?" he asked groggily.

"Yes." Her voice was terse. Angry.

"What... what are you doing here?"

"Looks a lot like I'm saving your arse again, doesn't it?" Yes, she wasn't happy. He'd known she wouldn't be.

"How did you get here?"

"The way any sensible human being with half a brain and a length of rope would. We came over the rooftops."

"But..." He barely got the word out before Allandria started again.

"Oh, for fuck's sake, Rasa found us. We were already on our way from the White Hart. We found Bear—he's fine. She led us here. What did you honestly think you were doing trying to blast your way through half a city of the Dead? Were you trying to get yourself killed?" She slapped him on the shoulder repeatedly in rhythm with her last sentence.

"No, I..." he began, but she was right. The roofs were a much better plan. He could have done that. Why hadn't he thought of it?

"God damn it, Aranok! Will you stop trying to do everything yourself?"

"I...I didn't want you to get hurt," he said honestly.

"I can look after myself. But even if you were trying to keep me safe, were you seriously going to walk in to face a demon-summoning necromancer and not take the holy knight specifically trained in killing demons? Are you fucking stupid?"

"I wasn't...I didn't..."

"No, you didn't think, did you? You didn't think about the people who care about you. The people you'd be leaving behind after you got yourself killed in blaze of idiocy, because you were feeling sorry for yourself after your friends died!"

That stung Aranok into silence. Not least because she was right. Maybe he hadn't thought of the roofs because it was safer. Because he was angry or...worse.

Allandria's tone was softer when she spoke again. "I know how much Conifax meant to you, and I'm sorry. I really am. But if he was here he'd be screaming at you. And you know it." She sat on the side of the bed and took his hand. "It wasn't your fault, Aranok. You're not responsible for everybody. You're one man."

"I got him killed," Aranok said quietly. "I got them all killed." Allandria opened her mouth to protest. "It's true. Conifax was killed because I put him onto something. Like the messenger. She was killed to stop her from talking to me. Glorbad's dead because we didn't go with him—or at least because we took Samily."

Allandria took a deep breath. "Are you a seer?"

He looked at her blankly.

"Are you?"

"No." Seers, he was fairly sure, didn't exist. Not real ones. Plenty of folk claimed to have "the sight," but nobody had ever proved real, that he knew of.

"How were you supposed to know?"

"I didn't! That's why I couldn't bring you with me. I keep getting people killed."

"Aranok, nobody knows what's going to happen. But you don't get to push us away. You don't make decisions for us. We're grown women; we make our own choices."

Aranok looked at the door. "Samily's here?"

"She is. I'm glad too. We had to fight our way through some of the Dead to get to the first building. Turns out she's very good at that." She cocked her head and offered him a flat smile.

Aranok laughed gently. "Who would have guessed?"

Allandria smiled genuinely this time. "It's almost as if she trained for it."

"All right." Aranok sighed. "I'm sorry."

"Don't be sorry. Just don't fucking do it again."

He nodded.

"A little birdie tells me you fell over." She nodded to his swollen knee, propped up on the pillow.

"Yeah."

"If only there was such a thing as a healer."

"If only." He smiled.

"How are you feeling otherwise? Rested?" She stood and moved toward the door.

"I think so. Why?"

"Because the best time to get out of here is in the dark. So as soon as Samily fixes that leg, we're going."

"Where?"

She looked at him as if he'd asked a ridiculously stupid question.

"Dun Eidyn."

---

Samily shifted in the seat. She felt oddly uncomfortable and slightly agitated. Rasa stood across the room, looking out the window. She found herself staring at her.

"It's bad," said Rasa.

"Sorry, what is?"

The woman turned from the window. "The Dead. They're everywhere."

"Hmm." Samily nodded.

Rasa lifted a poker from the hearth and idly drew lines in the ash. "What do you think they're talking about?"

"In there?" Samily jabbed her thumb toward the door. "Allandria was very angry with him for leaving without us. So, that, I imagine."

"What did she say?" Rasa asked.

"Nothing specific. It's more what she didn't say."

Allandria had said very little at all on the journey here—which was how Samily could tell she was scared and angry. When they'd arrived at the White Hart and found Bear, she'd raced up the stairs, throwing open doors in search of Aranok. She was agitated and fidgeting when she came back down alone. Samily wondered then if they'd see him alive again. Relief had washed over Allandria's face when Rasa found them. Knowing he was injured, trapped in a building surrounded by the Dead, was better than fearing he'd already joined them.

She heard Allandria's voice raised through the door. The silence suddenly became uncomfortable—not just because they could almost hear the argument, but because Samily felt a visceral need to speak to this woman, to know more about her. She wanted to hear her voice.

"Rasa? May I ask—when did you know you were *draoidh*? I mean, how old were you?"

Rasa looked up at her and stood. "Why?"

"Oh, I'm sorry, I don't mean to be rude. I just wondered. I only recently found out that I'm..."

"You're *draoidh*?" Rasa warmed instantly. "What skill?"

Samily had intended to talk about Rasa, not herself. But her cheeks flushed with Rasa's reaction, so she carried on.

"I believed I was a healer." She saw Rasa's brow furrow. "But Conifax explained that it's actually time."

Rasa's face blanched momentarily at the mention of her teacher but quickly regained its enthusiasm. "Time? That's so exciting! I don't think there's been a time *draoidh* in generations. It's all but legend."

"Oh, it's not as impressive as your ability. I mean, you can turn into...anything!"

"But I can't go back in time!" said Rasa, as if Samily had said something ridiculous. "And you can heal too, did you say?"

"Well, yes. Until I tried to heal Vastin, I thought..."

"What?" Rasa prompted her to finish.

"I thought God had granted me the power to heal. It felt like a miracle, I suppose."

"Does it matter? What you have is so much more! You can heal and literally change time. You can go back and fix your own mistakes; you can…" Rasa waved her hands as if to indicate the whole of creation. "The possibilities!"

"I suppose I flattered myself that I was special. That God chose me alone to heal."

"Oh," said Rasa flatly. "And just being a *draoidh* was disappointing."

"Oh no, no," Samily protested, realising she'd insulted her. "It was just…I don't know. I suppose I felt closer to God because of my ability before. And now I don't."

"I see." Rasa sat in the chair by the fire, gazing into the dark hearth. "I was ten," she finally said. "I was unhappy. I didn't want to be me. I suppose I never really had. I was watching a dog, running in the fields behind our house. It looked so joyous, so utterly happy just to run; the wind in its fur, the grass on its paws. I wanted to be that dog. Free. I can't explain the feeling." She thought for a moment. "I suppose it's like having warm water poured over you, but everywhere, all at once—and on the inside. Like you become the water, and then it hardens again in a new shape. I was a puppy, wrapped in my own clothes. I was terrified. But when I realised what it meant, what I could do…I ran into that field and didn't look back."

Rasa smiled at the memory, and Samily wondered if she'd ever seen a person look more serene.

"It took me three days to work out how to change back. I almost starved—drank from a horse trough. Nearly got stood on. Only on the third day, when the hunger was so bad I thought I'd die, did I change back. I suppose because I wanted to—enough."

"Why didn't you want to be you?" Samily asked. "You're so beautiful."

Rasa turned to her, smiling again. "You're sweet."

Samily felt her cheeks warm again. Why did this woman make her feel so awkward?

"How many *draoidhs* are there?" she asked, to change the subject.

"That we know of? Maybe a hundred, in Eidyn. Maybe less. Most of them come through Traverlyn. Some don't. Like you."

"What can they do? I mean, what other skills are there?"

Rasa turned in the chair to face her.

"Well, there's metamorphosis"—she pointed to herself, then to

Samily—"and time. Aranok is an earth *draoidh*, so he can control natural things, like fire, water, air, light, stone…"

Samily hadn't seen him use the air ability, but she remembered well
the wall of mud that had shielded them from the Blackened on the
Auld Road. That had seemed miraculous too.

"The other common skills are illusion, energy, physic and nature."

Samily had known illusion and nature *draoidhs*, and she'd heard of a
physic one. "What does an energy *draoidh* do?"

"They can be dangerous," said Rasa. "They draw energy from things
and can either give it to another thing or use it as a weapon."

Samily couldn't picture that at all. "How does that work?"

Rasa rolled her shoulders. "Say this fire was lit. An energy *draoidh*
could draw its energy and hit you with it." She pulled at the air in front
of the fire and thrust her hand out at Samily. "Or, she could just pass
the energy to you, to bolster your own. To give you more energy for
your own skill."

"Oh. I suppose that could be dangerous."

"Oh no, that's not what's dangerous," said Rasa. "As much as they
can put energy in you, they can take it out too. A powerful energy
*draoidh* could drain the life right out of you."

"Oh! That's awful!"

"They'd have to be extremely skilled, though," said Rasa. "The worst
most of them could do is put you to sleep. It would take a powerful
*draoidh* to kill. There are a few at the university, including Principal
Keft."

"Who could kill?"

Rasa frowned and looked to the ceiling. "I suppose. Possibly. Keft,
certainly."

Samily felt a chill run down her back.

"And, of course, there are the dark skills: demon summoning and
necromancy," said Rasa.

Samily instantly thought of Mynygogg. Nobody in Eidyn could hear
about demons or the Dead and not have the monster brought to mind.

"Is it true that he's the first? The first to have two skills?"

"As far as we know. Certainly, there are no records of another. Until
Mynygogg, we didn't believe it possible. But then, there are rumours

of other skills too. Ones we haven't seen in many years. Or at least, haven't confirmed. There was a report a few years back of a boy who could make himself invisible. He could be a skilled illusion *draoidh*, I suppose, but actual invisibility is one of the theorised skills. As is flight—though that might be about the ability to influence weight, or density, or gravity. We don't know really."

Samily thought back to their experience at Caer Amon. "What about the power to amplify another *draoidh*'s skill? Is that possible?"

"It's not one I've heard of," said Rasa. "But then, I've never met a time *draoidh* before, so..."

"Samily?"

She turned to see Allandria at the door she hadn't heard open.

"Could you come in, please?" the archer asked.

"Of course." Samily stood and turned to Rasa. "Excuse me."

Rasa looked at her with a kind warmth. "Go do your miracle."

Samily paused in the doorway. She turned back to Rasa, who was still looking at her—which she liked. "Did you...want to...watch?"

Rasa stood and strode toward her. "I would love to."

---

"Nuhing?" Nirea was still sluggish from the opium. It would have been very easy to drift off again. But she needed to stay awake.

"Nothing," Meristan confirmed. "We searched his rooms from top to bottom. No book. Nothing to suggest he's in league with Myny-gogg. If he did kill Conifax, there's nothing in his room to prove it."

There was a brief hammering on the door and it swung open. Morienne stepped in, panting, her face bright red.

"He's dead! Calavas is dead."

"What?" Meristan stood. "When? How?"

"His office," she said. "I went to keep an eye on him, to follow him, as you asked, but when I got there, he was dead. Egretta's there now. She says it looks like poison. I thought you'd want to know."

"Yes, yes, thank you." Meristan sat back on his bed, deflated. No wonder. Their most likely suspect was now a victim. Nirea felt a twang of guilt for disliking the man so much. For suspecting him.

"Now what?" Meristan's face had a grey pallor. Nirea wondered how much he'd slept these past few days. He'd been through a lot for a man whose previous daily exercise was chopping wood. "I mean, it must be connected, right? It can't be coincidence, can it?"

If Calavas killed Conifax—why? Why would he be killed? Because Nirea had gone to his office? Because Meristan and Morienne had searched his rooms? Because both of those things told someone they were suspicious? The records keeper was their best and only lead into Conifax's death—and the answer to that would most likely, she thought, lead to the hand behind everything. The fake mission to Barrock, Glorbad's death, her wounds—it was all connected, she was sure of it.

"Missing somehing. Wha' missing?"

The monk shrugged. She looked to Morienne, who did the same. They'd hit another wall.

"All connegged."

"Agreed," said Meristan. "But how?"

"Who invessigaing Calavah?"

"Opiassa is there, with the guard," said Morienne.

One of their suspects overseeing the investigation of another's murder: messy. They were missing a key. One piece of information that would make sense of everything. Nirea drummed her fingers on the book by her side. The one for which Conifax was probably killed.

Wait. Maybe that was the answer. She looked down at it, and up at Meristan. She'd have to write it down—it was too complicated for her to explain through the ache in her face. But for now, they just needed to know the basics. She'd have to say it carefully, so they'd understand. Taking a deep breath, she carefully licked the spittle from her lips and swallowed.

"We. Lay. Trap."

# CHAPTER 45

Tiny droplets of rain whipped in the swirling wind, hitting Aranok's face like needles. From three stories up it was difficult to tell one from another in the heaving mass of rotted flesh below. By the faint moonlight breaking through the cloud cover, they could see the bodies spread at least two hundred yards in each direction. Of course, Aranok could provide them with some light—but that would defeat the purpose of them coming up to the roof in the dark.

"God almighty," said Allandria.

"God had nothing to do with this," said Samily. They'd used soot to darken her armour, but with the spitting rain it wouldn't stay grimy for long. They needed to move.

Aranok turned to Rasa. "Thank you. I owe you...everything." He opened his arms and she stepped, smiling, into the embrace.

"Look after yourself, Envoy. Eidyn needs men like you." She kissed him gently on the cheek and stepped back. "Goodbye," she said to Allandria, "and good luck."

"Thank you," the archer answered. "For everything."

Rasa crossed to Samily and offered a hand. "It was lovely to meet you, Samily. I hope to see you again."

Samily took her hand without really shaking it. "So do I." The two of them seemed to have made friends in a very short time.

"Tell them everything," said Aranok. "Especially about the relic.

Make sure they get word to Janaeus." They'd given Rasa the full story—Mournside, Weyr, Caer Amon—all of it. None of them had said it out loud, but if the three of them didn't make it out, someone needed to know what they knew.

"If necessary, I will visit the king myself, Laird Envoy." Rasa turned her back to the three of them and unclasped Aranok's cloak. In a moment, it crumpled to the ground and a bat fluttered into the night.

Samily sighed and shook her head. "Miraculous."

Allandria leaned in toward him. "You two seem close."

He smiled. "She's a good kid."

"Should I be jealous?" she asked playfully.

"Always."

She tutted and rolled her eyes.

"Right, then," said Aranok. "How are we doing this?"

The buildings were mostly close together, and though they varied somewhat in height, none were so vastly different as to make getting from one to the next overly difficult. For the wider gaps, which were too far to jump, Aranok used *gluais* to throw the women over, then a quick burst of *gaoth* for himself. It was quicker than the method Allandria and Samily had used to get to him—using the rope to drop to the ground between buildings, then scaling the next one.

Within about half an hour, they'd reached the end of the buildings without alerting the Dead. The street below was sparsely populated with corpses. The Royal Mile ended at a crossroads. East and west, the tenements of Auldun continued to spread on one side of the road, while the three-foot wall marking the edge of the great Nor Loch ran along the other. In better times, families had walked there.

To the north, the Crosscauseway: the wide white stone bridge that ran a mile into the loch, leading to the gates of Dun Eidyn. Two great stone torches stood sentry at its entrance. They'd been alight for generations, only snuffed out to mourn a lost regent, relit three days later to celebrate the new. Like the rest of Auldun, they were cold and dark.

In the middle of the crossroads, the Heartsquare. Amongst the cobbles, a red stone heart the width of two people across. The symbolic heart of the kingdom. A body lay strewn across it, one arm ripped from its socket. The skull was bashed in. Must have been too badly damaged for resurrection. Or maybe, Aranok thought, smiling morbidly to himself, the man just needed a lie-down. They crouched on a rooftop at the southwest corner of the square.

"I make one to our west, three to the south, one, as far as I can see, to the east, on the corner there, and at least three on the bridge," said Allandria. "Plus the one on the heart—assuming it's not already dead."

"They're all dead," said Aranok.

"Shut up."

"If you drop me down, I can take care of them and then you can join me," said Samily.

The casual ease with which the Thorn discussed "taking care" of almost a dozen Dead was oddly comforting, and Aranok smiled despite the situation.

"We need to be quiet about it," he said. "If we make noise, we'll bring that horde we just escaped from."

"Good point," said the knight.

"Suggestions?" said Aranok.

"Well, it's dark," said Allandria. "And these things are stupid. Can you use *gluais* to drop them in the loch?"

*Gluais* used less energy than *gaoth*, and summoning the wind again was likely to get too much attention. But thinking back to his first attempt to get through Auldun reminded Aranok of his original plan, which had not worked then, but might now.

"*Solas.*"

The glowing orb appeared in the palm of his hand.

"What are you . . . ?" Allandria moved to cover the light with her own hands, but Aranok waved her away. With a flick of his wrist, he sent the light to hover above the corpse on the heart. Immediately, the three Dead on the bridge rushed toward it, as did the ones from the east and west. The prone one on the heart didn't move, confirming his belief it was truly dead.

Aranok looked to his right. The Royal Mile stretched away to the south. Of the three Dead within his sight, two were already moving toward the light. As soon as he knew he had all three from the bridge, he waved his hand and sent the light back the way they came. The Dead shuffled, hobbled and stumbled after it, clearing the Heartsquare in moments. The noise from the south intensified as other corpses caught sight of the light and became agitated. He'd keep it moving for a few more minutes, then let it die.

"Nicely done," said Allandria. Aranok effected a small bow, choosing not to mention how he'd tried it once already with less success.

Once they were sure there were no more Dead to appear from the closes, Aranok carefully dropped Samily and Allandria to the ground, then stepped off the roof himself and landed on a cushion of air. Allandria was looking round the corner, back the way they had come. She gave him a quick thumbs-up, and they carefully stalked across the Heartsquare to the Crosscauseway entrance.

Aranok dropped the *solas* spell as they walked along the bridge. Dun Eidyn's great silhouette loomed ahead of them. The first castle in Eidyn, it had been built on the most defensible piece of land imaginable. A mile offshore in the Nor Loch, a huge slab of rock stabbed up from the water with a great crack right up the middle, within which the land naturally sloped down from the top to sea level. It was as if it had been designed to put a castle on top.

At first, only boats could access what was once called the Nor Rock, and building materials were ferried back and forth. It was dangerous work—many of the stonemasons who raised the castle did not live to see it finished. But it was clear that accessing a castle by boat alone was impractical, and so the Crosscauseway was built simultaneously— a bridge between the castle and the mainland. That had required *draoidh* assistance, to lay the foundations in the treacherous depths of the Nor Loch. Auldun was founded on the shore as a village where the stonemasons and other tradesmen lived. First, travelling merchants arrived, and when it became apparent the work would take many years, a permanent market was set up, quickly followed by taverns, inns and brothels—everything a thriving, working community needed.

A decade later, the Nor Rock had been renamed Castle Rock and Auldun was a permanent settlement. Since it was largely inhabited by stonemasons, they took to building their own homes. The limited materials were used for tenement buildings, which housed as many as six families in each.

Of course, he only knew this history because he'd been able to go to the university in Traverlyn. All *draoidhs* were accepted as a matter of course, but the rest had to pay—unless they were in some way exceptional and impressed the masters with their talent. That had always been the way; it was how the university was funded—until Janaeus. He wanted his people educated, so he diverted crown funds to support the university and encouraged the wealthy to do the same. Many had—some because they accepted his argument that a better-educated populace would build a better country, some to gain favour with the new king. Either way, it had worked. The university had expanded, bringing in new masters, building new accommodation—expanding their reach. They'd brought the Traverlyn hospital under their auspices and trained more medics than ever before.

It was all part of Janaeus's vision for Eidyn. The better future.

"Should we be concerned about being followed?" Samily glanced back over her shoulder.

"No," said Aranok. "If we are, I'll put a wall across the bridge. That'll stop…"

He was cut off, as the rain suddenly turned from spitting to downpour. The deluge thundered against the loch, bouncing off the stone of the bridge. It was difficult to hear over the roar.

"Fuck!" Aranok vainly tried to shield his face with his hands as he pulled up his hood. A quick glance at the others and their stealthy march toward Dun Eidyn became a run. The stones were slick beneath them, so they couldn't go full pelt. Aranok was passingly impressed, again, at how quickly Samily could move in her white armour—which was getting more and more white by the second as water streamed down it, leaving streaks of gathered soot in its wake.

Water poured out of the drainage holes in the side walls as the deluge worsened. It was difficult to see more than a few yards in front of them. The wind was making it worse, of course, slapping them in the face one moment, knocking them sideways the next.

"What's that?" Samily, who was slightly ahead of them both, had stopped and drawn her sword, holding it across their path as a warning.

Aranok shielded his eyes and tried to look ahead. All he could see was the shadow of Dun Eidyn—they were nearly at the gate, where the bridge met Castle Rock.

*Shit.*

She was right. Something was moving up ahead. Something big.

Allandria drew her sword—her arrows would be all but useless in this weather. Aranok charged his armour. Without a word passing between them, Samily shifted her sword to a ready position and they began moving again, cautiously.

After twenty yards he could just about make it out. It must have been twenty feet tall and had at least four legs—maybe six. If it wasn't for the white stone of the bridge and the rain, it would have seen Samily already. For a change, her white armour was camouflage.

Suddenly, the shadow jerked into life. It came bounding through the rain toward them—so wide, its feet were on the side walls of the bridge. Samily held up a hand. Aranok and Allandria both stopped, bracing themselves for whatever was coming.

They weren't ready.

A huge, gaping mouth lurched toward them.

"Fire!" Samily shouted as she and Allandria both rolled away to the sides.

*"Teine!"* Aranok followed the order and a plume of fire burst from his hands.

The beast reared its head back with a resonant shriek. In the burst of light, he'd seen it better. It was a giant lizard, with green-gold scales and a red streak on its head. Its huge mouth had two rows of ice-pick teeth, and three yellow eyes glowered down at him from each side of its head. He'd never seen a demon that big before. It roared and swiped a leg toward Samily. Her sword dripped blood. She must have wounded it already.

"Allandria! Leg!" the knight shouted. Allandria rolled toward the demon and brought her blade across the back of its knee. It shrieked again, losing its footing and falling toward Allandria.

*"Gluais."* Aranok pulled her back toward him as the monster landed hard on its side. Aranok flicked his head, trying to shake off some of the rain running down his face, into his eyes. His hood had come down at some point, and water was pouring through his hair.

Samily appeared on the demon's other side as Aranok helped Allandria to her feet.

"Eyes!" the Thorn bellowed as she plunged her sword down into the beast's side.

Allandria threw down her blade and lifted the bow from her back, nocking two arrows in one fluid movement. At this distance, hopefully the wind wouldn't make too much difference. One arrow flew wildly past, but the other struck the largest eye in its exposed side.

The beast screamed again and rolled back, throwing Samily off-balance. She slipped and disappeared from sight.

"Samily!" Aranok bellowed into the rain.

"Go!" Allandria nocked another pair of arrows, moving closer to the beast's head. Aranok tried to move around the right side, to see where the knight had landed. The demon roared again. Allandria must have taken another eye.

"No!" Samily's voice came from somewhere beside the demon. "Help Allandria!"

He paused. Was the knight warning him off because she was fine or because she was prepared to sacrifice herself? He didn't have time to consider. If anyone could look after themself, it was Samily.

He moved back to Allandria's side. She'd got too close. The demon jerked its head and caught her, knocking her backwards onto the stone. It turned its great head sideways and snapped toward her.

"*Gaoth.*" A powerful wind knocked the head back the way it had come, away from the archer. She scrambled to her feet but looked unsteady—whether because of the weather or the fall was hard to tell.

All three of the demon's eyes on the left were now closed and bleeding. One still had an arrow jutting from it. It shook its head as if to remove an annoying insect.

Allandria lifted her sword from the bridge and raised it defensively. The beast regained its footing. Its elongated neck moved like a snake, the head dancing back and forth before them. It was wary of them now. It knew they could hurt it. But maybe that made it more dangerous. More careful.

It roared again and half turned on the bridge, snapping at something beneath it.

Aranok took the distraction as a cue and threw another burst of flames at the exposed right side of its head. At the eyes. It worked. All three smoked and crackled under the barrage. The blind monster howled with rage. It thrashed its head and stomped toward them. It might not be able to see, but it could still crush them. He and Allandria turned and ran—they had nowhere to go except over the side and in this weather that meant they'd be as good as dead the moment they hit the choppy water. The only question was whether they'd drown before they were crushed by the huge waves.

The demon roared again and reared its head. This time, it stopped completely and turned, its tail slashing across the bridge. It caught Aranok's legs and knocked him sideways. He scrambled to get a handhold but slammed against something and the wind was knocked from him. For a moment his eyes went black and he felt the rising panic as his lungs tried and failed to breathe in. He felt a hand on his shoulder.

"You all right?" said Allandria. He rolled onto his side and reached for her, gesturing frantically at his mouth. His heart was pounding in his chest. He needed air. *Now. Now!*

Allandria grabbed his head and pressed her lips against his. With a rush of breath, his lungs burst open. He coughed it out and sucked in more. Hells, he'd never been more glad to take a breath of cold wet air. He gasped another few lungfuls before his head began to clear.

"Can you stand?" Allandria shouted over the wind.

He got up to one knee, then used the wall to get back to his feet. The wall. That was what he'd crashed against. Probably saved him from the loch.

"Come on!" Allandria jogged back toward the fight. But they had another problem. The fight had drawn attention. Attention they didn't want.

The Dead were coming. He could only see the first of them—the fastest, the ones with the most sinew and muscle, but there was no doubt the rest were coming. He needed to stop them.

"*Balla na talamh.*" The bridge ripped itself apart and re-formed as a wall of white, cutting them off from the Dead. It also blocked their escape. They'd have to worry about that later.

Aranok turned back to the fight. The demon's head darted about. It stomped its front feet. Samily was still fighting somewhere on the other side.

Allandria tried to get close, but the demon's thrashing tail kept her back. Aranok was still breathing heavily and feeling light-headed.

"Aranok!" Samily's voice carried over the cacophony. "Wind!"

Hell, did he even have enough left for a *gaoth* spell? And where?

The monster reared up onto its back legs and he knew exactly what she wanted. He breathed deep and, with every ounce of strength left in him, bellowed, "*Gaoth!*"

He threw his arms together, blasting the demon with everything he had, battering into its side. Even with the huge toes it had gripping the walls, the gale was too much. It jerked to the side, head thrashing, trying to regain its balance. With a strangled cry, the huge mass lurched over the side of the bridge and into the tempestuous waters. As it rolled over the side, Aranok saw the macabre pattern of bloody slashes on its belly—Samily had hit it hard.

Damned thing never stood a chance.

They both rushed to the knight, who was panting heavily. She leaned on her thighs, her sword dangling against the stone.

"Brilliant!" shouted Allandria.

Samily put up a hand in acknowledgement. She'd been exceptional—not just a brilliant soldier, but a leader. The knight had marshalled them, used their strengths and made them work together. She'd easily taken charge of her elders. The Thorn had been taught well and would make a brilliant general.

"Come on." Samily stood straight again. "Let's move."

Despite the continued downpour, they moved more slowly now. With the immediate danger past, Aranok could feel the throbbing pains where his back had hit the wall. The muscles were beginning to seize up, and pain shot down his right leg with each step.

Finally, they reached the end of the Crosscauseway. They were sheltered from the wind, if not the rain, by the crevasse in Castle Rock. It felt like a reprieve. The rain seemed to be easing off too, though it was still pouring. They huddled against one wall.

"How are you doing?" Allandria asked.

"Tired," said Samily. "We lost. Three times."

"What?" Surely not. She didn't have that kind of power. Did she?

"We lost. I had to go back."

"I don't understand," said Allandria.

Aranok did. Samily's planning, her reactions, had seemed almost prescient. Because they were. She'd seen it before.

"Rasa said I could fix mistakes," said the knight.

"Who died?" asked Aranok.

The knight looked up at him with hooded eyes. "Both of you. You on the first attack," she said to him, "and then you," to Allandria. "It ate you."

Allandria gasped, covering her mouth. "Honestly?"

Samily nodded.

"The third time?" Aranok's mind was still trying to wrap itself around the impossible story she was telling.

"I slipped on the wet stone. When I fell—it stamped on me. Broke my back."

Hells. That must have been agony. And yet, the girl had stayed conscious. And strong enough to turn back time—for a third time!

"You must be exhausted," he said.

"No more than you." But she could barely stand, now he got a better look at her.

"Samily—you did that once at Wrychtishousis. It wiped you out. How did you survive three?" he asked.

She smiled weakly. "My teacher told me to practise conserving my energy."

He put a hand on her shoulder. "Incredible. Miraculous." It was all that and more.

Samily looked up at him with delight.

"Agreed." Allandria still looked a little rattled at the idea she'd just been eaten by a demon but would never remember it. "Thank you."

"Can you walk?" he asked. The rain was finally slowing down now. Of course.

"Let's give her a minute," said Allandria.

Aranok nodded. He could do with a rest too. Samily slid to the ground and sat with her arms resting on her raised knees. Aranok daren't sit, or his back might not let him up again. He realised with a chill that even if he'd got this far alone, he'd be dead. Had he really expected to make it on his own? Hells, that line of thought led down a dark path he wasn't ready to walk. The cold excused his shiver.

They stood for a while silently in the wet dark—exhausted, sore and very, very lucky to be alive.

Mynygogg waited above.

# CHAPTER 46

There are many ways to lock a gate. The best is magic. While the gates of Dun Eidyn would of course open from the inside, they could also be opened from the outside under certain circumstances. One of these was when the person outside knew exactly which part of the sheer rock face was concealing a secret lever. Aranok ran his hand over the area where he roughly knew it to be and found the edge of the hatch. He pushed on it and it clicked open, revealing the iron handle inside. The huge iron gates groaned open as he pulled it.

"Isn't that a risk?" asked Samily, as the three of them approached the stone steps rising to the castle.

"Only if anybody knew it existed." Aranok pulled the lever's more obvious companion on the inside to swing the gates closed again.

By the time they reached the top, Aranok's knees were on fire. He'd burned through too much energy in that fight, and so had Samily. She looked as bad as he felt. Should they abort this attack? How could they hope to take on Mynygogg in this state? But what was the alternative? Getting this far was always going to be hard. Especially if he summoned an even worse demon to guard the entrance. There was half a chance the storm had disguised their battle, but there was also a good chance he knew they were coming.

Allandria was the only one still fit for anything. As brilliant as she was, she couldn't take down Mynygogg on her own.

"Let's take a minute in here." He gestured to a guard hut. They quickly ducked inside. It was good to be out of the rain, even if they were already soaked.

There was a pair of chairs and a table inside, and a small hearth. It smelled of damp and dust. Aranok and Samily took a chair each. He ran his hands through his soaking hair, wringing water down his shoulders and shaking the rest off his hands.

"We can't do this." Allandria looked at Samily, then back at him. "Look at the two of you. You can hardly walk. If we go into that castle now, we might as well have let that demon eat us."

Aranok shivered. Probably the wet and the cold. "I know. I've been thinking about it."

"Good." Allandria's face changed. "Wait. Is it good?"

She wasn't going to like it.

"This is our best chance. If he's asleep, or he just hasn't seen us coming, he won't be expecting us. By tomorrow, at best, he'll look out a window and see his demon's gone. Then he'll be on guard, and our chance is lost. It has to be tonight."

Allandria rolled her eyes. "So what are we going to do? Throw rocks at him? Or are you expecting me to take out the most dangerous *draoidh* in history with this?" She proffered an arrow at him.

"No," said Samily. "He's going to have me heal him."

"Do you think you can?" Aranok wasn't sure it would work. But if it did, it was their best option. Their only option.

"In theory. If I take you back to before the fight, your energy levels could be replenished."

"What about your energy levels?" Allandria asked the knight.

"I'm not coming with you."

She understood.

"Absolutely not," said Allandria. "We can't leave you here alone."

"No, we can't," said Aranok. That was the part she wasn't going to like.

Allandria stared at him. "No. Not a chance."

"It's the only way. We need one of us at full strength. Now. And somebody needs to stay with Samily."

"No, Aranok. We've had this discussion. You are not going in there alone."

He didn't want it to be this way. After everything, he'd rather have them both with him. But they couldn't wait. If Samily could restore him, at least he'd have a chance. "Listen, summoning demons takes time and energy. If Mynygogg planned on the one we killed keeping us out, he might not have any inside. Maybe some shifters, like Weyr. I can handle them. They burn. There shouldn't be any Dead. We evacuated the castle." He took her hand and looked her in the eye. "What other choice do we have?"

She pulled her hand away. "We wait, and we go in the morning. You two sleep."

"We can't risk that. I've already said..."

"Then we sleep for a few hours. Both of you get some time to recover, get yourselves to a decent level..."

"It won't be enough." Aranok traced his finger across the table. "This is the only way."

"No. I'm sorry, Envoy, it is not," said Samily. "There is a better solution. Leave me here and you both go."

That was a ridiculous idea. He wasn't leaving her here to die. He could be wrong about more demons, about the Dead. She'd be completely defenceless. "Samily, you're likely to be unconscious."

"Then I will be well rested when I wake."

"So it's all right for you to go alone, but not to leave Samily alone?" Allandria paced in the small space she had to move.

"I'll be awake!" Aranok threw his hands in the air. Surely she could see the difference.

"I may well be fine, Envoy," said Samily. "I could sleep here soundly, undisturbed. You are definitely walking into a fight. You need Allandria more than I do."

"No," said Aranok. "I'm not leaving you alone."

"Oh really?" Allandria crossed her arms. "And how do you propose to make me stay here?"

He hadn't thought of that. He could order her to stay. But then he'd have ordered her—and she'd have ignored it.

"Aranok." Samily reached across the table and placed her hand on his arm. "You do not believe in God. You do not believe that God has put us together on this path. I do. It is as clear to me as you are, sitting before me. I saved your lives. You taught me how. Our fates are intertwined, Laird Envoy. And I do not believe God is finished with us yet."

Aranok stood and was sharply reminded of his injuries as pain shot down his back and through his legs.

"Damn it!" he shouted. "We're not doing this!"

"Fine," said Allandria. "Then let's all rest up and go home."

"We can't do that!"

"Then stop fucking arguing with me and let's go!"

The two of them stood and stared at each other. Why wouldn't she listen?

"Envoy, with respect, this is not your decision," Samily said calmly. "I will heal you or I will come with you. If I heal you, Allandria is coming with you, with my blessing. Your choice is only between the three of us going, like this"—she waved a hand over her own body—"or the two of you going. Those are your only choices."

Aranok ran his hand over his head. What kind of choice was that? Get them all killed or just leave Samily to die?

"Come on, Aranok." Allandria's voice had softened. "Please, let's not have this argument again."

"Fine," he said, exasperated. "But if she dies…" He jabbed a finger at Samily.

"If I die, then it is my time to be with God," said Samily. "And I will be at peace."

"Meristan will never forgive me."

The knight smiled. "He will, when you tell him it was my choice."

---

They found a bedroll stashed in a cupboard in the wall of the hut and set Samily up on it before she healed Aranok. Allandria hadn't realised just how grey he had been looking until she saw him revived. It was ridiculous to think they could have faced Mynygogg with him in that state. As Aranok had expected, using the last gasp of her energy knocked Samily out cold. Allandria laid Samily's head down carefully before checking her breathing and heartbeat. There was no key for the door, so Aranok used *gluais* to close the latch behind them, locking Samily inside. She was as safe as they could make her.

Back out in the rain, Allandria wondered whether the knight was the lucky one.

They crossed the square in silence, passing the giant Princes Fountain. Rain rattled in its limpid pools. It was odd seeing it still. She'd never been here before when it wasn't running—like a joyous welcome home.

It was somehow fitting, she thought, that after everything they'd been through to get here—everyone who'd been with them, everyone they'd lost—it came down to Aranok and her facing Mynygogg together.

Aranok raised a hand and pointed ahead. She saw why. Despite all the security they had faced getting here, the portcullis was raised and the heavy iron gates that should have barred their way lay open.

"Odd," she said quietly.

"Very."

They'd briefly discussed getting into the castle, but finding the entrance open was not an option they'd foreseen. She grabbed the *draoidh*'s arm.

"What if he's not trapped? What if this is a trap? For us?"

He nodded with a resigned grimace. They were going anyway.

But they were going carefully. She crept back around the fountain to come at the entrance tunnel from the left. Once she had a good line of sight, she signalled him and they slowly approached. At the outer wall, she crouched and peered around the corner. Nothing. It looked dead, abandoned. It was horrible seeing the place that had been home for so long now just an empty shell. She couldn't reconcile the two—it was like a different place entirely. A bad dream.

She waved Aranok on and the two of them crept in. The smack of their wet footsteps echoed off the tunnel walls. Light kindled around Aranok's fist, and she drew the bow from her back. They reached the end of the tunnel unassailed and looked carefully out into the courtyard leading to the inner doors. Nothing. Just more rain.

Aranok stepped out, beckoning her to follow.

Something battered into her, knocking her on her back.

Allandria instinctively rolled over her shoulder and came up on one knee, bow raised. She frantically scanned the area. What had hit her?

It took her a moment to realise Aranok was standing looking at her, dumbfounded.

"What was it?" she asked. "Where did it go?"

"What was what? What happened?"

"The thing that hit me!"

Aranok stepped back into the tunnel. "Allandria, nothing hit you. You just... fell over."

"What? No." She felt her face where it was tender from the impact. "Something hit me."

"I don't know what to tell you," said Aranok. "There's nothing here."

He put a hand down to help her to her feet. She took it, looking around warily. "Seriously. Something hit me."

"I believe you. So this time, let's be on guard."

She had been on guard the first time.

Again, they approached the tunnel exit slowly. Aranok stepped out; Allandria was thrown back. This time, she stayed on her feet. "There! What was that?"

"I don't know. It was like you walked into a wall." Aranok stepped back inside the tunnel and waved his arms in the air. "I don't understand."

Allandria walked forward again and, this time, carefully reached out a hand. As soon as it was about to breach the end of the tunnel, she felt resistance. Just as he'd said—like a wall that wasn't there.

"What the Hell?" She looked at Aranok. The *draoidh* easily passed the apparent barrier again, but no matter where she tried to follow him, her path was blocked.

"Bizarre." He ran his hand over the stone at the edge of the tunnel. "It has to be magic, but I've never seen anything like it."

"Why isn't it affecting you? Why just me?" A horrible thought occurred to her. Surely not. But she had to ask. "Aranok... did you do this?"

The look of confusion and disbelief on his face suggested he hadn't, which was a relief.

"I don't even know how to." He spread his arms. "I don't know what it is."

"So it's Mynygogg?"

"Must be." He shrugged.

"All right. What do we do?"

The *draoidh*'s face changed, and suddenly she knew what he was thinking. "Aranok, no."

"What?"

"Do not tell me to go back. Do not go on your own." She was suddenly very aware that, as he was on the other side of whatever barrier was holding her out, she literally couldn't touch him.

"It seems like that's the only option, doesn't it?"

Allandria pulled her sword from her sheath and swung it wildly. It bounced back. He was not leaving her there. He was not going in alone, God damn it. She screamed with burning frustration and swung again with every ounce of strength she had. The force threw her back on her arse.

"Don't. Do it," she said tersely. After everything, if he left now, she might never forgive him.

"Allandria," he said calmly, carefully staying outside the tunnel. "What choice do I have? I don't know how to get you in." He turned and walked toward the inner doors.

"Aranok!" She got back to her feet, feeling the anger rising. "This is a trap. You're walking into a fucking trap! Stop."

He turned and quietly said, "I'm sorry."

She punched the barrier so hard she'd have broken her hand if it were stone. It just threw her arm back again as if it were nothing.

"Fuck you," she spat. "You spoiled, petulant idiot. I hope you get yourself killed. God damn you."

If he heard, he didn't react. She watched him cross the courtyard in silence until she could barely see him pass through the inner doors and into the dark of Dun Eidyn.

And then he was gone.

---

Aranok went straight for the king's chambers; if he were Mynygogg he'd certainly claim the nicest bedchambers in the castle for himself. But the room was empty. It did, however, show signs of recent habitation. The bedsheets were a mess and the room had some residual warmth—the fire had been lit recently. It smelled inhabited—that sweet, musky smell of sleeping bodies lingered in the room, which obviously hadn't been cleaned in some time.

Aranok had been forced to use *solas* once he entered the castle, since some of the internal hallways let in no light whatsoever, depending entirely on torches when the building was inhabited. The little ball of light now illuminated the grand doors to the second room he thought worth searching—the throne room. So far, he'd been right about the lack of demons and Dead. If there were any here, they'd be with Mynygogg.

He grabbed the large brass ring and turned the handle. The loud metallic clunk of the latch releasing echoed in the corridor. Light spilled into the room as the thick oak door swung open. The only light in the room. If Mynygogg was there, he was sitting in the dark.

Aranok entered slowly, his senses on high alert for any sound, any twitch of movement. He was probably at his most vulnerable here in the vast central hall of the castle. A demon that could see in the dark would… He increased the strength of his light enough to see the length of the room. The familiar vaulted arches ran down each side, with balconies above them where the "lesser" nobles traditionally gathered for ceremonial occasions. Janaeus had done away with that tradition, amongst many others.

The great banner bearing the Eidyn coat of arms still hung on the far wall, just above the dais, which held the true throne. The seat of power that his closest friend belonged on—not hiding in Haven, miles away. Seeing the throne brought an unexpected surge of bile in his throat. How dare Mynygogg sit there? How dare he occupy this castle, which represented so much good, so much hope for the people of Eidyn?

A faint scraping made him stop. The door at the rear of the hall, behind the throne, creaked open. A figure stepped in, wearing a nightshirt and robe, carrying a plate in one hand and an oil lamp in the other. His long black hair was bedraggled and his beard was unkempt. But Aranok knew him.

*Mynygogg.*

"*Teine.*" An arc of fire burst across the room. Catch him now, off guard, and he might be able to end this quickly.

Aranok's mouth fell open. Somehow, the bastard had been prepared. The fire arced around him, as if hitting another invisible sphere, striking the door behind him instead. It blackened, then caught.

Mynygogg stood completely unharmed.

"Well, that was a new experience." The dark *draoidh* turned and looked back at the door. "Would you mind putting that out, before it burns down the castle?"

# CHAPTER 47

Mynygogg walked calmly to the throne and sat, setting the oil lamp on the stone table next to him. Aranok rubbed his fingers across his palms. How had he deflected the fire? Was it like the wall in the tunnel? Did Mynygogg have a *draoidh* skill he'd never seen?

"It's good to see you, Aranok. How are you?"

"*Creag.*" Three stones pulled free of the floor and hurtled at the throne. Mynygogg instinctively put up a hand in defence, dropping the plate. The stones smashed and fell to the ground inches in front of him as the plate landed with a clang, spilling its contents across the floor.

Mynygogg, wide-eyed, gave him a chastising look. "Please stop that. We have a lot to talk about."

Aranok felt the rage burst inside him. He ran at the *draoidh*, screaming. If magic wouldn't work...

Mynygogg stood. Aranok punched wildly with his right hand, but the man wasn't there. He stepped to the side and deflected Aranok's arm, his fist crunching against the throne. Pain shot up his hand. He turned and swung again with his left. Again the *draoidh* was too quick. He stepped back, deflecting Aranok's swing up and over his head. Again, Aranok swung, again; each time Mynygogg simply stepped away and deflected the punches. Exasperated, Aranok threw himself at him. Mynygogg crouched, grabbed Aranok's arm, pivoted and threw him across the floor.

Aranok rolled onto his front, ignoring the pain throbbing in his right hand. Mynygogg stood, looking down at him. "You can't hurt me."

Aranok scrambled to his feet and backed against a pillar. He was prepared for demons, for Dead, but not for this. How could he beat him if he couldn't touch him?

Mynygogg turned and walked back to the throne. He tutted, lifted the plate and carefully picked at what appeared to be bread and cheese amongst the rubble of the stones.

"Seriously." He looked back at Aranok. "Could you put out that door?"

The fire was getting worse. Fine. If he had to burn down Dun Eidyn to rid it of Mynygogg's plague, he would. The *draoidh* appeared to recognise his lack of action for the defiance it was.

"Aranok, I don't want to fight you. I'm not going to hurt you. We just need to talk."

"I'm not helping you get out of here. Nothing you say is going to work."

Mynygogg sat on the throne again and Aranok felt another surge of anger, seeing the bastard who'd half destroyed the kingdom sit in his best friend's rightful place.

"I'm not trapped," said Mynygogg. "Nothing's keeping me here. You must have seen for yourself. I presume you weren't stupid enough to come here alone? Allandria wouldn't have let you, surely?"

He knew about Allandria? Their names were relatively well-known amongst the public, but he was genuinely surprised Mynygogg knew them both. Knowing the name of the king's envoy was one thing, but knowing his bodyguard...

"The wall," Aranok said. "In the tunnel. How did you do that?"

"I didn't. Odd that it only let you in, though, isn't it?"

*Fuck.*

Mynygogg wanted him here. Allandria had been right. It was a trap. But why? So far, all the man seemed to want to do was talk. Was he stalling for time? For a demon to arrive? Aranok hadn't seen him perform any gestures or incantations—both of which were necessary for demon summoning. The most he seemed intent on doing was having dinner.

"Seriously, Aranok. Put out the door." His voice was oddly imperious, and Aranok actually felt a compulsion to do what he said.

The flames had started licking at the stone ceiling and were in danger of reaching the cloth banner on the wall. Whatever Mynygogg was planning, Aranok was part of it. Maybe he needed to see it out. He could always set another fire.

Never taking his eyes off the usurper, he crossed to the burning door and used *uisge* to extinguish the flames. The floor was slick with water. What was left of the door was a black, charred mess.

"Thank you," said Mynygogg. "Now, pull up a chair and we can talk."

The side walls were lined with ornate wooden chairs for visiting nobles. Aranok lifted one and dragged it under an arch. He sat, holding his right hand protectively in his left. His middle knuckles were already swollen and purple.

"You're going to sit over there?" Mynygogg crossed his legs. Aranok stared silently back at him. He had to work out what the *draoidh*'s game was—and he needed a safe distance between them to give him time to react to whatever was coming. "All right. How about increasing the light, at least? So we can see each other?"

That was a good idea. Aranok cast *luisnich* on one of the giant stone tiles in the middle of the room, and the whole of the great hall was lit. Now he could clearly see it all. The intricate painted frescos above the arches, depicting the history of Eidyn. The beautiful vaulted ceiling. The stained-glass windows, celebrating God, which Janaeus had chosen to leave in place despite his own lack of faith, because it showed acceptance of those who believed.

"That's better," said Mynygogg. "All right. Let's begin. Your name is Aranok. Your parents are Sumara and Dorann. Your sister is Ikara. You were born and raised in Mournside, thanks to your father's clothing business. You have a complicated relationship with your father. He never accepted you as a *draoidh*."

Aranok felt a chill run through him. Was he threatening his family? He felt another urge to rush him but resisted the instinct. He needed to think. To understand what was happening.

"Ikara is married to Pol, who you hate, understandably, since he is an arsehole," said Mynygogg.

Aranok snorted and almost laughed.

"They have a daughter, Emelina. Pol is not her father. Her real father was Korvin."

The chill worsened. How the Hell could he know that? Outside of his family, only Allandria and Janaeus knew that. They hadn't even told Korvin's family, at Dorann's insistence.

"Korvin was murdered by a group of anti-*draoidh* bastards. You found him."

Aranok was beginning to shake. How did he know all this?

"His death almost destroyed you. You spent months finding his killers." Mynygogg looked him straight in the eye. "And you burned them for it."

Aranok's mouth fell open. Three people knew that. One was dead.

"Do you understand?" Mynygogg asked.

Aranok shook his head.

"I know you, Aranok. First, we need you to understand that."

It was a threat. What was he going to demand? Aranok felt his teeth grind.

"You know me too," said Mynygogg.

"What?" Aranok had seen Mynygogg in person only a few times, but they'd never spoken. He had actually been a little surprised the *draoidh* recognised him.

"All right. All right." Mynygogg ran his hand over his chin. "Let's start at the beginning. Who do you think I am?"

"Who do I think you are?" asked Aranok. "A fucking lunatic who murdered half of Eidyn."

"All right." Mynygogg nodded. His voice was deep and dark, but measured. "That makes sense. How did I do that?"

"With your demons. And the Dead."

"Demons and Dead? Both?"

"Apparently."

"Hmm." He was quiet for a bit. Aranok chose not to fill the silence. He wasn't going to accidentally give away information the bastard wanted.

"Has a *draoidh* ever had two skills before?" Mynygogg eventually asked.

"You'd know better than me."

"All right." Mynygogg rolled his eyes. "Let's try something else. This might be uncomfortable. I'm sorry. What's the last thing you can clearly remember doing, maybe two, three weeks ago?"

"I'm not playing games with you." Whatever he was doing, Aranok needed to move it along. If Mynygogg was waiting for something, some things, to arrive, Aranok needed to act first. He just had to figure out exactly what to do. Burn the banner and pull it down on him? Maybe...

"You don't have to answer me," said Mynygogg. "I just want you to think about it. Find the oldest moment you clearly remember from that time."

Drinking with Allandria. Vastin. The forge.

"Now," said Mynygogg, "what were you doing the day before? How did you get to that place? Try to remember something specific. What did you eat? Who were you with? What did you talk about?"

"I told you, I'm not playing your game."

"What about the last few weeks? Have you come across things that don't make sense?"

He had. Plenty. His face must have betrayed the answer. Mynygogg smiled oddly. "All right. Have you had trouble remembering anything? Maybe something you were sure you should know? Or maybe you've had difficulty thinking clearly? Especially under pressure?"

Aranok stared back at him, doing his best to keep his face a blank mask. He had made some bad decisions. Throwing himself at the demon in Mutton Hole; not using the rooftops in Auldun. Things that, looking back, he should have done differently.

Mynygogg fixed him with a hard stare. "Aranok, this is going to be difficult to believe, but please try to open your mind. Don't speak, just think about this. If you do, you'll see it makes complete sense. In fact, I'll wager it will explain a number of things for you.

"Aranok, your memory has been altered. I'm not who you think I am."

Aranok swallowed hard. How to react? Maybe playing along, for now, would draw out his plan. But still, he needed to move the conversation. No way to know how much time he had. "By who?"

Mynygogg smiled wearily. "Truthfully? By a *draoidh* we underestimated. We thought his skill was just a trick—a gimmick for the stage. We didn't allow for him getting the heart. We didn't think it was real. By the time we realised... it was too late."

*The relic.* Of course. It had to be here somewhere. If Mynygogg didn't have it with him, it must be somewhere safe. The bedchamber. Damn it, he should have searched it properly. Too bloody eager to find Mynygogg. Careless.

"There's no such thing as a memory *draoidh*." There was no record of such a skill anywhere in the history books. He'd never even heard it suggested as a possible skill. Even healing had been conjectured for centuries despite there never being a recognised *draoidh* with that skill.

"Of course." Mynygogg nodded. "He would've taken that. Better if you didn't believe it possible."

He was quiet again. Having Allandria for backup would have been ideal. She would have put an arrow in him several times over by now. Maybe a real weapon would pierce whatever barrier he'd created around himself.

"Let's see what you do remember," said Mynygogg. "Why am I here?"

Aranok blinked in incomprehension. "What do you mean?"

"I'm trapped here, right? Who trapped me? How am I trapped?"

Aranok felt the world tilt beneath him, as he realised... he didn't know.

How could he not know? He was the king's envoy. And yet, all the time he'd been sure Mynygogg was trapped in Dun Eidyn, he hadn't known how. Or who had trapped him. He'd never thought about it. How could that be?

"All right, good, good," said Mynygogg. "That's a good sign. You're pushing at the boundaries."

The sudden nausea must have been evident on his face.

Why didn't he know?

"Do you remember the Hellfire Club?" asked Mynygogg.

The words sparked an odd emotion in Aranok's gut, but he couldn't remember hearing the name before. He shook his head but regretted it as the nausea was joined by dizziness.

"The Hellfire Club was a group of people who met in Auldun. There was an earth *draoidh*, an illusionist, a demon summoner, a necromancer and... a memory *draoidh*."

The dizziness got worse. His head began to pound.

"They were kids. Rejected by society. They were angry and resentful. Understandably. They practised their abilities and talked about changing the world—taking over, some said. They helped one another survive. Some had an easier time of it. Eventually, all but one went to Traverlyn. The eldest. The demon summoner. He was too resentful. Too angry. The masters rejected him. They worried teaching him to better use his abilities would be dangerous.

"After that, the group drifted apart. They made other friends. They continued to meet—once or twice a year—but the meetings were fractious. By then, they disagreed about the world. About the future. Things had changed for some. Not for others. When the illusionist was murdered, the earth *draoidh* withdrew completely. He never went back. But the others... the others were emboldened. The others were angry. The others made plans."

Aranok's head was throbbing. Knives stabbed at his temples and his eyes felt too large for their sockets. What the Hell was happening?

"Aranok, where were you the day before that memory?" Mynygogg asked. "What did you eat? Who did you speak to? Think about it!" The *draoidh* stood and walked to Aranok. He couldn't even lift his head. The room was spinning.

Where had he been the day before the tavern? Riding. He remembered it vividly, but... what about the day before? The day before?

"When was the war declared over, Aranok? How did you hear that you had won?" Mynygogg stepped closer and closer. Aranok slid off the chair onto his knees. He felt the cold stone floor beneath his hands and desperately tried to focus on it—to find his balance.

"Aranok, you're the earth *draoidh*. Korvin, the illusionist. You know that, don't you? The Hellfire Club. Remember."

His stomach churned, flipped and finally surrendered. Aranok fell forward onto his elbows and vomited across the floor of Dun Eidyn's great hall.

"The others were your friends. The necromancer—Shayella."

He didn't know anyone called Shayella. Why did the name feel familiar, though? A rush of discomfort, regret, fear.

"The demon summoner, Anhel Weyr."

"No!" Aranok shook his head. He knew about Weyr. "No. He's your ally."

Aranok vomited again, feeling his stomach squeeze itself into a tight knot. When it stopped, he spat to clear his mouth. Saliva dripped from his lip. He could barely see.

"He tried to kill us. I'd never met him." But now, the odd thing Weyr had said—"You really don't know me. He did it."—came rushing back.

Hells, could it be true? Aranok's eyes were streaming, his head pounding worse than any hangover.

"You had, Aranok. You were friends. You, Korvin, Shayella, Anhel Weyr... and Janaeus."

"No!" Aranok threw himself at Mynygogg. Still the *draoidh* was too quick. He sidestepped and avoided the lunge, leaving Aranok to land in his own puddle of vomit. He rolled onto his side, gasping for breath.

"Yes," said Mynygogg. "We were at war with Weyr and Shayella. They wanted the throne. For *draoidhs*, they claimed. We didn't think Janaeus was a threat. But he found the relic, Aranok. He found the heart of devastation. We sent Meristan after him, but he never came back."

That made no sense. "Meristan?" Aranok spat again. "The monk?!"

Mynygogg was stunned silent for a moment, then burst into a full-throated laugh. "I'm sorry, I shouldn't laugh, but... a monk? The Great Bear, God's Own Blade... thinks he's a monk? My God, that's almost brilliant."

Aranok was still light-headed. He wasn't getting enough air, and he couldn't slow down his breathing.

"Aranok, I can fix this," Mynygogg said gently. "We planned for this."

The *draoidh* reached into the neck of his nightgown and brought out two pendants. Aranok's eyes struggled to focus, but it looked like one was made of stone with carved runes, and one was a dark yellow ball. Was that how he did it? Resisted Aranok's magic?

Mynygogg held up the stone first. "You gave me this. Do you remember? You made it for Allandria, after you wounded her in a battle. You made it to protect her from your magic. Remember?"

Aranok couldn't even speak now. He wanted to scream no, but his mouth wouldn't work. He could barely even breathe. His heart pounded in his chest.

*Fuck.*

"Aranok, you're in shock. Try to take deep breaths, slowly." His voice was warm. Gentle.

Familiar.

"Can you see what I'm holding?"

Aranok's head was swimming.

"Come on, Aranok, slow breaths. You can do this. In the nose, out the mouth."

He focused on his breathing. His whole body was shaking.

*In.*

*Out.*

*In.*

*Out.*

*In.*

*Out.*

Aranok looked up at Mynygogg. His limbs were like water. He couldn't feel his feet.

"Can you see this?" Mynygogg asked again.

The yellow ball. There was something inside it. Something small.

"You gave me this," he said. "The barrier let you into Dun Eidyn because you created it, Aranok. You created it specifically only to let you in. I'm here because you left me here and told me to stay until you came back."

Aranok felt his heart pounding again, as if it would burst at any moment and rip his rib cage from his chest. God, he'd waited too long. Whatever Mynygogg was doing to him, he couldn't fight it.

"You left me the key to removing the spell." He crouched down beside Aranok. "All you have to do is hold this"—he took the leather strap from around his neck and held the yellow ball out to Aranok—"and say the word *clìor.*"

"No!" Aranok tried to bat the jewel away, but Mynygogg caught his hand and placed the ball in his palm.

"Come on, Aranok. You have to know this is true. You have to feel it. He can change what you remember, but not what you feel. Come on. You trust me. You trust me. Listen to my voice."

"No!" Spittle flew from Aranok's lips and tears streamed down his face. "No!"

Mynygogg wrapped his hands around Aranok's fist, holding the jewel in place. "Come on!" He sounded desperate for the first time. "Please, Aranok. Please trust me! Just say it. *Clior*. Say it, and it's over."

The room started to go dark. His body was numb. Somehow... somehow, he was dying. Somehow, the *draoidh* had done this to him. Leached the life out of him, while keeping him distracted. An energy *draoidh*? Could he do that too?

"Come on!" he heard Mynygogg scream, as if from a long distance. What was that necklace? What had it done? What was it doing? The darkness closed in around his vision, leaving just a tunnel of light ahead. His hand, wrapped in Mynygogg's fist. What power did it have? What did he want? Why would he need Aranok to say the word? It was now or never. He was dying.

"Please, Aranok! Please..." Mynygogg's desperate voice was moving farther and farther away. "Say it! *Clior. Clior*... Please!"

...

"*Clior*."

Aranok's entire body jerked as a wave of pain wracked him. He banged his head on the stone floor and felt air rush back into his chest. His lungs sucked it in greedily, as if they'd never breathed before. Every muscle in his body tensed, relaxed, tensed again, pulsing with life. He felt a hand under his head, another on his shoulder.

Images, thoughts, memories rushed into his head, overwhelming him.

A woman with sad lilac eyes.

A crown, nestled in red.

A blonde boy's hopeful smile.

A warrior's story, told in ale.

A mocking smile beneath cruel eyes.

A friend in the dark.

He retched again, but his stomach was empty, so nothing but bile dripped onto the stone as his stomach convulsed. When it stopped, he rolled onto his side again, exhausted. Wordlessly, Mynygogg lifted him back to his chair. He slumped onto it, weak as water, but stronger. Better. Whole.

The *luisnich* spell had gone out, so the whole of the great hall was lit only by the small oil lamp next to the throne. But even in the murky half-light, he could make out the figure standing before him. He looked him in the eye and felt a wave of relief. It made sense now. Everything made sense.

"Hello, Aranok," said the man, smiling.

His closest ally.

His brother-in-arms.

His best friend.

Mynygogg, the true king of Eidyn.

# CHAPTER 48

I'll murder that sleekit little bastard."

Aranok wiped his face dry. They'd moved down to the kitchen, where he could use the water pump to clean up and find some towels to dry off. The cold water had helped clear his head. Having two sets of contrasting memories was unpleasant. Slowly, though, the real ones were becoming more solid, while the ones Janaeus had planted in his mind were more like stories, fading dreams.

"I know," Mynygogg said calmly. "First, let's see if we can work out exactly what he's done."

"What do you mean?" They'd established what Janaeus had done. He'd rewritten the memories of everyone in Eidyn. He'd made himself king—worse, he'd made himself Mynygogg, taking credit for everything the real king had done. He'd literally overwritten people's memories of Mynygogg with himself.

The vain little prick.

And he'd made Mynygogg the enemy. Taken people's memories of the Hellfire War and twisted Mynygogg into a dark *draoidh* with impossible abilities. No *draoidh* had ever had more than one skill. He should have known. He should have realised it couldn't be true.

The truth was that Anhel and Shayella had led an assault on Eidyn, their demons and Dead savaging the country. Allies felled by demons rose again as enemies. Their combination was devastating, not least in the vicious and virulent Thakhati. Eidyn's dead became their own dark army.

They hadn't seen Janaeus coming until it was too late.

"For a start, tell me what he's got people believing," said Mynygogg. "What's the state of the country? What do people think is happening?"

Aranok sat down. "Hell, where to start? He's got us at war with the Reivers."

"Damn it, honestly?" Mynygogg shook his head. "I suppose it makes sense. His power must be limited in scope—if he couldn't make the Reivers believe he was king, the best alternative would be to convince Eidyn they're our enemies. People are easier to manipulate when they believe they're under attack. Fear makes them pliable."

He was right. In truth, the Reivers had been Eidyn's allies for years, and had fought with them against the remains of the Hellfire Club. Aranok counted a number of them good friends. Many had died beside him. Now some had died at his hand.

"The Reivers who were in Eidyn at the time—when he did it—do believe, though," said Aranok. That explained the actual raids they'd experienced, reaffirming the lie. It was hideous.

"What else?" Mynygogg asked.

"Shit. Glorbad."

"What about him?"

Glorbad was Mynygogg's general. The head of the armies of Eidyn. He hadn't fought in an actual battle since they took the throne from Hofnag. More than that, he was a friend—to both of them. A new wave of grief hit Aranok, with the realisation that he'd lost two good friends, not one.

"He's dead. Janaeus...Damn it!" He looked at the ceiling, feeling his eyes filling. Mynygogg didn't speak. He sat forward, covering his mouth with his interlocked hands as he leaned on the table.

"How?" the king finally asked.

"It's...I don't understand why he did it, but...Janaeus summoned a council. Me, Glorbad, Meristan and...Hells, Nirea!"

Mynygogg raised his head. "Is she...?" He clearly couldn't finish the question.

"She's fine, I think. But she doesn't know she's the queen. She thinks she's still in the navy."

"Thank God. I hoped, of course, but..." Mynygogg nodded anxiously. "She's alive."

Nirea had been a pirate queen and led the navy after Mynygogg recruited her to his rebellion, along with many of the ships under her command. They wouldn't have won without her. It wasn't long before she became Mynygogg's queen too. Unusually for a royal consort, she'd kept direct control over the navy. She'd been Mynygogg's equal in every way, which was why she'd been in Leet, organising forces, when Janaeus struck.

"So...what happened to Glorbad?"

Aranok explained the whole story: how Janaeus had sent them to Barrock, how they'd separated, how it had been a trap. Taneitheia really had evacuated the castle long before, just after the war began. Janaeus hadn't needed to wipe that knowledge from them—just lie convincingly. Aranok realised that he'd always thought something smelled wrong about the whole thing. Was that partly why he was in no hurry to get there? If he hadn't trusted Janaeus completely, maybe they wouldn't have...

"Fuck!" Aranok stood abruptly. He'd been so thrown, so addled by having his memory restored, he'd completely forgotten about his companions.

"What?" Mynygogg stood too.

"Allandria and Samily—they're outside—in the guard hut. I need to get them."

Mynygogg put up a hand. "All right...Hang on...who's Samily?"

"White Thorn. Brilliant White Thorn. Raised by Meristan. She's the only reason we got here alive."

"Then I owe her a debt. But wait, before you go, how are you going to explain this? You'll have to clear their minds too."

"It's fine." Aranok put a hand out for the amulet. "Allandria will trust me—and Samily is probably...not conscious."

He hoped Allandria would trust him. She was likely still angry at him. The last thing she'd done was wish him dead. Hopefully that would be water under the bridge when she learned the truth. Hopefully it would stay that way when she realised the particularly cruel thing Janaeus had done to the two of them.

Mynygogg took off the amulet and handed it to him. "All right." He rubbed his hands and looked around the kitchen. "I'll make food."

Aranok bounded up the stairs toward the throne room.

———

It had taken Allandria some time to rouse Samily enough to get her to open the latch and let her back into the hut. She had barely stayed awake long enough to hear why Allandria was back. With nothing else to do but fume about what a stupid, selfish bastard her lover had been, she'd built a small fire and hung her wet clothes over the chairs to dry. A dusty old cloak she found in the corner was unpleasant, but dry and warm.

She'd lost track of how long she had sat there, worrying about what was happening in the castle above them, pondering how they were ever going to get out of Auldun. The Crosscauseway ended at a sheer wall across a drop into the Nor Loch, with the Dead on the other side. Even when Samily was rested—what then? If Aranok didn't come back, they couldn't follow him into the castle.

Unless the magic was limited to the tunnel. Could she scale the wall? In daylight, when the wind died down, she could attach some rope to an arrow. Would it be enough? Would it hold for the two of them to get in? Normally, the rampart would be guarded, but with no soldiers inside—maybe.

She jumped at the sound of knocking. Her first reaction was to reach for her sword, but she quickly realised neither a demon nor the Dead would knock, which meant...

She lifted the latch and flung open the door.

"Oh, thank God!" Aranok stood in the rain. She threw her arms around him and pulled him into the hut. Then she remembered what he'd done and released him. "You fucking idiot! I can't believe you're alive! What happened?"

Aranok looked at her with an expression she couldn't read. He turned and closed the door against the weather.

"Is she...?" He looked down at the sleeping knight.

"She's out. Why?" Why was he so calm? It was weird.

He took a deep breath and blew it out. "Allandria, I know you're angry at me, and I understand why. But I need you to trust me. I mean really, really trust me."

She looked at him hard. What was it? What had happened in the castle?

"I trust you." She always would, even when he was an arsehole.

"Good. You should sit down."

This was becoming ominous. She sat and looked up at him. He seemed nervous—uncomfortable. What would make him like this?

"I'm going to try to make this easy for you," he said. "Easier than it was for me, anyway. Like I said, please just trust me. Everything I'm about to say is true. And when I'm done, I'll prove it."

"All right." She couldn't imagine what he could say that would be so shocking. "Go on."

"Your mind—all our minds—have been tampered with. Our memories changed. We've been made to believe things that aren't true." He crouched down and took her hands in his. "Allandria, we lost the war."

"What?" That made no sense. Even if somehow their minds had been affected, they would know if they'd lost. The country would be overrun.

"It's the truth. We were never fighting Mynygogg. It was others. A demon summoner. A necromancer. And a memory *draoidh*. The heart of devastation is real. He has it."

Allandria blinked. She was starting to feel dizzy. "No..." She raised a hand to her head.

"Ach, damn, I was trying to avoid this. Here, hold this." He put something into her hand—something cold, hard and round—then wrapped his hand around hers. "But listen, there's one thing, particularly, that's going to upset you. Just...try to be ready."

Allandria did her best to nod, but she couldn't open her eyes without feeling dizzy.

"*Chor.*"

A wave washed over her, and everything went black.

When she came to, the world was different. She remembered.

Mynygogg was king, Janaeus was a minor *draoidh* and... She opened her eyes and looked up at her best friend. The man she trusted above all others.

The man who, for some twisted reason, until this moment she'd believed was her lover.

"What the fuck?" she barked.

"I know. I know."

"Why would he... of all the things... Why would he?"

"I don't know why he put us together, Al. Maybe there was some twisted logic to it, maybe he thought it would put us off-balance. Maybe he thought it was funny; I don't know. But he did. I'm sorry."

"Hell, it's not your fault," she answered, suddenly aware of her state of undress. She pulled the cloak closer about her.

They'd been as close as friends could be without being lovers. What possible reason could Janaeus have for making them believe they were?

*The little shitbag.*

"He even made my family believe it," said Aranok.

He had. And made them believe it needed to be kept secret. Now, looking back, there was very little reason for that. Had it ever really made sense to her?

"Listen, I know this is a lot to take in, but do you think you can move?" Aranok asked.

Allandria planted her feet beneath her. Her legs felt weak, but she was strong enough. "Yes."

"Good. Let's get Samily inside. We can dry, eat and rest. Mynygogg is waiting."

Those words had such new meaning. Instead of dread, they were hope. And home. Allandria stood. "Fine. Turn around." She gestured to her damp clothes.

A hint of a smile curled the corners of Aranok's mouth, and his tired eyes sparkled, just a little. "It's a bit late for that."

"No." She raised one finger in admonishment. "We are not laughing about this yet."

The smile disappeared and he nodded solemnly. "Fair enough."

"I don't understand." Samily sipped the tea Mynygogg had given her. She'd awoken in the afternoon, confused both by her surroundings and by the muddle of memories in her head. She'd found Allandria before long and been brought to the king's chambers, where Aranok and Mynygogg had obviously been deep in conversation.

Learning that Janaeus had usurped the throne, using the relic and his memory skill, had made sense of her confusion, and she understood the crux of what had happened, but she could not for the life of her imagine why the *draoidh* would want to convince Meristan, the greatest White Thorn there had ever been, that he was a simple monk.

"Between us, we've pieced together as much as we can," said the king. Samily felt very odd drinking tea in his private chambers, but all things considered, it was amongst the least of the oddities of this situation. "We learned Janaeus was after the heart of devastation. We weren't even sure it was real, but I sent Meristan to intercept him, just in case. He was obviously too late. Presumably Janaeus had already reached Crostorfyn and used his skill to make the priest…" He waved a hand at Aranok.

"Dalim."

"Dalim. Convinced Dalim to give him the relic, then wiped his memory. We assume Meristan met him on the Wester Road. That makes sense, with him travelling from here to Caer Amon and Janaeus presumably making for Haven. With the added power of the relic, Janaeus was able to completely rewrite Meristan's memory of who he is."

"We think we found his armour on the road," said Aranok. "It explains why it was just abandoned there. He took it off."

"S'grace," said Samily. No Thorn would abandon their White. It was blasphemy.

"Presumably he sent Meristan to Baile Airneach with some purpose. We don't know what," the king continued. "But when he reached Haven, he cast the spell, the one that rewrote every memory in Eidyn— except his. And mine."

Mynygogg nodded to Aranok, who held out a small yellow ball he wore on a leather strap around his neck. "Janaeus gave me this. A long time ago. We were friends. All *draoidhs* can make charms to protect against their power. They're difficult and time-consuming, but he made them for all of us. So we would know he wasn't interfering with our memories. Ironically, so we would trust him. When we knew there was a chance of Janaeus doing this, I ordered the castle emptied and left Mynygogg here, alone, with this. Allandria and I went after Janaeus.

"When we took Dun Eidyn from Hofnag, we knew there was a possibility he'd come back. Try to retake his throne. So I did some research. Carved runes into Dun Eidyn's walls—the foundation for an enchantment to protect us from siege. When we left, I engaged it." He turned to look at the king. "You thought I was being overly cautious."

"I did. But I listened." Mynygogg smiled. "I still wonder if it wouldn't have been better to have you take the charm."

"And if he'd convinced you to kill yourself?" said Aranok. "You're more important than I am. We both knew you'd get through to me."

Amid a flood of questions, something was nagging at Samily, and she suddenly realised what it was. "I am confused. Why were the Dead in Auldun? And the demon we fought? What purpose did they serve?"

Aranok sat back and sighed. "Anhel and Shay laid siege to Auldun after we evacuated Dun Eidyn. I assume they saw it as a chance to take the throne—symbolically, at least."

"But the spell held." There was reverence in the king's voice, and he winked at his envoy.

Aranok nodded. "An enchantment written by better *draoidhs* than me."

"But never used on such a scale. Right?" Mynygogg countered.

"Not that I know of." Aranok opened his hands and turned back to Samily. "Anhel and Shayella took Auldun, but they couldn't breach Dun Eidyn. Janaeus used to say that when we wore his amulets, he could still sense our minds with his skill, he just couldn't touch them. He must have been able to sense Mynygogg in Dun Eidyn. They knew they couldn't reach him, but once Jan rewrote our memories, they needed to keep him there and keep us—me—away from him. So they left sentries—to keep Mynygogg in Dun Eidyn, and everyone else out."

That made sense. If they couldn't kill Mynygogg or change his memory, they needed him isolated.

"So you really were trapped here?" Samily asked.

The king nodded. Allandria seemed oddly subdued. She hadn't said much at all and just sat looking at the ground.

"How did it work?" Samily still didn't fully understand. "How can we all remember the same wrong things but also still lots of right things? Like, I remembered Meristan raising me, but as a monk, not a Thorn."

"It's complicated." Aranok shifted in his chair. "I'll try to explain. First of all, memory is tricky. We all have inaccurate memories—some stronger than others. Many things are gone from each of our memories, and we all, in our hearts, know that. So we don't examine them too closely if they seem a little hazy. In your case, he changed Meristan into a monk, but otherwise left your memories alone—except where he had to change them. If he had been dealing with you alone, he could have done a more delicate job, but since he was dealing with the whole country, he would have had to be blunt. That would mean replacing all your memories of Meristan, the man you know, with Meristan the monk. It would also mean removing any memory you had of him as a warrior. Otherwise, he will have tried to leave as many memories as possible intact. The less he changes, the more real it feels."

Of course. Her first demon battle, when Merrick was injured. The fourth Thorn she hadn't been able to remember. It was Meristan. And that constant, nagging feeling she'd had that something was wrong with him—there was something wrong *about* him. Samily shook her head. "It's awful."

"It is," said Aranok. "There are people he changed more, of course. Why he did what he did to Meristan we don't know, but Nirea...She would have been difficult."

"How so?"

"Janaeus can only change memories," said Mynygogg. "Not feelings. For everyone else, he could write himself into my place. But he couldn't make Nirea love him. She would eventually have known something was wrong. So he had to take me from her completely. Replace our lives with a false history in which she never left the sea."

*Heaven, to have her love taken from her.*

"Fucking arsehole." Allandria bounced her fist on her thigh.

"Can I ask, Samily, were you aware of problems with your memory? Was Meristan?" Aranok asked.

The great man had known in his soul something was wrong with him. A warrior's heart would not become a monk's without a struggle.

"'The war was a blur,' he said. He could remember very little. He was deeply troubled. I think he believes himself a coward because he does not fight." Samily felt an unexpected rage rising against the man who had done this to her mentor, her father. Saying the words out loud had somehow released it. She took a deep breath and tried to focus, to let it go. Anger was unhelpful. It clouded judgement.

"Mmm." Aranok nodded.

"Wait." Samily remembered something. "The Thakhati."

"Yes, we don't know why he took our memory of them. Maybe so we'd be more vulnerable," said the envoy. "I think they're an experiment. My guess is they're the result of Anhel and Shayella attempting to combine their skills. The dead reincarnated as demons through those cocoons. We knew they died in sunlight, though. I imagine Janaeus wanted us to forget that."

That was interesting, but not what she meant. "Allandria remembered them."

Three heads turned to look at the archer. She still gazed at the floor.

"Allandria?" asked the king.

"It was the smell," she said, not raising her head. "That bastard smell. From the time..." she trailed off.

"Allandria was..." Aranok started.

"I'll tell it," she snapped. The envoy sat back as if he'd touched flames. Allandria's tone was unnerving. Samily hadn't seen her this way. "I was in one of those things. The cocoons. It was..." She looked up. "It was Hell. He got me out." She nodded to Aranok. "But that fucking smell. I was covered in it."

Samily remembered it. Her armour had been splattered. It was the nauseating stench of decay. That was just from splashes. To be immersed in it... S'grace, what a thought.

"Smells often evoke strong memories," said Mynygogg. "That one would have been particularly strong, Allandria. I'm sorry."

"Wouldn't have minded if that memory had stayed gone," she said darkly. Aranok looked at her hesitantly. His hand moved as if to touch her, but withdrew. There was a strange tension between them. Was she still angry that he left her behind?

"In addition to all that, Janaeus has made enemies of the Reivers, had a demon attack the farmlands and had king's messengers spreading lies about the state of the country," Mynygogg said in what seemed to Samily an oddly chirpy tone. "Leet may or may not have been taken by pirates. We don't know. I suspect that's another lie."

"Why would he do that?" asked Samily. "Why more lies?"

"Well, his hold on the crown depends on nobody questioning him," said Mynygogg. "Anybody looking too hard might find inconsistencies. He made the Reivers enemies to prevent anyone from believing them when they send their envoys to tell people the truth. If enough Reivers are attacked, eventually the war will be real—exactly what Janaeus wants. Wars keep down rebellions. Nobody questions the king in times of war.

"As to Mutton Hole—making food scarce for commoners is another way of keeping them down. They're more concerned with feeding their children than questioning their ruler. And it's not his fault anyway—it's mine—evil Mynygogg, locked away in Dun Eidyn by heroic Janaeus, yet somehow still a puppeteer, responsible for all that's wrong in the kingdom.

"But he kept up deliveries to Mournside, of course. Can't have the wealthy turning against the king. If they stop paying taxes, the treasury runs out of money. But by isolating them with threats of Blackened and Reivers, and sending them news that all is well elsewhere in the kingdom..."

"They have no reason to do anything except live their lives, safe behind their walls," Aranok finished. It was horribly, hideously devious. And yet it made perfect sense when Mynygogg explained it.

"Of course, you can only lie to an entire country for as long as you can keep people from speaking to one another. The truth is always one chance meeting away," said the king.

"Like when you tried to see that messenger..." Samily said.

"Yes." Aranok's voice was small. "Janaeus presumably sent that wretch to keep an eye on her, suspecting I'd ignore his order. He really believed I was having an affair with his wife. She wasn't his wife, and she probably believed the news she delivered was the truth. There's no better lie than one told in earnest. She was likely innocent. I expect the murderer came from a gaol. Janaeus set him up and sent him away. I walked in and got her killed."

"You couldn't have known," Allandria said quietly.

"No. None of this is your fault, or any of ours," said Mynygogg. "Janaeus alone is responsible for what he's done."

There was silence then for some time. Samily sipped her tea again, trying to get her head around it. "I'm still a little confused. I understand that the relic allowed Janaeus to cast his spell wider—across the country, but how did he do that and make specific changes, like Nirea?"

Mynygogg looked to Aranok.

The envoy shrugged. "We're guessing, but the heart must be ridiculously powerful. We saw what it allowed the girl to do in Caer Amon."

Samily remembered it well. Those poor people.

"Face-to-face with Meristan, the relic must have given Janaeus the power to completely rewrite his memory of himself. That's well beyond any normal *draoidh*."

Samily nodded, feeling the anger stirring again.

"For the rest, I imagine it's like layers. The whole country had to believe that he was the king, that Mynygogg and the Reivers were the enemy, and that there was no queen. Anyone who knew Meristan had to believe he was a monk. Memories of Anhel and Shayella were changed. I mean, my God, the irony of Anhel Weyr being the most righteous man in Eidyn. It's twisted. Janaeus could project all that onto everyone.

"Once he'd done that, it would have been focusing on individuals. The power to do that at a distance, again, it's terrifying. He had to change things for us, for Glorbad, but especially Nirea. It would have taken time. It's likely we all lost time as it happened—the whole country in a trance for I don't know how long. He planned this. He planned it well."

The envoy was right. It was terrifying. Not only how powerful the relic had made Janaeus, but how detailed his plan was. She was almost impressed, which tasted sour. "What about the king's council? Why call it? Why send you all into a trap? Why kill Master Conifax?"

"I think he hoped to control us, at first," said Aranok. "To keep us close. He'd already split us. He took our memories of each other. Except for the two of us"—he glanced briefly at Allandria—"and Nirea and Glorbad. Commanders of the army and the navy—they were close. A lot of memories together. A lot of drinking together. To take Mynygogg from her and then take Glorbad too—that would have been messy, I imagine. And Allandria is such an innate part of my life..." He opened his hands. Allandria shifted in her seat but didn't look at him.

"At some point, maybe he decided it was too much of a risk. He couldn't just have us killed—his hands had to be clean. Heroic deaths for the king's advisors, ambushed by one of Mynygogg's demons. He's rid of us, and the people have one more reason to fear the evil *draoidh*."

"Conifax, we're not sure about." Mynygogg placed a hand on Aranok's leg. "We guess he must have found something that led to the truth. Janaeus likely has an agent in Traverlyn. Just in case. He must have been plotting this for an age. It wasn't only his magic we underestimated."

"No," said Aranok. "He was always clever. It's just...of the three, Anhel and Shayella were so much more of a threat. I never thought he was capable of..." He shook his head mournfully.

"Shayella is also most likely the one who cursed the Blackened," said the king.

Aranok nodded. "She's from Lepertoun. And it makes perfect sense it would be a necromancy *mollachd*. It all but turns them into the walking dead."

"Do we know where she is? Who she is?" Samily asked.

Aranok shook his head. "But she probably summoned the Blackened to the Auld Road. In fact, that's likely how Janaeus expected us to die, before we even reached Barrock. She's still around. Somewhere."

Samily finished her tea with a gulp. It was all well and good the four of them understanding this, but what could they do about it? "What now?"

"We've been discussing that too," said Mynygogg. "There are many risks. The worst is, if Janaeus discovers we know the truth, he could use the relic and rewrite our memories again. The whole country. But if you're with us, Samily, we do have a plan."

She nodded. "Of course, Your Majesty."

"First, we get our allies. If Meristan and Nirea are in Traverlyn, we go there. We clear who we can and get them with us. The university could be an ideal base."

Of course. A place full of the best-educated men and women in Eidyn, and a good number of *draoidhs*. *Rasa*. Samily's heart jumped at the thought of seeing the metamorph again so soon. "Wait." The joy turned to dread. "The last thing Rasa said…"

Aranok's face fell. "That she would go to Janaeus herself. Fuck." He turned to Mynygogg. "If she tells him everything we know—that she knows…"

Mynygogg nodded. "He'll kill her. And recast the spell."

Mynygogg stood. For all he was unkempt and dressed in simple clothes, he still looked every inch the king. There was something compelling about him, something that demanded attention.

"All right then. It's the four of us. We have no time. But we have the most formidable *draoidh* in Eidyn, the best archer I've ever seen, the first *draoidh* White Thorn I've ever heard of, and an old blowhard who talks too much."

They laughed. It felt wrong, but good.

"Right here, this is the moment." He raised his cup in salute. "This is what we'll all look back on one day and smile. This is the beginning of the new rebellion.

"Let's take our country back."

# EPILOGUE

Darginn Argyll woke to the smell of roasting meat and the taste of blood in his mouth. It took a moment for him to realise he wasn't in his bed, and that the pleasant afternoon he'd been spending with his granddaughter was a fading dream.

He lifted his head, shaking off the opium haze, trying to focus on his surroundings.

The pain bit, and he screamed.

His wrists burned. The rope holding him in place had rubbed the skin raw days ago. His shoulders—probably broken from holding his weight for so long—throbbed in agony.

He remembered.

When he couldn't scream anymore, he looked around. The fire still burned, illuminating the little stone room. How long had he hung here? Days? Weeks? In and out of consciousness, it was hard to tell.

Darginn breathed in carefully, trying not to move too much. Every inch hurt like the fires of Hell.

He looked down at the place where his legs used to be—the stumps tied off with leather straps, the board he hung from streaked with his blood. He tried not to look at the spit over the fire, but his eyes were drawn against his will. When he saw it, he sobbed from the depths of his chest.

The door opened and closed again. Darginn watched her slowly, silently cross the room. With a long blade, she carved a slice off the roast into a flat pan. Walking toward him, she lifted the meat and nibbled at it. Small bites. She stopped in front of him, looking up at him as an artist at a canvas only half-complete.

In that moment, Darginn Argyll wished for nothing more than that she would take pity on him and kill him.

But she just stood there in silence, chewing on her food—the little blonde girl who never breathed.

The story continues in . . .

*THE BITTER CROWN*

Book TWO of The Eidyn Saga

Keep reading for a sneak peek!

# ACKNOWLEDGEMENTS

This is a second release of *The Lost War*, so it has something of a storied history, and therefore a long list of people to thank. I'm going to try to do it chronologically and not forget anyone:

First, my endless thanks to Nathan, who literally made it possible for me to write this book. Without a hint of hyperbole, I couldn't have done it without you.

Sean, who has been GMing our roleplaying evenings for decades and not only allowed me to take over the characters we played for years but also made me a map to work with while writing the book. And the other players, Kirsten, Neith, Juliet, Craig and Jan, who allowed me to take their characters and build them into something new. Thank you all.

My one and only alpha reader, the only person who gets to read the first draft, and without whose threats of violence this book would have ended one chapter earlier: my wonderful, patient and ever-supportive wife, Juliet. Thank you.

My beta readers, Andy, Kelvin, Kathryn, Maryanne and Marya, whose feedback greatly shaped and moulded the final story. Thank you all.

My first editor, John Jarrold, who helped me smooth the rough edges and produce a vastly superior book. Thank you.

Anna Stephens, who generously read and reviewed the first release and got it the beginnings of a lot of attention from bloggers, notably

Petrik from *Novel Notions* and Alex from *Spells and Spaceships*, who were both effusive and supportive in its early days. Thank you, guys.

All the reviewers, authors and community that make the brilliant SPFBO awards happen, and specifically D. M. Murray, who picked *The Lost War* as his BookNest semifinalist, and Petros Triantafyllou, who picked it as his finalist. And especially my fellow finalists, who built a little support network to keep us all sane for the year! Thank you all for a wonderful experience.

Mark Lawrence, who not only gives a huge amount of his time and energy to make SPFBO happen but also introduced me to his agent after *The Lost War* won. Endless thanks, not just for what you've done for me but on behalf of the fantasy-writing community.

Ian Drury, now my agent too, who enjoyed the book enough to take a chance on me and take it to market. Thank you!

Bradley Englert, who saw the potential in the book and made this wonderful Orbit edition happen. His and Nadia Saward's edits, along with all of the team at Orbit, have again made this a better book, and I am eternally grateful for their faith and support.

And, of course, everyone else: my family and friends, who are always quick with support and encouragement; the huge number of authors in the SFF community whom I've met in recent years who have been generous with their time and advice, but especially Heide Goody, Iain Grant and Rachel McLean, who took me under their wings at my first FantasyCon in 2017 and have all become friends; and the readers who follow my progress on social media—your patience, enthusiasm and encouragement keep me going. Thank you all.

It occurs to me that this list includes a significant number of people who were not only critical to helping me tell this story, but whose actions and support have literally changed my life. I think that's worth noting. I'm grateful to every one of you for it.

*Slàinte!*
Justin

# CREDITS

**Writer**
Justin Lee Anderson

**Publisher**
Tim Holman

**Editorial**
Bradley Englert
Nadia Saward

**Agent**
Ian Drury

**Production Editor**
Rachel Goldstein

**Copy Editor**
Emily Stone

**Proofreaders**
Vivian Kirklin
Eileen Chetti

**Production**
Xian Lee

**Cover Artist**
Jeremy Wilson

**Design**
Lauren Panepinto

**Marketing**
Alex Lencicki
Paola Crespo
Natassja Haught

**Publicity**
Angela Man

**Early Readers**
Juliet Cavanagh-Anderson
Kelvin Aston
Marya Hemmings
Andy McIntosh
Maryanne Nielsen
Kathryn Wood

**First Edition Editor**
John Jarrold

**Map Artist**
Tim Paul

# extras

orbit

# meet the author

Melody Joy Co.

Justin Lee Anderson was a professional writer and editor for fifteen years before his debut novel, *Carpet Diem*, was published and won the 2018 Audie Award for Humor. His second novel, *The Lost War*, won the 2020 SPFBO award. Born in Scotland, he spent his childhood in the US thanks to his dad's football (soccer) career and also lived in the South of France for three years. He now lives with his family just outside his hometown of Edinburgh.

Find out more about Justin Lee Anderson and other Orbit authors by registering for the free monthly newsletter at orbitbooks.net.

# interview

This author interview contains spoilers for the ending of *The Lost War*.

*What was the first book that made you fall in love with the fantasy genre?*

When I was about twelve, I found a copy of *A Spell for Chameleon* by Piers Anthony in my school library. I devoured it and went on to read Anthony almost exclusively through my teens, moving from the Xanth books to Incarnations of Immortality, Bio of a Space Tyrant, Apprentice Adept and Tarot. He was definitely the one who got me hooked on fantasy. I still have my copies of the Incarnations, Bio and Tarot series from the late eighties.

*Where did the initial idea for* The Lost War *come from and how did the story begin to take shape?*

*The Lost War* came from three places: the first was my desire to write a political allegory about truth and manipulation, which led me to the premise of a book which begins with all the POV characters having had their memories changed—that was also slightly inspired by an episode of *Star Trek: The Next Generation*. The second was that I wanted to write a story using characters that friends and I had roleplayed for years. The third was an idea to write a book set in a fantasy country based on the history, mythology and etymology of my hometown, Edinburgh. When I realized they all fit into one book, that's when *The Lost War* took shape.

*What was the most challenging moment of writing* **The Lost War**?

I think it was making the twist pay off as dramatically as it did in my head. Writing that scene between Aranok and Mynygogg was a bit daunting and I had to really just lean into it and hope it worked as well for readers. The other thing was also making sure I had seeded enough through the book that it didn't come completely out of nowhere, but also wasn't given away.

*The characters in* **The Lost War** *are fascinating, and it's exciting to watch them come together as this sort of ragtag team. If you had to pick, who would you say is your favourite? Who was the most difficult to write?*

I don't know that I have a favourite, because I enjoy writing them all for different reasons. Maybe Samily, a little, because she's so striking in how she sees the world. But then I loved writing Glorbad's bombast and Aranok's inner demons and Allandria's sass and…yeah, I don't know if I have a favourite. The most difficult to write might have been Nirea, I think, and that's mainly because in the first draft I hadn't differentiated her enough from Allandria and they sounded too similar. There was a point where I sat down and wrote an A4 page of history for each main character, just to get them clear in my head, and that really helped me find Nirea's voice and character. I think she comes out even more strongly in book two.

*Aranok is striving to find his place in a world that doesn't necessarily love him. He's often pushing against the boundaries of other people's assumptions. What was it like writing this character?*

Cathartic, complicated, fun, exciting, liberating…all of those. Aranok was my character in roleplay and so there's a lot of me in him. I hope he's a complex character that people maybe even have difficulty liking. He's been shaped by his life in a way that he has this great power but also a wealth of mental health issues and emotional baggage to deal with. Again, I think that comes out even more in book two. Allandria was my wife's character and our kids have said they see a lot of our relationship in their dynamic, which I like.

**Without giving too much away, could you give us a hint of what happens in the next novel?**

Well, now that the four know the truth, they have to figure out how to convince the entire kingdom that they've been manipulated and lied to. And maybe they don't all agree on how to do that. And maybe some loyalties and alliances will be tested as they try to find a way.

**Who are some of your favorite authors and how have they influenced your writing?**

Neil Gaiman's imagination is almost peerless, I think, and one of his Sandman stories provided the inspiration for my first novel, *Carpet Diem*. I think Joe Abercrombie's characterisation work is incredible. Tom Holt's wit is magnificent and his sense of humour completely matches my own. Patrick Rothfuss's prose is just glorious. Ed McDonald's worldbuilding in the Raven's Mark trilogy, particularly of the Misery, is brilliant. Anna Stephens's weaving of a huge tale of warring nations and their gods in Godblind is beautifully executed and one of her characters' deaths was the most emotionally powerful I think I've ever read. I also read a lot of Jo Nesbø, who knows how to write a mystery thriller, and I also love Stieg Larsson's Millenium trilogy for that. I hope I've learned something from all of them, and a lot of others!

**Finally, if you were a draoidh, which power would you prefer (and no spoilers if new draoidh powers are yet to be revealed!)?**

When I roleplay a mage, my first instinct is always to get telekinesis, because it's just so versatile. But out of all the *draoidh* abilities, I think it's hard to look past Samily's time power. Being able to rewind and fix mistakes or heal wounds would be amazing. That power just has so much potential, and she'll be exploring that as the story goes on.

# if you enjoyed
# THE LOST WAR

look out for

# THE BITTER CROWN
## The Eidyn Saga: Book Two

by

## Justin Lee Anderson

*The fog of war is lifted and the conspiracy at the heart of Eidyn is finally exposed. Now that they know the truth, Aranok and his allies must find a way to free a country that doesn't know it's held captive. But with divided loyalties and Aranok's closest friendship shaken, can their alliance hold in the face of overwhelming odds? The quest to retake the country begins here.*

# Chapter One

Fetid air whipped across the chasm. Only yesterday, Aranok had torn fifteen feet of the majestic white stone Crosscauseway from its place and remade it as a wall, protecting them from the Dead during their battle with Anhel's great lizard demon. Then it had been protection. Now it was a barrier.

Once they got to Auldun's roofs, getting out would be straightforward. But the path to the rooftops was now across a fatal drop to the Nor Loch and through an agitated horde of Dead.

So he was going to try something he'd never done: use his wall spell to make a second bridge, connecting them directly from the north Crosscauseway to the nearest buildings on land, bypassing the Dead completely.

With his mind clear, Aranok was remembering things lost. If he focused completely on the earth, pictured what he wanted, it should run the path they needed. But if he tore too much from the depths of the loch, he'd unsettle the foundations of the Crosscauseway and dump them all in the freezing water.

A hand on his shoulder.

"Aranok, I've seen you do a hundred miraculous things. This is just another one."

Mynygogg was almost unrecognisable. The king had shaved his striking black hair and beard and wore a simple set of black leathers.

In contrast, Samily appeared hewn from marble—the rock upon which Eidyn could rely. Maybe the greatest warrior he'd ever seen, but for the man who'd raised her, or the woman beside her.

Allandria. His own rock. It had been awkward since they discovered Janaeus's trick—convincing them they were lovers. Instinct said she was angry with him. But they had no time for the kind of discussion she might want—might need. Hopefully, that storm would blow itself out, given time.

This was their army. The four of them carried the truth that would restore Eidyn.

Having Mynygogg with him again was comforting. He felt his friend's confidence in him like air, buttressing his belief. Aranok looked down at the water, up to the rooftops, breathed deep and closed his eyes.

*"Balla na talamh."*

*Focus.*

The loch roiled as sodden earth broke the surface. It rose like a beast from the deep, and Aranok was reminded they'd left a demon's carcass down there just the night before. In moments, the mound reached the edge of the causeway. Now it had to stop going *up*, and go *out*.

Another deep breath and he watched as it extended, mud and rock surfacing in a rough line toward the shore. His mind was barely clinging to the magic. At any moment, it felt as though he'd lose his fragile focus and the bridge would collapse back into the water.

The ground shifted beneath Aranok and a shock of pain stabbed as he dropped to a knee. Someone caught his arm. He couldn't look up, couldn't look away. The bridge crashed through the sea wall and he was no longer pulling up loch bed, but the stone and cobbles of an Auldun street. Almost there.

"Ari!"

Aranok was yanked back as his makeshift barrier against the Dead came crashing back through its old position, taking several feet of the causeway's edge with it.

He landed against someone, confused.

Unfocused.

*Out of control.*

Another rumble.

A festering avalanche of Dead poured into the loch as the other side of the Crosscauseway crumbled.

"Fuck! Move!" Allandria pulled Aranok to his feet as their side of the causeway shifted and lurched to the east, away from the new bridge.

"Go! Go!" Aranok gestured urgently to the others. The earth bridge was only about eight feet wide, and they slowed as they reached it. The earth was slick with seaweed—move too quickly and they could fall, too slow and the bridge might collapse before they reached safety.

Allandria reached the edge just before him. She slipped, recognising what he already knew, but her balance was sound. Aranok followed, stepping off the Crosscauseway as it finally lurched away.

He was on. With a sigh of relief he turned to see the north half of the Crosscauseway groan and stretch away.

Then, horrifyingly, it slowed, stopped and swung back.

"Run!" Aranok scrambled to keep his feet. What was left of the northern Crosscauseway battered through the earth bridge, sending debris plummeting back to the depths.

Twenty feet ahead Allandria danced along the ridge, each step finding solid ground. Aranok forced himself only to look ahead. If he looked back... He had to keep running, keep moving, keep...

A sickening lurch as the dirt sank beneath his foot.

And Aranok fell.

A second of panic, of terror, was all he had. In moments he would hit the freezing water and, if he survived that, be crushed by falling debris. Instinctively he pulled his hands tight into his sides and tensed his arms.

"*Gaoth.*"

The burst of air threw him upwards, back toward the makeshift bridge. He could see the others, looking down at him hurtling toward them. It just had to be enough to reach them. He reached out as their faces came closer and... went rushing past.

He'd overshot.

Aranok reached the zenith of his rise, slowed and fell again. They were maybe ten feet below him. But he was going to miss the bridge. *Gaoth* was a blunt instrument. Another uncontrolled burst could overshoot him so far he'd never make it back. Using it to cushion his landing would blow the others off the edge.

Aranok stretched, willing his arms to reach the edge, hoping he might catch just enough purchase to...

He screamed as his shoulder wrenched out of its socket. Ribs crunched, battering air from his chest, and something in his back popped as he slammed against wet stone.

It took him a moment to realise he was half on the bridge, his legs dangling, useless, over the edge.

A second pair of hands grasped his free arm and yanked him, agonisingly, the rest of the way on.

"Are you all right?" Allandria asked.

Was he? Half of him screamed in pain, the other was numb. He coughed up a glob of bloody phlegm.

Aranok tried to move, but his back seized, forcing him still.

"No," he wheezed.

"Where?" Samily's voice was urgent.

Aranok tried to point with his good arm. An awful, rasping sound and a nauseating sensation in his chest suggested his lung was torn.

"Never mind." He felt hands on him. *"Air ais."* The shoulder clicked back into place, ribs snapped into shape and his back popped in a way that was somehow more painful than the injury. Aranok sucked in a deep breath of damp air.

"Can you move?" the knight asked.

He could. He had to. With a grunt and support from Allandria, Aranok forced himself to his feet. It was another five hundred yards to the edge of the water. The bridge wasn't perfect. The lurch at the end had cost him, and the wall of earth had carried on too far, carving a great gash into the stone tenements.

"Who caught me?" Aranok moved carefully along the slick surface now that it wasn't actively collapsing.

"Samily," Mynygogg shouted. "She's everything you said."

"Thank you!" Aranok called to the knight.

Samily did not turn to shout her answer.

"I am sorry I missed you the first time."

"Bloody Hell." Aranok stifled a gag as a dank fug of horse effluent seeped from the White Hart's doorway.

"Good country air." Mynygogg grinned. He thought he was funny. He wasn't funny.

Aranok pushed a small *solas* ball into the dark. Whinnies told him the horses were alive.

"Hey!" Mynygogg slapped his shoulder. He was being bloody annoying about Aranok using magic "unnecessarily."

"What? It's a tiny spell—hardly any energy. We need to see."

"People always need to see." The king strode into the tavern. "They invented candles. Stop wasting energy."

"I already have a mother." Aranok followed him in.

"She'd be on my side," he answered without turning.

"He's right. She would," Allandria agreed. "You need to stop relying on it for everything."

Now there were two of them. Though it felt as if there was more in her words than the face of them.

After a short search, Samily sparked life into a candle behind the bar. Another few were enough to give them a view of the whole room, and Aranok dropped the *solas* spell. All three horses were there, disgruntled but alive.

The hay Aranok had brought in for Bear had been sorely depleted but not exhausted. Several large empty bowls told him the women had left more water out.

So despite their own fatigue after travelling across Auldun's rooftops, and the five miles to the inn, they had three well-rested horses. Good. They needed to keep going.

Mynygogg took a seat, pulled out rations and gestured for the rest to join him. Aranok itched to keep moving, but he was not in charge—not in the way he was used to. Nobody there would take his word as an order if it contradicted the king. Hell, nobody there would take his word as an order if they disagreed with him.

Maybe a quick rest and some food was wise. They had a long way to go.

Allandria took a share of the bread and cheese and leaned on the bar, just across from Mynygogg's table. She was being evasive, and he could do without it. It was well into the night and for all Mynygogg's coddling was annoying, he wasn't entirely wrong. Aranok had used a lot of energy creating that bridge and, worse, Samily had used her time skill twice—once to catch him and once to heal him. Add fighting their way through the Dead at Auldun's gates and they'd already burned too much.

But nothing was ever ideal. If they didn't stop Rasa from going to Janaeus, they'd lose before they began. Besides which, she'd saved his life just, what, yesterday? A great bear dropping from the sky. How could he do less than anything to save her?

"Three horses, four riders," said Allandria. "Bear will take two."

"Bear's the big one?" Mynygogg spoke through a mouthful of cheese.

"Aye." She pointed to the others. "That's Dancer and Midnight."

Samily walked to the big horse and stroked his huge face. Bear snuffled amiably and nudged her hand. Aranok doubted he'd get the same reaction, considering how hard he'd ridden the great beast. It was good Bear had had the chance to recover. He was going to work hard again tonight.

Seventy miles, minimal sleep. They could arrive late tomorrow night, at a push. Hopefully.

"Huh," said Samily. "Bear. I have just realised. That is why it felt familiar."

Of course. One of Meristan's nicknames was "the Great Bear." While she didn't remember that, the name Bear must have sparked a reaction. Fascinating how memory was entangled with emotion.

"Right." Mynygogg stood, packing away the remaining rations. "Let's get moving, then. Samily and I will take the smaller two. Aranok, you ride with Allandria. We could do with your hands free without us having to slow down. All right?"

Allandria's eyes flickered. She didn't like it. But she wasn't going to argue with the king.

"Of course, sire. Makes sense." She didn't even look at him as she brushed past to the horses.

*Oh good. This won't be awkward at all.*

It was painfully awkward.

Allandria tried to focus on the horse. The ride. The rhythm of the hoofbeats.

But what she felt were Aranok's hands on her waist and his chest against her back. It was familiar and nice and awful and wrong.

There was no conversation. No banter. No playful nudges. Just nothing. A door had closed that neither of them knew how to open. The awful truth was she'd been happy. It had been good. Right. All of it. Despite hating that little prick Janaeus for lying to them, she missed it.

But was it real? Did she like it because she remembered liking it, or because she actually did? She couldn't trust her own mind.

Had she had feelings for Aranok before? It was all a muddle. Maybe? Maybe she'd been attracted to him. Maybe she just remembered being attracted to him.

There had been moments, she thought, when it seemed like something might happen. Like there was a spark between them that was...more.

Her memories of the war—the real war—were returned. Instead of fighting Reivers, she remembered the waves of Dead. Running from the Blackened. The Thakhati—the bastard Thakhati and that cocoon. And the demons. Mostly smaller ones. The big ones were usually taken by the Thorns, with help from what *draoidhs* they could muster. So many chose to stay neutral, stay out of the fight. And who could really blame them in a country where they were despised by so many?

The skilled masters had stayed at the university to protect their students—and the skilled students were children. Allandria had come across three *draoidhs*, other than Aranok, that she remembered. What was the physic's name? Gast? Gost? Gart? Poor bastard had been torn in half by a demon north of Gardille. Held it for a long time, protecting a farm. Allandria and Aranok had arrived with a battalion of soldiers too late to save him. Just in time to hear his spine crack and rip as his strength finally gave out against that huge, red, four-armed thing. They'd forced it back. Aranok threw everything he had at it. He'd seemed to find energy from nowhere. From rage. The soldiers too—flaming arrows had stuck like pins from the thing's hide, and they'd done their best to hurt it up close, but reaching it was challenging, past all those damned arms. There had been Reivers too. Men and women she'd thought her enemies until yesterday. Hells, she'd hated them; thought them the worst traitors imaginable. But they'd died just like Eidyn's soldiers, protecting strangers from nightmares.

It was Thorns who saved them. A pair of them. To this day she didn't know their names. They were gone almost as quickly as they arrived. Green blades cut through the demon's skin in a way no other weapon did. They worked together so perfectly, their movements coordinated, fluid, like water—two bodies acting with one mind.

They took the backs of its knees, bringing it down. One attacked head-on, taking the demon's attention, while the other came around behind and, somehow, leapt high enough to reach the base of its skull, where they buried the blade that ended the fight.

When it was over, the knights didn't even remove their helms. Allandria couldn't have told if they were men or women, never mind what they looked like. They slit the thing open, reminded them to burn it, and were mounted and gone again, as if they'd just returned a lost sheep.

They lit the remains next to a pyre for the *draoidh* (Gort?) and the four soldiers they'd lost. Burning was the best they could do for their fallen. So many were left to carrion and rot—no chance to return and offer them dignity. Precious little dignity in war.

They'd limped back to Gardille to recover, and Allandria remembered that night, lying on a bedroll beside his, looking into his sad, exhausted eyes, she'd felt something. Something *more*. It had come and gone, but it was there, and it had shifted the world beneath her. In the middle of all the slaughter and death and exhaustion, she'd felt something real. But was it? Was it just a moment of shared emotional extremes between two souls who'd been through a new Hell together every day for months? Of hope for an end? For tomorrow? Was any of it real?

*God damn it!*

Whatever the truth of it, they'd spent weeks as lovers. They couldn't put that arrow back in the quiver.

They were going to have to talk about it. Eventually. Not yet. Not until she figured out what was real and what that fucker had put in her head. Not until she could work out what she actually wanted from the conversation. From him.

Aranok's hands lifted off her waist and she sat upright.

"*Gluais.*" To her right, a Blackened boy, no more than eight, disappeared back into the darkness. He was the third they'd seen.

Aranok sighed heavily as he replaced his hands. Gooseflesh rose on her neck, the tingle running down her spine. He'd be thinking about how he could have saved the boy, and whether he should have. And then how the time they spent doing that might make them miss Rasa, and cost them everything. And how the boy might not survive without a medic anyway. And how he should have found a way to do both.

He was a good man. And an idiot.

Mynygogg slowed ahead and raised an arm. Samily slowed Dancer to match Midnight's pace, allowing them to ride alongside.

"What?" Aranok asked sharply.

Mynygogg pointed ahead. Just visible from the *solas* orb was the edge of what looked like a clearing.

"We should stop here. Camp for a few hours and the sun'll be up. Then we have less to worry about in daylight, right?"

"All right." Aranok didn't argue. He must have been exhausted.

A few hours' rest here would be good for everyone, including the horses. They'd made good ground, but they weren't even half-way, and it had been a long night. Thank God they'd had no sign of Thakhati. The monsters had probably been on the road into Traverlyn to keep them away from the university. So it was more likely they'd come across them when they got closer. Sometime tomorrow night—or tonight, as it would be. Or tomorrow morning? God, she'd lost all notion of time.

*Sleep now.*

# if you enjoyed
# THE LOST WAR

look out for

# THE SWORD DEFIANT

## Lands of the Firstborn:
## Book One

by

# Gareth Hanrahan

*Set in a world of dark myth and dangerous prophecy,* **The Sword Defiant** *launches an epic tale of daring warriors, living weapons, and bloodthirsty vengeance.*

*The sword cares not who it cuts.*

*Many years ago, Sir Aelfric and his nine companions saved the world, seizing the Dark Lord's cursed weapons along with his dread city of Necrad. That was the easy part.*

*Now when Aelfric—keeper of the cursed sword Spellbreaker— learns of a new and terrifying threat, he seeks the nine heroes once again. But they are wandering adventurers no longer.*

*Yesterday's eager heroes are today's weary leaders—and some have turned to the darkness, becoming monsters themselves.*

*If there's one thing Aelfric knows, it's slaying monsters. Even if they used to be his friends.*

# Chapter One

His story had not begun in a tavern, but Alf had ended up in one anyway.

"An ogre," proclaimed the old man from the corner by the hearth, "a fearsome ogre! Iron-toothed, yellow-eyed, arms like oak branches!" He wobbled as he crossed the room towards the table of adventurers. "I saw it not three days ago, up on the High Moor. The beast must be slain, lest it find its way down to our fields and flocks!"

One of the young lads was beefy and broad-shouldered, Mulladale stock. He fancied himself a fighter, with that League-forged sword and patchwork armour. "I'll wager it's one of Lord Bone's minions, left over from the war," he declared loudly. "We'll hunt it down!"

"I can track it!" This was a woman in green, her face tattooed. A Wilder-woman of the northern woods – or dressed as one, anyway. "We just need to find its trail."

"There are places of power up on the High Moor," said a third, face shadowed by his hood. He spoke with the refined tones of a Crownland scholar. An apprentice mage, cloak marked with the sign of the Lord who'd sponsored him. He probably had a star-trap strung outside in the bushes. "Ancient temples, shrines to forgotten spirits. Such an eldritch beast might . . ."

He paused, portentously. Alf bloody hated it when wizards did that, leaving pauses like pit traps in the conversation. Just get on with it, for pity's sake.

Life was too short.

" . . . be drawn to such places. As might other . . . legacies of Lord Bone."

"We'll slay it," roared the Mulladale lad, "and deliver this village from peril!"

That won a round of applause from the locals, more for the boy's enthusiasm than any prospect of success. The adventurers huddled over the table, talking ogre-lore, talking about the dangers of the High Moor and the virtues of leaving at first light.

Alf scowled, irritated but unable to say why. He'd finish his drink, he decided, and then turn in. Maybe he'd be drunk enough to fall straight asleep. The loon had disturbed a rare evening of forgetfulness. He'd enjoyed sitting there, listening to village gossip and tall tales and the crackling of the fire. Now, the spell was broken and he had to think about monsters again.

He'd been thinking about monsters for a long time.

The old man sat down next to Alf. Apparently, he wasn't done. He wasn't that old, either – Alf realised he was about the same age. They'd both seen the wrong side of forty-five winters. "Ten feet tall it was," he exclaimed, sending spittle flying into Alf's tankard, "and big tusks, like a bull's horns, at the side of its mouth." He stuck his fingers out to illustrate. "It had the stink of Necrad about it. They have the right of it – it's one of Bone's creatures that escaped! The Nine should have put them all to the sword!"

"Bone's ogres," said Alf, "didn't have tusks." His voice was croaky from disuse. "They cut 'em off. Your ogre didn't come out of Necrad."

"You didn't see the beast! I did! Only the Pits of Necrad could spawn such—"

"You haven't seen the sodding Pits, either," said Alf. He felt the cold rush of anger, and stood up. He needed to be away from people. He stumbled across the room towards the stairs.

Another of the locals caught his arm. "Bit of luck for you, eh?" The fool was grinning and red-cheeked. *Twist, break the wrist. Grab his neck, slam his face into the table. Kick him into the two behind him. Then grab a weapon.* Alf fought against his honed instincts. The evening's drinking had not dulled his edge enough.

He dug up words. "What do you mean?"

"You said you were going off up the High Moor tomorrow. You'd run straight into that ogre's mouth. Best you stay here another few days, 'til it's safe."

"Safe," echoed Alf. He pulled his arm free. "I can't stay. I have to go and see an old friend."

The inn's only private room was upstairs. Sleeping in the common room was a copper a night, the private room an exorbitant six for a poky attic room and the pleasure of hearing the innkeeper snore next door.

Alf locked the door and took Spellbreaker from its hiding place under the bed. The sword slithered in his grasp, metal twisting beneath the dragonhide.

"I could hear them singing about you." Its voice was a leaden whisper. "About the siege of Necrad."

"Just a drinking song," said Alf, "nothing more. They didn't know it was me."

"They spoke the name of my true wielder, and woke me from dreams of slaughter."

"It rhymes with rat-arsed, that's all."

"No, it doesn't."

"It does the way they say it, *Acra-sed.*"

"It's pronounced with a hard 't'," said the sword. "Acrai-*st* the Wraith-Captain, Hand of Bone."

"Well," said Alf, "I killed him, so I get to say how it's said. And it's rat-arsed. And so am I."

He shoved the sword back under the bed, then threw himself down, hoping to fall into oblivion. But the same dream caught him again, as it had for a month, and it called him up onto the High Moor to see his friend.

The adventurers left at first light.

Alf left an hour later, after a leisurely breakfast. *Getting soft,* he muttered to himself, but he still caught up with them at the foot of a steep cliff, arguing over which of the goat paths would bring them up onto the windy plateau of the High Moor. Alf marched past them, shoulders hunched against the cold of autumn.

"Hey! Old man!" called one of them. "There's a troll out there!"

Alf grunted as he studied the cliff ahead. It was steep, but not insurmountable. Berys and he had scaled the Wailing Tower in the middle of a howling necrostorm. This was nothing. He found a handhold and hauled himself up the rock face, ignoring the cries of the adventurers below. The Wilder girl followed him a little way, but gave up as Alf rapidly outdistanced her.

His shoulders, his knees ached as he climbed. *Old fool.* Showing off for what? To impress some village children? Why not wave Spellbreaker around? Or carry Lord Bone's skull around on a pole? *If you want glory, you're twenty years too late*, he thought to himself. He climbed on, stretching muscles grown stiff from disuse.

At the top, he sat down on a rock to catch his breath. He'd winded himself. The Wailing Tower, too, was nearly twenty years ago.

He pulled his cloak around himself to ward off the breeze, and lingered there for a few minutes. He watched the adventurers as they debated which path to take, and eventually decided on the wrong one, circling south-east along the cliffs until they vanished into the broken landscape below the moor. He looked out west, across the Mulladales, a patchwork of low hills and farmlands and wooded coppices. Little villages, little lives. All safe.

Twenty years ago? Twenty-one? Whenever it was, Lord Bone's armies came down those goat paths. Undead warriors scuttling down the cliffs head first like bony lizards. Wilder scouts with faces painted pale as death. Witch Elf knights mounted on winged dreadworms. Golems, furnaces blazing with balefire. Between all those horrors and the Mulladales stood just nine heroes.

"It was twenty-two years ago," said Spellbreaker. The damn sword was listening to his thoughts again – or had he spoken out loud? "Twenty-two years since I ate the soul of the Illuminated."

"We beat you bastards good," said Alf. "And chased you out of the temple. Peir nearly slew Acraist then, do you remember?"

"Vividly," replied the sword.

Peir, his hammer blazing with the fire of the Intercessors. Berys, flinging vials of holy water she'd filched from the temple. Gundan, bellowing a war cry as he swung Chopper. Gods, they were so young then. Children, really, only a few years older than the idiot ogre-hunters. The battle of the temple was where they'd first proved themselves heroes. The start of a long, bitter war against Lord Bone. Oh, they'd got side-tracked – there'd been prophecies and quests and strife aplenty to lead them astray – but the path to Necrad began right here, on the edge of the High Moor.

He imagined his younger self struggling up those cliffs, that cheap pig-sticker of a sword clenched in his teeth. What would he have done, if that young warrior reached to the top and saw his future sitting there? Old, tired, tough as old boots. Still had all his limbs, but plenty of scars.

"We won," he whispered to the shade of the past, "and it's still bloody hard."

"You," said the sword, "are going crazy. You should get back to Necrad, where you belong."

"When I'm ready."

"I can call a dreadworm. Even here."

"No."

"Anything could be happening there. We've been away for more than two years, *moping.*" There was an unusual edge to the sword's plea. Alf reached down and pulled Spellbreaker from its scabbard, so he could look the blade in the gemstone eye on its hilt and—

—Reflected in the polished black steel as it crept up behind him. Grey hide, hairy, iron-tusked maw drooling. Ogre.

Alf threw himself forward as the monster lunged at him and rolled to the edge of the cliff. Pebbles and dirt tumbled down the precipice, but he caught himself before he followed them over. He hoisted Spellbreaker, but the sword suddenly became impossibly heavy and threatened to tug him backwards over the cliff.

One of the bastard blade's infrequent bouts of treachery. Fine.

He flung the heavy sword at the onrushing ogre, and the monster stumbled over it. Its ropy arms reached for him, but Alf dodged along the cliff edge, seized the monster's wrist and pulled with all his might. The ogre, abruptly aware of the danger that they'd both fall to their deaths, scrambled away from the edge. It was off balance, and vulnerable. Alf leapt on the monster's back and drove one elbow into its ear. The ogre bellowed in pain and fell forward onto the rock he'd been sitting on. Blood gushed from its nose, and the sight sparked unexpected joy in Alf. For a moment, he felt young again, and full of purpose. This, this was what he was meant for!

The ogre tried to dislodge him, but Alf wrapped his legs around its chest, digging his knees into its armpits, his hands clutching shanks of the monster's hair. He bellowed into the ogre's ear in the creature's own language.

"Do you know who I am? I'm the man who killed the Chieftain of the Marrow-Eaters!"

The ogre clawed at him, ripping at his cloak. Its claws scrabbled against the dwarven mail Alf wore beneath his shirt. Alf got his arm locked across the ogre's throat and squeezed.

"I killed Acraist the Wraith-Captain!"

The ogre reared up and threw itself back, crushing Alf against the rock. The impact knocked the air from his lungs, and he felt one of his ribs crack, but he held firm – and sank his teeth into his foe's ear. He bit off a healthy chunk, spat it out and hissed:

"I killed Lord Bone."

It was probably the pain of losing an earlobe, and not his threat, that made the ogre yield, but yield it did. The monster fell to the ground, whimpering.

Alf released his grip on the ogre's neck and picked up Spellbreaker. Oh, *now* the magic sword was perfectly light and balanced in his hand. One swing, and the ogre's head would go rolling across the ground. One cut, and the monster would be slain.

He slapped the ogre with the flat of the blade.

"Look at me."

Yellow terror-filled eyes stared at him.

"There are adventurers hunting for you. They went south-east. You, run north. That way." He pointed with the blade, unsure if the ogre even spoke this dialect. It was the tongue he'd learned in Necrad, the language the Witch Elves used to order their war-beasts around. "Run north!" he added in common, and he shoved the ogre again. The brute got the message and ran, loping on all fours away from Alf. It glanced back in confusion, unsure of what had just happened.

Alf lifted Spellbreaker, glared into the sword's eye.

"I was testing you," said the sword. "You haven't had a proper fight in months. Tournies don't count – no opponent has the cour-age to truly test you, and it's all for show anyway. Your strength dwindles. My wielder must—"

"I'm not your bloody wielder. I'm your gaoler."

"I am *bored*, wielder. Two years of wandering the forests and backroads. Two years of hiding and lurking. And when you finally pluck up the courage to go anywhere, it's to an even duller village. I tell you, those people should have welcomed the slaughter my master brought, to relieve them of the tedium of their pathetic—"

"Try that again, and I'll throw you off a cliff."

"Do it. Someone will find me. Some*thing*. I'm a weapon of dark-ness, and I call to—"

"I'll drop you," said Alf wearily, "into a volcano."

Last time, they'd reached the temple in two days. He'd spent twice as long already, trudging over stony ground, pushing through thorns and bracken, clambering around desolate tors and outcrops of bare rock. He'd known that finding the hidden ravine of the temple would be tricky, but it took him longer than he'd expected to reach Giant's Rock, and that was at least a day's travel from the ravine.

That big pillar of stone, one side covered with shaggy grey-green moss – that was Giant's Rock, right? In his memory it was big-ger. Alf squinted at the rock, trying to imagine how it might be mistaken for a hunched giant. He'd seen real giants, and they were a lot bigger.

If this was Giant's Rock, he should turn south there to reach the valley. If it wasn't, then turning south would bring him into the empty lands of the fells where no one lived.

Maybe they'd come from a more northerly direction, last time. He walked around the pillar of stone. It remained obstinately un-giant-like. No one ever accused Alf of having the soul of a poet. A rock pile was a rock pile to him. The empty sky above him, the empty land all around. He regretted letting that ogre run off; maybe he should have forced it to guide him to the valley. Turn south, or continue east?

The valley was well hidden. There'd been wars fought in these parts, hundreds of years ago, in the dark days after ... after ... after some kingdom had fallen. The Old Kingdom. Alf's grasp of history was as good as could be expected of a Mulladale farm boy who'd could barely write his name, and nearly thirty years of adventuring hadn't taught him much more. Oh, he could tell you the best way to *fight* an animated skeleton, or loot an ancient tomb, but "whence came the skeleton" or "who built the tomb" were matters for clev-erer heads. He remembered Blaise lecturing him on this battlefield, the wizard wasting his breath on talking when he should have been keeping it for walking. Different factions in the Old Kingdom clashed here. Rival cults, Blaise told him, fighting until both sides were exhausted and the Illuminated were driven into hiding. The green grass swallowed up the battlefields and the barrow tombs, and everything was forgotten until Lord Bone had called up those long-dead warriors. Skeletons crawled out of the dirt and took up their rusty swords, and roamed the High Moors again.

Last time, Thurn the Wilder led them. He could track anything and anyone, even the dead. He'd brought them straight to the secret path, following Lord Bone's forces into the hidden heart of the temple. All Alf had to do was fight off the flying dreadworms sent to slow them down. Even then, Acraist had seen that the Nine of them were dangerous.

"No, he didn't," said the sword. It was the first time it had spoken since the cliff top.

"Stop that."

"If Acraist thought you were a threat, he'd have sent more than a few riderless worms. He was intent on breaking the aegis of the temple, not worrying about you bandits. You were an irrelevant nuisance. You got lucky."

"Well, he got killed. And so did Lord Bone, and you can't say that was luck."

A quiver ran through the sword. The blade's equivalent of a derisive snort.

He took another step east, and the sword quivered again.

"What is it?"

"Nothing, O Lammergeier," said Spellbreaker sullenly. Alf hated that nickname, given to him in the songs by some stupid poet drunk on metaphor. He'd never even seen one of the ugly vultures of the mountains beyond Westermarch. They were bone-breaking birds, feasters on marrow. And while Alf might be old and ugly enough now to resemble a vulture, the bloody song had given him that name twenty or so years ago. He'd broken Bone, hence – Sir Lammergeier.

Poetry was almost as bad as prophecy.

The sword only used the name when it wanted to annoy him – or distract him. What had that pretentious apprentice said in the inn, about creatures of Lord Bone sensing places of power? Alf drew the sword again and took a step forward. The jewelled eye seemed to wince, eldritch light flaring deep within the ruby.

He shook Spellbreaker. "Can you detect the temple?"

"No."

Another step. Another wince.

"You bloody well can," said Alf.

"It's sanctified," admitted Spellbreaker reluctantly. "Acraist protected me from the radiance, last time."

Alf looked around at the moorland. No radiance was visible, at least none he had eyes to see.

"Well then." He set off east, and only turned south when prompted by the twisting of the demonic sword.

Another day, and the terrain became familiar. Some blessing in the temple softened the harshness of the moor. Wildflowers grew all around. Streams cascaded down the rocks, chiming like silver bells. Alf felt weariness fall from his bones, sloughing away like he'd sunk into a warm bath.

Spellbreaker shrieked and rattled in its scabbard.

"It's too bright. I cannot go in there. It will shatter me."

"I'm not leaving you here."

"Wielder, I cannot . . ."

Alf hesitated. Spellbreaker was among the most dangerous things to come out of Necrad, a weapon of surpassing evil. It could shatter any spell, break any ward. In the hands of a monster, it could wreak terrible harm upon the world. Even that ogre could become something dangerous under the blade's tutelage. But maybe the sword was right – dragging it into the holy place might damage it. When they'd fought Acraist that first time, down in the valley, the Wraith-Captain wasn't half as tough as when they battled him seven years later. The valley burned things of darkness.

Would it burn Alf if he carried the sword down there?

"Look," sneered Spellbreaker. "You're expected."

A tiny candle flame of light danced in the air ahead of Alf. And then another kindled, and another, and another, a trail of sparks leading down into the valley.

Alf drew the sword and drove it deep into the earth. "Stay," he said to it, scolding it like a dog.

Then down, into the hidden valley of the Illuminated One.